Precious Matter

—

Belinda Roberts

LENDAL PRESS

First published in 2021 by Lendal Press
Woodend, The Crescent, Scarborough, YO11 2PW
an imprint of Valley Press · lendalpress.com

ISBN 978-1-912436-91-0
Catalogue no. LP0007

Original cover image by Belinda Roberts
Cover and text design by Peter Barnfather
Edited by Paige Henderson and Jo Haywood

Printed and bound in Great Britain
by Clays Ltd, Elcograf S.p.A.

PRECIOUS MATTER

To Sophie, John, Alice and Ralph.

For adventures past and adventures yet to come.

1. Soaring skies

Earth, you could fit inside the sun a million times and more. And remember, the sun is only an average-sized star.

The skies soared above the sandflats; great bleached skies that rose from a thin line of salt marsh and pale-wash seas up into an endless blue. But Wilfie, nine years old and curious, knew that this was only the start of things – *the sky is a front to the big black openness behind, the beginning of something so forever, so beyond, that it hurts to think about it.*

Hurt almost as much as Wilfie's beating heart. His breath came hard as he tore across the expanse of beach, up into a mass of hummocky sand dunes and along a ridge of barely formed trails. Spying a sandy crater, he flung himself off the winding path and took shelter, wriggling his bony body into its giving curve.

The sky held above him, watery, eternally blue – a friend of wonder, who he would get to know better one day. Much better. He was not afraid of the sky. Not like the old people. He had seen fear flicker over their wrinkled faces when they looked upwards. Some were so ancient they had been there when the meteorites had come tearing down, blasting into Earth, smashing up cities, wiping out villages. As he lay on his back scooping up handfuls of sand, letting the grains fall through his fingers, the waving grasses rustled with their stories.

'We were lucky – dashed to safety in the arms of our screaming mothers. But many were not. Pink-cheeked babies tucked up in cosy cots in snug little bedrooms were blasted as they slept. But it wasn't just homes. Oh no. Great iron bridges, towering office blocks, magnificent churches, palatial government buildings – all hit and turned to drifting clouds of dust.'

Wilfie, captivated, was never frightened. Not at all. The meteorites falling made the unknown closer: space to earth, the sky the visible invisible entrance. He stretched up a freckled hand as if to touch the sky, to move himself into its dreamy infinity and the unknown inky blackness beyond.

The sound of bare feet padding on sand, closing in, tore Wilfie from skies and meteorites. He shrank back, squeezing his skinny body into as much of nothingness as he could. But the hunter was close: smell of sweat, lightest of breaths, faintest flap of shirt on the breeze. A shadow touched Wilfie's elbow. He tightened his arm to his side and tried to hold still, fighting the tickle of sand in nostrils, prickles of marram grass on bare legs, bare arms, that threatened to make him wriggle, to cry out and give himself away. Then it came. An eclipse of the late afternoon sun as a muscular giant blocked out the light, bent down and, with one large hand, tore Wilfie from his hiding place.

'Gotcha.'

'Let me go!'

Wilfie kicked and punched and the two fell to the ground, fighting and furious. Within seconds, another boy, smaller than Wilfie, ran up and dived on top of them. The boys scrapped and fought the man and each other.

'Oh, you've got me,' the man protested.

As the boys clung to him, he stood up, sending them rolling off his towering frame. Wilfie squealed, loving the roughness of the tumble.

'Hey, dad,' he cried, grabbing at his father's shirt.

But his father, Peter, laughing, peeled off his shirt and flicked it at the boys, inflicting stings on their bare skin.

'Dad. Stop it. Stop it!'

The boys scrabbled away, trying to escape. One last flick, then Peter slung the shirt over his broad back, shoulders freckled like Wilfie's, a silver scar crossing his spine – the relic of more vicious childhood scraps – and started threading his way back along the trail. The boys followed, still playing, pushing at each other, their fight diminishing to a hand-on-shoulder shove, a missed kick.

On the high edge of the dunes, the three paused, side by side: fine warriors, princes and kings, mighty and glorious. Heart calming from battle, breath steadying, it seemed to Wilfie the whole universe was before him: the beach an endless stretch of gold, the sea a foreign glittering grey, drawing its fading line with the sky which soared above, waiting for him. He felt intense possibilities, his confidence high, his spirit open.

Way below, a slight woman was sitting hunched on the sand, bare legs folded up to her chest, reading a yellow book, absorbed; a lone, other world island. But Wilfie wanted to share his perfect moment with her, wanted her to see him up there with dad and Pip – all of them, sky high.

'Mum!' he shouted, cupping hands to mouth, his voice sweeping along with the cry of a single peewit. The woman turned towards him, snatching at escaped strands of long dark hair that flicked across her face, catching in her fierce blue eyes, her expression, even at the distance, radiant with love.

She waved.

'Mum! Mum!'

Pip joined Wilfie in the cry, his voice piercing, his pixie-like frame waving, hopping about, keeping her attention. Wilfie, arms held high over his head, leapt up, again and again, stretching himself taller with each launch, his fingertips reaching to catch a comet, to trail in the fairytale dust of a shooting star, to dip into the sucking vacuum of a black hole.

'First one back to mum is a supernova. More energy than our sun in the whole of its lifetime. Think of that,' said Peter.

The boys were off; exploding stars, bright and fully charged. Whooping and leaping off the mountainous marram hummocks, they tumbled down onto the wide stretch of sand below and raced towards their mother.

Agatha Whisper, interrupted, dwelt a moment more in far-off lands, then closed her book. She slid it to the bottom of her canvas bag, hiding it away, though its images of caverns measureless to man, of sunless seas, of forests ancient as the hills – all only half understood but familiar and loved – lingered. The book – the only banned book Agatha possessed – had a false cover: standard bright yellow with the title of a state-approved novel stamped across the front in a heavy black font. She had been unable to resist bringing it to the beach: it was a pleasure dome, her treat

– they were on a day's holiday after all.

'Hurry up,' she teased, as Wilfie – a red-headed green-eyed Viking like Peter – and Pip – dark, delicate and strong like herself – closed in. Only feet away, the boys dived, crashing into their goal.

'Hey, look out!'

Agatha caught them as they tumbled against her. She fell to her back, slender arms wrapped around them, loving them, holding them tight.

'Got you. You're my prisoners now and I'll keep you forever, locked in my castle.'

'Let me go. Let go.'

'First to the sea.'

The boys wriggled free and were off – stick legs flashing across sand – lured by the coming and going of the water's edge.

As the boys ran, Agatha saw Peter race after them. Though she remained alone, she was part of them, wincing as they splashed into the icy sea, screaming at the cold. Peter snatched up Pip and swung the little boy around and around as if he weighed nothing. Pip was shrieking. Peter was laughing, his head thrown back, red hair bright against the low sun. Agatha shivered, hugging herself, willing Peter to leave the boys and join her – to sit beside her, to hold her, bare skin on bare skin. But that was for later.

'Again! Again!' cried Pip.

Peter swung Pip onto his shoulders and dipped and dived, threatening to drop him. Wilfie, dancing around them, pulled at his dad's swimming trunks, revealing a flash of white buttocks. The boys screamed with laughter. Agatha smiled and bit her lip, admiring.

'Hey!' yelled Peter, pulling at his trunks, lurching to catch Wilfie and trying to balance Pip on his shoulders at the same time. But he stumbled, falling into the shallow waters, taking Pip with him.

Wilfie, escaping, ran off down the beach.

That was the moment that Agatha, happy in her imaginings of Peter and herself – of intimate times past, of times to come – saw Wilfie running away and felt the chill of danger seep into her like an incoming tide over dry land. She tensed, her senses sharpened. Somewhere high above the cries of returning birds, over the lapping of sea on sand, beyond the murmurings of the restless dune grasses, she heard Wilfie calling out. Gentle, kind and, oh, so brave Wilfie, crying out for her.

'Mum! Mum!'

But it wasn't the cry of confidence he had clamoured from the top of the dunes. This cry held fear.

Agatha's fingers flew flat to the sand, ready to propel herself up, to leap forward, to attack, to defend. That sense of high alert, normally triggered when reprimanded by the state for making a slip – filling in a form wrong, missing a payment deadline, saying something inappropriate in a public place – caught in her throat, set her heart pounding.

'Mum! Mum!'

His calls evoked chaotic images from a distant memory – a young man calling, wanting her help, the flashing of a knife, the blur of spurting blood. Her fault! She had failed to see the signs then. She would not fail Wilfie too.

'Mum! Mum!'

'Wilfie, come back.'

But Wilfie was spinning away, whirling round and round, arms flung out, red hair flaming against fading blue sky.

'Wilfie!'

Still he spun. And still, from somewhere far beyond, she could hear him calling, wanting to come home.

'Mum! Mum!'

'Wilfie.'

She started to walk, to run a little towards him, not wanting imagined horror to buckle into reality. But he was moving ever further away, as if drawn by an invisible thread into another world. Then he stopped and crouched, foetus-like, head bowed to wet sand and picked something up – a fragment of meteorite? a pebble? a shell? – turning it over, considering. He stood and tipped sideways, bending his thin white arm back then thrusting it forwards, hurling the object – yes, it must be a pebble, flat and smooth – sending it skimming out across the sea, watching it bounce once, twice, sink into the unknown. Twisting round, he saw her and raised his hands skyward, waving wildly. He chose another missile and sent it flying before trotting back to her along the sea's white-laced edge, darting in and out of the tide.

'Did you see my skims, mum? Three bounces.'

'I did,' she said, her voice light, her hug playful, her fear hidden. 'Good skimming.'

Together they searched out more stones – smooth, flat – and skimmed again, chiming the count of bounces; one, two, three, even four.

'Good one,' said Agatha.

'Race you back,' said Wilfie.

She ran with him, back to the towels, the baskets, the bats and balls, the small treasured lumps of meteorite waiting to join Wilfie's collection in his bedroom – all normal, all their world. She began to pack everything away, though her gaze constantly flicked to Wilfie.

Checking. Just checking.

Peter, with Pip on his shoulders, jogged up the beach towards them.

'Coming in to land,' he said, discarding Pip upside down on the sand, and leaving himself free to grab Agatha instead. He caught her wrists and pulled her towards him, twirling her round, forcing her arms to cross in front and wrap around her waist. He slid his bare arms over hers, overlapping, holding tight. His muscles tightened to lock her in, in jest and in promise: as he rocked her side to side, kissing her shoulder, fear slipped away.

At their feet, Wilfie dived onto Pip, pinning his younger brother down.

'Mum. Save me,' cried Pip, squirming, squealing, laughing.

'Get off. Get off.'

Wilfie leapt up.

'Catch me if you can,' he challenged, running off, Pip on his tail.

'Boys, stay close,' said Agatha.

But Wilfie, still in the fun of the moment, kept going, trying to shake off Pip, racing away. Away.

'Wait. Wilfie. Wait!'

Agatha pushed away from Peter.

'The boys,' she said.

'The boys are having fun,' he said. 'Our turn.'

'Later,' said Agatha. 'I … Wilfie!'

Fear destroyed the closeness she had so desired with Peter only moments ago, disappointing him, disappointing herself. Breaking free, she ran after the boys, eyes flicking from sand to sea, sea to sand, searching out danger in the very places that earlier had provided such pleasure but now could be the sinister custodians of unknown terrors.

Quicksand?

A roaring surge from the sea?

As people did when sensing danger, she glanced to the skies.

Heart pounding, she closed in on the children.

'Wait, Wilfie. Wait!'

The command in her voice surprised Wilfie into immediate obedience. He turned and waited. And because Wilfie waited, Pip waited.

'Good boy. Good little boys.'

Agatha took their hands, squeezing tight. The familiar feeling of palm on palm, fingers – small and strong – cupped within hers, pushed at her terrors, steadied her heart and though tears came, they were tears of thanks, of a sweeping relief that all seemed as normal as it could be. Pip. Wilfie. Agatha.

And now Peter too, stuffing towels and T-shirts into the beach bag as he jogged to join them. Pip held out his free hand, small and fine boned like Agatha's. Peter took it and started to swing.

'Whoosh,' said Peter.

'OK?' he added, as they swung the little boy into the air.

'Yes,' said Agatha. 'I'm sorry. It… it was nothing. I don't know why… Sorry.'

'Again,' said Pip and they swung again until Peter, catching Agatha's eye, leant over Pip's head, trying to reach her, to kiss her. He dropped Pip's hand to pull her towards him, to claim her affection; the touch of his hand, strength of his arm, roughness of his cheek on hers was so comforting that she laughed out loud, expelling fears, joyful to be wrapped in love. They were together again. Together and safe, for now.

2. Stuffy Ted

Be prepared! In less than five billion years the Milky Way and Andromeda Galaxies will collide.

On the drive home, Agatha twisted round to check the boys. Pip had rolled up into a ball, peaceful, sleepy. Wilfie was staring out of the window, captivated by the early evening stars. Reassured, she turned back, her mind drifting. Wilfie, Peter, space: the three so intertwined, so hard to separate. Right from the start she had loved Wilfie's endless fascination, his questioning, his challenges, the way he mixed his life on Earth with his imaginings of what was out there. How he teased her. Yes, he teased her, knowing his knowledge soared above hers and he could catch her out again and again.

'Wilfie have you done your homework?'

He would scribble out a reply.

Sorreeeee. Cant here. In space.
NO SOND IN SPACE DON"T FOGET.

Then later, calling from the bath.

'Water's boiling. What's the hottest planet in our solar system, mum? You must know that. Mum!'

'Mercury.'

'No. Venus. VENUS. 460 degrees. Like this bath. Don't get in Pip. You'll be vaporised in under a millisecond.'

Astronomy, celestial bodies, constellations: he sucked up facts from a stream of school library books, which was odd as he could barely read the books school wanted him to read. She often watched him, absorbed, looking at the pages of complex, science based space books and wondered how the magical transfer of information leapt through the air from page to brain. How was there room for so many facts in such a small person? But they were there, and the questions were relentless.

'Hey mum, do you know the difference between the aurora borealis and the aurora australis?'

She was glad she didn't know, and he did. It made him special. Yes, most children were better at reading and spelling than Wilfie, much better, but how many children had heard of the aurora borealis? How many of his teachers had heard of the aurora borealis? Agatha flinched at the thought of his teachers, of disappointing school reports: *slow learner, distracted, more interested in the moon than maths, lives in his own world, finds it hard to relate to his classmates, must make more of an effort, trailing at the bottom, to be blunt – peers find him odd, have you considered a specialist school?* How blind they were. Could they not see Wilfie was not wrong, just different? Agatha glanced at her son's upturned face, his green eyes searching the sky, squinting as if he knew something was there but couldn't quite see it.

'Looking for the man on the moon, Wilfie?' she whispered.

'There isn't a man on the moon. But there is something,' said Wilfie. 'I'm going to live in space and you can all come and visit me.'

'Shall I bring you spinach soup?'

'Not spinach soup, Milky Way soup!' Wilfie and Agatha chimed, the joke familiar.

'And I'll do a spacewalk. For dad,' said Wilfie.

The spacewalk. Everyone had dreams. It had been Peter's dream once, after all. And it had so nearly been his to touch – the moment when he got so, so close to propelling himself beyond man's knowledge, to float alone in the void.

'I am going,' said Wilfie.

The little phrase brought back a sliver of fear: Wilfie calling from far away.

'You can visit me.'

An icy blast of air hit the back of Agatha's neck.

'Wilfie, what are you doing? Close the window.'

'I am going you know, mum.'

'Yes, I know, Wilfie. And me and dad and Pip are looking forward to coming to see you for our holidays,' said Agatha, but her pleasure in the conversation was gone; fear was upon her and her heart filled with dread.

'I am going though.'

A stark blue flashing light, alien and clinical, invaded from behind, flooding the interior of their car. A police patrol car sped past and cut in front of them, slowing, forcing Peter to pull over.

'What is it, dad? Why are they stopping us?'

'Just keep quiet. Keep still.'

Agatha knew it must be her forbidden book. How did they always know everything? Had they been spying on them on the beach? Seen her reading? She shoved her bag under her seat, but it stuck out, easily found if they were searched. She scrabbled about, trying to push it right in.

A policeman heaved himself out of the patrol car's passenger door. He shuffled straight past, stopping behind their car.

'What's he doing?'

'Ssh. Wait,' said Agatha, watching in the mirror. The policeman stooped, picked up something and took his trophy to Peter's open window.

'This has been danglin' behind your car.'

The policeman was young but overweight and puffing: baby face pasty white, bulky mass squeezed tight into his uniform. Podgy fingers handed Peter a small, battered teddy bear.

Stuffy Ted. Not the book. Stuffy Ted.

Agatha suppressed the urge to laugh out loud in relief.

'Danglin' stuff is a dangerous driving offence. Four points on your licence and a level three fine.'

Peter passed Stuffy Ted back to Wilfie.

'Keep Stuffy Ted inside the car from now on.'

'Stuffy Ted?'

'My son's teddy bear. The bear that was flying.'

'Why would he be doin' something like that?'

'Just for fun.'

'Fun?'

With pale round eyes, the policeman stared at Wilfie. Wilfie wriggled down into his seat. Agatha knew her son realised he had done something wrong and been caught and that he could be in big trouble. He had told her stories from school about classmates being put on community correction programmes, like the boy who was taken for putting a cardboard cereal packet in the wrong bin. It was a mistake, but he still had to go away for four days. It was part of trying to make the country a better place for all. Agatha leaned over and touched Wilfie's knee.

'Don't worry.'

'Worry?' said the policeman. 'Somethin' else up?'

Agatha snatched back her hand. Wilfie shut his eyes tight against danger.

The policeman peered into the dark of the back seat.

'Hang on. Little un's not buckled up.'

'I'm sure he is,' said Peter, sharp, insistent.

'I am. Did it myself,' said Pip.

'We always make sure their safety belts are done up. Always.'

'Let's have a look then.'

The policeman trundled round to Pip's side of the car. Peter twisted back to check Pip's belt. Pip pressed at the lock. Agatha heard it click, click, click. Open or closed? Closed? Open?

'Don't fiddle, Pip,' whispered Peter.

The policeman opened Pip's door and leant in obliterating Agatha's view of her youngest son, the smell of sweat flooding their space. Fat fingers fumbled with Pip's lock, pressing, pushing. She could hear Pip whimpering like a small animal – trapped, fearful.

Then, from beside Pip, Wilfie – gentle, sweet, considerate Wilfie – broke. He lashed out, kicking viciously at the invader, screaming, his voice high-pitched, furious.

'Get off! Leave Pip alone. Get off. Get off!'

The policeman, trapped by his bulk, struggled to escape. Agatha swirled round, her fingers snatching at Wilfie's flailing foot.

'Stop! Stop! Wilfie! Stop!'

But she could not stop him. His trainer smacked into the policeman's face, splitting open his pink fleshy nose. Blood spurted, pumping red. The policeman's head rocked back. He opened his mouth, a great black gaping hole, and howled, his cry marking his pain and his shock at Wilfie's unforgivable crime against authority.

Peter leapt out of the car. He threw open the back seat door and grabbed Wilfie, dragging him out. The policeman, shrieking in pain, hauled himself from Pip's side, hands cupped to his face, blood bubbling red from his nose, seeping through thick fingers. Dark, wet blood.

'Sorry! Oh, I'm so, so sorry,' said Agatha, scrambling out. Her small white hand hovered over the policeman's shoulder, wanting to comfort, terrified to touch. She might make it worse, like she had done before. And, like then, there was blood, so much blood.

'I'm sorry. Are you ...'

But her voice, white edged with horror, was drowned out by the anguish of the victim.

'My nose. What's he done to my nose? What's he gone and done?'

Above the threat, the blood, the danger, Agatha heard the moan of the vulnerable.

'Pass me a towel, Pip. Something. Anything.'

Pip squirmed around, hunting. He pulled out a T-shirt from the beach bag. It was damp and smelt bad.

'Here,' said Agatha.

The policeman took the T-shirt and dabbed at his nose.

'It really hurts.'

'I'm sorry. He just thought ... I don't know.'

'He shouldn't have kicked like that. I was just tryin' to help. Oh no.'

Blood was dripping onto his uniform, spreading dark patches.

'I'm gonna' have trouble for this. Big trouble.'

Sniffing, he wiped at his jacket with the T-shirt.

'Let me do that,' said Agatha, not knowing what to do and not wanting to touch the blood.

The policeman let her wipe at the glistening stains.

'Only tryin' to help,' he mumbled.

'I know. I know,' said Agatha.

To her surprise, he laughed.

'Thought it was goin' well,' he said. 'Oh, it still hurts.'

'Let's see.'

The policeman cautiously moved his hand from his nose, revealing a red mess, blood bubbling from nostrils.

'What is it?' he said. 'What's happened?'

Agatha, squinting to see, their faces close, suppressed a gasp. A lump of bone stuck awkwardly to one side.

'Is it broken?'

'It … I don't know,' said Agatha. 'It looks… maybe.'

'Broken,' said the policeman. 'That'll impress my mates. Broken nose on my first day.'

'Just don't tell them it was a child,' she said.

He laughed. Then groaned, pushing the T-shirt against his face.

'Our secret,' added Agatha. She smiled at him.

'Thanks, miss. It still hurts.'

'I bet. Peter, come and look.'

But as Agatha called to Peter, a second policeman stepped from the patrol car and marched towards them.

'Back in the car,' he ordered his colleague.

'Thanks again, miss,' mumbled the young man as he shuffled off, the T-shirt still pressed against his wound.

'He's on first level training. I've observed and recorded the incident. Or should I say incidents. Let's have your personal registration numbers.'

'Why?' demanded Agatha.

A tiny glance from Peter halted her. It was better not to protest, not to exacerbate things. Peter knew all the family's registration numbers by heart. It was a requirement of all citizens. As Peter rattled them off, Agatha shuddered at the thought that the numbers relayed everything the state needed to catch them out: vaccinations, negative attributes, misdemeanors, causes for concern, potential areas for protection.

'Dangerous driving, driving without a seatbelt, assaulting a member of the police force. That's quite a list. You need help.'

The officer tore off a sheet from his pad and handed it to Peter.

'Remember, that's what we are here for. To help.'

He returned to his car and drove off, leaving the Whisper family on the roadside.

'What is it?'

'Nothing,' said Peter as they got back in the car.

'Show me.'

Peter handed Agatha the slip of paper.

Child Assist Order (1)

'No! They can't!' cried Agatha. 'If we get three Assists they will take our children. Peter, what have we done?'

Peter didn't answer. Silence hung between them, neither wanting to voice the implications of such a form, one of many churned out by well-meaning but incompetent governments pushing control. Agatha was terrified of the threat the form brought with it. Everyone was: children from families failing to live up to governmental expectations could be sent away to learn the truth and light of the new order. Agatha had seen it at school, the scythe of misguided, poorly conceived legislation devastating families. Now an Assist had wormed its way into her own family.

'How can they do this? What right do … what …'

'Put it away,' said Peter. 'It doesn't mean anything on its own.'

'Sorry,' said Wilfie from the back. 'I just thought the policeman was going to …'

'Doesn't matter,' interrupted Peter. 'We need to be careful, then these things can't harm us.'

Agatha pressed her fingers to her forehead, trying to calm herself. Peter was right. She leant across to kiss his shoulder, grateful that they could take control. It was only their first Child Assist Order. If they were careful, it would mean nothing. But there were so many ways you could be tripped up: tiny things you did not even know you had done wrong. And she was frightened of her own impulses – of putting the family in danger. She glanced at the boys. Pip was asleep. Wilfie had retreated back into his seat, safe and sound for now. She folded up the Assist, pulled her bag from under her seat and stuffed it deep inside. Out of sight. Then she took out her precious forbidden book. She ran her fingers over the cover, thinking of the beloved words within, how their poetry brought her so much joy. Then she opened her window and gently let it fall. Maybe someone else would find it and take pleasure in its imaginative landscape, so feared by the state. But for her, with a Child Assist Order hanging over her family, it wasn't worth the risk.

3. Circles
Grow younger: time goes more slowly in orbit than on the surface of the Earth so you can return younger than when you left.

The city traffic slowed to a stop-start crawl, creating a tedious journey round the outermost city circle, number twenty-nine and in to circle thirteen, before heading out again; a poor system that gathered cars into great lumpy nodules, lurching them from one standstill to the next.

As they edged round yet another island, Agatha gazed up at an immense angular rock in the centre. She shuddered. How beautiful, the way it balanced like a ballerina en pointe – yet how sinister, a relic of the meteor catastrophe. She had heard stories recounted many times by surviving grandparents, great-aunts, ancient uncles, of the night the meteorites had struck, pouring down, peppering Earth, a thousand bright lights tearing into the atmosphere, smashing into the ground at random, a spectacular show, joyful in its beauty, terrifying in its carnage.

No home, no village, town or city, no baby, no child, no woman or man, insignificant or important was safe, they said. Death came raining savage blows, wildly and indiscriminately. It could be me. It could be you.

Cups, saucers, milk jugs, sugar bowls, and teaspoons were laid out on tea tables to illustrate the new circle city plans.

'So here in circle one, the very centre, are the government buildings, monumental, imposing, stately, with indestructible underground shelters. Safe havens should meteorites strike again. Police are circle two, prisons circle three, hospitals and health circle four, and government officials, along with other prestigious members of society, live in circle five so that's the place to be. Professionals and businesses on the up operate from circle six. The outer circles, numbers seven to twenty-nine are a hotchpotch: businesses, schools, leisure, shops, homes – progressively more impoverished as you move further away from circle one. Beyond that are villages and, further still, recluses. You definitely don't want to live out there.'

Then a great-aunt, with a twinkle in her eye, would add, 'Well, at any rate, *they* don't want you to live out there. Shall we have another cup of tea?'

The ring road ran around circle thirteen, bordered by towering buildings and brightly lit windows: giant office blocks, homes in the sky.

'Do you think everyone wants to get out?' said Agatha, breaking the silence, as she watched the silhouettes of people moving about, pausing by windows on high, birds in a cage. 'Get away from the cities, the systems; live freely, out on the open moors?'

'Who wants to tramp about on an open moor when you can see them on TV?' said Peter. She smiled. It was a poor effort at a joke but between them they had batted the threat of the Child Assist Order aside, refusing to let it dominate and allowing their thoughts to wonder on better things.

4. Ostrich

A fairytale planet floats forty light years away in the constellation of Cancer, its rocky surface glinting with graphite and diamonds.

As the Whisper family headed home, a young man, arms folded, was leaning his forehead against the window on the twenty-second floor of one of the circle thirteen office blocks so disliked by Agatha, knowing he was on the verge of something big but as yet unable to pin it down. Weston W B Wright was an advertising creative; a wishful hotshot. Weston didn't think outside the box: he thought outside the universe. Thirty, thin and thirsty for success, he was the number one creative at Ostrich Advertising Agency and was leading the OSH – Other Side Homes – pitch. He was actually the only creative at Ostrich, as well as the founder and boss.

A lingering hammering in his head clouded Weston's thought. So many vodkas the night before. He had slipped from the bar stool. Twice. A bruise on his elbow was testament to that. So, he was at the bar and got talking to this bloke from OSH who thought he was a genius. Or was the bloke from OSH the genius? Perhaps they both were. Anyway, amongst the banter and hilarity, he must have said something that cut through. And he must have given his new pal his business card. Or perhaps the guy had picked one up when Weston crashed off the bar stool, spilling the contents of his wallet onto the sticky floor. It was sticky. He remembered that. Anyway, it didn't matter now. The result was a call to Ostrich HQ that morning for Weston to pick up a brief: the opportunity to pitch for a major OSH project. This was serious stuff, the greatest challenge in Ostrich's three year history. They would be up against some of the big boys in the ad industry. Despite his brain fog, Weston was elated. A break at last! It was also top secret, hush-hush, can't say more. So much so that to get hold of the brief Weston W B W had to travel all the way in to circle six to meet an OSH contact by the train station departures board.

'Sign here.'

The contact presented Weston with a contract.

'What is it?'

'Confidentiality agreement. Top secret. If you want to pitch, you need to sign.'

Weston signed. You had to take chances in life. And he was rather thrilled by the cloak and dagger approach. The contact handed him a brown envelope and disappeared into the crowd of commuters.

Weston headed into the station cafe, ordered a double shot black coffee, ripped open the envelope and started to read.

There was a whole load of company-speak nonsense about OSH which he skimmed over. Mega property company. Design, build and retain. Brightest people. Great steps forward. Innovative. Yawn, thought Weston. Massive investment in design over decades. Yawn. Yawn. Yawn. They all say that. Weston had seen it all before. Ready to go. Developed homes for living. Leader in its field. Now world leader. Bought by the state to push things forward. He skipped down to the brief itself and read:

Develop a campaign to encourage mining companies to take space in OSH living accommodation.

Dull. Dull. Dull. Another boring old property company desperate for tenants. Weston flicked through the designs that OSH was trying to let. He didn't think much of them. They were weird. And tiny. Especially the Pennysides, which were the 'cottages' of the scheme. How did they have the nerve to suggest they were in any way cottages? Where was the thatch? The little picket fence? The roses rambling over the door? The only similarity the Pennysides had to a cottage was that they would be a tight squeeze to live in. He hated these modern architects' designs. All metal and reflective glass.

Weston slammed the document down on the table in disgust. He stood up, about to leave, when a word on the open page caught his eye.

'Intergalactic.'

The word jumped out at him. He read it aloud.

'In-ter-ga-lac-tic.'

Was there something he had missed? Something "in-ter-ga-lac-tic"?

He dropped to his seat again, picked up the document and re-read a few sentences.

OSH designed, built and let property in space.

In space.

Whoa. This was really something…

And he had nearly missed it. Living spaces in space.

Weston read fast. Earth was running out of precious minerals. Yes, yes, yes, everyone knew that. The papers were always banging on about it. The science stuff about minerals baffled him, so he skimmed over it, drilling down until he hit *asteroid mining*. Ah ha! So, asteroid mining was the big thing at the moment, done remotely. But remotely was too slow, too limited. The industry needed to move on. Get men up there. Mining properly. Not scraping the surface but sinking shafts. *Picks and hammers on the coalface.*

The phrase pulled him up sharp. His dad had died from a lifetime working with picks and hammers on the coalface. Lungs spewing black slime, coughing himself to death. And now they wanted to mine in space. Weston stirred his coffee. It wouldn't be mining coal, of course. Precious minerals, whatever they were. Silver, perhaps, like his teaspoon? Although that, of course, was stainless steel. But mining. Mining was dangerous. And what on earth could he have to do with it?

'Progress,' his dad would say, voice rasping. 'It's all about progress. World's got to move forward. And that includes you, son. Make the most of yourself. Take chances. Be your best. Not like me. Wasted.'

Weston felt the tears prick, as they always did when he thought of his dad. He read on, trying to concentrate.

To summarise, our marketing campaign needs to grab the hearts and minds of mining companies and miners. OSH living spaces need to be seen as real homes. Safe homes. Comfortable homes where miners can live happy, fulfilled lives. Not one or two men, but thousands. Remember our key objective – to turn mining in space into a commercial reality. The survival of the world depends upon it.

The survival of the world. And he had nearly walked away. Weston stuffed the document back in the brown envelope, his heart racing. He swept out of the coffee shop and scoured the departures board, searching for the next fast train back to circle thirteen. Frustrated by having to take a slow train that inexplicably paused in a siding and took the best part of the day, at last back in his office block, he jabbed at the button to call the lift. Too impatient to wait, he raced up the stairs, slowing by level four, and slogging the rest of the way, up to floor twenty two, promising himself between puffs, that it was still quicker than the lift. Sworn by the contract not to tell anyone else, he would have to think through the ideas, the concept, the strategy, the launch all alone. He needed to get going. It was a big deal.

5. Smiley face
Gamma ray bursts. Not to be messed with. Count ten seconds and they will have given off as much energy as the sun does in its lifetime.

'Top secret. One man only brief,' Weston announced as he burst in on the Ostrich team: Miriam on reception and Lazarus, the part-time graphic designer, tucked in a dark corner. Weston put a finger to his lips, muttered 'shh' and disappeared into his office, the only other room – so far – in the Ostrich empire. He yanked at the door twice, failing, as always, to click it fully closed behind him, loosened his tie and took two purposeful strides across to the window, wishing he could throw it open and breathe in inspiration whilst he gazed at the humming cityscape before him. But the window was jammed, so instead he leaned his forehead against the glass and tried to ignore the bleak view of the brick wall opposite.

'Weston. This is it. Big break. We're going places. Don't mess it up. Think, think, think.'

The mist of Weston's breath lay opaque on the pane. Instinctively, with his left index finger, he drew a smiley face, added a stick body, shorts, T-shirt, five upward marks for hair. What was he doing messing around doodling? He flung himself into his director's chair, swivelled round to face his desk, slammed his ideas pad down on the leatherette top, scrabbled around in the drawer for a thin black marker pen and started work.

'Ideas Weston. C'mon. This is what you're good at. Think. Think.'

He doodled again. Smiley face, stick body, shorts, T-shirt, five upward marks for hair, a rocket, a moon, stars, planets...

Miriam, olive skinned, soft featured and with eyes like inky pools edged with deeply dark kohl, pushed the door open and backed into his office, carrying a mug of tea, brimming to the top and threatening to spill. The mug was emblazoned with the Ostrich company slogan: *Simple Minds. Simple Ideas. Simply Brilliant.* Weston had thought of it himself. Painfully slowly, she reached his desk and, her wrist jangling with an excessive number of golden bracelets, put the mug down on a coaster – also printed with the slogan, the words just visible beneath a history of tea stains. He found her billowing white shirt distracting.

'Tea time, Weston. How's it going? Creative juices flowing?'

Weston snapped his ideas pad shut.

'Yes, Miriam. Oh yes.'

'I won't disturb you then. Exciting isn't it? Just so you know, I'm ordering some more toilet rolls. We're very low.'

Miriam exited, the bouncing of her abundant dark glossy curls proving disturbing. She reappeared almost immediately with two garibaldi biscuits on a plate.

'Nearly forgot.'

She put the plate down beside the mug. There was

31

something about that white shirt that was a bit hippyish for an ad agency. There was nothing wrong with being hippyish. It could be creative, he supposed. But he was trying to be sharp and the hippy look was not sharp. But what was it that made him think hippy? The floatiness? The embroidery? What were those little blue flowers all over the front? Cornflowers? Forget-me-nots? Buttercups? No, obviously not buttercups. They were yellow. Obviously. It was such a long time since he had seen flowers growing in the wild. He had seen the odd one between the cracks in paving stones. But they never looked the same as in a field. No, not a field. A meadow. An endless meadow filled with something to do with nodding flowers. He wondered what it would be like to take Miriam's hand and run through a meadow full of flowers. Naked.

'Won't disturb you,' Miriam was saying. 'Great minds and all that.'

Miriam pulled at the door, trying to close it behind her. Click. Click. The latch never quite made it. Weston sighed. He sipped at his tea and without noticing it, ate the biscuits. He shrugged his shoulders and rolled his head, trying to relax. Ideas were not flowing. He had to get into the zone. Clear his mind. Open it to infinite possibilities.

Instead he opened his pad.

And there it was.

The great idea.

Simple. Brilliant. Like all great thinkers on the edge of giant leaps forward, Weston could not believe it for a moment. Then, in glorious colour, he had a vision of other great moments in mankind's progress: the fall of an apple from a tree; the displacement of water from a bath; how to calculate the long – or was it the short? – side of a triangle. Added to this string of genius was his own,

Weston W B W's idea. Simple. Brilliant. An idea that could save the world.

He wanted to shout out, dance around the room, bang his fists on the table, punch the air. So he did. He shouted, danced, banged and punched.

'Yes, Weston, boyo. Yes!'

'More tea?'

Miriam, poking her head round the door, her big dark eyes opened wide, stopped Weston in his tracks. He felt a fool but didn't care. She wasn't really offering him more tea. She was being nosy. But strangely, at that moment, another cup of tea made by the white-shirted hippy temptress seemed the perfect way to celebrate.

'More tea? Oh yes, Miriam. Oh yes!'

6. Watercress soup
Sometimes raindrops can be diamonds: look to Jupiter and Saturn.

I love you, Agatha. You are my beginning. Before, I was lost to darkness. I am writing to you in a book with a pale blue cover they have given me. My hand aches already and my writing is slow. But I want to do this for you, Agatha. To explain everything. The woman watching me as I write has dead eyes. Dead eyes like the first who should love me. I am born in the light of love but am lost by a split second of thoughtlessness. I wriggle my woolly mittened hand free from mummy and toddle, tripping, slipping, sliding out onto a lake of glassy ice. My breath comes out in puffs. Puff! Puff! Puff! 'Peter!' she screams. 'Come back!' But I slip and slide onwards. Faster. Faster. Further away. Can't catch me! Daddy is on the ice, chasing me. He shouts for me to come back but I shriek and giggle and fall and pull myself up and totter onwards, further out. Daddy is getting close. We play chase, just us on the freezing cold of the ice. He has nearly caught me. He reaches out. Long arms, giant hands grabbing. 'Come back!' But he is slow on the ice. I twist away and slither back to mummy. First one home. I win! Daddy is still out there, moving slowly like he is trying not to put his feet down. The ice screeches and screams and splits open and he looks wild-eyed at me and mummy and his arms fling up and he goes down, fast. Gone. My mittens are soaking and my fingers hurt. I shiver. I am so cold. Mum howls and I am tipped into a black hole: misery closes in. Home is a stink of mould, hunger gives me sharp bleeds from jagged tin. Moonlight. She, too, sinks below muddy waters and nights become as silent as one. I should have reached out. But I am not brave. Not brave at all. Not like dad. Not like Wilfie. I try to escape. To lose myself in others: crows in a tree taking flight; moor ponies galloping in a herd; sewage rats running to higher ground. I long to feel the thick softness of friendship. I wait. Then I start to take chances. One person smiles and I am rising. But I am still cold. Another smiles. And another. Now I am rising fast. I swim dark lakes, make them my own. I shrug off lurking horrors of razor-toothed green-scaled pikes. I race slow-flowing rivers, kicking at green fronds and thick mud that tries to suck me down before I reach the other side. I am rising through the ranks. My cold heart will take me to the top. Chances come and I grasp them. And a passion grows. Space. Its infinite possibilities for Earth, its infinite possibilities for mankind. And here I am. A student at the University of Future Earth Sciences. I am heading for the MSc in Practical Space Astronaut Exploration. Ha! Peter Whisper, ready to battle for a place on the most prestigious space course known to man. Ready to launch into the above and beyond. To forge the future for the people of Earth. To push the boundaries of the impossible. To become an intergalactic space mining explorer. But I am still alone. Still cold. And then suddenly, watercress soup. You are there. Hair black as a starless night, dancer's limbs, eyes of speedwell blue concentrating on a bowl of soup, making sure it doesn't spill. You smile a waitress smile as you place the white, wide-rimmed bowl before me, holding it carefully with slender fingers, nails chewed raw. The soup is safe and you glance at me, smiling a true smile, lost as anxiety ripples over your fine features. 'Hang on,' you say, picking up my spoon to taste the bright green slurry. 'Yes, watercress. For a moment I thought I had brought you spinach.' You laugh with relief that you have not made a mistake. Then you clasp your fine white hand over chapped lips. 'Oh, sorry! I tasted your soup. I'll get you another. I can't believe I tasted your soup. That's awful. I mean, not the soup, but that I tasted it. I'll get you another.' But before you can go, I take the silver spoon from you, touching for the first time those fingers, those hands I come to love and I taste the soup. 'Perfect,' I say.

7. Pool of gold

Hot space. The heat of a supernova can be five times that of a nuclear explosion.

'Meteor! Look! A meteor!'

Wilfie's shout from the back seat woke Agatha.

'Shooting star,' said Peter.

'Same thing, dad. Same thing.'

The dense suburbs became patchy until the city vanished altogether as they dropped into the night blackened contours of countryside. The Child Assist Order seemed to lose power in the magic of the full moon that hung in the ink of a sky, a pool of gold, its brilliance catching the edge of shadowed blackthorn hedges, the ridges of deep ploughed fields, the outline of a copse of huddled trees; landscapes familiar. Agatha felt a growing joy as they dipped into the village and up and out onto the endless expanse of moonlit moor, with its far off silhouettes of strange granite giants that whispered into the night the secrets of hushed heathers, of gorse, of great primeval ferns, of sucking blanket bogs and the graceful gossiping of grassy moors, where wild ponies gathered, tails to the wind, to protect themselves from the night chill. Turning off the moorland road, they bounced down a rough track. Their own land at last. Their own space. Their home. No one could tell them what to do there.

8. Grey Cottage

As one: the Moon is the Earth's only natural satellite.

Home was Grey Cottage, a compact, sturdy pale grey stone farmworker's cottage at the end of a rutted track, protected on each side by long, low dry stone walls. Nobody else had wanted it: too remote. People felt safer huddled in cities with meteorite shelters built into every new home, or even in villages with their community shelters, but Agatha and Peter had known Grey Cottage was where they wanted to be, even if the attack from above came again. It was a risk worth taking. And anyway, Agatha did not trust those flimsy meteorite shelters. Just propaganda; the government pretending to do something. And it was not the meteorites they needed to fear. It was things like Child Assist Orders. And now with one CAO slapped on the family, the remoteness of Grey Cottage was more valuable than ever. It had protected them before and would protect them again. Of that Agatha was sure.

Agatha's affinity with her home had formed fast and firm early one morning a year after her marriage. Alone in the black cast iron bed, she had felt pains in her abdomen, sharp and growing. Peter was already up and busy downstairs. No, outside. The bedroom window, set deep in ancient whitewashed walls, was open, letting in chill air from the moor. She could hear him whistling, clucking at the hens, stamping about the yard. She called for him but his sounds grew fainter. He must be going up the track. Or perhaps clambering the stone wall to stride out across the heathery expanse beyond. Painful spasms drove her out of bed. She threw aside the sheets and blankets and descended the narrow wooden stairs to the kitchen. On the bottom step, her foot caught the edge of *Raising Children To Form*, a government issue book; required reading for all parents-to-be. She had meant to take it upstairs to read the night before but had forgotten. Now her ankle flipped over with a sickening pop. A screaming stretch of ligaments snatched her balance and flung her down onto the flagstone kitchen floor.

'Peter!'

The back door was swinging on its long black hinges and she could see out into the yard. No Peter. The pain in her ankle was overwhelmed by a rush of agony that tore at her torso, gripping, squeezing.

'Peter! Peter!'

Agatha closed her eyes, fighting the pain and the fear of what was to come. Amongst the screaming red heat of it all, she registered that the fall had been caused by the book she was meant to read but hadn't. If the government hadn't sent the book, there would have been no danger. They had caused the danger. They didn't want people like her to have children. But hadn't she left it on the stairs? Was this her fault? Slicing through the chaos came a thought of such unspeakable horror that her body shook with sobs: had she lost her child, unborn, unknown?

'Agatha.'

Peter, a black mass framed in the doorway, quickly crouched by her side.

'I fell. It had already started. Upstairs. I might have lost…'

They were meant to get in the car, drive to hospital, get everything done correctly, measured, recorded. The authorities insisted that births take place in hospitals, registered, all in order. But, gripping his hand, Agatha begged Peter to let her lie on the stone a moment or two – to let the cottage care for them. This was where they should be. Half an hour later, Wilfie was born. Alive. Perfect. Wilfie cried and Agatha and Peter cried with him, for the sheer joy of the moment they had kept for themselves. And, above all, for the sheer joy of becoming three.

9. Infinite possibilities

Space is infinite. But what is the other side of infinite?

For Agatha, this was a precious time at Grey Cottage – looking after her baby son, loving her husband, growing greens in their vegetable garden and later, when her body had recovered, working as a cleaner for six households in the village. It was physical work which she enjoyed and, for the most part, she could just turn up and be alone with her thoughts. She tried to stay under the radar, avoiding a government that meant well but in its chaos caused chaos. It built legislation on shifting sands, brought fear where friendship was intended and replaced respect with anxiety in people's hearts. To avoid trouble as best she could, she filled in the endless requests for statistics about Wilfie – his weight, his height, his first steps – and sent in the statutory requirements for tiny fingerprints, locks of his red downy hair, a drop of blood, a phial of saliva. It was imperative to keep on the right side of things. And she never wasted a precious moment with Peter and Wilfie.

'Before the meteorites came it was as if no one apart from scientists had noticed space before,' Peter told Wilfie, who crawled about, exploring the cottage, as Agatha cooked them soup and steamed up the kitchen. 'There were a few astronauts who made it up there. But they didn't do much. Just had a look around. Like visitors. Space as something to use or be part of seemed way off in the future. Then suddenly it seemed that space got fed up of waiting and came shooting down, screaming, "Hey! Hello. Look at me. Here I am!".'

Agatha paused in her stirring to watch Peter swoop and dive, making Wilfie gurgle and hiccup with laughter.

A year later, Wilfie, on uncertain little legs, would stumble and trip as he tried to swoop and dive too.

'Then, Wilfie, the idea of space mining took off. Scientists looked at the remains of the meteorites and it blew their minds. What was the point of arguing about scraps of precious minerals left on Earth if there was millions and billions and trillions of tonnes of the stuff up there? It was like space mining had come crashing out of the future into the present. It was suddenly exciting and the impossible seemed possible. And I wanted to be part of it.'

'So do I,' said Wilfie, now five years old. 'So do I. So do I!'

By now, he had a little brother: Philip, who cried and yelled and squealed. Wilfie would lean over Philip's cot and let him suck his finger with his gummy mouth to quieten him. But the minute Wilfie took his finger out the yelling would start again. So, he would stick his finger back in.

'Pip, Pip, Pip,' he would say. 'Look at the sky, look at the moon. Can you see the man in the moon? He's waving at you. Look, Pip!'

And Wilfie would gently turn Pip's head so he could see the moon shining in through the stone-framed window; the big, yellow, beautiful moon. And sometimes Pip would stop crying and gurgle a little. Wilfie would wave Pip's arm for him.

'That's it, Pip. Say hello to the man in the moon. Look, he's waving back at you. Waving from space. Like I'm going to one day. Wearing a space suit like daddy. Look Pip. Look at the picture.'

Amongst a few photographs of Wilfie and Pip, a watercolour of the moors, a pressed leaf from their first autumn at Grey Cottage, Agatha had pinned a tatty photograph of a man in a space suit: Peter, a month after they married, on the day of his acceptance onto the MSc in Practical Space Astronaut Exploration.

Wearing a space suit like daddy.

The photograph still had the power to bring tears to Agatha's eyes. How often as she stood by the sink would she glance across and see Peter in his moment of triumph. He had wavered, not sure he wanted to leave her. He knew the risks, that he might never return. But she did not want to stand in his way. And he had set his course.

'Everything is different now,' he would say. 'I will come back. I used to think I wouldn't but now my world is here. Right here.'

And there was something else. She knew he needed to push himself beyond safe barriers. How proud she had been as she watched him accept his commission at Future Earth Sciences, conferred by the great and the good, standing in line with the other successful candidates; the brave young, eager to stretch mankind's existence to the limit and beyond.

They had laughed and joked as Peter squeezed into one of the latest space suits to have his picture taken. It was a tight fit. Photographs were taken. Standing. Sitting. Helmet on. Helmet off. Afterwards, Agatha and Peter, hand in hand, watched the others, enjoying the moment until Peter was called aside, ordered to take off his shoes and stand with his back to the wall. A book was levelled on his head, a little black line drawn and a tape measure pulled from the floor up to the mark. Agatha remembered staring at that little black line, fearing its significance.

'He can't be,' said an official.

The group of three who had done the measuring were looking aghast at the tape measure.

'Are you sure?'

'Yes. Six foot three and a half.'

'But that's no good. No good at all. Look, it says here.'

'I know what it says. Get the chief over.'

An elderly man with wispy hair and a cup of tea in his hand was brought across.

'What's all this? What's all this?' he sang.

'Peter Whisper. One of the candidates, sir. We've measured him and he's six foot three and a half.'

The old man's eyes strayed towards Peter. He tipped his head to one side and looked Peter up and down.

'My, a fine height, but no. Impossible. Can't be done. Shame.'

He held out his empty cup and saucer for someone to take, then shuffled back towards the cake table.

'Sorry, mate,' said the man who had done the measuring. 'On the updated specification for the modern range of spacecraft, the maximum height permitted for an astronaut is six foot two. 'I'm afraid you're too tall.'

'Too tall?'

'Yep.'

'But they knew my height from the start.'

'I know, but the specification has been changed.'

'So what do I do?'

'Nothing. You'll have to leave the programme. Thanks for coming, though.'

There was no more discussion.

At six foot three and a half, Peter was simply too tall.

For days after, Agatha stormed about Grey Cottage shouting about the unfairness of the world. How could they change the rules like that? She tore up the spacesuit photograph, then pieced it together again and stuck it on the wall. At least they would have that. She was proud of

Peter's achievement and he should be too. Peter appeared to take the setback lightly but she knew his disappointment ran deep. 'That's good,' she said the day he returned with news that he had got work labouring on a building site. But she still had to stop herself from worrying when he was out, evenings, weekends, hours at a time, traipsing the moors, the endless lanes, the coastal paths. Their future seemed uncertain.

10. Walk on the wild side

A giant object once collided with Earth. It broke off a great chunk. This dismembered part orbits the Earth forever. Our Moon.

So, again, I fail to care for those I love, Agatha. It tears me apart to see you and the boys suffer. I escape to a cliff path. Here the wind gusts off heaving seas, pushing at yellow gorse. The swell of grey-green far below swallows jagged rocks, then sucks back, revealing black tips, even as surf gathers to surge again. Two figures emerge from the mists, pale green coats flapping. Stooping. Frail. In colour and form they seem as natural to the landscape as the gorse, the heathers, the bent over storm blown hawthorn. Escaped wisps of white hair dance in the wind, the lightest of vapours from their steady breathing merging with the dampness in the air. I press into the hillside to let them pass on the narrow path. 'Lovely walk,' the first, an elderly woman, says, her face cowled in green waterproof. 'Yes, cold and damp but lovely,' I reply. She laughs, a light, merry laugh and I feel my load lighten at the small pleasure we have shared. As the second figure – an old man – approaches, he nods and smiles at me with crinkled eyes. I push further into the gorse. But as he passes, he stumbles. He stumbles and crashes towards the cliff edge. He cries out. He flings his arms wide, spreading them like wings as if he is leaping, flying – a bird, an angel – as death rushes towards him. I grab his hand and pull him back. Back into the living world. He is breathing hard and holds onto me, hugging tight, trembling. I hold him until he is steady. 'That was close,' he says, letting go at last. 'Thank goodness you were here. What a blessed thing.' And he chuckles, casting out the last vestiges of fear. 'A blessed thing, indeed,' laughs the woman. But I am not a blessed thing for him. I brought him close to death. 'How quick you were,' says the man. 'Did you see? Did you see?' he asks the old woman. 'My arms were out. I nearly went!' 'Yes. Snatched you back from certain death. In an instant. What a thing!' 'A miracle!' 'A miracle!' They laugh together and I see it differently. I stop fighting and see the miracle. I laugh with them. 'How wonderful, how simply wonderful it is to be alive,' he says. He is speaking joyfully to me, to the old woman, to the seagulls, gorse, grass, wind, spray, salty waters. 'Just look at that view,' he says. And I look with him and the old woman; the three of us sharing in its unfathomable beauty. Then they turn and stride away into the oncoming sea fret. I stare at the mist where they once were. I can no longer see them or the waters swirling below. But I can see the palm of my hand where, seconds ago, I pulled a human life back from the brink and I am thrilled. I think I can care for you, Agatha. I think I can.

11. A fine career

Spin. Spin. Spin. In the time it takes to count to one, a neutron star will have spun six hundred times.

Agatha could tell something had happened. When she was busy tying up canes for green beans, Peter came and watched her. But he wasn't really watching. He wanted to talk.

'Agatha?'

'Yes,' she said, cutting twine.

'I'm going to retrain. If I can't help people in the skies, I want to help people here on Earth. Make up for things.'

'Peter, You don't need to make up for anything. You…'

'Agatha, I've thought about it. I'm going to be a medic.'

'A medic? What sort of… why do you…?'

But the questions could come later. This was something moving forward. She dropped the scissors, the twine, the canes and hugged him, joyful that now they were at the start of things again.

The application process was a labyrinth of paperwork and endless form filling but, once on the course, Peter sailed through the elementary level exams and basic training and Agatha revelled in his renewed confidence. The hospital that they had failed to reach for Wilfie's birth became his workplace. Seventeen miles away.

He would set off for work up the track from Grey Cottage, drive along the top road, down into the village and up again over the high moor until, through a cutting between two great hills, he would see the city splashed out, spreading across the valley below him, its circle format like a work of art, a concept, an idea in which people lived their lives. The hospital – vast, white, hard, shiny – dominated circle four.

The hospital became Peter's second home. Whilst Agatha worked cleaning houses in the village or digging the vegetable garden at Grey Cottage, her fine fingers coated in soil that turned with the smallest of living creatures, Peter scrubbed his freckled hands, eradicating all dirt, all danger, to give the living, as best he could, more life, more hope, less pain. He set his sights on becoming a surgeon, consumed by an unremitting drive to bring light into darkened lives. Agatha was entranced by his endless stories and shared in his joys and sorrows. How glorious it was that, despite the setbacks, he had at last found his perfect career.

Perfect, that is, until one winter's day, after three days isolation due to a severe snowstorm, Peter tramped across to the workshop and picked up the axe to chop firewood.

12. Airlock
Space is not so far way. Cross the invisible Karman Line sixty two miles above Earth and you can touch the void.

Agatha listened to radio warnings of the snowstorm on and off all day; news of city traffic coming to a standstill, cars skidding at right angles, gritters unable to keep up. Falling snow created great soft white drifts that filled the track up to the top road. No vehicle could get up or down. School and work were an impossibility and quickly forgotten, giving way to the pleasures of sledging and snowballing. They were bound up in their own world, glad they could not get out and no one could get in. Agatha delighted in being alone without being lonely: at night she and Peter had each other and in the day they had Wilfie and Pip.

The small kitchen window framed the chilly early evening landscape, a monochromatic contrast to the warmth in which Agatha peeled red earthy skins off potatoes, revealing their startlingly pale water starch within. Wilfie sat at the kitchen table, his illustrated school library book on planets gripped in his small freckled hands. His eyes flicked across the pages, not reading side to side, but hopping about, as fact after fact, picture after picture, caught his attention.

Reading was a challenge for Wilfie, and the state fiction books for children, in Agatha's opinion, were dull, off-putting. But non-fiction was different. The state ploughed money into these and they were lavish. It was important for young people to have knowledge. Wilfie sucked up knowledge, letting it flow into his very own space information bank: black holes, comets, neutron stars. She knew he planned to go up there one day to find out what it was really like, just like his dad had nearly done – so, for now, he was busy learning everything he could.

'Supper's ready.'

Agatha placed vegetable stew, hot and steaming, on the table.

'Dad, how close did you actually get to going into space?'

'This close.'

Peter held up his finger and thumb, an inch apart.

'Could you touch it?'

'Practically.'

'But you can't touch space. It's space.'

'You could touch an asteroid. Or a planet.'

'Not a shooting star.'

Supper finished, Agatha chased Wilfie and Pip upstairs. Washed, pyjamas on and into bed. Hugs, a story, more hugs: small strong arms round her neck, the sweet smell of clean skin, a touch of breath on her cheek.

'Love you,' she said. 'Lights out.'

She left them, ready to cross the threshold from mother to wife, her senses switching to being with Peter, wanting him. But there was the sound of heavy steps on the wooden stairs, climbing fast, three at a time.

Pip giggled in excitement. The boys wriggled under their covers as the bedroom door opened.

'Time for a spacewalk?' whispered Peter.

'Yes! Yes! Yes!'

The bedtime spell was broken: the boys were wide awake again. Peter lifted Pip out of his cot and Wilfie scrambled out of bed. They stood side by side. Agatha, her bedtime work undone, didn't mind. Her time alone with Peter would come later, and waiting made her longing all the stronger. And how wonderful it was to break with routine, to do things with those you loved because the moment was there, a chance to be taken, nobody saying, 'no, it's past bedtime, that's the rule'. She leaned against the wall by the window, half ready to play, half distracted by the moon shining bright on the snow, and thinking of seeds in the frozen earth, like her, biding their time.

'Attention crew,' said Peter. 'Space suits on. Helmets on. Check your batteries. Oxygen masks. Breathe in that oxygen. Pure oxygen. Acclimatise. Acclimatise. Expel nitrogen. Ready Team Whisper? Let's go.'

Peter crossed the wooden floor with soft, slow spaceman strides and clicked open the iron latch of the narrow tongue-and-groove door that led from the boys' bedroom to the bathroom. The young astronauts followed: soft, slow strides and a final giant step into the white enamel bath. All three stood together, awaiting instructions.

'Airlock One, Astronaut Pip. Have you locked Airlock One behind you? Airlock One confirmed?'

Pip scrambled, slipping and sliding, out of the bath, and trotted back to the door. He pushed it closed. Alone in the boys' bedroom, Agatha could hear Pip jumping as he tried to reach the bolt above the latch. She knew it would be too high.

'Emergency. Call in Astronaut Wilfie,' commanded Peter.

Agatha heard Wilfie step out of the bath and cross the room to lock the door.

'Confirm Airlock One locked.'

There was a click as Wilfie pushed the bolt across.

'Airlock One confirm locked?'

'Ground Control, Airlock One confirmed. Are you receiving us?'

'Yes,' said Agatha, deepening her voice. 'Ground Control receiving loud and clear.'

'Message received. Thank you. We are now – hurry up Astronaut Wilfie – ready to start countdown.'

Peter counted down sixty seconds exactly, after which Agatha heard the command confirming it was safe to move on.

'Open Airlock Two, Astronaut Pip.'

Pip was scrabbling out of the bath.

'Emergency. Astronaut Pip too short to reach Airlock Two. Call in Astronaut Wilfie.'

She heard the click of the door as Wilfie reached the bolt for Airlock Two on the door that opened out onto the landing. There was silence as the three astronauts floated out. She waited for the noise, the shouting, the screaming that always followed. Sometimes one of them would have forgotten to put their tether on and would find themselves floating away along the landing into darkest space, or worse, sucked down into the whirling vortex of a black hole, forcing the others to rescue them from the bottom of the wardrobe. Sometimes a shooting star would whoosh past, so close it knocked them to the ground, or a solar storm send them spinning out of control. Tonight, aliens attacked and a fierce battle commenced. Pillows. Shoes. A toothbrush. Anything they could find was used to defend themselves from the terrifying space monsters.

Whilst the fighting raged around her, Agatha watched the moon and thought how, if it was springtime, such a moon would be good to plant by. And she knew, if it was springtime, she would go downstairs and pull on her boots and go outside, knowing that once her three astronauts had escaped from the black hole or beaten the aliens, they would float to the bedroom window and watch her digging and planting down on Earth.

Later, when bedtime finally came, Wilfie lay watching his mother, her dusky presence outlined against the window in pale gold, and knew for sure that the moon was a magical place with special powers. He wondered what was past the moon and, if you kept floating on and on, what would be next and what would be next? His dad had nearly gone into space long ago, but couldn't because he had grown too tall. Which seemed odd to Wilfie because he was small and tall people seemed closer to the moon and more likely to reach space than small people like him. But he was learning about space from school library books and that must count for something. He liked to look at the pictures. Tried his hardest to work out the words. A hushed 'night boys' caught his attention and he watched his mother's shadowy figure glide across the creaking floorboards and slip out, gone with a click of the latch. Then, in a whisper that floated with the gentle breathing of his brother's oncoming sleep, Wilfie told Pip everything he knew.

13. Mining beyond

Hard to imagine. The Milky Way galaxy is over 100,000 light years in diameter and filled with 800 billion stars and planets. And there are at least 200 billion galaxies in the universe.

On the second day of the snowstorm, Weston battled to get into work. His bus slid on ice, slammed into a drift and Weston, thrown forward, smashed his temple on the 'Stop Bus' request button. The driver revved into reverse, slewing the vehicle side to side, going nowhere. Weston had had enough. He leapt off the swinging back platform, trying to ignore the fact that he would be caught on camera and get a fine, and sank immediately up to his knees in snow. By the time he had struggled onto the pavement, his shoes and lower trousers were soaked through. And yet small discomforts like damp feet numb with cold, a throbbing in his left temple and yet another fine for a minor misdemeanour were not going to shake his spirits. Weston knew he had discovered gold with his idea and now it looked like he would have the chance to let it shine.

OSH had prevaricated, delayed and put off the date of his presentation for weeks, so much so that Weston thought they were trying to get rid of him. He had thought about getting on with the research, working up his idea, but with no deadline to work towards it was hard to focus. And then yesterday they had dropped the bombshell. A firm date for his presentation. Two days time. Suddenly,

Weston needed to know his facts. He would have his work cut out to be ready, his planned schedule severely under pressure.

Miriam was already in the office when he arrived.

'Morning,' she said. 'You look as if you've seen some weather!'

Hadn't she had to battle through the same snow? Yet here she was, looking immaculate. No. Alluring. The word rolled around Weston's mouth. He tested it out, saying it silently, slowly, his lips, tongue and jaw moving in unison. All-ur-ing.

'You swallowed something, Weston? You all right?'

Her big brown eyes were following his every contortion. He had been caught, an eel in a net.

'Yep,' he snapped. 'Great. Ready for anything.'

In a gesture designed to distract her from his ridiculous behaviour, Weston threw his damp coat over the visitor's chair. They never had any visitors so the chair had become home to coats, jackets – anything that didn't have a place. Still, they always called it the visitor's chair. But things were about to change. Soon they would have visitors. No, not visitors. Clients. Streams of them. And the chair would come into its own. On reflection, no. It was tatty. Just look at it! Stuffing coming out. And stained. Horribly stained. It would have to be replaced.

But first things first. Research. If he could prise Miriam from her magazines, she could look things up, check things out. He knew she was a smart cookie underneath all that smoky make-up. What would she look like without make-up? First thing in the morning? He needed to focus.

'The OSH presentation is fixed for tomorrow.'

'I know. I took the call yesterday, remember? You were out. Long lunch. Good contact?'

'Yes. No. Look, Miriam, I need to get to grips with this space mining game. Put those magazines away and put on your research hat.'

'Hat?'

'Speaking meta-whatsit-ly Miriam.'

She needed educating. Probably didn't go to a very good school. Probably good at sport, though. She had that sort of body. Lithe. Soft and lithe.

'Find out everything you can about OSH. Who they are. What they have been doing. Where they are going. I need it now. No, yesterday, please Miriam.'

Weston stormed into his office, swung down onto his revolving chair, kicked off his shoes, rubbed his toes to bring them back to life and tried to focus on the great idea. It was on the tip of his tongue to tell Miriam, to get her opinion, but he was still confined by the OSH contract to keep the whole thing secret. Research was different of course. That was finding out what people already knew, stuff already in the public domain. Miriam might as well use the brief for starters. The company information was a bit dense, hard to grasp if he was honest. He tore off the confidential first few pages, called her in and gave her the rest.

'Use that as your basis, Miriam. Consolidate. Simplify.'

Later that morning, Miriam slapped a fat document down on Weston's desk.

'Info on OSH. Pretty interesting, actually. A game changer, if you ask me. They've spent billions developing a Space Mining Village. Sounds cute, but it's actually state-of-the-art, ahead of the game. Travels through space, trawling the solar system for precious metals and gases for consumption back down here on Earth.'

'I know. What sort of metals and things?'

'Loads. Gold, for starters. I've listed them somewhere. Here we go. Iridium, silver, osmium, palladium, platinum, rhenium, rhodium, ruthenium, tungsten. It goes on. A real treasure chest. Tea? Coffee?'

The document was stuffed with newspaper clippings, accounts, memos, even a stack of OSH's company reports. How had Miriam got all this stuff? It was all very well for her but he had to read, digest and commit everything to memory; facts, figures, the whole lot.

'You don't have to remember it all. I've summarised it on this sheet.'

The single piece of paper slipped from her hand and swooped under Weston's desk. From opposite sides, they bent to pick it up. Fumbling under the desk, their fingertips touched, a connection in the dark. Weston snatched back, shocked by the intimacy. Miriam giggled. A girly giggle. Utterly charming. Bewitching. Or was he imagining it?

'Got it,' she said, putting the sheet back on his desk. Nimble fingers.

'Like mining in space under there,' she added. 'Who knows what treasures we might find.'

Ridiculous, thought Weston, distracted by the tingling in his fingers.

'I'll get that coffee. Or was it tea?'

An hour later, Weston's mind was racing. He tried to summarise, clarify, get up to speed. Remote mining from Earth was all very well, but limited. The capsules that were sent up and down, up and down to Earth on a weekly basis were hardly covering their costs. And some were making heavy losses. Bringing back scraps. Yes, they had made a few products. There had been big excitement when the first bunch of children went off to school with lunch boxes made from a new material mined from Near-

Earth Asteroid NJ34. But that was hardly enough. OSH was focused on the real solution: extensive workforces of skilled miners were needed to live and work up there, sinking shafts, digging out industrial quantities. And to do that, they needed homes. OSH homes. Proper places to live. And extended communities where they could socialise and their kids go to school. Then, the future of Earth would be secured.

'It's the future,' said Miriam, bringing in more tea. 'But what do you think of the rim disaster?'

'The rim disaster?'

'Yes, the rim OSH invented to attach the houses to. Where they had the catastrophe. Wasn't it awful?'

Was it awful? And why was it that Miriam always seemed one step ahead?

'I remember my gran telling me she had nightmares about it. The idea of those sixteen miners tipping off the rim and being sucked into space. I mean, where are they? Where are their bodies?'

She left Weston pondering. He flicked through her notes again, hunting out information on the rim. Why did she always have to make such a drama of things? Of course there would be disasters if you were trying to create new frontiers. That was science. A newspaper article caught his eye. Thirty-eight OSH Pennysides, tiny ten foot by ten foot by twenty foot lozenge-shaped capsules, had been installed on the rim. There was a picture of a group of men in old fashioned looking space suits. A caption ran below:

Asteroid miners: the first seventeen miners to live and work in space in the new Pennysides, before take off.

Aha!

'It was seventeen miners, actually Miriam.'

Weston fired the information through his closed door and regretted it immediately as Miriam reappeared.

'Seventeen? I'm sure it was sixteen.'

'Nope. Seventeen. Look, there's a picture of them here. And listen to this: "Tragedy on the rim. Seventeen Pennyside miners in unprecedented disaster. Returning from a day's work mining on Asteroid N482, the OSH rim lock failed. The Pennysides were ripped off by surging solar storms and sucked into the blackness of space, lost along with seventeen lives and billions of pounds." Facts, Miriam. We've got to get the facts right.'

'Sixteen or seventeen. That's still a lot of people to die. Everyone is someone's baby.'

Miriam returned to reception, walking, Weston noted, in a particularly bouncy manner. Or was she flouncing? Her jewellery jangled in a distracting way. Annoying when he needed to concentrate.

Weston returned to the story.

Miraculously one of the miners regained control of his Pennyside, reattaching it to the rim and bringing the initial reported total of the disaster down from seventeen to sixteen lives lost.

Sixteen. Weston stared at the door for some time. He shut his eyes, counting the Pennysides. The ones lost, the ones still there. Confusing. He had to get this right. And why was she always so… so…

Weston rocked back on his chair. He imagined the embryonic ghost village unmanned, floating aimlessly in space, gobbling up money. Vacant. Tenantless. He saw planets made of gold, seams of mysterious green minerals running thick through asteroids, volcanic mountains puffing out priceless red dust. No wonder the government wanted to get involved. He imagined the new Pennysides. Redesigned. Flashy. He imagined himself up there. A man for the modern age. Perhaps with Miriam. No, there was only space for one. Could they squeeze in together. Could be fun. But for now, the challenge was to get the miners up there. Prove it was safe. And that was where the creative genius of Weston W B Wright of Ostrich Advertising came in. A simple mind to save the world.

14. Splitting maul

How brightly shines the supernova! Brighter than an entire galaxy of millions and millions of normal stars.

On the third day of the snowstorm, Wilfie pulled on his coat and followed his dad outside to split logs. They would load a barrow, wheel it inside, fill the log basket and pile the rest beside the open fireplace. Then, if the snow kept falling, they would keep warm and not have to go out. But they were outside now and the snow was blowing up across from the valley below, forming deep drifts against the stone walls. When Wilfie had pulled open their kitchen door, the harsh cold flung itself around them, sharp and shocking.

'Galactic freeze blast!' cried Wilfie, rushing headlong into the flurrying snowflakes. Gasping, they pushed forward against the icy wind, crossing the yard and stumbling into the shelter of the wooden stable where, in the summer months, Peter had added to the log pile by throwing in branches and sticks and broken up old pallets. Some logs were the right size for burning on the open fire in the cottage, but there was no kindling.

'Stand by the manger,' said Peter. It was safer there, out of reach of flying shards of wood. 'Splinters of anger that can maim or kill,' he told Wilfie once when he had come too close.

Wilfie watched his dad pick up the splitting maul. He wedged a row of old floorboards between two stocky beams the width of railway sleepers, raised the axe and swung down, hitting hard, splitting the first board in two. He struck the next board and the next. Sticks fell either side, their inner wood revealed, startlingly pale. The cobbled floor was soon littered with wooden shards. Wilfie gathered them up into a steel bucket and, together, they loaded the wheelbarrow with larger logs and boards and made the arctic journey back across the yard. They pushed open the kitchen door and wheeled the barrow into the kitchen and up to the fire. Sweating from the warmth of the room, they unloaded the logs into a great woven basket. Wilfie stacked the few that wouldn't fit at the other side of the fire.

'Nice and tidy,' Wilfie told Pip. 'One, two, three.'

'Whoosh!' he added when a blast of freezing air swept in again as Peter opened the door to take the wheelbarrow back outside.

Agatha, my heart is warm against the cold. It makes me happy to do things for you. Put the wheelbarrow by the gate to the garden path. You will need it when the snow melts and spring wakes sleeping seeds and the earth you cherish erupts in a glory of green. Your paradise. But now the snow itself lies asleep, covering all. I turn back to the glow of Grey

Cottage, my heart drawn to the stone and slate that cares for us all, but as I move I am tricked by a treacherous dip. A ridge? An unexpected edge? I twist, out of control, my balance lost. I fling out my hand, snaring it on the wall. Something razor sharp, jutting, digs deep. I cry out but cannot save myself and plunge forwards. Snowy whiteness closes dark over me. I am drowning in frozen waters, my chest filling to an impossible fullness. I am trying to pull myself up, but my own weakness presses me down. Holds me under. So, this is the last – like those I first loved. This is my ultimate failure. I see your face swimming above me. You smile and reach out. Slender hand. Reaching. I take it and we rise together. Up and out. I gasp and suck in the beauty of fresh, sharp air. Out, but you have gone. Alone, fearful, I burn with cold. Warmth emanates from Grey Cottage and I cry with love for that place and all who live there. I stumble closer. The sun bursts from behind heavy cloud and the moors light up, stretching away with the promise of eternity. And right here, right before me, is a dazzling, dancing show of sparkling light. But my joy is a deception: thrust into the whiteness there are dark patches that speak of horror. I know what it is. It is my working day; the bright red response to sharp slicing steel. Crimson blood springing from split pale skin. But here it is all wrong. So very wrong. A splinter has caught Wilfie. Slashed his leg? His hand? His face? Wilfie! I burst into the kitchen. Wilfie is brave. So brave.

'Wilfie, come here!'

Wilfie, playing with Pip by the fireplace, looked up, surprised by the aggression in his father's voice.

'Dad?'

Peter grasped Wilfie's hands in his. Against Peter's black gloves, Wilfie's hands were white and tiny.

'Look Wilfie. There's blood. Does it hurt? Where does it hurt?'

'Daddy, it's you, not me. It's your blood.'

Wilfie could see his dad's right glove was slashed through, soaked with blood.

Wanting to help, he pulled gently at the sodden material.

'Stop!' said Peter. 'Stop! Something's not right.'

Wilfie stood back, obedient. His dad started tugging at the glove with his left hand. Wilfie, wanting to help, took the scissors from a jam jar on the shelf above the table and held them out.

Peter took the scissors and, wrong handed, cut at the thick padding. He peeled back the material to reveal a mess of smudged red. There was a deep gash across the base of three of his fingers. Blood spurted onto the stone floor. Wilfie could see the pain starting in his father's face.

'Does it hurt a lot, dad?'

'Of course,' said Peter, panting.

'It's bloody,' said Pip. 'Bloody. Bloody.'

'Bloody?' called Agatha, coming from the pantry, a black cake tin in hand. 'What's bloody Pip? You know… Peter? Oh no! Wait. I'll get a… oh, Peter! What have you done? Not the axe?'

'No. I think the wall… I don't know.'

'The wall? Quick. The sink.'

'It's dripping, dad. Stop chewing your sleeve, Pip. Pip! It's dad's blood.'

Peter, the surgeon-in-waiting, stumbled to the sink. Water from the silver tap swished his blood round, swirling it into the scrapings of marmalade cake mixture left in a mixing bowl.

'Wait!' cried Agatha. But as she took out the bowl she cracked it on the hard ceramic.

'Oh Peter! Sorry! Sorry!'

Agatha snatched the jagged pieces from the pool of buttery cake mix, blood and water and piled the muddle onto the draining board to make room for Peter's damaged hand under the tap. Water, powerful against the pumping red, revealed flashes of white bone. The cut was deep and the blood kept coming, swirling down the plug hole.

'Dad, your blood is going away,' said Wilfie. 'Down, away. Where's it going?'

Peter did not answer. Wilfie put his arm round his father's leg and squeezed.

'You'll be alright, dad. You will.'

Peter closed his eyes.

'My fingers...'

'Oh Peter, it's bad. It's bad,' said Agatha. 'Your fingers are hardly...'

'Just get a bandage. Hold it together.'

'Yes. Yes. I'll get one. A bandage. A bandage. Can't find one. Not here. Where...'

'Upstairs? The bathroom. I don't know. Hurry.'

'Yes! Yes. Stay with daddy, Wilfie.'

Agatha rushed upstairs.

Wilfie squeezed Peter's leg again.

'It'll be alright dad. Don't cry.'

Agatha returned, her face white.

'Not upstairs. Where else could I...'

'I need a bandage.'

'Yes. Yes,' said Agatha. 'I can't…'

Agatha grabbed a stool and started searching on the top shelf of the kitchen cupboard, pushing things to the side, spilling them onto the floor.

Peter fell against the sink.

'Help me sit down, Wilfie. I need to…'

Wilfie stretched to put his arm round his dad's waist, but Peter's balance failed him and he fell, crashing to the ground.

'Dad!'

Agatha jumped down from the stool and knelt by Peter's side. His fingers lay at the wrong angle. Not like fingers at all.

Peter covered his eyes with his other arm.

'Bandage it. Please.'

'Yes. Yes, of course. Maybe in the bathroom…'

Crying, Agatha fled upstairs again. Wilfie grabbed a cushion and put it under Peter's head. He stroked the freckled forehead, pushing back damp hair.

'It'll be alright, dad. I promise.'

But he wasn't sure. His father's blood was pumping out onto the floor. Bright red, terrifying blood.

15. One minute pitch

Once upon a time four and a half billion years ago the Solar System was born.

The day of his presentation, Weston planned to take a taxi to OSH's headquarters. An extravagance, but it was still snowing hard and he knew his shoes would not stand up to the freezing conditions. A taxi would enable him to arrive fresh, sharp, snappy.

'Snappy, Miriam. That's what I'll be. Snappy.'

Weston marched out of the office.

'Good luck, Weston. Don't forget your presentation file.'

Weston marched back.

'All up here,' he said, pointing to his temple, wincing from the forgotten bruising. 'All up here.'

He snatched the file from Miriam, marvelling as he often did how she managed to type with all those rings and bracelets, jangling with beads and baubles and things tied with string and bits of leather round her fragile yet dimply wrists, and marched, faster than ever, to hail a taxi. But it proved difficult. He could not even see a taxi. Perhaps they didn't come to Borage Green, circle thirteen. And his feet were getting cold and wet. He returned to the office.

'Miriam, get me a taxi.'

Ten minutes later than he wished, Weston sat back into the torn, dogtooth patterned seat of an outer circle taxi, opened the window to let out the stale smell of sandwiches and tried not to think how much the ride would cost. Or be cross with Miriam for getting the wrong sort of taxi. She was probably thinking of costs. He was always reminding her that they needed to be careful with expenses. Run a tight ship and all that. Although, on this occasion, he had imagined travelling in style in an inner circle taxi, slipping smoothly through the traffic, whilst he calmly ran an eye over his presentation. On arrival, the driver – smart, attentive – would hop out and open the door for him. Perhaps salute. But this was jumping the gun. Weston closed his eyes and ran through the presentation, trying to focus. Trying not to think about coffee stains, or the broken window in his office or embroidered, billowing shirts.

'Here we go, mate. Wake up. We're here.'

Weston strode up the wide steps of the OSH offices, swung through the revolving, tinted glass doors and crossed the marble entrance hall in ten manly strides. He addressed the receptionist, perched behind a high desk the length of a large public bar. It had a screen of pale green, semi-transparent glass running along the top, making it difficult to see who you were talking to.

'Weston W B Wright. Ostrich Advertising Agency. I have an appointment with the OSH marketing team,' he announced to a crown of shiny, brunette hair. The owner did not look up.

'Over here, sir,' chirped a high pitched voice. 'Can I help you, sir? Over here.'

A girl three metres further down the desk stood up and waved. Young, hair tinted pink and brushed into a firm bob, and wearing joke shop-like giant glasses, she waved again.

'Still snowing, is it?' she said, as Weston hurried across. 'You're covered.'

Weston brushed melting flakes off his shoulder.

'Like your tie, sir. Emus are they?'

'Ostriches, actually.'

'Head in the sand?'

'What?'

'That's what ostriches are known for, isn't it? Putting their head in the sand. So they don't have to see danger lurking. Lions. Tigers. Crocodiles. All the main predators.'

'Right.'

Weston had chosen the ostrich as his company symbol, imagining a graceful bird, head and shoulders above their other feathered friends. He was not aware of the head in the sand bit. Perhaps it wasn't such a great image, after all? Perhaps that was why business wasn't so good. Maybe he should change the name.

'So, how can I help you, sir?'

'Weston W B Wright. Ostrich Advertising Agency. I've come to see the OSH marketing team'

Weston stressed 'Ostrich'. He had committed to the bird and he would pin his colours to the board. Bird? Whatever the saying was.

'Nice. Take a seat on a leaf bud in a pod in our green space, Mr White. I'll let them know you're here. Would you like a glass of iced lime water with a sprig of mint?'

Weston perched himself on one of the green leaf bud seats in the area reserved for visitors, sales reps, interviewees and anyone else OSH wanted to feel uncomfortable. Silent, massive TV screens running news programmes filled one wall and towering glass windows the other. Soothing music made Weston anxious. He fiddled with his black pen. The lid flipped off and rolled under a bud. He leant down to find it. It was nestled at the back of the bud against the wall. He got down on his knees. He couldn't reach it. Dusty. It was really dusty under there. That surprised him.

'Mr White, come this way. They're ready for you now.'

Weston became aware of the faint smell of a peachy perfume before he saw Big Glasses' trim ankles waiting for him. Attractive. A tiny tattoo just above the left ankle bone said *Go. 4. It.*

Not many people, he thought, would have seen that close up.

He gave up trying to retrieve his pen lid, got to his feet, stuck the pen, topless, in his suit breast pocket and hoped it would not leak or run out. Weston followed the young woman into an all-glass lift. He kept his eyes down, trying to focus on his pitch, but actually focusing on the little tattoo.

It said it all.

On arrival at the top floor, the door slid open, straight into the heart of OSH.

'Presentation seven. Mr Weston White, Emu Agency,' announced the girl.

'Ostrich,' whispered Weston.

'Apologies, correction. Mr Weston Ostrich, of course, head in the sand, from another agency.'

She scurried back into the lift.

Weston tried to clarify his name, his company, but his own words tumbled in confusion from his lips. He fell silent, a hot flush rising up the back of his neck.

Before him was a long, silver boardroom table. Thirteen OSH executives – suited men, sharp-looking women – sat round, expectant.

'Mr White?'

Weston nodded, hesitantly.

'You have one minute to pitch. Starting now.'

Only one minute? Weston looked at his watch as if to remind himself what a minute looked like. The second hand ticked away, counting down. Fifty seconds. He had practised his pitch: eight minutes. Now he only had one. Actually, forty seconds. Where could he start? Where was Miriam?

'Yes, Mr White?'

Weston had to begin. Trying to overcome rising panic, he launched in, talking fast, his voice unusually high and squeaky.

'Miners are nervous about going into space…'

'We know that. Forget the long winded, boring preamble. What's your idea?' shouted an exec from the far end.

'Yes. Spit it out.'

'Come on. Let's hear it.'

Weston had not expected this – the jeering tone, the naked hostility. Well, he would give it to them. No, as Miriam would say, 'sock it to them'.

He didn't need a minute. He didn't even need thirty seconds. His idea was so concise, so perfect, so hit-the-nail-on-the-head, so right button pressing, that he only needed five seconds.

He stood tall and defiant.

'My idea...' said Weston W B W, eyeballing every single conceited, big-headed, pompous suit in the room.

'My idea' he repeated, 'is to send a child.'

16. Chaos and change

Sleeping beauty. The dark side of Uranus lasts for twenty-one years on Earth.

Wilfie stared at his father lying helpless on the floor. He stared at the blood dribbling in streams between the flagstones. He stared at the space on the stairs where his mother had been. He felt the chaos and change.

Three babygrows were drying on a wooden rack by the stove. Clean. That's what you needed. Something clean. Wilfie took one. His dad's eyes were still closed. Wilfie looked at the bloodied hand again. The cut was deep. One finger was nearly sliced right off, showing tiny flashes of white bone stark against the dark red of muscle, brighter red still flowing. Wilfie put the babygrow on the flagstone, its arms and legs outstretched. He slid it gently under the wounded hand. He arranged the fingers neatly, soldiers in a row, as they should be and wrapped the babygrow round the hand. Neatly. But blood seeped through, staining, spreading. He heard his mother rushing about upstairs, now crashing down the stairs carrying a sheet.

'Mum, I've done it. But more blood's coming. Get another babygrow.'

'I've got a sheet, but I can't tear it. Where are the scissors? What are you…?'

'Another babygrow. Quick mum.'

Agatha dropped the sheet and helped Wilfie tie a second babygrow around Peter's hand. It looked big and fat, like a rugby ball.

Now they could not see the wound, they felt safer, braver.

Peter opened his eyes.

'Oh, Peter,' Agatha cried. 'Your poor, poor hand. Wilfie you were so… Pip. Pip, where are you?'

Pip was back playing with logs. He saw the family grouped together and toddled over to join them. That was where he belonged. All four together.

They hugged Peter and he hugged them.

'Lucky I'm a surgeon and knew what to do.'

It wasn't funny, but they tried to laugh all the same.

17. Be prepared

Oh floating sphere! Liquid, moving free in outer space, make thyself into a sphere, pulled by your own surface tension.

Agatha, your breath comes gentle as you sleep beside me. But I cannot sleep. My hand throbs with pain. And my heart burns with love for Wilfie. We are the children, Agatha. You and I, still burdened with our past. If I could return to the water I could have saved her. Oh, how I wish I could feel her palm in mine. Like the man on the cliff. Yes, I saved him. But even then, I feel he saved me. I am not brave like Wilfie. Wilfie can touch others. He sees and acts. A babygrow! My hand is saved but damaged. If it doesn't mend... If I cannot work. A surgeon. Ha! I do not have the wisdom to save my own family. No bandages. No plasters. No antiseptic. It could have been you, Agatha. Or Wilfie. Or Pip. I have failed you again. Not like Wilfie, who fights my battles for me.

18. Wild birds

Flying start. It only takes one and a quarter seconds for the sun's rays to bounce off the moon's surface and reach Earth.

As morning broke, Peter fell asleep and Agatha awoke. Seeing his hand soaked with blackened blood lying helplessly beside him, she felt a rush of love, of desire to care for him. How shocked she had been by his wound; the blood, the bone, the horror. How she had panicked. It was Wilfie who had done the right thing. Ashamed, she whispered Peter a promise she would do all she could to look after him. He deserved all the care in the world.

She slipped out of bed and crept downstairs. Dressed only in her nightdress, she wrapped herself in Peter's heavy coat, wanting to feel him around her. She pushed bare feet into cold rubber boots and unlatched the kitchen door. Snow was still piled in drifts but had stopped falling and the sky was clear blue.

Wild birds circled high above, swirling and rising, dipping then soaring back up into the sky, veering east then flicking as one to swoop west. Agatha, trudging across the yard to feed the hens and check, as she had all week, for the first of the eggs, paused and watched their spectacular dance. She started to dance herself, tipping and diving, mirroring their freedom. How knowing were those birds. They knew what to do without thinking. They knew when to leave – before the air in the north developed a freezing bite. As one, they would take off from the endless plateaus, the forests, the steppes, and fly south looking to keep warmth on their wings. How cold it must be in those lands if they came here in winter to find warmth.

And did they find this annual exodus exciting?

Did they wake up and think: 'How marvellous! We are off on an adventure today. We are flying over iced mountains, great frothing seas. There will be beauty and danger. Hunger, even death for some of us. But still we will go. Of course. And nobody will cheep, "I can't be bothered this year. You go."'

So great in number, the individual does not count anymore. But down here, where the black granite wears its snow-white coat, we are not free to fly. Not free at all. At birth, we cast a net, linked and knotted, affecting those close. One move – a shrug of the shoulder – and those we are intimate with will feel it and deeply care. So, here at Grey Cottage, four makes the perfect square, criss-crossed with diagonals. Each affecting the other. None free to fly. Not yet.

Agatha pushed open the stable door. Inside, it was dark and warm, the hens murmuring to each other. Squabbling a little. Pecking for grain from a cobbled floor, presented to them with no danger. No big adventure like their fellow birds outside. For a moment, Agatha felt sorry for them. In the manger, one pale brown egg lay warm on a bed of wood chippings. The first egg. Perfect in form.

'Thank you,' she murmured, taking the egg and, feeling hopeful, returned to the cottage.

19. Did I think of that?

Water, water, enough for all but, oh so far away! Know this: a water vapour cloud, one hundred and forty trillion times the mass of water in Earth's oceans, is waiting for us, ten billion light years away.

After his pitch, Weston did not get a taxi back to his office. He stumbled four miles through slush from the OSH head office to his bedsit in Borage Green. It had been a crushing embarrassment. They board had met his idea with guffaws of laughter. How could he have thought of such a stupid, stupid, idiotic thing? A child in space! What was he thinking? Ashamed, he had slunk home, unable to face Miriam.

But he would have to face her today. The buses were not running on time, so he had to walk. By the time he got to the office, his feet were wet and numb again. Miriam was at her desk, reading a magazine. She was already eating the garibaldis. Annoying. She had no respect. Sitting there with her silky green trousers tucked into long boots. And what was that orange shirt? Hideous. He hated that orange shirt. It even had crumbs on it. No self-respecting ad agency would allow such clothes in their reception. No wonder he was getting nowhere. Useless. The whole thing was useless. Miriam smiled when she saw him. Her dimpled cheeks really got up his nose. How could she look so chirpy when he faced disaster? That was the thing about Miriam. She had no idea. No. Idea.

'Weston Wright, you genius,' she sang.

Her voice was all up and down and silly, her body animated as she moved towards him. That was inappropriate. Disrespectful. He thought for a terrible moment she was about to fling her arms round him. He could not deal with that. Not right now.

'Mr Black from OSH rang. Only a second ago. He was ever so chatty. Said your idea is spot on and the team wants to know how it would work. They want to see you again after their board meeting. Friday. Six o'clock.'

Miriam handed him a sheet of paper with all the details neatly written. She might look terrible, but she was efficient. He would give her that.

'Sure it was Mr Black from OSH?'

'Absolutely certain.'

'Are you sure he meant to ring me?'

'Yes, defo. It must have been you because he said he liked your ostrich tie. He wanted you to know it wasn't an emu. I mean, why would it be? But I explained we were Ostrich Advertising. I think he understood. He was ever so friendly. Had a lovely voice. You look cold. And those shoes. They're coming apart. Shall I get them mended for you?'

'Thank you,' said Weston. 'Thank you very much.'

20. Go. 4. It.

Be strong! Weigh a teaspoon of neutron star. Four ounces? Four pounds? No. Four billion tons.

On Friday, at four minutes to six, Weston approached the OSH reception, braced for a rebuttal. The receptionists were probably grumpy about having to stay late for a board meeting. The brunette looked up. She smiled, attentive.

'Good evening, Mr Weston. Please sign in and I'll take you up to the board room.'

He noted her plain white shirt. Smart but dull. That was the difference, of course, between someone working for OSH and someone working for Ostrich. An orange shirt said so much more about a place. Creative. A bit out there.

Big Glasses, back behind the desk, waved and gave him the thumbs up.

'So, who's won some brownie points, hey?'

'Guess I'll just have to Go. 4. It.' said Weston.

Big Glasses giggled. Surprised. Found out. She went into a hands-only dance routine: pointed, held up two fingers from both hands, and measured a small amount of fresh air with finger and thumb.

Weston tried the routine but got confused, so he gave her a thumbs up.

The brunette was waiting by the lift, patient, polite.

'Please,' she said, as the lift door slid open.

Her attention made Weston feel even more nervous than the first time.

Obediently, he stepped inside. Her elegant finger, the elongated nail a commanding vermilion, lightly touched the button for floor twelve. Weston threw her a chummy smile. She kept her eyes fixed on the rising floor numbers. Weston became uncomfortably aware of the sound of his own breathing. He held his breath, only daring to exhale as the lift came to a halt and the door slid open. Before him was a room full of OSH executives. The board room table had disappeared. Weston had expected them to be sitting, focussed, ready, but instead they were all standing round, ties off, drinks in hand. When they saw Weston, they broke into spontaneous applause.

The big cheese of OSH, Franklin Black, bounded forward and shook his hand vigorously. Franklin was a striking man; small with dark features, quick movements, a ready smile. He exuded action, dynamism, excitement. Only a year or so older than Weston, he had the charismatic presence Weston was trying so hard to cultivate in himself. How on earth was he already in charge of this great empire when he only had Miriam and Lazarus? And Lazarus didn't really count.

'Come in. Come in. The genius himself. If you weren't a six-foot giant, perhaps we could send you up there. You look fit enough.'

Franklin looked up at Weston. Weston noted he was making out that he was a big guy, physically impressive, which he knew he wasn't. But it was nice of him. Thinking about it though, when did he last do any serious exercise? To the point when the muscles in his legs begged him to stop and his heart felt like it belonged at the front of a marching band. Not since he had set up Ostrich, that was for sure. And Miriam was always commenting that he looked peaky, under the weather.

'Not working too hard are you, Weston?'

'Getting enough fresh air are you, Weston?'

It annoyed him. If you were going to succeed in business, you had to spend your days in an airless office the size of a dog kennel and which smelt just as bad. At least in the early, pioneering days. Eventually he'd have an impressive art gallery of an office like this, with paintings of brightly coloured naked bodies doing gymnastics and a cocktail bar in the corner. Anyway, what business was it of Miriam's? And if she cared so much, why wasn't she here with him now? Part of the team. In her orange shirt. Making a statement about their creativity. He should have asked her to come along.

'Come on then. Let's have it,' said Franklin.

Weston went blank. He could hardly remember why he was here. Why all these people in sharp suits were looking at him. Grinning. One was wearing an orange tie. Probably a shade lighter than Miriam's shirt. Not the same full-on depth or resonance of foreign sunsets.

'Your idea,' pressed Franklin. 'We cut you a little short at the pitch. We had a lot of agencies to get through but I have to say, sir, we liked the cut of your jib the best and, if something feels right, we like to make snap decisions in this company.'

'Snappy,' said Weston.

'Snappy. Of course. So hit us with it.'

Weston forced himself to focus.

'We have got to prove the Pennysides are safe. So my idea is to send a child.'

'Love it, love it, love it.'

'In other words, send a minor not a miner.'

'Great line. Great line.'

The executives, fuelled with after-work drinks, fired off questions.

'Where will you find a kid who wants to go?'

'What parent in their right mind will let them?'

'How will the kid get time off school?'

'You can't just pluck a child off the street and blast them into the solar system.'

'Quiet.' Franklin Black raised his hands. 'Give Mr Wright – Weston – a chance. He's the expert. Listen to him. Come on young man. Tell us how it works.'

All eyes turned to Weston. His mouth was dry, his palms were damp and he was sweating.

Tell us how it works.

How did it work? Weston had not thought about the detailed mechanics of his idea and had never in his life been called an expert. All he knew was that this was his big chance and he was a fraction of a millimetre close to blowing it. His only option was to take evasive action. In other words, pretend he knew. Better still, pretend he was someone else who knew and say what that person would say. Method acting for an ad exec. And that person would, of course, be Miriam. Miriam in her orange shirt and green silky trousers. Relaxed but clever. So, she was here with him after all. And she was brilliant.

'OSH will set up a charity. A programme not just for miners, but for the advancement of living in space, of expanding opportunities for living beyond the bounds of an overcrowded Earth.'

Applause threatened to break his train of thought.

'But how do you get the kid?' someone called out.

Kid sounded relaxed, friendly, non-threatening. Weston used it.

'The charity would be called the Kid's Intergalactic Space Something. KISS for short.'

'KISS?'

'KISS.'

The word echoed round the board room.

A charity was an excellent idea. Gave credibility. Looked like they were doing the right thing.

'But you still haven't told us how you would get the kid,' persisted the voice from the back.

'KISS would run a competition, backed, of course, by OSH.'

'What? To find the brainiest space geek in town?'

'No,' replied Weston. 'A child with a passion for

space. A child who has always wanted to see what it's like up there. Has a curiosity.'

And from some deep memory of a whispering ancient uncle with no teeth and a lot of spittle, a turn of phrase sprang to Weston's mind.

'Blessed are the curious for they shall see the stars.'

The room fell silent. Instinctively, Weston knew he had got it wrong. Not the phrase, but the language. Why did he say 'blessed' of all things? And, thinking about it, curious wasn't the right word. Or stars. Weston glanced at Franklin. His lips were pressed together, suppressing a smile. The rest of the room was stony-faced.

'Young man, forget the fancy wording. Stick with the idea. We want a curious kid – yes?' came a voice angry, impatient.

'Yes, of course.' Weston ploughed on. 'To select the child, we must make the competition appear run-of-the-mill; family friendly.'

'How are you going to do that?'

Weston was ready.

'Put it on the back of a cereal packet.'

'Cereal?'

'Which cereal?'

Weston began to feel now that he might just pull it off. The concept was accepted. They were discussing the detail. The deal was almost done. Weston paused for effect.

'Brexypops,' he said, 'are very popular.'

Thirteen top executives considered the nation waking up and coming face to face with the possibility of their son or daughter being the very first child in space. And they loved it.

'Brexypops. That's genius,' echoed round the room as clapping broke out again.

'If this mission is accomplished successfully' continued Weston, 'OSH's reputation as a world leader in space living will be assured. Funding will not be a problem.'

It was a big claim, but worth a push. The clapping returned louder than ever. Weston was surrounded, patted on the back and a drink thrust in his hand. He had done it.

'You are one hell of a creative and entrepreneur,' said Black. 'Be in my office on Monday morning, seven o'clock sharp, and let's get this ball rolling.'

21. Ask the questions

Are there enough stars? Our galaxy, the Milky Way, holds maybe two, three, four hundred billion stars. Hold this, then remember there are billions of galaxies out there.

Franklin Black was daring to hope. He liked Weston and he liked his idea. At last, he had come across someone he could work with; his spirits lifted at the thought of having a one-to-one with the adman on Monday morning. He'd get to know him. Find out what made him tick. Franklin was the new head of OSH and he knew the job could overwhelm him if he wasn't careful. He needed allies. He was still reeling from the recruitment process; ruthlessly headhunted, pursued and appointed by people considerably older than him who wanted someone else to blame for the next inevitable OSH failure.

It was odd how he of all people, who didn't crave fame or fortune, was making his way up the corporate ladder at breakneck speed. He wasn't flattered by the appointment but took it because saying no wasn't an option; it simply wasn't allowed. If he had refused, the repercussions could have been catastrophic – they had a way of dealing with anyone stepping out of line. His knack for leadership, for turning things around at speed a process that thrilled him – had put him dangerously in the spotlight. He should have been more careful, curbed his enthusiasm, held back. But now here he was, expected to pep up OSH, get things moving, make decisions, light the fire.

From day one, he had been shocked by the despondency of the OSH directors. They had run out of steam, were drifting around, bickering, getting nowhere – because they had no idea where to go. With confidence low, investors were pulling out. And the government was no help: a bunch of fading ministers who floundered about in cabinet meetings, fed up of throwing money at the project and then defending themselves to the public for losing it all. Franklin was expected to come up with something fast.

To Franklin, the solution seemed obvious. OSH needed one thing: belief. If he could revive the space mining companies' belief in OSH, make them eager to send their people up there again, to start living the dream, everything could get back on track. But belief wasn't going to come from within OSH. It would have to come from outsider.

'We'll launch a new campaign to rebuild confidence in OSH,' he told a weary board. 'Invite the best marketing companies in the industry to pitch. They'll give us the answers if we ask the questions.'

That was what Franklin was good at. Asking other people.

Ruefully, Franklin realised if he hadn't been so good at asking, he wouldn't be in this situation now. He had risen on this one skill. He asked people what they thought, what he should do, how things should be done. And when he had finished asking, he listened to their answers.

And when he got the answers, he asked others what they thought and what should be done. And then he was, generally, able to make the right decision. His lively manner and quick-fire questioning impressed, and people called him clever, astute, a fine young mind. But Franklin knew he was none of these things. He knew it was easier to fire off questions than think of answers, and he also knew, by some odd chance, how to ride the wave. And boy, was he riding the wave. Chairman of OSH. It was a big job.

And it terrified him.

After the board meeting, a company car took Franklin to circle five, quarter seven. He slid onto the leather back seat, uncomfortable with his senior status, the lifestyle, who they wanted him to be. He could not come to terms with living in circle five – the most expensive residential area – and worse, in quarter seven, the most exclusive area. It irritated him that there were seventeen quarters in circle five; it was odd, illogical – there to catch out the uninitiated, separate the ordinary man from the elite. And quarter seven was elite, reserved for level eight government officials and selected high fliers. You had to be invited. And if invited, you had to accept. On the day of his OSH appointment, Franklin had been given a stiff envelope. Inside was a key card and a slip of paper which read, *Franklin Black. Number 73, Colorado 85. With compliments.* Colorado 85 – a tower block of eighty-five exclusive living spaces. To Franklin, it didn't feel right. But he knew better than to object.

At the heavy, ornate metal gates, the security guard, sheltering in his hut from the cold, shuffled out and pressed a button to lift the barrier, allowing Franklin's car to sweep in, right up to the pillared front doors.

'Night, sir,' said the driver. 'Six thirty pick up Monday morning?'

'Yes, thanks. You have a good evening. Hope the pitch is clear for Callum's team tomorrow. Striker, isn't he? Let me know if he scores the winning goal.'

The driver left with a cheery wave. Franklin knew the drivers thought he asked a lot of questions about their jobs, families, aspirations. Even what they would do if they ran OSH.

'What do I know?' they would say. 'I'm just a driver.'

Nevertheless, they were happy to give advice. Franklin valued that – and envied them. Their families. Their wives. Especially their wives.

The bleep as Franklin entered the building with his key card was jarring. How much more homely would a click of a key turning in a lock be. He took the lift to level seven. An elderly resident he had never met before joined him and they chatted. He helped her out at level five and she thanked him by name. Franklin was having to get used to being a public figure. He knew people liked it in Colorado 85. It reflected well on them. But although Franklin was known, he was careful not to be *known*. His nature meant that he was always friendly, resulting in multiple drinks invitations from neighbours. He knew that in their eyes he was considered a social catch. Over cocktails, they would tell him so, quite blatantly.

'Such a handsome young man. And doing so well. You must have a girlfriend, surely?'

Franklin chatted, was polite, funny and flattered one and all by asking questions, showing interest in their lives. But he never dropped his guard. Never told them about himself.

'You seem a little lonely, dear,' probed one elderly partygoer.

'It's endearing,' said another.

'A lone wolf,' said the first, and they giggled like young girls.

Getting out on the seventh floor, Franklin marched along the corridor and turned sharp left onto the suspended high-level walkway that crossed the formal landscaped garden below – its grass and box hedges patchy white with remnants of snow. A man in short sleeves, braving the cold, waved across from his balcony. Franklin waved back cheerily. Reaching the other side, he turned right and entered the Colorado 85 gym. He headed straight to his personal locker and carried out a routine perfected by repetition: he pulled out a rucksack and removed his folded running kit, placing the shorts, top, socks and trainers side by side on the bench. Then he untied his shoes and placed them at the bottom of the locker and hung his suit on a hanger. He took off his shirt, tie and socks, folded them and put them into the rucksack. And finally, with increasing eagerness, he put on his running gear. Feeling the trials of the day drop away, he secured his locker, pulled the rucksack onto his back, scooted down the stairs to the south exit and jogged off through the slush towards circle fifteen. As he dodged damp pedestrians on crowded pavements, his mind cleared of OSH, of boardrooms, of execs, of space mining, giving way to thoughts of a small terraced house, what he might buy from the local supermarket for supper that night and if, with any luck, there would be a young woman on checkout seven whose dimpled cheeks made buying rice and cabbage and milk a moment of pure joy.

22. Blackened

Pluto has icy mountains, but where did the energy come from to make them? Not the sun. Not gravity from other planets. A mystery of missing energy.

On Monday, five days after Peter's accident, Agatha and the boys, wrapped in coats and boots, tramped up the track to see if the minibus could get up the road from the village. They heard the familiar engine, mechanical against the still white landscape, and then the minibus itself came creeping up the hill, tyres skidding but pushing onwards and upwards.

The boys were back to school at last. Agatha waved them off, sad that their time cut off from the rest of the world had come to an end. She slithered back down the icy track. It looked passable by car. Just about. An hour later, hands gripping the wheel as the car skidded side to side, Agatha drove Peter up onto the top road.

At the hospital, Agatha felt helpless – hopeless – as nursing staff took over Peter's care. She had replaced the babygrows with cotton strips torn from a pillowcase. Even so, as Peter lay his arm on the sanitised hospital table, his hand looked like an overwrapped present – an amateur botched job.

'Not that impressive for a surgeon,' joked Peter.

Not that impressive for a wife, thought Agatha, ashamed.

A nurse cut into the pillowcase bandage with razor sharp surgical scissors. She peeled away crusty layers of dried-up stickiness – the outer white cotton mottled with deep red blemishes; the innermost layers, once soaked crimson, now dried to dead black. And, at last, flesh. But a mockery of flesh. The skin was blanched with ghostly patches of pale green and the gash – a strip of venomous maroon, edged with blackened blood crusts – was punctuated by seeping yellow pus. The smell of meat hovered in the air. Peter's thumb twitched, a cruel contrast to the inert digits that lay slashed and dying. Agatha felt sickened by the smell, by the sight, by her own failure.

23. Broken wing

What we know is not always true. Look to the sunset on Mars. It's blue.

Time brought healing. On Saturday, two weeks later, Agatha was out early, throwing corn to the hens. The day was fresh. Green tips of bulbs, with their promise of spring, were pushing up through the last of the snow. Peter's fingers had been stitched and Agatha's heart had leapt when yesterday, for the first time since the accident, he had picked up a glass with his right hand and his bandaged fingers curled. Just slightly.

The sound of an engine coming up the top road caught her attention; the red splash of the postman's van. He stopped at the top of the track, dropped something in their post box, then sped back towards the village. Agatha hurried up the track. They hardly received any post – bills, the occasional letter from school, a new government requirement, perhaps a fine. That was about it. Their post box, a grey tin with a slit in the top, was nailed to the gatepost. It had been there when they arrived and Agatha had painted *Grey Cottage* in white letters on the front; now faded but still visible. She lifted the lid and took out a slim envelope.

'Mr P W Whisper.'

Agatha read the name aloud, running her fingers over the words as she traipsed back down the track. She was proud of her husband. She said his name again, her words mixing with the cries of starlings swooping overhead. But, from the swirl of sound, a cheeping that was different from the confident cries of above caught her attention. Where stone track met grassy verge, a small bird was fluttering, beating its wings against the ground but failing to rise – panicked, trapped by injury. Agatha cupped it in her hand and, cradling it close, hurried back to the cottage, whispering promises it would fly again.

The boys, eating their breakfast with Peter, were building a tower from their empty eggshells.

'Wilfie's go to spin.'

Wilfie spun the teaspoon.

'It's me!' cried Pip.

He picked up the spoon and smashed it down on the eggshell tower.

'Shot!' said Peter. 'A real smasher.'

Agatha leant over Peter to hand him the letter. Then she took the wounded bird over to the sink. She could feel the rapid beat of its tiny heart. Its terror. She turned on the tap, letting a splash of water wet the ceramic. The bird, set down, ignored the water and flapped in alarm at the strange white world.

The boys tried to grab the letter off Peter but he held it up, just out of reach – laughing, teasing – until his eye caught sight of the lettering.

'Whoa. Looks official. Game's over, boys.'

He held the envelope in his left hand and tried to tear it open with his right thumb but the bandage made him clumsy. Wilfie took the envelope from him, slit it open and held it out so his dad could pull out the letter.

'Dear Mr Whisper,' Peter read.

'Mister!' echoed Pip.

'We have received the results from your tests of the thirteenth of this month. Mobility and dexterity are severely impaired and unlikely to improve to any significant degree. In view of this, we hereby give you notice that your position as a surgeon...'

Peter hesitated, steadying himself.

'...your position as a surgeon is no longer tenable and will...'

Peter paused again, rolled his head back, closed his eyes and sighed as he spoke.

'...will cease with effect from the date of this letter.'

'What's it mean, dad?' whispered Pip.

'Just... I suppose...'

Peter looked at his right hand and tried to bend his fingers. They bent. Just slightly.

'It says... because of the damage to my hand I can't... sorry boys... sorry, but I'm no longer a surgeon.'

Agatha, by the sink, felt his pain, his desolation as he rocked back and closed his eyes, breathing deeply, trying to take it all in. His life had slewed off course again, everything chaotic, thrown in the air. She stood immobile, tears falling.

The bird cheeped.

Peter screeched his chair back against the slabs, the sound loud and aggressive. He strode over to the sink to look at the bird, the boys in his wake.

Wilfie put his arm round his dad's waist.

'Don't worry, dad. It'll be OK.'

The bird cheeped and fluttered.

'Broken wing,' said Peter. 'Let's see what we can do about that.'

24. Hey There, Woman!

Together forever: when pieces of metal touch in space they bond, never to be torn asunder.

Weston Wright was worried. Franklin Black seemed to have faith in him. A lot of faith. And even more worryingly, Franklin seemed interested in him. Weston W B Wright. Nobody had ever seemed particularly interested in him before, and it unnerved him. Miriam certainly wasn't interested in him. And now Franklin had booked a host of OSH executives and media types to thrash out the details of his child in space idea at some mega meeting. Weston needed help. And the only person he could think of was Miriam. He strode out of his office and stood in front of her cluttered desk. She looked up from her magazine.

'Miriam, I am going to tell you something. It's top secret. What is said between these walls must stay within these walls.'

They both looked towards Lazarus's seat. It was empty.

'I am going to tell you my idea. My concept for the OSH project.'

'Go on then. Hit me with it.'

'My idea, Miriam, is to send a child into space.'

'A child?'

Miriam's hand – a flash of gold rings, sapphires and opals, bangles and bracelets – flew to her ruby red lips in horror.

'Oh no, Weston. No! No! That's cruel.'

She shook her head, her gold earrings jangling.

'A child will be horribly homesick.'

'Not this child. We are looking for a real keen bean. An eager beaver. A kid who has spent his life dreaming about intergalactic space missions. And this is his chance.'

'His?'

'Well, I sort of imagined it would be a boy. I mean boys are more interested in space than girls, aren't they?'

'Not necessarily, Weston. But, that aside, what about their little bodies?'

'What do you mean?'

'It's bad enough for an adult going up into space. The impact of microgravity is pretty serious on a fully formed human body, let alone a kid. It causes chaos with your metabolism, heat regulation, heart rhythm, muscle tone, bone density, eyesight, respiration…'

Miriam ticked off the problems on her heavily ringed fingers.

'…and your immune system can be sent right up the spout. Imagine what it could do to a child.'

'How do you know all this stuff?'

'Always been interested in the stars. You know me, Weston.'

'No, seriously. How do you know?'

'I read, Weston. I read.'

To prove her point, Miriam picked up her copy of *Hey There, Woman!* magazine and waved it at Weston.

'If you think this is just full of lipstick and eyeliner, you're wrong. All this Earth running out of resources business means that space and living in space are hot topics – yes, Weston – even in women's magazines. When it comes to actually going up there, the hints and tips we women have picked up means we'll be light years ahead. Look at this. "Recipes for Mars", "How to Breathe Calmly in the Above and Beyond", "Cutest Baby Names for The Space Age". Why do you think Iridium, Tungsten, Osmium and Osmi are top of the pops at the moment? And then there's this.'

Miriam slapped the magazine down, open on a double-paged spread. The headline, *Your Body in Space: Could It*

Really Cope?, swam before Weston's eyes. Miriam was bombarding him with facts, figures, moral issues. All he wanted was her blessing for his great idea.

'You should read it yourself, Weston,' Miriam was saying. 'Keep in touch.'

Miriam picked up the magazine and pushed it towards Weston. Reluctantly, he took it and started to flicked through. There were some pretty long articles. He'd never get round to reading them. He didn't have the time. Not like Miriam sitting on reception all day – and now lecturing him. Wasn't he meant to be the boss? His attention was caught by a picture of a model in a plunging, violent lime green dress. Even though he was irritated by her, he couldn't help feeling Miriam would look better in the dress. The lime green would complement her olive skin. The model's skin was white. Unhealthily white. Not warm and glowing like Miriam's. Yes, Miriam would definitely look better in the dress. He wondered if she had ever thought about being a model. Probably too short. But she had the figure otherwise. Especially for a plunging neckline. Or maybe she was a little bit too curvaceous. The model in the lime dress was pretty flat chested. No hips, as far as he could tell. Generally models didn't. No, thinking about it, there was no way Miriam could be a model. No way.

'See,' said Miriam.

'Yes. No.'

He flipped the magazine closed. Perhaps he would have another look later. After Miriam had gone home. Unless she took the magazine home with her. She probably went home and put on some relaxing clothes, then got into bed and read. Or perhaps she ran a bath. Read the magazine in a nice hot steamy bath. With bubbles. No. No bubbles. They could get in the way. Although bubbles could be romantic.

'The dangers of sending a kid into space. What it might do to its poor little body?'

She was back lecturing him. It was annoying.

'So you think it's a non-starter?' he challenged.

'I didn't say that. I just think you can't play with people's lives. Not with the technology as it is. We can't even regulate the heating in our office. It's stifling in here, Weston.'

To prove the point, Miriam pulled her tight fluffy jumper off over her head. She was wearing a swirling green and cobalt shirt underneath. Almost as interesting as the orange one, thought Weston.

'How people can even think of sending a child into space is beyond me.'

Weston desperately wanted Miriam to believe in his idea. Ridiculous, but he needed her approval. He had to have faith in it himself, for goodness' sake. It was his idea. And it was a good one. At least OSH seemed to think so. So it must be. He wished she could see that. Acknowledge it.

'Yes, but obviously experts will sort out all the technical and medical stuff. They're working on having whole villages up there. They've got a long way already.'

Weston hoped to sound decisive, knowledgeable. He had a horrible feeling it sounded as if he was defending himself.

'But what if the child is sick? What if he vomits where there is no gravity? That is really nasty. It floats all over the place. Who would clear it up?'

'Those are details, Miriam. Details. We are still at the concept phase. And anyway, it's a charity.'

'Fair enough, Weston. Who am I to say? Just don't forget it's a kid at the centre of all this. Someone's precious kid.'

25. Another life

What am I? Solid debris entering the Earth's atmosphere and making it to the surface is a meteorite. Burn up on the way and you're merely a meteor.

Agatha took the letter telling Peter he would no longer be a surgeon upstairs and slid it into her drawer with all the other bits of paper that must be kept but which she didn't want to be reminded of. Like the Child Assist Order (1). Out of sight, even Peter's letter seemed to lose its power. But, still, something had to be done.

'Could you still work at the hospital? There must be other jobs in the department. You've got all that knowledge,' said Agatha.

It seemed the obvious thing to do. Peter still couldn't drive, so Agatha took him in to talk to the hospital's HR manager, Naomi.

'Nope, I'm sorry, but the senior jobs don't come through us. In fact, not that much comes through us at all. Shame, since we're sitting here.'

Peter knew all this – he had been through the system before.

'But it's different, isn't it?' said Agatha. 'The hospital knows Peter and he was good at his job. Very good. Can't he move sideways?'

'I'm not familiar with sideways. Most people go up. What level were you at, Peter?'

'He was on his way up.'

'So why do you want to go sideways?'

'He doesn't. It's his hand.'

'I see. I can tell you what we do have but it probably won't be a sideways move I'm afraid. Let's have a look.'

Peter got up and left the room.

Agatha, a man in blue overalls is dancing a screaming floor polisher around the hospital corridor. I circle the swirl of patients stumbling on crutches, visitors laughing, visitors crying, newborns in plastic cribs, doctors hurrying in flapping white coats. Nurses, nurses, nurses. My second home, but now I am a stranger. Life bleeds from the noticeboard: warnings, official statements, vacancies – and... 'Hospital Porter. Apply HR.' I stare at it. 'Hospital Porter.' I say it out loud. I say it again and go further. 'Hospital Porter. I am going to be a hospital porter.' A baby-faced doctor is passing. 'Good for you,' he says. 'We need powerful chaps. Get a good speed up.' I say it again and again. 'I am going to be a hospital porter.' It's easy. I have replaced 'astronaut' with 'surgeon' with 'hospital porter'. I will look after you, Agatha. I rush back to HR. You are sitting there with Naomi and look up at me in surprise. 'I would like to apply for the job of hospital porter.' 'We were looking at other options, Peter. Doctor...' you say. I interrupt. 'I need something now. I could start tomorrow. Here. In the place I love.' 'But your hand?' says Naomi. 'Test me. Right now.' So Naomi finds a trolley and you lie down. I cover your slender body with a thin white sheet and you smile at me, your beautiful blue eyes shining. We race along corridors, round corners, over ramps, in and out of lifts. We are children, me pushing you on a swing, spinning together on a whirligig, bouncing up and down on a seesaw. I am full of joy. But this is not a game. I am a hospital porter and I will care for all those who travel with me.

26. Lunar gardener

Let me count the grains of sands on all the beaches on Earth and I will know I have still not counted the number of stars there are in the universe.

While Peter was pushing patients, Agatha was growing vegetables. Since living in Grey Cottage, she had become a lunar gardener. She didn't believe in horoscopes or fortune telling or anything like that. But she did believe that planting certain vegetables, herbs or flowers at certain times in the moon's monthly journey led to better crops.

'It's obvious,' she told her boys. 'The moon is so big and round and powerful that it can pull whole seas backwards and forwards, so of course it can pull up a bit of moisture in the ground or in a teeny-weeny plant. Look.'

Wilfie stared at the chart Agatha had pinned to the plaster of the kitchen wall.

'So where's the moon now, Wilfie?'

Agatha knew the chart by heart, but Wilfie liked to look at the moon every night.

'New moon. Waxing crescent phase so that's green leafy vegetables and herbs.'

He was right. During a new moon – waxing crescent phase – they would sow green leafy vegetables and herbs. In the first quarter – waxing gibbous phase – they would sow vegetables that had seeds buried within: pumpkins, courgettes, legumes. During a full moon – waning phase – it was root vegetables, bulbs and tubers. In the last quarter – waning phase – it was not a good time for anything much, so they would do a bit of weeding or go down to the gorge on the moor and swim in the river or climb the high hill.

When they had first moved to Grey Cottage, Agatha had planted spinach seedlings which grew and grew. The moon had given them a good start. Not just on her first sowing, but forever. The baby leaves grew small and tender, transforming into great deep green spreads that shrank to nothing when she steamed them in the kitchen. Every year, as the warm weather came with longer days, the stems grew thick and tall, sending out small, bright, bitter green leaves and shafts with exotic, spiky seed heads. She fed the boys puréed leaves in soups, small leaves in sandwiches, young tender stalks dipped in butter like asparagus. The boys were not good gardeners and weeded out the spinach. But Agatha didn't mind. The spinach still came back and grew and grew. There was no stopping it.

And there was no stopping the boys growing. Agatha had already received a form to fill in for Wilfie's secondary school. There was competition for places. Agatha knew some parents cheated, but she wanted to apply with honesty. She sat at the kitchen table, glancing up every now and again to check on the boys playing outside. Especially Wilfie. Just in case – she hardly liked to admit it – he had disappeared. It was Wilfie she had heard calling on the beach and the sound still played in her mind, spiralling thoughts into imagined terrors that left her shivering in a cold sweat of dread. Sometimes, in the night, she would creep into Wilfie's bedroom to check he was still there. Just in case an invisible hand had come and plucked her little boy away. Somewhere beyond her knowing. It was always Wilfie, not Pip. Pip was grounded, scrabbling round on grass with the hens or hunting insects. It was Wilfie who wandered in other places, above and beyond, with dreams of living in other lands, other spaces.

Through the window, she could see the boys kicking a ball about. Two ordinary boys. She returned to the form and tried to concentrate.

Has your child ever been in trouble at their present school?

The questions were personal and hard to answer truthfully without reducing your chances. Surely every child had been in trouble at school? At least once. For Agatha, lying did not come easily.

Yes, she wrote.

Have you, as a parent, ever been disciplined by the school?

As a parent? Why were they asking about parents?

No, she wrote.

Have you ever deceived the state?

No, she wrote again. *Of course not.*

Are you sure?

The question was so absurd that Agatha laughed out loud. It was as if someone was in the room asking her. Of course she was sure. Wasn't she? Agatha glanced up to check on the children. Pip was kicking the ball against the stone wall again and again. But Wilfie was gone.

'Wilfie,' she shouted. 'Wilfie!'

Agatha leapt to her feet ready to rush out into the garden.

Wilfie stood framed in the doorway.

'Mum, I've cut myself.'

Agatha, laughing in relief, looked at the outspread hand and the thin red line splitting the grubby skin. Wilfie squeezed a drop of blood onto the scullery's quarry tiles.

'It's nothing,' she said. 'Nothing.'

'It's bleeding quite a lot,' said Wilfie.

'No, it's not.'

'It needs a bandage.'

Agatha scoured the store cupboard and found a small biscuit tin where they kept a few plasters. Ever since

Peter's accident, she had meant to get a proper first aid kit, but she had not got round to it.

'Put your hand under the water,' said Agatha, turning on the kitchen tap. The cut was deeper than she had first thought. She tried to keep calm, to dab the wound dry, but the blood kept pumping out. She got two, three plasters to pull the skin together, cover the wound, hide the blood from sight.

'There. Better?'

'Better,' said Wilfie, poking at the plasters, squeezing a few red drops out and turning the sink water the faintest pink.

'Don't,' said Agatha, swooshing the water away.

'Will my blood mix up with daddy's?'

'Probably.'

'My blood would like that. Say "Hello, daddy blood". And his would say "Hello Wilfie blood". Then they would go mix, mix, mix.'

'I don't think so. Daddy's blood went down the plughole a long time ago. It would have gone down the pipe, out into the septic tank and then seeped into the earth. It's probably somewhere out there under the moor by now.'

'Like it's buried?'

'Sort of.'

'So some of me and some of him will be buried out there on the moor?'

Agatha and Wilfie scanned the moor, wondering where they might end up.

'I like that,' said Wilfie. 'But I would prefer to be up in space. Perhaps I will evaporate.'

Wilfie ran outside. Agatha watched him show Pip the plaster. A trophy.

Agatha returned to the form, but her mind was elsewhere. Wilfie's cut was slight but, had it been more serious, she would have been unprepared. And the sight of the droplets of blood, watered down and whirling down the plughole, had disturbed her.

Danger had seeped into the place she should be keeping safe.

27. My beating heart

Earth's grazing fireballs are those dallying meteor that fly into Earth's atmosphere and out again. Farewell fireballs!

Franklin Black, chairman of OSH, stood at the head of the boardroom table.

'Welcome, team KISS!'

Clapping rippled round the room. Even grim-faced directors looked a little more hopeful.

'First I would like to thank Mr Weston Wright of Ostrich Advertising for coming up with such a terrific idea. Simple but brilliant.'

Everyone looked at Weston, perched on the edge of his chair to Franklin's right, and applauded again. Weston stood up, scraping his chair back and giving a bow. What was he thinking? Bowing! Making an idiot of himself already. His throat was dry. He was finding it hard to breathe.

Franklin read from the minutes, his voice friendly, charismatic, commanding attention – just as Weston aspired to do.

'Item one. Technology Summary. Welcome to Bert Weinberg, our lead designer. Bert, could you give us a rundown of how the Space Mining Village project will work, from take-off to landing?'

'Sure, boss,' said Bert, quick to his feet. 'As you all know, our potential tenants are asteroid mining companies.

Right now they are mining remotely and are already pulling out valuable minerals – platinum, rhodium, tungsten, silver, gold – but in tiny, tiny quantities. Volume is what they need. And to get volume they need to sink shafts. But how do you do that from a desk on the twelfth floor of a terrestrial office block?'

Bert paused for effect. Nobody spoke.

'Well, sir, you can't,' he continued, batting away an imaginary response. 'But if you could send working miners up there to sink the shafts, to dig the stuff out, that would be a whole new story. And we've cracked it two-fold. One, the shuttle won't burn up on re-entry. Yes sir, we've made heading into space as simple as flying from an airport – just hop on and zip off into space. Two, we have designs for the miners' space homes ready to go. Three styles – Victory Villa, Highpoint House and the Pennyside Cottages – all designed to be attached to our famous rim system. Just need to get the mining companies to fall in love with these beautiful homes then, oh boy, the world's our oyster. Or should that be the solar system and beyond is our oyster?'

Laughter flittered around the room.

'And it'll be fun. Miners will stroll along tubular walkways to socialise, to take exercise. In the village centre – and one day we'll have hundreds, no, thousands of villages up there – we are creating a giant tower, the Beating Heart, with restaurants, schools, cinemas. And, get this, on the twelfth floor will be a wild garden so that miners can get a daily fix of green. We'll have walkways, paths, benches, hills, even a stream trickling down a rocky hillside. We'll build the landscape on sliding plates so it can be moved daily. One day, we'll even be able to reflect the seasons and…'

'Tremendous stuff Bert. But to clarify, where are we right now?' interjected Franklin.

'OK. For now, the Beating Heart is a work-in-progress. Victory Villa, with a capacity of six, is on the drawing board. But, get this, the first Highpoint House – which sleeps three – is now under construction. And, as you all know, Pennysides have been up on the rim and operational for...'

Bert stumbled, tussling with something. Something, thought Weston, he did not want to mention.

'...well, operational for some time. And the latest versions are ready to replace the old versions as we speak. Bed made. Kettle on!'

'So only the old-style Pennysides are up there?' said Weston. 'Up there, but abandoned.'

The room fell silent. The word 'abandoned' had a ring of finality to it. And billions down the shoot. Weston got the feeling that OSH never had and could not afford to consider the word abandoned. Not even utter the three syllables out loud.

'Well, nobody is up there are they? And they used to be. Before the explosion. When sixteen people died. I mean how did you recover from that?'

Execs fiddled with pens, looked down at their notes.

'You are referring to the past Mr Wright. At OSH, we prefer to talk about the future. And the Pennysides are the future,' said Bert. 'Improved design. Technical hitches sorted.'

There was a round of applause.

'We've had chaps living in our new prototypes testing them out for over six months.'

'So people are up there,' quizzed Weston, 'living in the new Pennysides?'

'No. The new Pennysides are down here on Earth where they are being tested. Flexible. Functional. The white vans of space.'

Weston was bemused. It seemed like some ghastly fantasy land. Where was the reality? The truth?

'Let's move on to item two,' said Franklin. 'Charlene Cooper is our Ground Control Director. Charlene, could you take us through the launch?'

Charlene stood up, her voice crisp and bright, a relief from Bert's drawl.

'Thank you,' she said. Her look was directed at Franklin. Piercing. Admiring. Available. Women never look at me like that, thought Weston. Least of all Miriam. Franklin seemed to take it in his stride. As if he was used to it.

'Launch and return,' she was saying, 'will be from Growlers Drop. I know, I know, not the prettiest for publicity purposes but it's the nearest and has excellent transfer shuttles.'

Weston dropped his head into his hands. Growlers Drop was a well-known disaster area: moorland which had taken a massive hit from the meteorites, its villages and farms laid to waste. And it had a terrible reputation for air quality. *Contamination. Radiation. Poisoned air.* All the usual terrifying phrases had swamped the headlines. It was a swathe of abandoned country. But perfect for a launch site: noise, heat, fumes – not an issue.

'Look, Mr Ad Man,' said Bert, eyeing Weston, 'before you ask, everyone is kitted up in departures before they make the transfer. No contamination is possible. Safe as catching a bus. Got it?'

'Easy now. Thank you, Bert,' said Franklin. 'Tell us, Charlene, how you see the project progressing.'

'Delighted to, Franklin,' said Charlene. Piercing. Admiring. Available. All over again.

'Miners will launch and return on six months shifts. To begin with, operations will remain on Earth, guiding miners to their work spots and returning them safely to the rim. As for letting the Pennysides to asteroid mining companies, I think Rupert from Swish, Fish and Stopps can help you on that.'

Rupert, floppy fringed, got slowly to his feet. He raised a hand to wave generally at everyone in the room.

'Hi guys. Yep, so the Pennysides; as I see it, you'll be hiring them out primarily to space mining operation companies. I admit it's quiet out there right now. Not a lot of movement in the market. But we're stepping up the marketing. Yep. Done the measuring up. Five foot by five foot by twenty-five upwards.'

'Are you sure?' interrupted Franklin. 'I thought they were ten by ten by twenty?'

'Pretty sure but I'll get a check on that. Brochures are out. Yep. No enquiries as yet. I mean once let, the idea is, as I see it, or understand it, is that OSH as the landlord will pass over the key whilst the Pennyside is in occupation. So, yep, working on marketing, getting feelers out there. Just got to pull the punters in. So great to have this bit of publicity. Great. Yep. We're with you all the way.'

'Thanks Rupert. Keep us posted,' said Franklin. 'Any questions anyone?'

Weston had been trying to work out how big a ten by ten by twenty foot space would be. Certainly not much room for a kid to run around? Perhaps they were including floating?

'Next on the agenda is marketing the competition. Welcome to Evie Blick-Foxton, brand assistant representing Brexypops. Over to you Evie.'

Weston was surprised. Where was the senior management team? Evie looked as if she should still be in school.

Evie, clearly anticipating a break in her fledgling career, leapt to her feet, flicked frothing black curls off her face, gave everyone a little wave accompanied by a cheeky giggle and launched in – high pitched, chirpy and chatty – directing her most enchanting smiles to Franklin. Of course.

'Hi guys! First thank you all *so* much for choosing Brexypops as your vehicle for this super-important competition. Our exceptional design team have worked night and day to come up with an amazing concept to market the competition on our Brexypops packaging. And here we have it. Drum roll please.'

Evie slapped her well-manicured hands on her rounded thighs creating a rhythmic rat-a-tat-tat, then held up a box of Brexypops.

'Ta dah!'

Delegates leaned in to get their first glimpse of what would, after all, lead to a world changing event.

'Fab isn't it. Pass it round. But no munching on the Brexypops.'

The Brexypops box circled the table like a game at a kid's party. Pass. Pause. Inspection. Pass. Pause. Inspection. When it was his turn, Weston took the box and chuckled. The cartoon picture of a child in a rocket smashing through a bright yellow blast shape with the strap line WIN A TRIP TO SPACE! bursting out from a bowl of Brexypops cereal was right up his street. He flipped it over. On the back was the entry form. It looked so, well, *simple* for such a big deal. Miriam's words rang in his ears. 'It's someone's precious kid.' Someone's precious kid was going to fill in this little coupon, cut it out, end up in space and might never come back. Weston shuddered and passed the box on.

'Eye catching, huh?' chirped Evie. 'A child blasting into space. It's wacky. It's fun. It's irresistible. Form on the back. Simple and easy to fill in, even for a child.'

She uttered the last word of each sentence with a high pitched giggle. Weston was starting to find it irritating. Could she not take this whole thing a bit more seriously?

'So, the child needs to say in ten words why they'd like to be the first child in space,' went on Evie. 'But this is the real clincher. This project is *super*-educational, obviously, so let's get schools in on the act. Bag the attention of headteachers. Ask them to answer the question: *Why do you think your pupil should be the first child in space?* Competition credibility, hey? And, of course, I'm happy to act as school liaison officer if that's OK with you guys?'

She's bulldozing them, thought Weston. There was no stopping her.

'So, not forgetting the charity; along the bottom of the form it says: *This competition is run by the charity KISS, sponsored by OSH.* I think the charity bit reassures. Gives it double credibility along with the school bit. So basically, from Brexypops' point of view, it's a wrap. I'd say we're nearly ready for blast off.'

'What happens when we receive all the entries?' an exec asked. 'I mean there could be hundreds, thousands.'

Evie hesitated.

'Weston?' asked Franklin.

Weston was as white as a sheet. The momentum of his idea was building so fast. One moment he thought it was a brilliant idea, the next terrible. And now all these people were involved. It felt out of control. What *would* they do if thousands of children entered? He had no idea. But he had to say something.

'We interview the top twenty, chose the best five and hold the final on live TV.'

A murmur of excitement circled the room. Evie clapped her hands.

'Wow, Weston. Brilliant idea. Wow.'

'Can you fix all that for us Weston?'

'Done deal,' said Weston. He had never had anything to do with TV before, let alone live TV, but he was in so deep he was going with instinct not practicalities.

'Good man,' said Franklin. 'Good man.'

'Yes, all good. Very good,' said Weston. 'I just … it just seems too simple, a little coupon like that. What will happen when we have a winner? I mean, how safe will it be to send a kid up into space?'

'Good point Weston. Jerry this is your bite of the cherry. Is the idea safe?'

'Safe? I'd say so,' drawled an unhealthy looking fellow who sniffed as he spoke.

Miriam would find that unattractive. Very unattractive. And somehow suspicious. How could you trust a man with the safety of such a project if he didn't even own a handkerchief?

'I've been working on the Space Mining Village project since it began,' went on Jerry, still sniffing, 'and our safety record is exemplary. No serious accidents since, well, you know. And no fatalities since then either. And once we've sent a child up there for a couple of days and he comes back safe and sound, we'll have companies queuing up to send their workforce.'

'Yes, but that's if the child comes back safe and sound. What if…'

Tears pricked Weston's eyes. Everyone talking in riddles. How would he explain it all to Miriam?

'Don't you worry, Mr Wright. This mission is safe. Thousands of similar capsules are operating remotely all the time.'

'But that's different from sending a child.'

'Mr Wright, you focus on the ideas and I'll look after the safety side. Trust me.'

'We do Jerry,' said Franklin, 'but, even so, I want a full and detailed health and safety report on my desk within twenty-four hours. We're not leaving anything to chance.'

'It'll be on your desk in twelve.'

Franklin smiled at Weston. Weston tried to raise a smile back.

'Gilbert, Graham,' said Franklin, moving on, 'thank you for joining us. Gilbert and Graham of Gee & Gee are the interior design duo who have designed all the OSH offices. I'm sure you will have noticed the pods down in reception. The living space inside the Pennysides is limited but with your genius, Gilbert and Graham, can you make them child friendly? Perhaps even fun?'

'Oh, a dream of a project,' said Gilbert. 'I see a swirl of joyful yellows and playful oranges.'

'Swings and roundabouts. A treehouse in space. A castle of imaginations. Balloons and buttercups.'

'Our minds have been awhirl with thoughts but our designs are still under wraps. So, for now, mum's the word.'

Weston was incredulous. They were treating the whole project like a children's surprise birthday party.

Franklin was moving on. Final item.

'Do you have anything to add Norman?'

Franklin directed the question at an elderly gentleman.

'I believe it will be a fine and glorious thing for our nation.'

The voice was thin, hoarse and unmistakable: Norman Barron MP. Charming, affable, ineffectual. He had the knack of staying in government year after year. Age had given him seniority. He was now Minister for Future Affairs, which included responsibility for running the National Space Mining Programme

'Good news,' said Franklin to Weston. 'That's a thumbs up from where it counts. Now, let's have a break before we talk timescales. Twenty minutes, everyone.'

Franklin headed for the lift.

'Like to come with me Weston? Get some fresh air.'

28. Falling toads

Too far to understand. Great galaxies of the universe are two million light years long.

Franklin set off at such a pace that Weston struggled to keep up.

'So, Weston, were you curious as a kid? Always wanting to know what was on the other side?'

Weston wasn't sure if he was curious. Except about orange blouses. But a childhood memory about the other side did pop into his head.

'I once got in trouble for looking in a cupboard.'

Franklin's shout of laughter cut above the sound of traffic.

'Tell me about it.'

Weston had not thought about the tall thin pine cupboard that lurked behind him in class for, well, years. The sudden recollection made him shiver.

'Go on. What was in there?'

'A skeleton. Well, we *thought* it was a skeleton. Someone had heard the teacher say something about a skeleton in the cupboard so we believed it.'

'And was it? Did you look?'

Here he was on the biggest day of his career and Franklin had opened up memories of himself as a little boy, sitting on a school bench with an upright coffin directly behind him, holding its deathly secrets: white bone, a skull grinning in the dark. He would sit lesson after lesson in a state of terror, imagining the horror of a bony hand coming out and touching him on the shoulder.

'One day the teacher went out of the classroom and the other boys dared me.'

'Yes?'

'I pulled at the door handle but it wouldn't open.'

'Did you try again?'

'Yes.'

Weston could hear the cries of the boys as they abandoned their books and leapt from their benches to surround him.

Try again. Pull harder. Go on, Weston. Hurry up!

Egged on, Weston had pulled and pulled at the handle. With a bang, the door flew open.

'Was it a skeleton?'

'No. It was…'

Look out! It's falling. Get back.

The boys' cries trilled loud in Weston's memory as the door swung open and the cupboard tipped towards him, hurling its contents onto the floor. No skeleton, but a hoard of glass jars, each packed with stinking body parts. Dead fish. Putrefied toads. Pickled cockroaches. Legs of newt. Eyeballs in alcohol. They spilled out, smashing to the ground, spreading their vile slime across the classroom floor. The stench was overwhelming, the horror of death long trapped in jars worse than any dried up bones of a skeleton, the mess impossible to clear up before the return of the teacher.

'I got in a lot of trouble.'

'But at least you knew what was on the other side of the door. And you weren't scared anymore.'

How had Franklin turned the disastrous episode into something positive? It was like talking to Miriam. Things became the opposite of what you had thought before.

The two men strode on against the wind, turning right, weaving in and out of shoppers, office workers on breaks, the homeless sheltering where they could.

'So, would you have entered the competition, Franklin? Wanted to know what was up there?'

Weston bet to himself he would; the man was always asking questions.

'Not as a boy.' Franklin barely paused as he pressed a few notes into the outstretched hand of a man slouched in a doorway. 'My grandmother would have done it for me. She was a geologist. Loved adventures.'

'Like what?'

Franklin hesitated. Weston felt he had gone too far, been too nosy, but then Franklin seemed to want to talk. Perhaps he was lonely.

'When I was seven my parents died of influenza within a week of each other, and I was sent to live with my grandmother. The first thing she said to me when I turned up on her doorstep was "Guess what's in this?".'

'In what?'

'A small wooden box. Inside was a dried-up translucent greeny-yellow snake skin. Scales fragile as anything. "Forest pit viper," she said. "Deadly poisonous. I found it under my camp bed on an expedition hunting crocodiles." Then she closed the lid and said, "I hope you will be happy here."'

Weston followed, tripping along, trying to keep up, as Franklin marched down the street.

'One day, I came back from school with a detention for climbing onto the school roof. It was a dare, like your cupboard. But my grandmother wasn't cross. She took me into her back scullery and pointed to a thin pale gold frame hanging on the wall. It held a piece of embroidered material, the lettering faded. "I sewed that at school," she said. "We might have been in the jungle, but I still learned to embroider. I did it when I was six. Made it up myself. And never you forget it." I couldn't make much out. Just a bit of embroidered fabric, pressed behind glass. It was always dark in there. But she had sewn it when she was six and that was impressive, I supposed, so I promised never to forget.'

'No,' said Weston, not sure where all this was going.

They turned right again and the OSH building loomed into sight.

'My grandmother had been a geologist, travelling the world at a time when women didn't travel. She went down endless jungle rivers in a dugout canoe wearing a long dress and white gloves. As adventurous as travelling into space today. But it was only years later, when she died, that I understood what she had meant about her sewing. I had gone to sort out her house.'

'Oh dear,' said Weston. It was an involuntary remark. His nan had lived with them and her room smelt awful: stale smoke, sickly-sweet humbugs. And it was a chaotic jumble of stuff: tea cups with floating blue mould, dead mice trapped in crocheted cardigans, cream-coloured complicated looking underwear, forgotten false teeth. But Franklin was describing a different world. His nan, no, his *grandmother*, had treasures.

'They were her world,' said Franklin, 'from her everyday and her adventures; a painted, feathered spear, chests full of ivory buttons, bits of string, silk gloves, a shrunken skull, cut glass vases of dried flowers that crumbled when you touched them, a gilded dagger, a small soft leather book of treasured texts, a grotesque dancing monkey ornament, a crocodile jaw that opened and closed. And you know what, Weston?'

'No, what?'

'I took down the framed embroidery from the scullery. Out in the light of the kitchen, I read her neat little stitches, sewn in and out, over and over, faded but just legible. You know what it said?'

'Something about crocodiles?' guessed Weston, puffing as he climbed the OSH steps.

Franklin laughed, striding the steps with ease.

'Nearly,' he said, pausing at the swing doors. 'It said: *Off this narrow path I'll stray and seek a more exciting way.* And that's the sort of child we're looking for, isn't it? You said so yourself in the pitch. Something about them being curious to see the stars?'

Weston sensed something momentous had just occurred. He had no idea what, but his heart surged. He felt ready for anything.

The girls on reception touched their hair and adjusted their smiles as Franklin marched past, exchanging a joke with them. Weston skipped to keep up.

'Do you know,' said Weston as the shiny silver lift door closed, 'I like to think I would've signed up. I really would.'

Weston felt he had unexpectedly connected with Franklin, had become a *confidant* – the sort of word Miriam would use – and it made him feel confident. He was a confident confidant. He chuckled at his own joke.

'Good Weston, pleased to hear it. Let's just hope we find a youngster of your calibre.'

Your calibre.

If only Miriam had been in the lift to hear such praise.

29. Blood sticky on black leather

Where does the water flow? On Earth. And maybe Mars.

Agatha. Astronaut. Surgeon. Porter. I am most suited here, Agatha. Invisible. But close to patients. Nobody expects much of you. You can be yourself rather than having to be the right sort of person. Wide awake, semi-conscious or elsewhere, I have the chance to take those in fear to a better place. I bring the joy of Grey Cottage into a world that favours precision and control. I am pushing a middle-aged woman bandaged head to toe to surgery. 'Know what you remind me of?' I say. 'A chrysalis all wrapped up. But you'll emerge like a beautiful butterfly. Imagine that. Fluttering out of theatre like a purple emperor and landing on a great nodding buddleia. Imagine, those beautiful lilac flowers with their tiny orange centres bobbing about, waiting for you.' She is laughing. I push her into theatre and wait to take away the inevitable clinical waste. It is odd to divide a human being up like that. To have something removed that is part of you: chopped out, disposed of. I wonder if I should keep it so she can take it home? One day be put back together. At least be buried as a whole person. But I don't have time. I am rushing to take a motorbike smash up to surgery. I see limbs contorted, blood sticky on black leather, a young face in agony, fearful. I try to fight the lad's fear for him. I try to match humour to the person I see lying before me. 'Don't worry,' I say. 'I fell off my bicycle when I was five and look at me now. Two good legs, strong arms and pushing trolleys round the circle four hospital.

Complete recovery. You'll be back, right as rain, in no time. The surgeons here are tip top. They once sewed a severed hand right back on. Shame it was the wrong way round. Only joking, of course. You're in excellent hands. Not severed!' There is the faintest of smiles on his ashen lips. Next I am pushing frail bones and a pink scalp with a thread of white hair. She is whispering. The poetry is from another age. It is forbidden, but I don't warn her. Together our minds are dancing on something beautiful. She will stay in the past. I am happy she has no idea of the risks she is taking. No idea at all.

30. Homeless

Oh noble comet, tell me what you are made of? Rocky particles, dust and ice.

'Do you mind me only being a porter?' Peter asked Agatha as they lay wrapped together in bed early one morning, close in body, close in mind.

'Only?'

'Sometimes I wish I could do more.'

She sensed his thoughts shift from the bedroom to the hospital – his other world.

'Like what?'

'The time I have with patients seems so short. Wheel them down the corridor, into the lift, out onto another corridor, into theatre. That's it.'

'You can make a big difference even in a short time,' said Agatha, trying to sympathise but wanting to stay in the intimacy of their bedroom, not roaming stark hospital corridors.

'I suppose. But a surgeon can do more. Much more.'

'But you can't be a surgeon,' said Agatha. 'Not a good one with that hand. But you can be a good porter. Making lives a little more bearable. And that's a wonderful thing to do.'

'Promise you mean that?'

She kissed him.

Peter fell back to sleep but Agatha lay awake thinking about what it really meant to help others. She was proud of Peter and the stories he told her – the light he tried to bring to the lives of the vulnerable. But it was best not to go too far, get too involved.

She should know.

She closed her eyes and drifted back to the time when she was seven years old, a little girl buttoned up tight in her blue wool coat to keep out the winter chill. She could still remember the shock of seeing a hummocky bundle in a shop doorway and thinking that inside that slippery, thin nylon sleeping bag, under that damp bit of cardboard, was a human being. She remembered her outrage. Wasn't it unkind to walk past, pretending not to notice? Wasn't it wicked of her mother, holding her hand, to pretend not to notice? Shouldn't adults do something? She had reached down to touch the concrete pavement slabs and feel their hard iciness. How that would creep into your bones and freeze you to death.

'Stop pulling Agatha,' her mother had snapped. 'And don't touch the ground. It's dirty.'

But Agatha had wanted to know what it was like. Being homeless. So she had pretended.

She tried sleeping on her bedroom floor. It was different from sleeping on the street, of course. Her room had a thick carpet, a window with pretty floral curtains and a row of teddies and furry soft toy animals on her bed. Her parents – civil servant, lawyer – had been eating supper downstairs in their comfortable circle six detached home. Agatha closed her bedroom door, turned off the lights, drew back the curtains, and opened the window, gasping at the rush of icy night air.

In the gloom, she had flattened a cardboard box and laid it on the floor. She didn't clean her teeth or brush her long black hair or change out of her clothes but lay down as she was, covering herself with another piece of cardboard and closing her blue eyes she tried to sleep. But the chill from outside had crawled over her skin, into her bones. She had shivered all night. In the morning, she wrote a poem called *Too Cold to Sleep* but it didn't rhyme and she realised it would not help anyone anyway, so she threw it away.

If only she had left her desire to help the homeless there. Many times she had gone over how her interference, her desire to force events in a direction she thought best, had played such a catastrophic part in the story of one homeless young man.

Maybe if she hadn't gone to university it would never have happened? Eng. Lit. What a disappointing, tedious three years she was threatened with, trawling through lifeless, state commissioned books with their ugly black titles stamped onto yellow covers. It was the tutorials that saved her. What a thrill it had been when, one day, her tutor, a self-confessed 'bearded loon', checked the corridor, locked his study door, and began to pull down book after book from his top shelf.

He taught his trusted group of tutees about the treasures that lay behind the false canary covers, and Agatha had loved it: the poetry, the prose, the late afternoons when students and tutor would read in hushed voices, filling the room with whispered thoughts, emotions, bright images, one phrase rising above another. *Tread softly because you tread on my dreams* – Listen! – *whatever our souls are made of, his and mine are the same* – Oh, imagine! – *five fathom five thy father lies, of his bones are coral made*.

The beauty of the words and the thrill of subterfuge meant Agatha had read endlessly: in her bedroom, the library, the bus, the canteen. How young, bold and careless they had all been. As a parting gift, the tutor had given each student a single book wrapped in yellow: a thread to another world. How she had treasured hers. How she now missed its images of caverns measureless to man and the sunless seas.

But the pleasures of literature only intensified her sorrow for the homeless. She remembered how sometimes she might stop to give a young man with downcast eyes a cup of hot sweet tea before she headed into the library to read poetry that squeezed into verse the horrors of the human condition, or great novels stuffed with beautifully written prose about the torment of the poor. Her studies kept the real suffering of those on the streets outside the magnificent stone library walls at a comfortable distance – and that was wrong, surely?

Restless, Agatha got out of bed and crept across to the window to gaze out at the moor. In the end, it had been the books – the descriptions of the poor, the plight of the *homeless starving wretch* – and her realisation that these words had changed hearts and minds in the past and could do so again, that prompted her to act. She would still offer cups of tea, but maybe her own writing was where she could make a real difference.

She remembered how she had set out with trepidation to talk to hunched figures wrapped in layers of rags shivering in doorways. They seemed happy to spill their tales of sorrow from cracked and sore lips − so many were fallouts from families who had lost everything a few generations back in the meteorite strike. The economy had not been strong since − and the most vulnerable were the hardest to help. Easier for the government to turn a blind eye. Writing up their stories had been heartbreaking, but even now Agatha could remember the joy she had felt when at last she got a break; a story accepted by a national newspaper, and an interview with the editor.

'You're young and curious − things that can make a successful journalist. I'll give you a chance. Junior reporter. Features.'

But how frustrated she had been with her first commissions: 'Resurgence of the poncho'; 'Make an entrance: top tips for your hallway'. And how, with growing confidence, she had asked her editor if she could write about something she actually cared about: the homeless.

'Well, I loved your poncho article,' the editor had said. 'I'll give you a shot. Come back to me with ideas.'

It could have worked out, thought Agatha, leaning her forehead against the window frame, her fingers pulling at some lichen that was daring to grow over the sill into the bedroom. She tried to remember all the articles she had had published. Maybe she could have changed things. Her editor had thought so.

'Moving. Well written. Not bad. You've had readers in tears. Keep going.'

If only she had not started helping at the homeless hostel. It seemed a good idea at the time: making tea, coffee for the people who shuffled in, some every day, some forever strangers who sat in a corner telling no one their name and keeping their sorrows and secrets to themselves. And then, one day, there was Ben, a young man about her age, smart clothes reduced to rags, dirty and smelling of sweat and rubbish, his beard matted, dark circles under his eyes and filthy finger nails – the uniform of rough sleeping.

'Tea? Coffee? Sandwich?' she had asked.

He seemed surprised to be spoken to and, saying nothing, had gone to sit at one of the canteen tables. She remembered how he sat – upright, staring ahead. If only she hadn't gone over to talk to him. But she had.

'Nice place,' he had said, his voice gentle.

'I'm Agatha. What's your name?'

'Ben. No Barry. Barney. Something like that.'

She remembered how he smiled; a lovely, shy smile.

'Ben maybe?'

Gentle and bewildered, he seemed completely lost.

'Ben is a good name.'

'I like someone saying "Ben".'

Then he had put his hand on her knee.

'Mum,' he said.

The touching hadn't surprised Agatha. It had happened before. But calling her "mum" had made her stop in her tracks. He couldn't think she was his mum, surely? They were practically the same age.

'Mum,' he had said again, his hand still on her knee.

'I'm not your mum.'

'I don't know where she is.'

'Would you like me to help you find her?'

So, that was how it had started. She had just wanted to help him. He seemed so lost: no idea of his name, his family, where he was from, how he had come to be in the hostel – *In someone's car? It might have been a van.* She would spend hours and hours talking to him, looking for clues, something that might help her find out who he was, where he lived, find his mum. Funny that the vital clue turned out to be a sliver of a memory about a purple, green and orange striped school tie. That was unusual. It led her to his home town and, eventually, to his elderly parents. Not just mum. Mum and dad. Ben had been overjoyed when she had told him the news.

'Come with me. Please, please, please come with me,' he had begged her. 'You can tell them things for me.'

How thrilled she had been. This was what journalism was all about: getting to the heart of a story. Her words would be featured in the weekend papers – she would include a plea for shoppers to stop for a moment if they saw someone sleeping rough, get them a cup of tea and pass the time of day. It could be life changing, both for the homeless person and themselves.

She remembered how happy she had felt travelling up with Ben on the train, walking up the rose-lined path of his parents' neat semi-detached home, ringing the doorbell, waiting for the joyful reunion. Moments later, she was sitting next to Ben on a floral sofa facing his parents, old beyond their years, who sat deep in armchairs surrounded by books and cups of tea, trying to think of something to say to cut through the silence.

'I'm so glad to have been able to meet you,' she had said. 'Ben's keen that I tell you a bit about what he's been up to.'

'It's James,' the father had said, nodding at Ben. 'His name's James. Not Ben.'

'He's been away before,' added his mother, her voice barely audible. 'Goes away all the time.'

They seemed quiet, subdued. Unfriendly even.

And she remembered her bewilderment when, two days after the reunion, police had called at her door. How they took her to the station. How they questioned her about James.

'Ben,' she had said. 'He's Ben to me. What is it? What's happened?'

'Last night, James stabbed his father and mother with a kitchen knife. They were getting ready for bed. His father died at the scene. His mother died in hospital this morning.'

'No!'

'James's body has been recovered from a weir.'

Agatha's mind was a blur of nightmare images; red blood on white hair, a slashed nightdress, arms flailing in a feeble attempt at defence, the flashing silver of a knife coming down, sharp, slicing skin, white bone. And then Ben. His body bloated and stinking in the weir. How she had misunderstood him. And how she had misunderstood his parents. They had not been quiet, subdued. They had been frightened.

The story, of course, became big news covered by more experienced journalists. Agatha was sacked and unemployable. She was even implicated in a murder although she herself had committed no crime. But she *felt* guilty. How could she have missed the real story, not seen the clues, put Ben's parents in such danger? And how could she have had the audacity to think she could control the situation, influence things, when she clearly could not? Anger and guilt tormented her, lurking in her daily thoughts, stalking her dreams and threatening to overwhelm her.

Agatha turned to look at Peter, still sleeping. She felt a rush of gratitude, of love. How lucky it was that, in the wake of the catastrophe, she had become a waitress and, as a result, had met him. Waitressing hadn't been too bad. In fact, she had come to like it: the greasy spoon cafes, student canteens, the old people's home. She always tried to take extra special care of the elderly, trying in some tiny way to make up for what had happened to Ben's parents. She had noticed how so many of them seemed to have so little, struggling to make the best of their final days. The smallest of treats often made such a difference.

'We have cherry cake, coffee and walnut or lemon and lime drizzle today.'

'How lovely. What will you have, Dorothy?'

She loved to see how their eyes would sparkle as they weighed up the choices.

'Oh, it all looks tempting. But not today thank you dear.'

Agatha knew they had enough money for a cup of tea in a warm cafe, but a slice of cake was too expensive. Sometimes, she gave them a sliver anyway, just as a taster. She loved to see their smiles. It was the same sense of fulfilment Peter had as a porter. So, she was happy: for the patients, for the family, for him.

'No, Peter,' she whispered. 'You are not only a porter. You are a good porter. A great porter. A brilliant porter. And I'm proud of you.'

31. Dorcas
Take the size of the Earth and times it by one thousand. Jupiter!

Agatha, it could be Pip. The boy on the trolley is the same age. He is a muddle of tubes. Tubes protrude from thin white lips, little nose, strapped to arms. 'Like spaghetti,' I say to his parents. 'He fell on his head out of a supermarket trolley,' hisses his mother. 'Sorry,' I say. I wish I could take back my joke. 'We'll get him straight to theatre. He'll be in good hands. The very best.' I am racing down the corridor. Dorcas scurries along beside me. You remember Dorcas? She is struggling to hold the drip trolley. She could do with another few inches. In height. Not waist. Her blue tunic is tight. She is breathless. I count her taking three fast steps for every one of my strides. She is chattering about losing weight. 'If I don't, I'll be demoted. They told me if I don't shift some pounds I'll be in real trouble.' We reach the lift. Dorcas hands me the drip. 'Take the lad up to level four. I'll join you there.' Dorcas disappears through swing doors to climb the stairs. I take the boy up in the lift. I try a joke. Not a very good one, but his eyes soften a little. Dorcas gets in at level four, panting, her hand pressed to her side. 'Enough.' I press the button for level twelve. The boy is moaning. Pain flits across his features. Dorcas puts her hand over the young boy's pale hand and closes her eyes. I don't know what she is doing. The numbers light up green above the door. Five. Six. Seven. Dorcas is leaning closer to the boy, her face tilted upwards, eyes closed. She looks beautiful. My heart is beating fast. She is outside the rules. Eight. Nine. Something is glittering. A silver that should not be there is glinting against her chest. A cross. A shocking defiance of the rules of the state. I tear my eyes away and look at the rising numbers. Ten. Eleven. At twelve we come to a halt. I can hardly breathe. I am shocked by what I have seen. The danger she has put us in. 'You'll be fine, dearie,' says Dorcas to the boy. Her eyes are open now and she gives the child's hand another gentle squeeze. The lift doors open. I race the trolley towards the operating theatre swing doors at the far end of the corridor. Tears are in my eyes. I hope they will be able to save the little boy. His parents would do anything for that.

32. Fellows Light

Fifth of the force: gravity on the surface of the Moon is only a fifth of that on Earth.

Monday night was Wilfie's parents' evening at the boys' school, Fellows Light, a faded red brick Victorian village school with modern classroom add-ons. Mr Skillern, deputy head – and headmaster-in-waiting – had stationed himself in the panelled hall ready to welcome parents. To his annoyance, Mr Firth, an ineffectual fellow in his twenty-eighth year at the helm, was shuffling towards him. That man, thought Skillern, has no idea – he doesn't understand modern education. Only yesterday, Firth had started mumbling on about morning assembly.

'We used to sing *All Things Bright and Beautiful*, then have a quiet moment for, well, our own thoughts I suppose, maybe notices and then an ordered exit to the accompaniment of some uplifting music performed admirably by Mrs Bellows on the piano. Ah, Mrs Bellows. She was a splendid lady: exuberance squeezed into a floral dress. I loved those floral dresses. So joyful and gay. Such a shame to replace floral dressed pianists with a Tannoy system. Such a shame.'

Skillern checked his watch. He needed to get rid of Firth before parents started to arrive.

'Ah, Mr Skillern,' said Firth, closing in. 'A word. Someone has left a warning slip on my desk saying I should not pat children on the head. Since when have headmasters got warning slips? They should be giving them out! Things are topsy turvy. Oh, that's it. Topsy. Mrs Bellows' Christian name. Topsy Bellows!'

Firth, chuckling and muttering 'Topsy Bellows' over and over, trundled off back up the corridor.

'Mad,' muttered Skillern. 'Off his rocker.'

Thank goodness that his own grip on Fellows was getting stronger. Skillern was preparing for his takeover, promised when the board slipped Firth away into retirement. Already, Skillern was laying ambitious plans to make the school one of the best in the country. Academic accolades were the goal. Pupils would be drilled, examined, drilled again. Nothing would be left to chance.

'If we are going to achieve greatness for Fellows,' he preached to his inner circle of teachers, 'we need to conquer the minds of our children. And those we cannot conquer, those too weak, those falling behind, will be vanquished.'

Skillern was not sure what he actually meant by 'vanquished' but his speech seemed to make the point; under his leadership, Fellows Light would sit at the very top of the result tables.

'Hurry,' urged Agatha as Peter drove round the packed school car park. Every space was taken. Breaking the rules, Peter parked the car on rough ground under a beech tree.

'The boys will be better hidden here, anyway,' he said as they came to a jolting halt.

'Wilfie, Pip, don't get out,' said Agatha. 'Get comfy and go to sleep and if you see anyone coming, keep down.'

Agatha leaned over and tucked the boys in under a rug. School forbade children from parents' evening.

Should they have left them at home on their own? Bring them? Leave them? Bringing them had seemed the safest option. But if they were discovered. Agatha did not allow herself to think of the consequences.

'Come on,' said Peter, 'or we'll be too late.'

Pip had already slipped into a snuffling sleep. Wilfie was staring contentedly out of the window at the evening sky.

Peter took Agatha's hand as they hurried across to the bright lights of the school. She had plaited her long black hair, scrubbed her nails, made herself neat and tidy. She felt hopeful; Wilfie had been borrowing books on astronomy from the school library and had been actually reading them. Not just pulling out facts. He might have started slowly at school, but he was improving.

A list in the hall put Wilfie at the bottom of the year.

'Alphabetical,' joked Peter.

Agatha tried to pretend that it didn't matter, so long as the school understood Wilfie; could see what was special about him.

Mrs McDuff, the school secretary – comfortable, amiable – rang the bell vigorously to start the first meetings. Parents swarmed in, snapping up all the seats set round the teachers' tables in seconds. Agatha and Peter, slow off the mark, had to wait. Agatha watched the smiles, the nods, heard the light satisfied laughs of other parents. She clenched her fist.

At last, there was a space at Mr Furl's table. Biology. Peter sat awkwardly, a giant perched on a child's chair. Agatha leaned forward, keen to hear what Mr Furl had to say.

'Wilfie Whisper. Yes, so quiet I thought he had passed away. Lucky we didn't start dissecting him. Chopping him up and sending him home in little pieces.'

Furl, sweating and greasy skinned, snorted with laughter down his hairy, bulbous nose. But Agatha was not in the mood for such jokes. Far from it. Muscles spasmed in her cheeks, on her neck. Her jaw locked tight. Peter squeezed her hand.

Seven bruising reviews later, Peter and Agatha queued to see Mr Chillworth. Bottom set maths. Agatha's hands were clasped in tight knots, her breath coming in shallow bursts.

'Are you alright, dear?' asked Mrs McDuff, who was wandering around making chit-chat with parents, keeping everyone happy. 'There's tea and coffee in the dining room if you need refreshments.'

'I'm fine. Actually, I'm not fine,' said Agatha. 'None of the teachers are keeping up with Wilfie, with his daydreams, with his interest in space. None of them.'

'I'm sorry to hear that, dear. Perhaps Mr Chillworth will have something nice to say about him.'

Mr Chillworth glanced up at the sound of his name.

'He's such a lovely young man,' the school secretary continued. 'I know I shouldn't say so but I do have a soft spot for him. I always look forward to his visits to my office. I keep custard creams, you know. His favourite.'

Agatha was grateful for Mrs McDuff's kindness but her eyes were fixed on Mr Chillworth and his table, determined not to miss the next slot. Mr Chillworth, she thought, was paying more attention to what Mrs McDuff was saying than the parents in front of him. He was hanging on her every word, surprise flitting over his thin, angular face. Was it so odd that someone should put in a good word for Wilfie?

'Goodness,' said Mrs McDuff. 'Time's up already.'

Mrs McDuff clanged the bell. Agatha and Peter went to take their place at the table, but another couple pushed forward and sat down first, forcing them to wait. Again.

Agatha, staring at the backs of the other parents, felt angered by their strength, her weakness. How bullies always got in first. How the weak were left out and despised: children not good at reading, homeless people languishing on the streets, birds with broken wings. Even the parent pushed to one side.

A display of posters she hadn't noticed before brought her close to tipping point. *Remember. Do Not Fail.* Fail? Someone had made the 'i' into an 'l' to make it read *Fall* and had added a scribbled *Over*. Another said, *Remember. Your Marks Count.* Shouldn't it say something like, *Remember. Look Out For Your Friend* or *Put Others Needs Before Your Own?* Wasn't that how you should grow as an individual? Society was tilting the wrong way. Agatha felt the walls pressing in on her, the school a microcosm of the well-intentioned but feeble state. Authority had become sanctimonious, self-satisfied, perched on the moral high ground, yet ineffectual and misguided. Pretending to care for the individual. But they did not. Crushing people like Wilfie, the out-of-the-ordinary. Agatha bowed her head to hide her confusion, her tears of rage.

Mrs McDuff rang the bell again.

Peter squeezed Agatha's hand again as they took the vacated seats. But Agatha was on the brink, a storm of emotions – anger, disappointment, frustration – whirling, gathering, pushing her to breaking point.

'Wilfie is not good at maths,' said Mr Chillworth, his voice nasal, sneering. 'He has no interest in maths. What to do?'

Chillworth lent forward, his hands clasped, his pointy elbows wide on the table to form a neat isosceles triangle. He rested his narrow chin on the apex, tapping his little fingers together. His black eyes flicked from Agatha to Peter to Agatha, a clever little smile patterning his face.

What to do? was the final straw. Restraint, trying to keep under the radar, fear of the system – the pressure points that had stopped her again and again from standing up for Wilfie – rushed to the surface and Agatha erupted. She grabbed at Chillworth's tie with its little plus and minus pattern, and pulled hard, collapsing the isosceles and dragging him across the table.

'No interest in maths?' she hissed. 'No interest in maths? It's your job to make him interested in maths.'

Mr Furl jumped up from the next table to intervene, slapping and flapping at Agatha with great ineffectual paws. Mr Chillworth was choking. He was actually choking.

'Goodness!' cried Mrs McDuff, rushing across the hall to prize Agatha's hands off Chillworth's tie. 'Come and have some tea, dear. It'll make you feel better. Come along, dear.'

Agatha released her hold but, still gripped by fury, she grabbed the books on Mr Chillworth's table and hurled them at him, at Mr Furl, at Mr Skillern, who was charging towards them, at the parents who were watching, smirking, giggling.

'What is the point of this school? Where's the nature table? Where's the music room? Where's the astronomy club? Yes, astronomy for those that are interested in astronomy. Where are the rockets made out of paper tubes streaming with red and orange and yellow strips tissue paper? When do you make planets out of fir cones? When do you teach what the children are interested in? Never. Never. Never.'

Agatha directed her last remarks at Skillern before storming out.

Peter put his arm round Agatha as they ran back to the car. She was sobbing, heart racing.

'Well, that livened things up,' he said. 'I can't believe you grabbed his tie. You were so… oh, his face!'

'Not cross then?'

'Not a bit. What a woman!'

Peter squeezed her waist, laughing. Agatha felt his liberation, his joy in her rebelliousness.

She had done something at last. Snapped the shackles that bound them to regulations they didn't believe in. Dropped the pretence that they were part of the system. Agatha hugged Peter, not daring to think beyond the moment.

At the car, Agatha peeped in on the children. Pip was asleep but Wilfie…

Where his little body should have been was an empty space; a shocking void.

'Wilfie!'

The terror of Wilfie being lost slewed into her – nightmare images of him falling, begging her to save him. She pulled open the car door, scrabbling under the seat, searching the smallest spaces, willing him to be there.

'Wilfie! Wilfie!'

And, beyond her own screams, she could hear the whispered calls of Wilfie crying out, wanting to come home.

'Pip. Wilfie. Where is he?'

Peter was already rushing towards the playground, to the swings, the slide, the climbing frame, calling his son's name. Agatha dashed round the other parked cars, cupping her face against windows, looking for her little boy hidden among the back seats. Abducted. Perhaps tied up. Or perhaps in the boot. Not the boot. No!

Wilfie's tiny body trapped in a claustrophobic tomb, light cut out as the boot slammed shut. She flew to the playground entrance. To stop…

'Mum. Mum!'

Pip was shouting for her, waving something.

'Wilfie's written something. Look.'

Peter was back first. He snatched the paper from Pip.

'Unbelievable!' said Peter, laughing in relief. 'He's in the library. Just the library.'

Gown to the libererary. Pip sleep bac very son.
I have ended my book. I need blac hols.

'I'll get him,' said Agatha, her eyes brimming with tears as the madness of the last few moments evaporated.

A blaring siren cut Agatha short. Parents and teachers were pouring out of the main school door. Mr Skillern was barking commands.

'Orderly exit. No running. Teachers to the left. Parents to the right.'

Wilfie was running towards her.

'What's happening, mum? Is it a fire?'

'Just hurry.'

She grabbed his hand as they ran.

'You shouldn't have got out of the car.'

'Sorry, but I needed a book. I got locked in the library and the other door to the playground was really hard to push.'

'Is that when the alarm went off.'

'Yes. But I didn't see a fire. Or smoke. Otherwise I would have crawled.'

'Get in the car quick before anyone sees you,' urged Peter, the engine already running.

'What's the book, Wilfie?' asked Agatha, as she leapt into the passenger seat. She wanted to say something normal. Something a calm mum might say to their child, not a mum who had thought seconds early that their child had been abducted. Not a mum who could hear the deputy head shouting at them. Not a mum who had sent her family veering onto a dangerous new course.

'Come back. Come back! You need to be accounted for. Everyone must be accounted for.'

As they sped out of the car park, Peter snorted.

'What?'

'You,' said Peter. 'You were magnificent. That tie!'

Agatha burst out laughing. She could not believe what she had done. She had stood up for Wilfie.

'So, what's the book, Wilfie?' she asked again, wanting to hear his voice, feel his presence behind her.

'*Black Holes and How To Find Them*. I've read it before, but I want to be sure I know what I'm doing when I get there.'

33. Haunches to the wind
Mercury might be hot but be surprised – ice lies in its shadowy craters.

The following afternoon, Agatha traipsed to the top of the track to meet the minibus. Wild ponies were sheltering by the top wall, their broad haunches turned to the wind. She perched on the mossy stone wall, waiting for her boys. Her fury, which had transformed into exhilaration, even hilarity last night, was now tainted with disappointment. She had thought Wilfie was getting somewhere at last. She even thought she was getting somewhere. Learning to control her frustration. Becoming more patient, accepting. Now she felt a fool. A dangerous fool. She had a long way to go if she was to keep her family safe.

The ponies pushed forward. She rubbed the rough whorl of hair beneath the black-brown forelock of one, her hand moving down its nose onto its soft pink muzzle. She envied the ponies, their thoughts free from humiliation, living for the moment.

The school bus whined up the hill and the ponies, as one, cantered off. Only a few yards on, they stopped, terror forgotten, and dropped their sturdy, deep set necks to crop at the coarse grass.

The bus came to a halt and the only two children left aboard jumped down.

'Bye Mr Minibus.'

'Cheerio lads.'

As the bus headed back to the village, Pip climbed over the stone wall and offered the ponies grass from the flat of his palm. They pushed to take it from him. Pip trotted down the hill, ponies following. Wilfie jolted down the track with Agatha. He pulled out a crumpled envelope from his pocket and handed it to her.

Inside was a note. Agatha stared at the words, little black marks on white.

Child Assist Order (2)

A second.

Of course, the reprisal for her behaviour last night. She had been in denial, thought she could get away with such an outburst. But her behaviour was way over the mark. And they always had the power. At every slip, they tightened their grasp, suffocating her, her family, everything she loved.

A second Assist Order. A second. Could she avoid a third? Agatha was not confident. Not confident at all.

And there was another note.

In direct response to her irresponsible behaviour, the

school was suspending Wilfie and Pip for three days. What fools these people were. Punishing the children for her behaviour.

'What is it mum?'

Wilfie was trailing a stick along the top of the wall.

'You've been suspended. Sorry. My fault.'

Agatha tried to make light of it. She didn't mention the Child Assist Order.

'What's suspended?' shouted Pip.

The ponies, alarmed, rolled their eyes white and dipped away.

'You're off school. Three days.'

Pip whooped in delight and the nearest ponies, consumed by fear again, dug in their forelegs, halting suddenly, then swerved off, cantering a few paces to the left.

'Don't be frightened, sillies.'

Pip grasped one by its long raggedy forelock and led it down towards Grey Cottage.

Agatha felt a glimmer of hope.

'It's good news. I'll teach you instead.'

34. Home school

Explosive. The Red Planet has the biggest volcano ever known in the solar system. That's weak gravity for you.

The next day Agatha got the boys up early.

'We'll start with maths.'

But maths had changed. She could not understand the new methods. They moved on to English. Wilfie read aloud to her, the book dull, his phrasing awkward. Pip dropped crayons and crawled around searching for them. He stayed under the table for the whole of the session.

Outside, the sun illuminated the garden in a radiant brightness and the moors rushed away in an exuberance of bobbing purples and yellows.

'Nature. That was once a subject. Outside boys.'

They spent the rest of the day outside; playing, roaming, gardening.

'Back to maths tomorrow,' promised Agatha, more to herself than the boys.

But on the second day, Agatha gave up even sooner. She could not contain the boys in the cottage. With a sigh, she realised she was not an indoor teacher. By mid-morning she was gardening, the boys free to mess about – fighting, kicking balls. And later they started making planets out of pine cones, balls of grasses, woven twigs. Wilfie tied each globe onto a piece of string and hung them from the beams in his bedroom. Agatha knew he would lie awake watching them twirl and whirl in the breeze that crept in from the open window, their profiles caught by moonlight. For now, she felt that was enough. Time well spent. But, by the end of the third day, she admitted the boys were not being educated. Not properly.

'They need to be at school,' she said to Peter. 'I'll try and do the right thing. Conform. Behave like a normal person. I know I'll find it hard, but there it is.'

They both knew the dangers if she should fail.

Later, Agatha returned to the Secondary School application form.

'Have you, as a parent, ever been disciplined by your school?'

She crossed out 'No' and wrote 'Yes'. It was the honest answer, but she had to restrain herself from adding 'provoked'. She had to be careful from now on. Very careful.

35. Porter
Space is completely silent.

Agatha, I am looking into a mirror. A man my age
is lying on the trolley. Hollow cheeked. Yellow.
Eyes closed. Barely a breath left. Is it possible there
is one last chance of life left for him? A woman,
eyes frightened, hovers besides him. She is grasping
the hand of a fair-haired girl. 'Daddy's goin' be jus'
dandy. C'mon. Let's go and get a hot chocolate,'
she says. But they do not move. They just stare,
looking at the face of the husband, the father they
love, perhaps for the last time. 'Don't worry,' I say.
'He'll be fine.' What a stupid thing to say, I think
as soon as I have said it. How could I say this man
will be fine? He looks terrible. Yellow. Blue.
Green. Grey. Colours of death knocking on his
door. But I say 'Right-o, time to go. He'll be fine,
honest.' I push the trolley to the lift. Dorcas, trots
beside me. She turns to head off up the stairs. 'No,'
I say, holding the lift doors open. 'Come with me.'
I say this before I even really know why. Dorcas
enters and I feel peril steal in with us, but still I go
on. 'You once said, 'if two or more are gathered
together,' I say. 'Be careful Peter.' 'You be careful.
A little silver can be dangerous.' Dorcas's hand flies
to her chest. She covers the metal cross we both
know is hidden beneath her hospital uniform. 'You
shouldn't have been looking.' 'I've seen what you
do.' 'I don't do anything.' Our patient is lying passive
between us. I take his right hand in mine, conscious
of its dead weight. Surprise flits over Dorcas's face
then she smiles, gently takes the dying man's left

hand in her own and closes her eyes. Nothing more. But what if we are on camera? I let go of the patient's hand, but I keep the smallest touch, the slightest connection of skin to skin. I press the button to level twelve. The lift mirrors are distracting. I, too, close my eyes. The lift takes twelve seconds to ascend twelve flights. How long does it take for a miracle? Is twelve seconds enough? How do you pray for a miracle? I don't know what to do. The touch of the patient's frail hand seems to burn into mine. A hand that once had life – wielding a hammer, comforting a child, throwing a cricket ball. And now it seems to be nothing. Empty. I can't ask for a miracle. My thoughts and desires are known. So I am best to become nothing. An empty vessel to be filled. But it is not easy. My mind is wandering. I think of you, Agatha. Of Wilfie. Of Pip. I see you in the garden, in the moonlight. You are working away. Pip roams about. Wilfie looks to the sky, thinking of stars and black holes and what might be out there. The lift comes to a halt. The doors slide open. Was that it? Has anything happened? I wheel the patient out. Dorcas is still holding his hand. We transfer him to theatre then I push the trolley back down the corridor. The dent of a body gone is still visible on the sheets.

36. Gooseberry bush

From us nine, who is the hottest planet of them all? It is I, fair Venus.

The boys back at school the following week, Agatha, cycling across the moorland road to her cleaning work in the village, hit a pothole and was flung onto the verge. Winded, waiting for pain that never came, she lay still for a moment, face to grass, eyes watchful of the minute green world she had become part of: an insect, steady in its forest journey – predator or prey?; blossom fallen and lost, its pink beauty waiting to fade and shrink to nothing.

Life so unpredictable.

She rolled onto her back, squinting against the morning sun. So, here she was, a once bright young journalist, flawed and failed, spilled to the ground of a remote country road on the way to her job. Not even waitressing now. Cleaning. Oh, and married to a hospital porter. No, not what she or Peter had imagined, had dreamed. But would she change things? Probably not. Maybe even the Child Assist Orders had helped; made them realise how precious family life was. How they must treasure it, care for it, never take it for granted. Portering seemed to suit Peter; helping others, bringing light into dark moments. And cleaning wasn't too bad; houses large, small, detached, terraced – a glimpse into other lives. Today, she hoped to bring light into someone else's life.

Standing, she heaved up her bike and pushed the bag of spinach she had picked early that morning back into her basket. The spinach was a gift. Agatha had become fond of the old lady she cleaned for who lived alone in a small terraced house. She had no family apart from a nephew, Frankie, who she adored but who lived in circle fifteen and worked all hours. So she enjoyed daytime company from Agatha and asked her questions about her vegetables and her children and, in return, told her in a quiet, breathy voice about her vegetable garden and Frankie and a childhood far away.

'Call me Penelope, dear,' came the whisper one day. 'But don't make the mistake of shortening it to Penny. I don't like that. Penelope is my name. I like people to use it.'

'I've brought some spinach,' Agatha said at lunchtime. 'Would you like me to make you some soup?'

The two women enjoyed their lunch sitting on folding metal chairs squeezed into Penelope's lean-to, surrounded by wooden slatted shelves overflowing with clay pots, trailing geranium plants and a colony of beetles. Fennel plants, tall and majestic, grew either side of the garden door.

'When I was a little girl,' said Penelope, her voice so soft that Agatha had to lean in to catch the words, 'my sisters and I used to eat fennel seeds like sweets. Cram them into our mouths. And the feathery ferns. One day, I noticed tiny spiders crawling all over the ferns, but we didn't mind. We ate them all the same.'

Agatha watched Penelope holding her spoon; such a lightness and delicacy. The spinach soup sat like a bright green jewel in the dip of the silver spoon held by fingers, fine, pale, beautiful. So smooth for a woman of Penelope's age. Barely a wrinkle. The skin on her hands was tissue paper thin. Agatha could see little blue rivulets running just beneath. Life giving. Precious.

'I'm not well, you know,' Penelope whispered. 'I will be dead this time next week. No, don't be sad. You can pick the garden flowers if you like. Frankie comes sometimes and cuts flowers. I don't know what he'll do with the house when I'm gone. Perhaps he might come and live here. I don't know. He should marry. I think there might be somebody. Then there might be children. If he moves here, he might like you to clean the house. I'd like to think of the house full of life, children in the garden.'

She smiled a little and Agatha, sensing her excitement, smiled back.

'I do hope so.'

'I would have liked children,' Penelope went on. 'But I've been blessed with Frankie. And I have never been alone. Remember Agatha, always remember that He will never leave you nor forsake you.'

Agatha felt a flicker of fear: what was Penelope daring to utter aloud?

'We all have regrets, dear. Things we have done wrong. Misjudged. Some things small. Some things that have such terrifying consequences you might wonder if you can ever be forgiven. Can you be forgiven?'

The question was so direct that Agatha felt her throat tighten. Did she carry her guilt so clearly that others could see it – a black stain visible to all? Could she be forgiven? How could she be forgiven?

'I… What do you mean? I don't understand.'

'Come, come, let's settle this,' Penelope said. 'Though your sins are like scarlet, they shall be as white as snow; though they are as red as crimson, they shall be like wool.'

Penelope tinkled with laughter.

'I've always liked that. Like wool. You cannot be afraid of wool, dear, surely?'

Riddles or truth? Agatha felt deeply moved. Sunlight pouring into the lean-to flooded Agatha's darkest memory with light. She could no longer see the blood, the bone, the fear, she could only see the smile of a young man, the love of an elderly couple. And herself as a young woman, doing her best.

'No,' whispered Agatha. 'No one can be afraid of wool.'

She felt, somehow, forgiven and the guilt that she carried lose its hold.

Penelope closed her eyes. They sat for a while in a communion of silence.

'I'm going to hospital this afternoon,' Penelope said, her voice whispering into the quiet. 'A hospital car is picking me up. Not an ambulance, not at my age, not in this area. They say I must have an operation. They want me to live on as long as I can, spin me out. Something about the mortality figures for this circle. So competitive these days. Even how long they can keep us old people alive.'

What must it feel like knowing you are so close to death; to not existing anymore? Agatha stared again at Penelope's hand, that life giving blood running so close to the surface.

'I'm not afraid of death. It's not the end, you know. There is more. Whoever believes in Him shall not perish but have eternal life. We all used to believe that. Still do. Still do.'

Agatha listened, enthralled but fearful.

'I would like to be here for the end. Sitting right here. If an operation saves me, perhaps they'll allow me home again. Frankie will look after me. He's a kind boy. And I would be so very sad not to taste the gooseberries this year. It will be a generous crop.'

The two women looked out towards the gooseberry bush. The branches, once cup-shaped and pruned to stop them growing inwards, fighting for space and light, had become long and straggly. They couldn't see the fruits but knew they were there, growing close to the branches, hiding amongst the shimmering three-lobed leaves; some still small and hard with the tiniest whisker of hairs, others large, plump and sharply delicious.

'It might need netting,' said Penelope. Some years she netted, some years she didn't. Three sharp tings from the doorbell severed their peace. Agatha turned to look across the tiny kitchen. Through the front window, she could see the bright yellow of a hospital car in the street. So, these few moments might be the last Penelope spent in her home. What should Agatha say? What do you say to a living person so soon to be nothing? Or to a living person who believed there was life after the end? Could there be?

'Remember the gooseberries,' whispered Penelope.

Two medical operatives let themselves in and took Penelope away.

Agatha strayed out to Penelope's garden, overgrown and loved. Penelope was so full of life, not death, that Agatha failed to feel sorry about the old lady's departure. Gooseberries were hanging in secret clumps among small gatherings of leaves. She picked a fruit, ignoring the prick of pain from pointed thorns, and bit into its flesh. The sourness was too much. She spat it out quickly to get rid of the bitter taste. She hunted around the green leaves, picking the ripest to take home for the boys. Then she found netting in Penelope's shed and covered the bushes. She looked forward to returning in a week or two when the sun would have ripened the berries further to pick some for Penelope. Strange that they were growing to fullness as her days were ebbing away. Penelope should taste them at their best. Agatha would ask Peter to take some in as soon as they were ready. Peter the Porter. She liked to think of him in this way. Taking presents. Easing burdens. Looking after people. Passing things on. He was the perfect hospital porter.

37. Swirl
Little star! Be wary of black holes. Pass too close and you will be torn apart.

Agatha, I am sitting in the hospital canteen on my tea break thinking about miracles. 'Penny for your thoughts,' says Dorcas. She dips a chocolate biscuit into a swirl of milky coffee. 'Don't bother. I know what you're thinking.' Can she read me that easily? 'Just so you know,' she says in a loud whisper, 'the theatre team were in uproar this morning. Complaining that patient notes were inaccurate. Worse, wrong. Complete system breakdown. They said patients were being trolleyed up at breakneck speed for surgery, loaded onto the operating table, notes read, everyone ready to go and then, blow me, their condition didn't match the notes. Operation no longer required. And I'm not talking about run-of-the-mill varicose veins or hernias or appendicitis sort of jobs. No. It's the big ones. The scary stuff with devastating outcomes for the poor old patient: amputation, paralysis, death. Odd, isn't it? Just thought you should know.'

38. Purple stain
And who are the smallest of them all? 'We are,' sang the tiny neutron stars. 'Who else can boast a radius of only six miles?'

Mr Wigmore, owner, manager and boss of Wigmore's Grocery Store, had his own problems that Friday afternoon.

'Stop messing about.'

Heavy and sweaty, he had already had to go over three

times to checkout seven to reprimand the young woman on the till for not concentrating. It was not good enough.

'Sorry, Mr Wigmore,' said Susie, 'but my head is pounding.'

'Shouldn't stay out late if you're not fit to work the following day.'

Irritated, he pushed the few surviving lank strands of mousy brown hair back over his balding head. His pate shone under the strip lights and dark patches had appeared under each arm.

'I'd send you home if we weren't so busy.'

Mr Wigmore was not an unkind man. He'd known Susie since she had started packing shelves as a schoolgirl and, nine years later, she was still here, working full-time. She always greeted him with a merry 'Good morning, Mr Wigmore,' and a smile that showed off her dimpled cheeks and sparkling eyes, looking for all the world as if there was nothing she would rather do than work at Wigmore's. And he appreciated that. Better than the rest of the staff. She had potential too. Bright. Personable. Just as he would have liked his own daughter to be. Maybe she could take on management tasks. Release him from some of the burden. But she frittered away time chatting to the customers. Especially the older folk; helping them get money out of their purses, counting out coins for them. And that fellow Frankie, the one who came in every Saturday, had taken to chatting her up. Distracting her. Did he really need to ask for her entire family history every time he came in for a tin of tomatoes? She shouldn't be chatting to him or anyone else when they were busy. Busy like now. Giving customers the service they deserved was demanding. Half the time they didn't deserve it, but still demanded it. He could feel the tension rising; trolley traffic jams were winding back from the checkouts all the way to the cream crackers. Customers were huffing and puffing.

'Hey, you've already charged me for those.'

A customer's cry, shrill, whining, rang out from checkout seven.

What an earth was Susie doing now? Wigmore's never knowingly overcharged. Especially on a busy afternoon when there were lots of witnesses. Wigmore hurried over. Susie, her skin pasty and yellow, seemed to be in a daze, staring at a bag of economy sausage rolls. Why was she staring as if she had never seen those little parcels of fatty meat rolled up in ruff puff before?

'You definitely did. The sausage rolls were on the belt and you picked them up and scanned them, then scanned them again. Charged me double.'

The aggrieved customer turned round to engage support.

'Void it, Susie,' said Wigmore. 'I do apologise. Just a mistake.'

'Likely story,'

'Sorry, Mr Wigmore. My head…'

Susie was pressing her fingers to her eyes. She was a terrible colour. Perhaps he would take her off.

As he considered whether he had any spare staff to take her place, Susie reached for the next item moving towards her – a large jar of Piper's Pickled Beetroot. She seemed to be dragging it as if it was stuck to the conveyor belt. Suddenly, it rocked beneath her hand, fell sideways and smashed against the metal ridge along the edge of the belt. Glass shattered, releasing great primeval balls that rolled out in a purple river, staining packs of biscuits, bags of sugar and hair spray before cascading onto the lino floor.

'Turn off the belt,' ordered Wigmore. 'Turn off…'

'Didn't overcharge,' Susie was mumbling. 'Can't find

it. Can't find the button… sorry, Mr Wigmore… sorry… can't find the button. My head…'

And then, as Wigmore leant over the chaotic heap of gathering items to press the button, Susie slipped, unconscious, to the ground.

The girl on the next till screamed.

'Susie!' cried Wigmore. 'Susie, what… oh, my dear girl…'

Customers crowded in, shocked, excited, nosy.

'Stand back, everyone,' ordered Wigmore. 'Stand back.'

'What's happened?'

'The checkout girl's collapsed…'

'Is she breathing? She's not…'

'Watch the broken glass.'

'She looks terrible. Is she going to die? She's dead. I think she's…'

'What's all the purple?'

'She overcharged me, you know.'

'Will you shut up!'

'Someone should help her.'

'Move her off the floor.'

'Such a lovely girl. Lovely smile.'

'Watch the glass. It looks nasty. You could cut yourself.'

'Stand back. Just. Stand. Back.'

'She's coming round.'

'Lift her up.'

'No, don't touch her.'

'Call an ambulance,' commanded Wigmore. 'And get a mop.'

By the time an ambulance car arrived, Wigmore, in a fluorescent yellow jacket, had the situation under control: yellow and black striped tape cordoning off the incident area; beetroot mopped up; glass shards disposed of; Susie, the dear girl, made comfortable, supported by three unsellable cushions Wigmore had personally selected from the bargain display. Customers murmured in little groups, competing to show the most sympathy. Wigmore felt a glow of satisfaction; the supermarket was humming with the sense of community his grandfather had created when he opened Wigmore's Groceries on this very site over seventy years ago. This was what it was all about. People talking to each other. Pulling together in a crisis.

'Careful. Careful,' he warned, as medical operatives lifted Susie onto a stretcher. He patted her hand, knowing he would miss her more than he liked to admit, not just because she was a good worker but because he, well, yes, he was fond of her. He turned away to dab his eyes.

'I think we should send a get well card,' said one regular who had never passed a pleasantry before with anyone at Wigmore's – staff or fellow customer.

'Please choose a card from the card and wrapping rack, with the compliments of Wigmore's Store,' said Wigmore, trying to steady his voice.

It was the first time he had ever given anything away for free, and it felt good.

Peter got an emergency bleep to take a young woman up to surgery.

'Susie Field. Septic pneumonia. Blood blockage has already starved her lower leg of oxygen. Dead tissue. Amputation below the knee required. Emergency.'

Peter helped lift Susie onto the trolley. He made no jokes. He knew the poor girl couldn't hear him.

Dorcas held the drips, the tubes, as they made their way at speed along the ground floor corridor to the lift. Every second counted. Peter pressed the button for level twelve. The lift door closed. The three of them were held in the small silver capsule, a moment of respite before the horror to come. Dorcas put her left hand on the girl's right and closed her eyes. Her expression took on the otherworldliness Peter had noticed before and she became, in those few moments, beautiful. Tentatively, Peter placed his large hand next to the girl's left hand, barely touching. If he had thought too much, he would have cried. Instead, he let his thoughts drift. These were precious moments. He saw flowers on the moor near Grey Cottage. Small four-petalled splashes of bright yellow.

'*Tormentil*,' Agatha had said, 'I think.'

She had a book and was trying to learn the names.

'A medical marvel. Says it can cure…'

But Peter could not remember what tormentil could cure. Sore throats? Cholera? But he remembered how strong the wind had been, how the yellow heads danced on long slender stalks, back and forth, back and forth. Holding tight. So tiny in a giant landscape. Unafraid.

The lift came to a halt. The moment was over. Peter and Dorcas were ready to go. They rushed the trolley out and into theatre. It was less than three minutes since they had received the emergency call. Even so, time had run out for Susie; the surgeon would amputate her lower leg immediately. Theatre staff ordered Peter and Dorcas to wait to take away the severed limb. The mood was sombre. Planned amputations were bad enough, but emergency amputations brought increased risk: infection, deep vein thrombosis, poisoning, heart attack. The team were dancing on the cusp of the unknown, the unseen. But before Susie could be anaesthetized, a theatre nurse, wiping at the blue-black stains on Susie's leg, realised something was amiss.

'Goodness! Beetroot juice. It's just beetroot juice. I should know; I grow beetroot and make a lot of soup. Nothing that a little soap and water can't fix. The leg is fine. Susie, can you hear me sweetheart? You're going to be fine.'

Susie did not answer. She was sleeping, a little smile on her lips.

39. Witch hunt
So dearest meteoroid, survive the fall, collide with Earth and be known ever after as a meteorite.

Agatha cooked gooseberries for Wilfie and Pip; bright hard green buttons slowly softening in the pan.

'I picked them from Penelope's garden,' she said. 'You know, one of the ladies I clean for.'

'Your *favourite* lady,' corrected Pip.

'Yes, you're right. My favourite lady.'

'Why's she your favourite?'

'Because she's wise and kind.'

Penelope's whispers had been circulating again and again in Agatha's mind since the two women had enjoyed spinach soup together a little over two weeks ago. Penelope was not just wise and kind. She was special. She could change things.

'Does Penelope like gooseberries?' asked Pip.

'I think so,' said Agatha, putting two bowls of steaming green fruit on the kitchen table. 'I'll ask dad to take some into hospital for her tomorrow. If you like them, we could plant our own bush.'

'Oh, I don't,' said Pip, spitting out a mouthful.

'Put more sugar on. Nicer then,' said Wilfie, spooning sugar on to Pip's bowl.

'Sharp and bitter and sweet,' said Agatha.

'Nice,' said Wilfie. 'I like them.'

Agatha sat with the boys at the table, topping and tailing more gooseberries to share with Peter later and half watching Wilfie arrange the fruit round his bowl into a solar system. He was always arranging things into solar systems: peas on his plate, shells on the sand, bubbles floating in his bath.

'Mum,' he said.

She knew something was coming, some question she would have to wrack her brains to answer.

'Mum, if you grow something in the garden, then make it into a medicine, then use it to make someone better, would that be a bad thing to do?'

'No, of course not. That would be a good thing.'

'Silly,' chipped in Pip.

'We learnt it was a bad thing at school today.'

'What do you mean?'

Agatha paused. Why would school teach that helping people was a bad thing?

'Mrs Beech was telling us about a woman who was burnt in a fire for making a magic medicine from a dandelion and putting it on a child's boil. The boil disappeared like magic, so the people in the village thought she was a witch. She lived on a hill in a cottage, sort of away from the village. She spent all her time growing herbs and flowers and vegetables. She even talked to her vegetables. Like you do.'

'That's a sad story. People used to be superstitious and frightened in those days.'

Wilfie pushed the gooseberries round his plate. They were losing their form, turning into a green slurry.

'Mum. Are you a witch?'

'What? Me... what do you think?'

Agatha waved her knife at him.

'I'll put a spell on you if you say such things.'

'But you do make magic mixtures from the garden.'

'Yes, but that doesn't mean I'm a witch. I just use a few things like, say, feverfew leaves if you've got a headache. But I also buy medicine like everyone else.'

'Mrs Beech said you were a bit weird though.'

'She said what?' said Agatha, astonished, stopping her work to pay full attention. 'What do you mean, weird?'

'I heard her say it to Miss Mills in history when she thought I wasn't listening. Which was silly because I sit on the front row in history.'

'Tell me exactly what she said.'

'She said you were like the woman in the story who lived in the house on the hill and spent all her time in the vegetable garden. All the villagers thought she was weird. And she was a witch.'

'Wilfie, I am not weird and I am not a witch,' retorted Agatha, standing up. 'Look how normal I am. I am picking up your bowls and I'm carrying them to the sink. If I could do magic, I would send them flying on their own. I am normal. Totally, boringly normal.'

'I know mum. But Mrs Beech said you were weird. And Miss Mills said you could be a witch. Some people are. Even now.'

'Is that true?' said Pip.

'Yes, Pip.'

'What, now? Today?'

'Yes, now, today, this very minute.'

'Promise you're not a witch mum,' cried Pip. 'You've got long black hair.'

'I promise Pip. Don't ever think I am. Whatever people say.'

There was the muddle again. A medieval danger creeping into their lives. Although she felt angry, insulted even, that the teachers had called her weird, something in Agatha liked the power it gave her over Mrs Beech and Miss Mills and the gossips at school. Perhaps they were a little scared of her. Perhaps she could put a spell on them. Get them to see Wilfie as the visionary he was.

'But, just say, if you were a witch, mum,' persisted Wilfie, 'a good witch, would you be able to do magic spells? Fun ones.'

'Could you make us disappear? Pop!'

Pip clapped his hands. He didn't seem to mind the idea of a good witch so much.

'Pop! Gone!'

'No, I'd never make you disappear,' said Agatha. 'But if you did, I'd make you come back.'

'Could you fly and go into space?'

'Perhaps I could, Wilfie.'

'Could you magic me wings, too?' asked Pip.

'I'd magic us all wings so we could all go.'

'Only it wouldn't be wings, mum,' corrected Wilfie. 'You'd need a rocket to go into space. Wings are too fragile. They would combust before you'd even reached the edge of the atmosphere. And they wouldn't be strong enough to carry you in a space suit. You'd have to have a proper rocket.'

The gooseberries finished, discussions of witches and space travel lingering, Agatha and the boys drifted out into the garden. Pip started pulling up weeds and spinach and picking berries. He put them in a clay pot and added snails, a worm, some earth and water. The water ran out through the hole in the bottom.

'I'm makings spells,' Pip said to Wilfie.

'That's mean,' said Wilfie. He picked out the worm and put it gently back on the ground.

'It's a mean spell,' said Pip. 'It's going to turn you into a ghost.'

'Stop talking about spells,' snapped Agatha. Such talk could be dangerous. She had had enough of it. If the boys were overheard talking like this in the wrong place, it could be dangerous.

Peter, arriving home, bounded straight up the vegetable garden path and embraced Agatha. It was always a lovely moment, his return after they had spent a day apart, the promise of an evening together. It never failed to make her heart leap. It was a wonderful thing – precious, of the moment. And there was always time for that.

'What's the matter?'

'Nothing's the matter.' She smiled. Now Peter was here, any fears were banished. And she wanted to share things with him. It almost seemed funny. 'The school think I'm weird and a witch.'

Wilfie and Pip stared at their parents. The witch word again. Pip was looking at her long black hair. Looking at the bunch of spinach she was holding. Considering.

'But you are a witch,' cried Peter. 'Look at this garden. It's full of magic and mystery and curses and cures and … oh no! … worst of all, horrible, nasty little children!'

Peter snatched at the boys. Pip and Wilfie, shrieking and laughing, darted off into the great swathes of bolting spinach; a forest of brilliant green where you could vanish in an instant. They hid, crouching down, bare hands and knees on damp earth.

'Ha! Ha! Ha! When I catch those fat little boys, I'm going to give them to my witchy wife who will make them into soup for our supper. Ha! Ha! Ha!'

'He's coming! Hide boys, hide!' cried Agatha, enjoying the game.

Thick stems and spiky spinach tops swished as the boys crawled deep into the green. Peter, up to his waist in giant fairyland plants, twisted this way and that, hunting his prey.

'Got you!'

He leapt forward, long arm reaching down.

'Dad,' screamed Pip, laughing, Peter hauled the little boy out and whirled him round, up onto his shoulders.

'Now, let's find Wilfie,' said Peter. 'You're on lookout. Shhh. Listen.'

Agatha felt a prickle of alarm. Where was Wilfie? He had been gone too long. The spinach patch, a source of such goodness, suddenly became mocking, sinister. She imagined him trapped amongst the great green leaves, a jungle where death was a terrifying reality; larvae sucking the veins of plants, skeletonizing them, aphids crunched by the jaws of pretty ladybirds. Or maybe he had fallen down a sinkhole? One might have opened up. There were shafts all over the moors. He could be twenty, thirty feet down, wedged in the dark. Maybe a leg broken. Crying. But they couldn't hear him.

'Wilfie.'

She tried to hold back the panic, but her voice was shrill.

'Where are you? Show me. Now!'

'Wilfie, game's over,' said Peter and took Agatha's hand. 'He's fine. I promise you. Can you see him, Pip?'

They stood in silence, listening. Nothing but the sound of a gentle breeze in the spiky plant tops.

'Dad!'

Agatha swirled round. Wilfie was there, just behind Peter, leaping up at Pip, pulling him down from Peter's shoulders. Having fun. The terrors of the jungle, the sinkhole, the horror of Wilfie missing had vanished. Not down a sinkhole. Not in the dark. He was leaping about in the bright green of the spinach bed with his dad and little brother. Nothing frightening in that.

Agatha picked up her hoe and began wheedling out the little plants that should never have been there. Leaving them to wither on the surface.

Pip cried out. A bramble had torn the skin on his arm. Bright red burst from a scratchy, dotted line.

'Blood. I've got blood.'

Pip twisted his arm to show Agatha the wound.

'It's only a scratch. I'll make it better.'

Agatha pulled at a large floppy leaf. She rubbed the green over Pip's scratch, wiping the blood away.

'There we go. All better?'

'Looks better,' said Wilfie, inspecting.

'Better,' said Pip. 'That was a spell. You did a witchy spell, didn't you mum?'

She had made Pip's arm better, but it wasn't a spell. It was the leaf. The leaf and her knowledge. Did that make her a witch? No. She was just channelling power that existed in the natural world. But there she went again. Doing weird things outside the system. And talk of spells could raise suspicion. People would gossip. There could be another Child Assist Order. The third. On such a light touch, danger could fall.

'Talking of spells and witches is forbidden,' she said. 'Look! The final spell.'

She grabbed Wilfie's hands, encircling Pip, dancing around him.

'I banish all spells from this garden, now and forever more. Go! Fly away! And never come back!'

Wilfie laughed as she spun him round. Pip whirled in the opposite direction. Round and round. Round and round. Pip, dizzy, fell to the ground.

'Are they out on the moor now?' asked Pip, getting up, stumbling to his feet.

'No, not the moor. Much, much further away than that. And they'll never come back,' said Agatha. 'Never, ever, ever.'

She was flushed, feeling the power. Her secret.

40. Sanctity
Tread carefully friend. Your footprints will stay on the Moon forever for there is no climate to take them away.

Agatha's euphoria was shortlived. Two days later, Peter returned home with news: the hospital authorities had put him on Special Monitoring Observation.

'Why?' she demanded. 'How dare they?'

'I don't know. Admin said it was for my own good. They monitor everyone all the time, but only put you on SMO if they think you're up to something.'

'Well, are you?'

In her fury, Agatha let the knife of distrust slip between them.

'No, of course not.'

'So, why?'

'I don't know. They wouldn't say. Said it was confidential.'

'Confidential. But it's about you. You, Peter!'

'I know but—'

'How can they—'

'It doesn't matter—'

'It does matter. Of course it matters. They're watching

you, Peter. Why do they need to spy on you like that? Oh...'

The radio was broadcasting good news: another government policy success. No! The government governed on shifting sands. Made assumptions. Excuses. Got it wrong. Put good people like Peter under surveillance. Agatha grabbed the radio and smashed it to the floor, silencing the voice. She kicked it, sending it spinning across the stone slabs until it skidded to a halt under the oak chest where they kept shoes and footballs and the boys' drawings and old school books that Agatha didn't want to throw away.

'Agatha, you broke the radio. I know you are angry about the SMO. I can't exactly explain what's happened. But I'll tell you what I do know. There are rumours spreading in the hospital that patients are being wheeled into theatre and their notes are, well, not wrong exactly, but don't match up. A senior surgeon opened up a woman to remove a cancer and found the cancer wasn't there. You'd think that would be good news. But they got pretty angry about it. The notes, the surgeon insisted, were precise but incorrect. And they need someone to blame. They think I'm tampering with things – somewhere along the route from laying patients on my trolley to delivering them to theatre. I've heard them talking about it. In the corridors, in the canteen: "How is it that the notes of so many of the patients wheeled to theatre by the hospital porter with the injured hand are wrong?"'

41. Walnuts

Hold back from the black hole that will spin you in riddles, its massive gravitational influence distorting space and time, but never rushing you. Oh no! The closer you get, the slower time goes. And it whispers, 'No rush. No rush.'

Two days after Peter had been put on SMO, strong winds shook the branches of the ancient tree that grew beside Grey Cottage and bombarded the grass with green and blackened fruits that Agatha had never noticed before. Wilfie picked one up – a mushy ball – and squeezed. Black pulp oozed between his fingers.

'What is it, mum?' asked Pip.

Agatha rubbed at the soft dark flesh, revealing a heavily contoured shell.

'Walnuts,' she said. 'Get the nut crackers.'

Gripping metal levers, Agatha popped open the shell and inside was a pearly walnut, soft and rubbery like a tiny human brain.

'A gift,' said Agatha. 'Right under our noses and we never noticed. Come on. Let's collect some for dad. A surprise.'

It was a joy to do something for Peter. Agatha fetched a large basket and the three began hunting for the treasures nestled in secret places, deep in the long grass. Then the boys hurled sticks at the tree's branches, whooping when a little green ball lost its hold and tumbled – another prize saved from squirrels.

Agatha hurried into the kitchen, keen to sort the harvest. It was odd, she thought, how quickly you could learn a skill. Walnut sorter. She laid the hard green ones on a tray. Perhaps they might soften like the half-green, half-black ones that gave up their seed without too much trouble.

The soft mushy black ones fast became her favourite, so soft that the shells came out with ease.

'A present for you,' she called to Peter when he returned home. 'All from our tree. They have been there year after year and we never realized.'

He put his arms round her waist, kissing the back of her neck as she worked. She twisted to kiss him back, glad to have him home, glad to have something fun to do together – to take their mind off the outside world.

'Help me,' she said.

She tried not to mind that Peter found it hard to peel the semi-ripe ones.

'You wash the black ones,' she suggested, tipping the peeled shells into the sink. Some came away clean but black pulp stuck to most.

'I don't think it matters,' she said.

Together, they piled the walnuts on trays and put them in the pantry to dry. A hundred walnuts. Two hundred. And more.

'I love this place,' said Agatha. 'I love all the gifts it shares with us. And I love you Peter.'

Side by side, they stood at the sink to wash the black off their hands. Their skin felt soft and oily but, no matter how hard they scrubbed, the black stayed, stubborn and dirty looking. Agatha hoped they would not notice at the hospital. Even though Peter's hands were clean, they were stained and looked grubby. Not good for someone on SMO. Not good at all.

42. Custard creams

Frozen water and super cold methane, ammonia and carbon dioxide ices, rock, dust, metallic bits of solar system debris. What am I? A comet.

At Fellows Light, Mr Firth had passed out at his desk and been removed from school. Skillern immediately took over as Head and eagerly moved into Firth's office. On the desk sat a glass paperweight filled with snowflakes holding down a list of pupil performance ratios and the school's national position. Fellows Light was in the bottom third; too many pupils not performing well. Skillern snorted. Under his rule, this would stop. Stop dead. Fellows would climb the table. Pupils who let Fellows down would be dealt with. He started to jot down a list of culprits. Number one: Wilfie Whisper.

Wilfie was at that moment in the school secretary's office, sent to see Mrs McDuff about his injured hand. He had been fiddling with his plaster during maths and pulled it off, tearing the scab beneath and accidentally smearing blood on his text book. Mr Chillworth liked to keep text books pristine. He sent Wilfie out.

'And while you're about it, get a new plaster. Ask Mrs McDuff.'

Wilfie tapped on Mrs McDuff's door and, even though he knew she could see him, she said,

'Who's that knock knock knocking on my door?' like she always did.

Wilfie liked Mrs McDuff. All the children liked Mrs McDuff with her soft curly hair, her powdered cheeks and woolly cardies and the way she mothered them. It was rumoured that her husband had died on their honeymoon and she had no children of her own.

'The school is my family,' she would say. 'If I could live here, I would. It can be very quiet at home. Very quiet.'

She knew everything about the pupils: who cried if they fell over in the playground, who was frightened of the headmaster, who was miserable because someone in their family had been removed. Her office was warm and snug and smelt of a fruity sort of perfume.

'Come in, come in. Now, what can I do for you, young man? Oh, Mr Chillworth sent you, did he? And did he ask you if I had any custard creams? Not a day goes by when that man doesn't pop in here to ask for a custard cream. As if I haven't got better things to do.'

Wilfie thought she said the maths teacher's name in a way that made him think Mrs McDuff didn't like Mr Chillworth very much.

'A plaster? Let me see. Would you like a custard cream? I know they're your favourite. I'm afraid I have to hide them from Mr Chillworth otherwise he would eat me out of house and home.'

Mrs McDuff reached for a tin on the very top shelf, which it shared with files labelled 'crafts', 'nature' and 'cookery'. These files were no longer used and sat far above the more important files – 'exams (internal)', 'exams (external)', 'accidents', 'parents (disciplinary)'. She balanced the tin on her chest, prized off the lid and, as always, looked surprised by what she found, even though she put the biscuits in the tin herself.

'You're in luck, young man. A few custard creams left. Did you know Wilfie, in the good old days pupils always had custard creams at break time? Kept the Fellows Light spirit burning. I like to think, Wilfie, that my office is a little haven of how things used to be. Everything's moving so fast these days. Which reminds me, I have something for you. Something very special. I've been carrying it around in my bag for days. Days and days. What a lucky thing you popped in.'

Mrs McDuff hunted through her crocheted bag and pulled out a piece of card.

'I was eating my cereal when I saw this and straight away I thought, 'Wilfie Whisper – he'd be perfect'. Look at this, Wilfie.'

Wilfie took the card. It was torn from a Brexypops cereal packet.

Could you be the first child in space?

Wilfie stared at the question.

'What is it? What's it mean?'

'What it says, dear. It's a competition. And the prize is to be the first child in space. Imagine that!'

This was the chance Wilfie had been waiting for his whole life and now here it was, on a bit of card that had been tucked in Mrs McDuff's bag.

'Well, would you like to give it a go?'

Wilfie's lip trembled. Before he knew why, or how it had happened, he was sobbing and hugging Mrs McDuff, his arms wrapped tight around her, shaking and crying, unable to let go.

'I think that's a yes. Come on, dear. You're squeezing me to death. Let's read it carefully and fill in the form. Let me see. We need your name, age, height, weight and then you have to say in ten words why you think it should be you. Let's measure you.'

Wilfie, in a daze, rubbed his tears away. Here was a chance, a slim chance, that he might actually go into space. It was incredible. Unbelievable. He wanted to race, skidding and slipping down the corridor to tell Pip. He wanted to fly home and hug his mum and tell her he was going to have Milky Way soup at last. But above all he wanted to make himself invisible and suddenly appear in the hospital where his dad was working and say, 'Hey dad, I am truly, honestly, really, really going to do a spacewalk!'

But, instead, he helped Mrs McDuff pull the wooden height measure and the school scales out of her cupboard where they lived, waiting to measure children when they joined the school and when they left.

'I don't know why we do all this measuring,' said Mrs McDuff. 'I really don't. But lucky for you, we do. Best take off your shoes.'

Wilfie took off his lace ups and stood tight against the measuring stick, pulling himself up tall through his spine and tucking in his chin. Mrs McDuff lowered the level onto his head, flattening his thatch of thick red hair.

'Stand straight as a rod.'

Wilfie pushed up, trying to nudge the stick higher. He didn't know why but it always seemed to be important to be as tall as possible. People admired tall boys. He knew he was a bit small for his age.

'Lovely. Now hop on the scales.'

Mrs McDuff wrote down the measurements on her school notepad and then, in her very best writing, on the form.

'You better fill the rest in yourself, dear. You're the one going up in a rocket, not me. Can you imagine?'

Wilfie tried to think of Mrs McDuff in a rocket and it made him giggle. Then Mrs McDuff started laughing. Then they were laughing together. Wilfie felt overwhelmed by happiness, the sheer joy of the adventures to come. He took the pen and started to fill in the form. Wilfie Peter Whisper. Nine years old. The next bit was easy.

Hey there. Hit us with ten out of this world words.

Why do you think you should be the first child in space?

The next section was for the headteacher.

'Mr Skillern has got to do this bit,' said Wilfie.

Why do you think your pupil should win?

'I don't think Mr Skillern would think I'd be any good in space. He doesn't think I'm any good at anything. He told mum.'

'Don't you worry. I'll ask him at breaktime. Better still, I'll tell him.'

Then there was a section for the responsible adult and their address.

'I think you'd be best at this bit, Mrs McDuff.'

Mrs McDuff filled in the address.

'Wilfie, what am I thinking? I've put me and the school address, not your home address. What a ninny I am. Automatic. That's the problem. The number of times I write that address.'

Wilfie looked at the form and considered. Perhaps it was for the best.

'Doesn't matter,' said Wilfie. 'You've done it neatly. And when I win, it means it will be a brilliant surprise for mum and dad.'

'Surprise? Aren't you going to tell them?'

'Yes, but not yet. I just don't want to…'

Wilfie did not want to explain to Mrs McDuff. His dad had been sort of sad since he had been on SMO, and Wilfie wanted to bring him good news. Big, exciting news. Not disappointment.

'I want to wait. For now. When I win, I'll tell them.'

'What confidence! You mean *if*, Wilfie. Don't count your chickens before they hatch. Have another biscuit while I get an envelope. You write the address. Let's see.

KISS, PO Box 000, SOLAR 7. Well done. A stamp and there we are. I'll post it today. Then we just have to wait. Fingers crossed.'

Wilfie looked at the envelope and dared to wonder where it might lead.

The bell rang for the next lesson.

'Bye, Mrs McDuff. Thanks for the plaster. And the biscuit. And the competition.'

'Bye, Wilfie dear. Get ready for lift off!'

Wilfie trotted down the corridor. It was a thrilling secret. He couldn't wait to see his dad's face when he won. And he could not wait to see those shooting stars close up.

43. Skillern on top

Leftovers. That's what comets are. The leftovers of the creation of our solar system created four and a half billion years ago.

Skillern was in a bad mood. He always felt irritated when he felt things slipping out of control. Paperwork was swamping him: parent letters to answer, report forms to complete, bills to be signed off, endless forms for a court case against the school for an accident involving a slippery gym mat. Skillern swore and determined to plough through. He had forty-five minutes before he was due in the main hall for whole school assembly. He would do his best to clear his desk. The idea of a race against the clock was enough to help him focus. Ten minutes in and his desk was looking neater. Things had been dealt with. That was why he, Skillern, would make a success of Fellows Light – he would drag it up from Firth's era of ineffective leadership and transform it into a top-notch school.

Mrs McDuff sashayed into his office. Skillern glanced up, irritated. Why could she not knock like everyone else? Show some respect.

'Morning Mr Skillern, dearie.'

She was what was wrong with this place. Been here so long she thinks it's her right. What does she do all day in that office? He would sack her if he could.

'Busy, busy, busy, I see. But I have a favour to ask. I know you have a hundred thousand important little tasks, but I just have one more to add. Could you sign this coupon for me and put a few words of support? It's for a space competition. Won't take a sec. It's for dear little Wilfie Whisper.'

'Space competition? Mrs McDuff, I have already had a whole stack of these ridiculous entries to sign off. Look. Here's one. And another. Loads of them. Don't you think I have better things to do?'

Skillern hunted around his desk and brought out ten, twenty, thirty pieces of card torn or cut from Brexypops cereal packets. Attached to each one was a pleading note from a parent asking him to complete the headteacher's section.

'Ha, look at this one. For Dillon Gill. I don't even know who Dillon Gill is.'

'Oh Dilly is a delight. He has the most adorable blonde curls. In fact, he would be very good for the competition – an angel in the sky. Although, I must put in a good word for Wilfie. It would do him the world of good. All he ever talks about is space, space, space.'

Skillern sighed. Wilfie Whisper was the sort of boy Fellows Light did not need and what was Mrs McDuff doing talking about angels. In his office.

'Please, Mr Skillern. The deadline is looming. Imagine how wonderful it would be for Fellows Light if one of our pupils won.'

A wonderful thing for Fellows Light?

It would be wonderful, of course. In fact, not just wonderful but a triumph. Could this competition be the opportunity he had been looking for?

'Looming, Mrs McDuff? We better get a move on.'

44. Window display
My Milky Way has a central core to astound you. It contains not just a black hole but a supermassive black hole, and that black hole contains the mass of our sun times four million.

On Saturday morning, a runner, unshaven, in tatty shorts and a sweat-lined sleeveless vest had stopped outside Wigmore's store and was peering in at the window display. Mr Wigmore, staring out, did not like what he saw. It was that man Frankie. Loitering. Probably wanting to get a glimpse of Susie. Wigmore would be the first to admit that circle fifteen was not the classiest of locations but they still had standards. He marched outside to confront Frankie, move him on.

'Sold many Brexypops yet?'

Frankie got in first. His voice was pleasant yet commanding. Not the sort of person you could ignore. Certainly not ask to clear off.

'We always sell lots of Brexypops. Why?'

'The space competition. Sounds exciting. Has it made a difference? To sales.'

Wigmore considered the display. The sight of his own portly reflection standing next to Frankie, all muscle and tone, filled him with dismay. He would cut back on iced fancies. Straight after his coffee break.

'Do you like the packaging?'

Why was Frankie so obsessed with Brexypops? Wigmore hadn't really registered the competition until now – but, come to think of it, he did remember Susie chattering about the idea of sending a child into space. She had wasted time reading a Brexypops cereal package – front and back whilst she was meant to be packing the shelves. It had annoyed him.

And he felt her trip to hospital was somehow her own fault. The shop floor was still stained with splashes of beetroot juice. All very irritating. Although, of course, he had been pleased to have her back so soon. He had missed her. Yes, he would admit it. And looking on the bright side, his customers had bonded over her plight; they had only just had time to get a card to her in hospital before she returned. And he, Wigmore himself, had given them the card for free in the first place. Overgenerous, that's what he had been. Overgenerous.

Wigmore frowned at the display: Brexypop boxes piled up into the shape of a rocket. And some member of staff had even taken it upon themselves to add a homemade sign saying, IT COULD BE YOU!

'Would you want your kid to win?' asked Franklin.

Wigmore was taken aback by the question. He once had a child. The last of the Wigmores, as it turned out. A little girl. The thought of her up there, belting through space, sounded dangerous. Although it was too late for that. She was gone. Years ago. Choked to death on a radish. She could, he supposed, be up there already if she was anywhere at all. His eyes filled with tears – he would do anything to have her back. But no, he would never send her up there, to be all alone, dangling around helplessly in some black hole. A bit of fluff. A mite of dust. Flicked about like a piece of nothingness.

'No,' he said. 'Not in a million years.'

'A million?'

'Well, I suppose it might be safe in a million years, but not right now.'

Frankie laughed.

'What do you think of the packaging?'

Wigmore was glad to move away from philosophical riddles. With the wisdom of an experienced retailer, he considered the design. Bright. Jolly. Engaging. Actually, a bit scary.

'In my opinion, the er... kid looks scared.'

'Yes,' said Frankie. 'I think you're right.'

'Smiling faces sell. They give confidence. I'd want to reassure parents. Sending children into space must be a risky business.'

'As risky as running a supermarket?'

'Running a supermarket is a vocation,' began Wigmore. He felt he was confiding more, explaining more, becoming more excited about Wigmore's than he had for many years. Somehow this fellow made him open up, feel a problem shared was a problem halved, feel excited for the future. If only he had a son of such ability. Or his lovely little daughter had lived to become a talented retailer, marry such a man and continue the Wigmore name. His eyes began to tear up again.

'Thanks, Mr Wigmore,' said Frankie. 'Keep up the good work. Wigmore's is a fine institution. And it's wonderful to see Susie back in action.'

Wigmore was aware that Susie had been watching them from her post on checkout seven. And now Frankie was waving at her and she was actually waving back. What on earth was going on? Now, Frankie was off, running down the street. Wigmore returned into his shop, confused but in good spirits, pleased he had dealt with the situation without confrontation. And had given good advice. And how splendid it had been to chat man-to-man with a fellow like Frankie. Someone on his wavelength at last. Yes, there was a man you could do business with. Even run a supermarket. He shook his head. He was getting beyond himself.

A week later, he was surprised to see that the Brexypops packaging had changed. The cartoon kid was looking a whole lot jollier.

45. Making Neptune

'I'm going the wrong way,' said Venus, spinning backwards relative to all the other planets. How they laughed at her.

Wilfie started making more models of planets to add to his collection. He found some chicken wire in the shed and bent it, pushing it into the shape of a ball.

'What are you doing?' asked Pip.

'Making another planet.'

'Can I?'

Pip tried to push the wire, but it was too stiff. He gave up and followed Wilfie out of the shed. Wilfie climbed over the stone wall onto open moorland and dropped to his hands and knees, searching the ground: grasses, tiny blue flowers, moss, sheep wool blowing about, hummocks and tussocks.

'What are you looking for?'

Pip was struggling to climb over the wall.

'Bits of moss. To stuff in the planet.'

Wilfie ran back to pull Pip over.

'C'mon,' said Wilfie.

Moss came up easily as they pulled it from amongst the grass. Pip took a handful and scrubbed it over the back of Wilfie's neck.

'Hey!'

They fought; moss a green ammunition to be pushed in faces, rubbed into hair, shoved down shirts.

'C'mon' said Wilfie, spitting out little emerald fronds. 'Let's make the planet.'

They pulled up tufts again, stuffing them into the wire ball. Picking. Stuffing. Picking. Stuffing. The ball took in the moss. And then the wire took no more and the moss stuck out. They smoothed the hairy green, tucking it in, trying to get it under control.

'Green monster,' said Pip.

'Neptune.'

In the workshop, Wilfie took a galvanised bucket, turned it upside down, stood on it, reached up to the top shelf and threw down a ball of thick string. Pip caught it with both hands.

'Yes!' said Pip.

Wilfie took the end of the string and pulled out two arm's lengths. He opened the tool box and took out a Stanley knife, pushing the bright silver steel blade from its housing.

'Sharp,' said Pip.

The boys looked at the blade, loving its danger.

'That would cut you hard,' said Pip.

'Deep.'

Wilfie put the string on the workbench and started cutting. But it slipped and slithered, so he tied the string near the ball to a nail on the bench and handed the loose end to Pip.

'Pull tight.'

Even tight, Wilfie had to make lots of cuts. Again and again. One by one the fibres split away from the main string until only a few remained.

'Hold the end tighter, Pip.'

Wilfie cut again and the last fibres broke, the string freed from the main ball. Wilfie looked again at the blade.

'Sharp,' said Pip, again.

Wilfie slid the blade back into the handle and put the knife away in the tool box. Danger over.

He threaded the string through the wire ball and tied a knot. Then he held the ball up by the string. It dangled and twirled, green moss sticking out, bits failing off.

'Come on,' said Wilfie.

'Can I carry it?'

'Not it. Neptune.'

'Neptune.'

Wilfie gave Pip the planet.

The boys trotted across the yard, into the kitchen and up the short flight of stairs to their bedroom. On the ceiling were two wooden beams. The beams had an assortment of nails hammered into them. And from the nails hung an assortment of round objects – the solar system. Wilfie stood on a wobbly wooden chair and hung up the mossy ball, tying the string to a nail on the beam near the window. He jumped down.

'I like it,' said Pip. 'But Saturn is still my favourite.'

Saturn was made from newspaper. Wilfie had painted it pale yellow and added some orange stripes. It hung in fourth place away from the sun. Wilfie knew this was not right but he had not made Mars or Mercury yet.

'It's pale yellow because it's got ammonia crystals whizzing around in its upper atmosphere. Did you know that, Pip?'

'Of course I know that. Everyone knows that.'

'Even so, it doesn't look much like Saturn yet,' said Wilfie. 'We need to make the ring.'

Saturn without its icy halo of dust and debris swirling round wasn't Saturn at all. The boys clattered downstairs to get some newspaper.

'I've stopped buying newspapers,' said Agatha. 'Why don't you try this?'

A jam jar of greenery stood on the table. It was a mix of stalks and stems and whip branches.

'Pull all the leaves off and twist them like this.'

Agatha twisted the stalks together and wound string round to hold them in place. Then she bent them into a circle and, with the help of the boys, tied the ends together.

'Smaller, I think,' said Wilfie. So they untied the string and pulled the twist tighter and tied it again, smaller. Wilfie hurried upstairs to see if it would fit. It was too tight, so they undid it again and made it bigger.

'How will you get it to float around Saturn without touching it?' asked Pip. 'You can't let it touch.'

'We'll think of that upstairs.'

'It would have been much easier with newspaper,' said Pip. 'You'd get a long bit and twist it and tie it together and then that would have been finished. Much easier with newspaper.'

'Mum doesn't like newspapers anymore,' said Wilfie, knowing it was something to do with dad being on SMO and mum being angry with the world.

46. Hair space

'Say, black hole, how do you become a supernova?' 'Good question. Good question. It all comes about when a large star, and I mean large, much bigger than a sun dies. And when that star becomes a black hole, that is when it becomes a supernova. Got it?'

Wilfie and Pip were on the school minibus – a maroon sixteen-seater adorned with pale cream swirly lettering proclaiming the school's name: *Fellows Light*. The Whisper boys lived the furthest away, so each day they were picked up first and dropped off last. When they were very little, Agatha would walk up the track from Grey Cottage with them and wait at the top until they saw the bus come over the brow of the hill and stop at the end of their track. Now, the boys often walked up on their own. Pip and Wilfie always sat in the front seats directly behind the minibus driver.

'Morning, lads.'

The minibus driver said the same thing every morning.

'Morning, Mr Minibus,' the boys replied.

Everyone called him Mr Minibus. Mr Minibus whistled all the way to school, only breaking his tune to say morning to the next children getting on.

Wilfie suddenly realised the two girls on the seat behind him were talking about the Brexypops competition. He froze, trying to hear every word; it was the first time he had heard anyone say anything about the competition since he had entered. It was as if they were talking about his secret.

'Are you gonna give it a go, then?'

'Thinking about it. I might. I dunno. Not sure if I want to go into space really. It might be a bit boring. Floating around by yourself.'

'I've entered, but I bet I won't win. Nearly everyone in the whole world has entered. 'Cept you.'

'And everyone who doesn't have Brexypops for their breakfast.'

'Which is probably quite a lot of people.'

'What would you do if you did win? Would you go?'

'I won't win. You never actually win competitions. But my dad filled the entry in for me.'

'If you went, would you be able to do your plaits yourself?'

'I don't know. Wouldn't I be wearing a helmet?'

'You might. But if you weren't, your plaits might stick straight up.'

The girl held her friend's plaits up in the air.

They giggled.

Wilfie smiled to himself. They didn't know anything about space. He knew he had a better chance.

47. Creatives
Teenage years. The universe is fourteen billion years old.

An invitation to brainstorm the Pennysides project with Gee & Gee had unnerved Weston.

'Go along,' Franklin had said. 'Give them a pop of your creative genius.'

Weston did not feel he could give Gee & Gee a pop of anything. And he felt less able to do so as he stumbled into Gee & Gee's minimalist studio on the seventeenth floor of a block in circle six.

'Welcome, dear fellow, welcome,' said Gilbert, pumping his hand. 'Just going over the brief with Graham.'

Gilbert nodded at his partner, who was pacing up and down in front of the panoramic window, moaning.

'He's taking it badly, I'm afraid,' Gilbert added in a whisper.

'Right, Graham. Pay attention. Weston from Ostrich is here. First things first. Timescale. We have two days to come back with designs.'

'Impossible,' protested Graham.

'Graham does the designs. I do the briefing,' explained Gilbert. 'Here goes. Graham, are you listening?'

'No.'

Gilbert went on regardless. 'The capsule needs re-decorating before it's sent off and installed on the rim in orbit. The space is cylindrical. And compact. You needn't worry about the mining work station, which takes up fifty percent of the base area. That's sealed off. The bit we've got to put our minds to is the top end, the home living area: sleeping, washing, eating, the six screens for communicating with Earth, the control centre for heating, oxygen levels, decompression.'

'It's a cupboard and you want me to make it a fun place to live? That's not fair.'

'It may be a cupboard, Graham, but a hugely prestigious cupboard.'

'Graham always plays the melodramatic creative,' said Gilbert, turning to Weston. 'That's where he needs to be. So, good response so far.'

Gilbert and Graham had seemed interchangeable. Presenting together. Chipping in. Talking simultaneously as if with one mind. They even looked similar: short cropped hair, long noses, thin lips, medium height, muscular arms from working out. Both had soft, kindly eyes, Graham's blue to Gilbert's green. They seemed to enjoy dressing alike: light linen jackets, ties, Panama hats. But here, in their studio, Weston realised they were chalk and cheese, taking heart from each other's talents and strengths – like himself and Miriam. Graham came up with the ideas, Gilbert sourced materials, got things organised. And, of course, they both had lives outside the partnership: wives and children. Or a wife and children. Like himself. Maybe. One day.

Graham flounced over to his desk, a transparent perspex six-foot table – the sort of desk all creatives should have. The sort of desk, thought Weston, that he should have, where design ideas could float before him. Graham closed his eyes. Gilbert tiptoed across and silently placed a large sheet of watercolour paper in front of Graham. To the right of the paper, he set down a drawing pen, a block of watercolours, a fine paintbrush, a mixing palette and two cut-glass bowls of water. The final touch was a cup of black coffee. Maybe the aroma of the coffee was a signal. Graham opened his eyes and Gilbert retreated without a word to his own desk, putting a finger to his lips.

'Not a sound,' he whispered to Weston.

Weston nodded, and tiptoed to a white leather sofa, wincing as it squeaked as he sat down. He felt alert, excited. This was a masterclass in creativity playing out before his very eyes – and he was determined not to miss a second. There would be some changes back at Ostrich HQ. Oh yes! But after ten minutes his eyelids felt heavy and he fell into a world of paint brushes swirling watercolours into a landscape of cornflowers and orange shirts, all whirling round a black hole that was the plug hole in his bath. Try as he might, he couldn't save them. They were being sucked away. Far, far away.

'I don't know! I really don't know where to begin.'

Graham's cries woke Weston. The great designer slammed down his drawing pen and, with delicate, tapered fingers, pulled from his pocket a square of orange velvet. Footstools, thought Weston. That would be the ideal covering for a footstool. A nice present for Miriam. Would go with her orange shirt. Unless it clashed. Graham rubbed the velvet anxiously between his fingers.

Gilbert padded over.

'Just remember, this project is about a child. A child.'

'I know it's a child. I'm not used to children. Give me high end office blocks. I'm all about elegant minimalism. Not designing for a child.'

'I know you can do it,' said Gilbert, his arm around Graham. 'No one knows how to make spaces work like you, how to float people around buildings of metal and glass. Your delicate positioning of screens and dividers. No one has such a light touch with furniture that it appears as if by magic in the right place. And your sensitivity to colour is second to none; think how you make blues dance with yellows, taupe flow into greys, fawns surprise and delight with violets, purples hum with silvers. Yes, Graham, you are renowned for your incredible taste, your mastery of tone. And always, always your genius only emerges if you get to this point of anxiety. You know that, Graham. I know you do.'

'But I don't know what base colour to use, let alone what it can run alongside. It's impossible. I hate this Pennysides project. A working base for a space miner turned into a play home for a kid. It's beyond me. Never, never, never have I felt so out of my depth. It's not fair.'

Gilbert patted his partner's shuddering shoulder and gave him a squeeze. To Weston's embarrassment, Graham started to cry. Gilbert turned to smile at Weston.

'This,' he whispered, 'is where Graham needs to be. At his most vulnerable. At his most creative. When the tears flow, the ideas flow too.'

Gilbert picked up Graham's pen and put it into his right hand. Miserably, Graham pushed the velvet back into his pocket and started to draw. Gilbert retreated to his desk.

'Shhh,' he said, winking at Weston.

Weston nodded, determined to watch and learn. But it was so hard to keep his eyes open. So hard.

Sometime later, as if still in a dream, Weston was standing at the table beside a beaming Gilbert as an animated, excited Graham explained his concept. It was brilliant. The deadline would be met in time for the design to be implemented in Number 49 Pennyside before it was taken to the cargo capsule, launched into space and docked on the rim, ready for the competition winner's arrival.

48. Be prepared
Biggest of them all! Star RMC 136a1 sitting majestically in the Large Magellanic Cloud. Hottest (over 50,000 K). Most massive (mass of three hundred and fifteen suns).

Wilfie lay on the bracken on the open moor thinking about the competition. Pip was playing nearby, pushing little sticks into the ground to make a miniature twig tent, humming and talking to himself. Pip was always busy doing things like that. He was never still. He would be no good in a rocket. But Wilfie was good at keeping still and thinking about things. He would be the perfect first child in space. He knew he would.

But he would miss Pip.

He started thinking about the things he would need to take. He went inside to pack a bag so he would be ready.

49. Final Five

How many galaxies? Over a hundred billion in the universe, for starters.

Skillern banged his fist on his desk.

'Yes!'

He stormed into Mrs McDuff's office waving a letter.

'News, Mrs McDuff, news! Wilfie Whisper, of all people, has got through to the second round of the space competition.'

'Oh my!'

'Beaten off thousands of others to get down to the last twenty.'

'Oh my, I can hardly believe it.'

'They are coming here, Mrs McDuff, here to Fellows Light to interview him. Hunt out a decent cup and saucer to offer them a decent cup of tea. We mustn't leave anything to chance.'

'No, of course not. Oh, I still can't believe it.'

'If he gets through this round, he'll be in the final five. Fellows Light, Mrs McDuff, is on the way up!'

'Mr Skillern, you must take credit for your part. And what a wonderful thing for dear Wilfie. He must be so excited.'

'Yes. No. He doesn't know yet. Send him to my office, Mrs McDuff. I'll give him the news myself.'

Ten minutes later, there was a tentative knock on Skillern's door.

'Enter. Wilfie, I have news for you.'

50. Champion

All together. Fourteen billion years ago the universe was collected in one point of space.

When Peter arrived home that evening Agatha could see his weariness as he got out of the car. He rubbed his neck and rolled his shoulders, shaking off the strain of yet another day under SMO. The constant pressure seemed to affect him more and more each day. He had to make sure he toed the line. Any slip-up and a reprimand would follow. Reprimands took many forms, some trifling, some sinister.

So, it was a joy to see the two boys racing up the path, leaping at their dad in welcome. Peter laughed as he caught them, his anxieties seeming to drop away. The sun hovered, a great orange disc, holding on for his return. There was chill in the air, yet the boys were in shorts and short-sleeve shirts, their faces cherry-red from exercise, their eyes bright with excitement.

'Wilfie has got some news dad. Really, really big news,' cried Pip, opening his arms wide.

Agatha caught up with the boys. She had known something was up, but the boys had refused to tell until Peter was home. She liked that.

But now the moment had come, Wilfie seemed unsure what to say. He thrust out an envelope.

'You read it, dad.'

Peter opened the envelope and took out two sheets of paper. Agatha saw delight spread across his face.

'I don't believe it. I just don't believe it.'

Peter grabbed Wilfie and threw him up and down, up and down, in the air, telling him he was champion.

'Who'd have thought it? My little boy taking up where I left off.'

'I've not won yet, dad.'

'Not yet. But you're on your way.'

'Will you do the spacewalk Wilfie?' asked Pip.

The boys and Peter started larking about, mimicking the spacewalk, floating around the garden, taking great steps, shrieking.

'Aliens,' screamed Pip.

The three dived for cover.

'What is it? Won what? What's it say?' cried Agatha.

Peter escaped the aliens and turned to her. He was grinning, his eyes sparkling.

'Your little boy has done something remarkable. Supersonically amazing. Listen to this.'

He took the letter, already crumpled, and read:

Dear Headteacher.

Congratulations! Your pupil, Wilfie Whisper, has got through to the second round of the KISS competition.

'The what competition?'

'KISS. Just wait.'

We were impressed by his/her reason for wanting to go into space and felt that the information supplied by yourself as his/her headteacher makes him/her a good candidate. Read the attached information carefully for the next stage. The flight, should your pupil be successful, will last five days and will take place during term time. The Department for Education has been informed and will give permission for the winning child to have time off school. This will include an additional two days pre-flight training. Please confirm that you will attend the next round of the competition and that, if you are successful, you will accept the prize.

Yours Evie Blick-Foxton, Space Project School Liaison Officer

KISS. Kids Into Space Something

'So what, Mrs Whisper, do you think of that?'

Peter was triumphant. Agatha felt the blood drain from her face.

'Space? What are they thinking of?'

'Do the spacewalk mum,' said Pip, pulling at her hand.

'What do they mean? The second round. How did this happen? Tell me, Wilfie. Now.'

Agatha grabbed at Wilfie's wrist.

'Tell me.'

'Agatha, stop it,' said Peter.

'Stop it. What do you mean? Can't you see how dangerous this is?'

This was it: how Wilfie would be taken.

'Agatha, calm down. Wilfie has achieved something incredible. Isn't that what you've always wanted?'

'But not this! Space is no place for a child. You of all people should know that.'

'But he hasn't won yet. He's not definitely going.'

'But you want him to go Peter. They want him to go. Can't you see? They are trying to steal our son.'

Agatha was shaking – how could Peter not see the danger?

'You're not going Wilfie. No. No. No.'

'I'm not going yet, mum. I haven't won. You have to do tests. It says on the other bit of paper.'

'Give it to me.'

Agatha snatched the information sheet from Peter. She skimmed over the words, her face white, her breathing erratic.

Candidates will be tested on the following: empathy, resilience, sensitivity, craft, responsiveness, loneliness, anticipation, trust, sleep, pluck, motor skills, digestion.

Are they out of their minds? What does 'craft' even mean?'

'I think Wilfie would be good at all those things, whatever they are,' said Pip.

'Oh yes, Pip, he would be good. But he's far too precious to go.'

'Dad wanted to go,' mumbled Wilfie.

'What about the spacewalk?' said Pip. 'You wanted to do a spacewalk, dad. Can't Wilfie do it instead?'

'Agatha, I think we should give him a chance. This is an incredible opportunity. Can't you see that?'

Agatha flung her arms in the air in fury: 'How can you be so stupid? How can you trust these people?'

'We can find out...'

'Find out what? That they're idiots? By which time they'll have blasted Wilfie to...'

'Agatha, you're wrong. People are travelling into space safely every day. You don't know anything about it. I'm the one who studied for a PSAE. I'm the one who got close. I know...'

'Oh yes, you know everything. I'm just a cleaner. But I know what's right for my son. Our son.'

'Agatha, listen. You know Wilfie is special. This is something he was born to do. For others. For progress. It's not just a trip, Agatha. It's something truly amazing. It's—'

'What, so you would sacrifice your own son for those people? People we don't know. Who don't care about people like us?'

'No, Agatha. You don't understand. You—'

'Shut up, Peter. Just shut up.'

'What is it? Why are you so angry?'

'I'm not angry. I can't see why... how you can... oh, what is wrong with you?'

Agatha crumpled the form and hurled it to the ground as she turned from her family.

'Mum, come back,' shouted Pip.

But Agatha, her head ringing, tears falling, climbed over the wall and ran out onto the moor. She stumbled over the rough terrain, terrified for Wilfie and shocked by the chasm between her and Peter. On an evening like this, she might stride out here hand-in-hand with Peter, but tonight she felt only anger towards him; how could the man she loved drive this wedge between them? How could he put his own ambition – no, the fallout of his own failure – on the shoulders of their son? He was pushing the boundaries beyond his own comprehension, and that was dangerous. Her own guilt for the same crime welled up. She musn't give in. The consequences would be catastrophic. She swished fast through the long tough grasses that bordered narrow paths, gorse scratching against bare legs, and felt her anger set against Peter: he was wrong – so wrong – to contemplate putting Wilfie in such danger.

She climbed a black granite step to cross a dip in the stone wall. The moor opened before her, glorious in its beauty but not enough to penetrate the misery that engulfed her.

Sliding on loose earth, she scrambled down a steep hillside, following the stream that raced, ice cold, over exposed rock, splashing silver as it created waterfall after waterfall. Where the stream met a shallow river, water had carved out a gorge. Cliffs rose at each side, smothered in lichen and moss – a brilliant lime green. High above, the roots of ancient trees pushed outwards, floundering witchy fingers trying to get a hold where there was nothing to hold, while others buried themselves in thin brown earth, feeling their way into pitch black cracks in the rock. Against the sky, blackened leaves rocked on wind-blown branches, blots against fading blue. Agatha crashed her way down the river's course, slipping on stepping stones, careless on the familiar narrow stone path that ran like a ribbon along the water's edge.

A rocky handhold tugged at a memory. She could see Peter now, grasping a lowered branch for balance. She remembered how, against the giant underworld landscape, he looked vulnerable. She had put out a hand as if to help and, seeing her, he jumped, stone to stone until he was with her, kissing her, holding her, and she had pressed herself into him, wanting him. She flushed at the thought, not wanting him now. She was angry with him.

With herself.

She clambered from the gorge and crossed the base of the valley, skirting the bog that could swallow a man, and slipped and slithered up shale to the top of the high hill that rose behind Grey Cottage. At the summit, the wind was noisy, whipping up her hair. Far below, little window squares of light, glowing from under the slate roof of Grey Cottage told her so many stories: boys upstairs in bed, unhappy that she had been cross; Peter going to bed, ready for an early start, but half waiting for her, wanting to talk, make things right between them before they slept. She wanted that too, but what he was asking for Wilfie was madness. She sank to the damp ground, wrapped her hands round her knees, pulling them tight to her chest and wept.

Later, stiff and icy cold, Agatha fell into a jolting jog down the hill. In the gloom she came upon ponies cropping the moorland grasses. Small and stocky, they stood tails to the wind, their thick dark manes lifting, picked up and played with by swirling breezes. They raised their heads, dark eyes watchful behind long thick forelocks. One took a step forward. Agatha rubbed its soft muzzle. She rubbed between its ears, its mane. Then, daring herself, she lay her arm across its withers. The pony, ears forward, turned to nibble at her. She lay her body across its back and, heart pounding, inch by inch brought her leg over to sit astride, keeping her body low to its neck. The pony shuddered, shook its mane. If Peter had been there, he would have been fearful for her: a wild pony, the hooves, the bite, the sudden, unpredictable movement. But Agatha wanted to feel fear, to scare herself. She stroked the coarse, dark hair and slowly, slowly sat upright. The pony bent to crop again. Agatha sat motionless, calming, connecting with unknown dangers. One day, when the time was right, Wilfie could go, but not now. He was too young. If Peter could not see that, maybe it was best not to discuss it. Not confront him. Talk of other things. Let the episode fade away. She slithered off, pulled a handful of grass and offered it on flattened palm. But the pony, grazing, took no notice.

Back at Grey Cottage, there was the special quiet that comes when people you love are upstairs asleep. The competition form, lying smoothed out on the kitchen table, caught Agatha by surprise.

Peter had signed it.

Her fury reignited. She hunted for a pen to scribble out his signature. No pen. She searched through the wooden box of crayons, scissors, rubbers, sharpeners, homework stuff. She could only find a blunt pencil.

She scribbled out Peter's signature, scrawled a comment and signed her own name. Then she slid the form into the envelope, crossed out 'Mr and Mrs Whisper' and wrote 'Mr Skillern, Headmaster', licked the flap and stuck it down. With relief that the decision was made, she tucked the envelope in Wilfie's jacket pocket for him to take to school in the morning. Then she dropped onto the sofa and drifted into sleep.

51. Snowflake

The Moon is two hundred and thirty-eight thousand, eight hundred and fifty-six miles from the Earth.

At break, the next day, Wilfie ran up to Mrs McDuff's office to ask if she could give the envelope to Mr Skillern. And it was a bit more than that. He wanted her to open it. To see what it said. Mum had been funny about it that morning, saying they hadn't got time to talk about it as if she was still cross with dad. And he hadn't even seen dad, he'd gone so early. And now Mrs McDuff wasn't there. Wilfie stared at the envelope. Not wanting to wait, he crept up to the headmaster's office. The door was open. He could see right into the room. No Mr Skillern. Daring himself, he ran in and put the letter on the mighty desk and put the funny glass snowflake thing on top of it so it wouldn't get lost and ran out, his heart hammering. He hoped it was a yes. He really did.

Skillern was upbeat. Things were going well at Fellows Light under his leadership: failing teachers moved on, academic standards on the up. And now there was the possibility of one of their most useless pupils becoming the first child in space. He had talked to the teachers about space projects they should run, should Wilfie Whisper win. Make it easy for the press to report Fellows Light as a leading primary school.

Fellows Light: light years ahead. Headmaster Skillern: a shining star.

Skillern guessed the contents of the envelope someone had slid under Firth's ghastly snowflake paperweight. Credit to the Whisper parents for responding so speedily. If he was quick, he could countersign the form and, if Mrs McDuff ran, they might catch today's post and hit the KISS desk first thing tomorrow morning. Efficiency. That could only count in Wilfie's favour. Skillern pulled out the form and gasped.

NO WAY!

Mrs Whisper had scrawled the words in capital letters. He knew it was her. She had scribbled and then signed it herself. Ridiculous woman. A trouble maker. Fancy writing 'No Way' like that. And in pencil. So ignorant. Didn't the woman even own a decent pen?

On the other hand, writing in pencil did present opportunities.

Skillern scrabbled around his desk. He had a rubber somewhere. All children should come to school well equipped with a pencil case containing pencil, sharpener, ruler, rubber. An efficient, well prepared pupil was a successful pupil. So where was his rubber? He was a busy man. Things to do. No time to waste. He would have to have a tidy up later. Piles of paper. Broken pens. Overflowing wastepaper basket. At last a rubber! He erased Mrs Whisper's scrawl and, to his delight, saw Mr Whisper's signature intact. He added his own name in the appropriate section, hunted around for a another envelope and wrote the KISS address.

Wilfie Whisper would take part in the second stage of the competition. He knew what was best for the boy even if his mother didn't.

52. Decent cup and saucer

'Most moons? That's me,' sparks Saturn. 'I host eighty two, the most of all the planets in the solar system.'

A week later, Mr Skillern found himself in his office offering a cup of tea in a decent cup and saucer to a vivacious young woman, Miss Evie Blick-Foxton, School Liaison Officer from KISS. She had come on behalf of the OSH space competition to interview Wilfie Whisper and wanted to have a word with the headmaster first.

For Skillern, Miss Blick-Foxton's presence on the far side of his desk was a big tick that said he was taking the school in the right direction. Upwards. Adults sitting on the other side of his desk were normally parents: angry ones, red faced, perspiring, banging their fists; sanctimonious ones, full of adoration for their average kid; miserable ones who cried and wrung their hands, fearful of the future; and, worst of all, dull, pasty ones, who said nothing, thought nothing and were sitting there because it was their turn to waste his time. One thing they all had in common was that they had no style, no panache. Miss Blick-Foxton had panache. Oh yes! She worked in circle six. Skillern was impressed, and he aimed to impress. Make his mark.

He asked her about KISS, showed interest, compassion. It was a charity, after all. And she seemed interested in him, keen to get under his skin, find out what he was doing at Fellows Light.

'I so admire your focus, your determination, Mr Skillern. From my research, this school has not had the best reputation. But under your leadership – well!'

Evie lent forward as she spoke. Skillern was tempted to lean forward too, but caught himself and sat back instead, tapping his fingers together.

'Mr Skillern, I have to ask you, what do you know about space mining?'

'Space mining?'

'Yes. If Wilfie wins, the publicity will thrust Fellows Light into the spotlight. You're the headmaster – they will hunt you down to quiz you on space mining. It's a big topic. And between you and me, that's what this competition is all about: the future of mining in space. You will get hounded for your opinions, your expertise. How space mining might compare to mining in the past? Especially living here, near the moors.'

'The moors?'

'You know, tin mines. I expect you know a lot about that. Your pupils probably have ancestors who earned their living sweating away underground. And who knows, some of them might one day earn their living mining in space. Mining runs in their blood. So, it might be good to do some school projects, give a talk, go on a trip.'

'You mean on space mining. Or mining mining?'

'Both. Compare and contrast. That sort of thing. It's important for you to come across as having a grip on things. Just a friendly thought. Shall we move on to the test?'

'Test?'

'Not you,' Evie giggled. 'The test for young Wilfie. It will only take twenty minutes or so. Shall I do it here or is there a spare classroom?'

'We'll sort out a classroom,' said Skillern. The idea of Miss Blick-Foxton taking over his office, sitting at his desk, was too much.

He rang through to Mrs McDuff. Seconds later she burst into his office.

'Hello, hello. 4B is free. So, you've come to see little Wilfie Whisper – are you from the council?'

'Miss Blick-Foxton,' interrupted Skillern, 'is from KISS. She has come to test Wilfie for the next round of the space competition.'

'The space competition. Of course. Hasn't he done well? I have to tell you I was the one that brought the entry form in to school for him. Not that I want any credit. It was just when I saw it I thought, 'Mrs McDuff, if you don't cut that out and get young Wilfie Whisper to fill it in you will never forgive yourself.' He's perfect. He loves space. Obsessed, I would say. Although obsessed sounds a little unhealthy. What I mean is that he's really keen. I don't—'

'Enough, Mrs McDuff. Bring Wilfie to room 4B for testing. I will escort Miss Blick-Foxton. And make a note to ask all classes to run a project on mining. Mining in the past and mining in the future. Space mining, that is. And book a school trip to the tin mines.'

'The tin mines! I'd love to take the children to the tin mines. My father was a miner. The stories he told me.'

Mrs McDuff bustled off.

'There we are; mining does run in the blood of Fellows Light,' said Evie.

Skillern was not sure if Miss Blick-Foxton was teasing him. And he was not sure if Mrs McDuff was being helpful or ruining Wilfie's chances. Whichever it was, she was a tiresome woman and did not complement the professional approach of Fellows Light. Her days were numbered. He would make sure of that.

After the mining trip.

Wilfie was happy to be pulled out of maths but not so happy to be facing Mr Skillern in 4B.

'Wilfie, Miss Blick-Foxton has come to ask you some questions. Nothing difficult. Do your best. The school is relying on you, so don't mess it up.'

Skillern backed out of the classroom, nodding to Miss Blick-Foxton, who giggled.

'Hello, Miss,' said Wilfie, relieved by Mr Skillern's absence and deciding he liked Miss Blick-Foxton already.

'Well, hello Wilfie. Just call me Evie. We're going to play one or two games then I'll ask you a few questions and that's it. Happy?'

Wilfie nodded. He was used to people coming in and testing him. He was so behind everybody else that adults were always trying to find out what was wrong with him. It wasn't usually fun, but this was different. He enjoyed wearing a mask and earphones: he could see nothing, hear nothing, but the dark and silence did not bother him. He enjoyed the spaghetti challenge, speedily linking a host of coloured wires and connection points so they all joined up and not one was left without a connection. They even had refreshments. Evie had brought a picnic of shrink wrapped ham and a shrink wrapped roll. She asked if Wilfie could make it into a sandwich, which he did. Quite easily. Then she shared it with him and, yes, he liked it even if it was a bit rubbery. When Evie accidentally set fire to her notebook, Wilfie grabbed a school apron and smothered it out before the fire alarm could be activated. After that, she made some notes, measured his height, waist, arms and legs, weighed him, gave him a basic hearing test and shone two dots on the wall and asked him what colours they were.

'Red. Green. Green. Green. Red,' said Wilfie.

'That's it,' said Evie, flicking off her torch. 'Any questions?'

Wilfie thought. It was polite to ask questions.

'How far are you travelling today?'

Evie laughed. 'Not as far as you might be.'

She packed her bag.

'Three more schools to visit so I need to get a move on. Cheerio – and good luck.'

Wilfie ambled back to his maths lesson wondering why yet another person from Slow Learning Concern had come to check him out.

53. Reconstruction

There is no atmosphere in space. Sound has no way to travel to be heard.

Agatha, I am signing the form. What an opportunity for our little boy who talks of nothing else but space. Of course we will make sure it is safe. Of course we will check it out. The moor is taking your anger. I wait but you do not return. Thin light of dawn creeps into our bedroom, sheets still cool beside me. I dress and go downstairs. You look peaceful, blanketed on the sofa. I lean in to kiss your sleeping breath. Tonight we will heal the wound. But tonight comes and we are not healing. A pattern separates us. Overnight work. Early mornings. The chasm holds. We do not find the moment. Three, four days. I am miserable in our separation and I know you are too. And I am thinking about the competition. Maybe you are right. Wilfie is young. Perhaps too young. I will talk to him. I am pushing trolleys when I imagine us on an early evening walk by the stream, hand in hand, stepping across cool flat rocks, to reach the moss green bank and, beyond, the soft grasses where angelic flowers grow. My heart sings. I am smiling as I push trolleys up and down, up and down. You would laugh. Dorcas is here teasing me. You would like her. Oh Agatha, I am sorry a thousand times. My bleeper is going again. Not a patient. An order to go to Staff Welfare. 'Fingers crossed you're off SMO,' Dorcas says. She gives my arm a squeeze and trots off towards the canteen for her coffee break. 'Don't worry, I won't have a single biscuit,' she says. 'Not even two,' I call after her. She laughs and hurries away. Off SMO! Can you believe it Agatha? I am racing up the stairs three at a time to level four. The door to Staff Welfare is ajar. I knock and go in. 'Hi. Peter Whisper. You wanted to see me,' I say. Two men and a woman are sitting behind a table opposite the door. The pale faced younger man gets up and closes the door behind me then returns to his seat. He moves quietly. 'Sit down, Peter,' says the woman. She shifts on her seat, flicks her mousy brown hair, fiddles with her collar, pulls at her earlobe. She seems on edge. I smile at her and sit on the only other chair, facing them across the table. They look at me. Smiles flit about their faces, but smiles that unnerve me. Is it sympathy? Empathy?

Not cruelty, surely. Whatever it is, they are not a bundle of laughs in Staff Welfare. 'Have a drink,' says the woman. She slides a glass of water towards me. The glass rocks as it catches an imperfection on the wooden table. I grab it just in time. 'Thanks,' I say and take a sip. 'Drink up,' says the woman. 'You've missed your coffee break. You'll need refreshment.' 'You're right,' I say. I finish the water. 'Well?' They say nothing. 'So,' I try again, 'what's this all about?' 'Peter,' fires the man sitting in the middle. The sound ricochets round the room, high pitched, aggressive. I look at him and am caught by crow-black eyes that glitter from a face that, grey-skinned and infinitely wrinkled, speaks of death. 'Peter,' he repeats. 'We are putting you on Reconstruction.' The words slam into me. Physical bullets. I lose my balance. Grab at the table. Reconstruction. It can't be true. 'Ver… muzz… muzzle… summits… miss… take.' But my tongue is thick in my mouth and my words are blurred, stupid sounding. The water. What have they put in the water? I try to stand, to protest, but feel nauseous, dizzy. The crow-eyed man is speaking on and on, faster and faster, his voice screeching, piercing. I put my hands over my ears to cut it out. I try to dive into my mind, to swim out of the room, to ride on a roll of purring clouds and evaporate into the kitchen of Grey Cottage, knocking the breakfast egg with Wilfie and Pip, never to come back. Tap. Tap. Tap. But the voices are still coming. 'You have been recommended for Reconstruction by the senior staff of the hospital. You need help. Remember, Peter, Reconstruction is a privilege only given to those workers whose service we value. Your family will be proud. Proud. Proud!' The three people are merging into each other. My head is heavy. Too heavy. Something is banging in my skull, screaming at me. I can't go without making things right with you Agatha. I need to go back to Grey Cottage... now... never come back... stop the form... mix my thoughts with Agatha like the cake... The woman is standing, towering over me, a giantess, shouting orders through a megaphone but she doesn't have a megaphone and she doesn't need to tell me all these things. They are all mixed up because you are still angry with me. Don't be angry, Agatha. Please, please don't be angry. 'Removal for Reconstruction is immediate. Contact with family is not permitted. They will be informed. They will be sent a Family Reconstruction allowance which is twenty per cent of your pay for the duration. If you are unresponsive to the programme and the duration is increased for an indefinite term, the allowance will cease.' 'Remember, Peter, remember,' says the third, pulling me down into a milky stream that flows from pale eyes, rocking me with a gentle melody, pitching me side to side as he sings a lullaby. 'Your family will be proud of you. So proud. Reconstruction is never a punishment. Never. It is a great compliment offered only to the best – the very best – of our society. You have been chosen, yes chosen, as someone who is considered important in your role by the state. You may only be a porter but you are a good and loyal worker and we look after good workers. Always.' I slump forward onto the table. From far away, the pale stream pulls thoughts from my head, singing a hundred thousand times again, 'Time to go, Peter, time to go.' Out of a mist comes a chair with wheels that float and roll and squeal. Hands press into my flesh and I am being taken and there is nothing I can do about it. Hum. Hum. Hum. We are in the car and you are beside me. But there is a tightness across my chest, my abdomen, holding me down, trapping me, and my eyes are heavy. I force them open and they flit like moths' wings, brown, orange, brown, orange. You are not there. It is not our car. I see high rise buildings, a blur outside. And now fields, fields, fields and we are sucked into a forest of towering black pines, slender and dead looking. Black. Sliver of light. Black. Sliver of light. Black. Black. Black of trees. Light beyond obliterated. We are slowing and the forest is opening out, letting in a brilliant white circle of open sky and there is a building. Four storeys. Regimented windows. We slow to a halt and a woman in a pale blue uniform comes towards us and opens the door. The belt that has held me so tight, releases. 'Get out now,' she says. 'No,' I say. 'You're not being… no… not this place…' But my tongue is still thick in my mouth and the words are coming from elsewhere. Her grip is strong as she leads me into the building. I lurch, my legs heavy and slow. It is so quiet inside. And there is a table with forms. Not forms. 'Sign to say you have arrived,' she says. I cannot write. She pushes a pen into my hand and bends my fingers, forcing me to take hold, to sign. And I can't. So she is writing my name for me. 'Now you will shower. I will be waiting.' I don't want to shower but she keeps talking. 'Leave all your things in this locker. They will be perfectly safe. Put on this gown when you've finished.' I feel weak. I try to focus, try not to slip on the tiles in the cubicle but my knees buckle and I fall and the water is so hot, so cold. I don't want to leave my things in a cubicle. I don't want to put on a gown. But all the time the woman is there, so I do. 'I'll take you to your room. Do you need a wheelchair?' A wheelchair? Am I not the porter? I tread step by step, watching each rising of my legs, placing of the foot, as we travel dimly lit corridors, passing numbered doors spread at equal distances on each side. I am becoming stronger. We stop outside 373 and she slides a card into a silver mouth below the door handle. The door clicks to unlock. She tells me to go in. 'Make good use of your adjustment period. Do not rush.' I take three steps into the middle of the room. The door clicks shut behind me. I am here in the absolute silence of a small white space. 'Agatha.' My cry is shocking in the quiet. I step to the window. Are you outside? Waiting to take me away? The window is a slit of horizontal glass. High up. But eye level for me. Clouds reflect grey on a lake, the water lapping the shingle shore. And around is the forest, pine trees growing in ranks. Lines of despair. My stomach rolls and I rush through the doorless gap into a bathroom. I slam my hands onto the side of the toilet and my head is down and I vomit again and again. I am sweating, shaking. I stand and want to fill the sink with water but there is no plug. So I run the water, splashing it over my face, taking handfuls into my mouth, trying to spit away the bitterness of bile. I snatch at the thin grey towel that sits on a narrow shelf and dry my face, rubbing hard. I look to see my face in the mirror over the sink. But there is no mirror. I touch the space where it should be. This omission frightens me. They are rubbing me out in my own mind. There is no razor of course. My chin feels smooth, but even this they will take from me. I hold out my hands and turn them over to see the freckles, to remember myself. You would tell me to make the best of it. I laugh. I take a step back into the bedroom. The single bed mocks me. I find two metal boxes under the bed and drag them out and dump them onto the thin mattress where they sit alongside a folded grey blanket, a pillow, a blue and white striped sheet and pillow case. The first box is labelled 'Day Wear'. I pull out a grey T-shirt, shorts, socks. There are no shoes. 'Sleep Wear' holds a white T-shirt and shorts. I pull off the gown, damp and wet, and throw it in the corner and put on the day clothes. They fit. The gown lies in a heap. My doing. I pick it up and fold it neatly. So neatly. I will look after things like I do at home. I feel calmer. I will deal with this Reconstruction and then be sent home. It is just a question of waiting. 'Agatha.' I say your name out loud and it feels good. Yes, I will deal with this. I will leave this room and look around. Someone once said there was a library in Reconstruction. Although that was breaking leavers' rules. You are not allowed to talk about Reconstruction on your return. I will not talk about it. I press down on the door handle but it will not open. I try it again and again. Not stuck. Locked. 'Hey! The door's locked!

Hey!' I slam my fist against the door, again and again. 'Where are you? Hey! Let me out. Unlock the door. Someone!' And now I think of the form and I am swamped by fear. I have to get out. I have to. I am sobbing. 'The form. Don't send the form. Let me out. Can anyone hear me. Tell Agatha. Don't send the form. Don't send Wilfie. Someone!' But nobody comes.

54. Saturday Smash

Look out for exoplanets; planets outside our solar system. Four thousand spotted so far.

Weston was doodling on his ideas pad, thinking about getting a new desk, when Miriam burst in, flushed and excited, bracelets and earrings catching a tiny stream of sunlight that had found its way into his office. He was glad of the distraction. And even more pleased that it was Miriam who was distracting him. Certainly preferable to Lazarus.

'Weston,' she said, leaning over his desk. 'It's a smashing big "Yes" from *Saturday Smash*.'

'*Saturday Smash*?'

'Yes, you know. Saturday morning programme for children to watch while their parents are still lounging around in bed?'

'So what?'

'They've said yes to screening the final of the space competition. They say they'll have time for a slot if we can get all the kids there this Saturday morning. And, if we do, they'll broadcast it live. How exciting is that?'

Weston put his head in his hands and groaned. This is what happened if you gave people like Miriam too much of a free rein. Yes, he had asked her to do a bit of homework: ring round, contact a few highly regarded, intellectually challenging science programmes stuffed with gripping features on the latest in dark matter, exploding supernovas and the birth of new planets to see if they might – just might – be interested in screening the final. Or maybe even a current affairs, state of the nation programme in its looking-to-the-future slot. She had been busy all week on the phone and, as far as he could tell, not getting anywhere. So, why had she gone and rung *Saturday Smash*? How could she even begin to think *Saturday Smash* would be a good idea? Infantile. Juvenile. Slapstick.

'I know you're thinking it's infantile and juvenile and slapstick but parents watch it with their kids. They hang around on Saturday morning in their pyjamas and have a good laugh. It will bring the whole living in space business into the family home. The last thing you want is the final stuck on some ghastly science programme that nobody understands.'

Miriam was gabbling on. Somewhere along the line Weston realised she was talking sense. He took his hands from his face. There she was: impassioned, imploring. Her dark eyes, heavily rimmed by kohl. Beautiful. Soulful. Her orange shirt rising and falling with the intensity of her expression. She was right of course. She must be right. How could anyone so full of fervour, so animated, so intense, so attractive be wrong?

'You, Miriam, are a genius.'

Weston leapt up, dashed across his office and, before he knew it, had kissed her. Nothing serious. Just an impulse. Just a light-hearted lips-to-cheek as the result of her excellent idea. Or had he been meaning to do it for months? Without knowing it. Kiss Miriam. Had he? What was going on?

Embarrassing. She would probably leave now.

'Thank you, Weston. Pleased to help.'

Then she put her jangly arms round his neck and kissed him back.

'You deserve a bit of success.'

Weston was reeling. Miriam kissing him. *Saturday Smash*. What. A. Woman. He had spent hours trying to get a TV programme to host the final but with no success. It had been a low point when OSH had taken on a string of expensive PR companies to prop up the competition, get some airtime. He had lain awake at night sweating, worrying that they had lost confidence in him. But the PR companies had been a washout too. It seemed any programme running stories on space mining wanted news about new mineral source discoveries, remote mining innovations. Boring stuff. Some were happy to run a minute or two about the competition, but getting a programme to host the final was a different thing. Nobody wanted to be that involved. A child in space could be a joke at best, a catastrophe at worst. Time was running out for OSH and their credibility. People were talking about it. Asking who, what, where? And they didn't even have a final organized, never mind a winner. Weston had not in his wildest dreams imagined the final taking place on *Saturday Smash*. But it seemed that Miriam – of all people – had cracked it. Simple mind. Simple idea. Simply brilliant. That's why they were a creative agency. That's why the big guns like OSH would come to a small company like Ostrich. Head and feathers above the rest. Weston chuckled: feeling success, feeling relief, feeling that Miriam was so...

'You never know, Weston, influential mining company directors might be up early watching with their kids. All cuddled up on the sofa. It's perfect.'

Weston resisted the temptation to kiss Miriam again.

'You're right. Spot on. I'll get on the phone to Franklin. You ring Evie. Tell her to tell the final five they're on *Saturday Smash* this weekend. On Saturday. Obviously. If they can't make it, we'll have to drop them from the competition. Birthday parties and balloons and jelly will have to wait. Get me the name of the *Saturday Smash* producer. This is going to be epic!'

55. Open wound

Hard hitter. How much energy does the Earth use? Less in a year than the amount of energy that hits the Earth from the Sun every hour. Hour after hour.

Agatha stomped up the track with Wilfie and Pip to wait for the minibus. Peter had not come home the night before and she was missing him. It frightened her that the argument still hung between them. She wanted to talk to him. Get everything back as it had been before. But he had been so busy at work that they hadn't had the chance. There always seemed to be something keeping him late, even overnight: motorway pile-up, crowd stampede, major fire, protest out of control. She promised herself that when he came back tonight she would make it right with him again. It would be hurting him as much as it was hurting her and she felt guilty for that. What a waste when their togetherness was so precious, so desired. Her heart leapt in anticipation.

Agatha waved the boys off and checked the post box. There was a small envelope. No stamp, hand-delivered, which was odd. Anything odd made her uneasy. Inside was a note. She read it once. Twice. Her legs buckled.

She hunched down by the roadside, trying to understand.

Peter in Reconstruction?

It couldn't be true. It could not! She stumbled back down to Grey Cottage. As she passed the stone that had caused Peter's accident, she slammed down hard on its sharpness, hating the world, hating government incompetence, misguided legislation, powerful do-gooders who were no good for her family. Pain seared her palm, cutting the skin, opening a wound. She needed to share Peter's suffering. Oh, how he would be suffering.

At the kitchen table she read the note again. *Reconstruction is a privilege*. A lie. It was a prison sentence. They were liars. Liars! She flung aside a mug, a plate, a state-issue book, sending them crashing to the floor. She screwed up the note, hating it's cruel message. Hating it! She leapt to her feet, the chair screeching as it scraped against slabs. Out of the kitchen, she crossed the yard, climbed over the stone wall and stormed off onto the moor. At the top of the high hill, she slumped to the damp grass and sat, her arms wrapped tight around her knees, her hair caught in the wind, flapping across her face, tears streaming.

What could she do?

Only a few nights ago, Peter had been down there. In their home. Their bedroom. And she had been up here, angry with him. Oh, what she would give to turn back time and run from the hill. Run down and be with him. What folly it was to waste time being angry with those you love and then find they are gone.

The moors stretched away – dark green softened by purple heather, dashed by yellow gorse. Grey rocks lay, ancient, steady, forever. What certainty they had. What uncertainty she felt. What impotence. Pushed into a corner – tight, suffocating. If she rebelled, caused a fuss, they would punish her family with another Child Assist Order. A third. But to bow her head? To be passive? Become a non-person? That was what they wanted from people like her. And she was not sure she could do that. But if she should fail. For the love of Peter. Wilfie. Pip. The tears came again.

When the minibus dropped the boys off after school Agatha was waiting.

'Is dad home?'

Pip always asked if dad was home. First question.

Agatha told them straight.

'He's in Reconstruction.'

'No!' said Wilfie.

Agatha heard shock in Wilfie's voice.

'Is it because of me?' whispered Wilfie. 'Because you argued?'

Agatha thought her heart would burst.

'No, Wilfie,' she said, hugging him. 'Not you. Not you at all. I don't know why but it's not because of you.'

Wilfie hugged back, sobbing, great deep sobs.

'I want daddy,' cried Pip. 'I want him.'

That night the three of them slept together in Agatha and Peter's bed. In the morning, waking to the nightmare, Pip started crying again.

'It won't be long. I promise,' said Agatha.

The promise offered the boys comfort, but in truth Agatha had no idea how long the separation would last. You were never told such things.

56. Huff and puff

Always the same. Wherever we stand on Earth we always see the same side of the Moon.

When Skillern got the phone call from Mrs McDuff telling him that Miss Blick-Foxton was on the line he pulled his tie straight, cleared his throat and stood up. He had once read that if you stand up while speaking on the phone you sound more masterful.

'Mr Skillern, headmaster, how are you?' Miss Blick-Foxton's voice was candyfloss.

'All the better for speaking to you.'

Ridiculous. What an earth made him say that?

'Then I'll huff and I'll puff and I'll tell you the news.'

Skillern managed a weak laugh.

'Wilfie Whisper is through to the final five.'

'The final five? Wilfie Whisper? I can't believe it!'

'Oh? Surprising?'

'No, not surprising I just can't believe it.'

'You're confusing me, Mr Skillern.' Miss Blick-Foxton laughed – a sprinkling of fairy dust. 'And there's more. I know you're a busy man. Important things to do. But, as they say, listen carefully and I'll begin.'

Was she teasing him?

'Are you sitting comfortably?'

Skillern sat, trapped by embarrassment.

'Yes, very comfortably, thank you.'

'Then I'll begin. Have you heard of *Saturday Smash*?'

'Unfortunately yes. Dreadful show.'

Skillern could not abide tomfoolery.

'That's a shame. They have agreed to host the KISS final this Saturday. Marvellous news, hey? I know it's short notice, but that's the media. All five finalists need to be there. Could you check that Wilfie will be able to attend? And,' Evie paused, 'guess what, Mr Skillern? The programme has invited each child's headteacher to be there too. Live on telly. Mr Skillern, you're going to be a star!'

Skillern put the phone down, not sure if he was excited or terrified. *Saturday Smash* was run by idiots: cream cake in the face, slipping on banana skins, silly whooping noises. Perhaps he should invite Firth back. It was the sort of idiotic thing he would enjoy. Skillern's hand hovered over the phone. No, he could do it. He would do it. What was he afraid of? Taking part would show his light-hearted side. In touch with young people and all that. It could make his name. He rang through to Mrs McDuff.

'Get Mrs Whisper on the phone. I need to have a word. Urgently.'

'Is it about Wilfie? Is there news?'

'Just get Mrs Whisper.'

Later, during the school lunch hour, Mrs McDuff burst into Skillern's office.

'I've tried and tried, but I can't get through to Mrs Whisper. She's probably out cleaning. That's her job, you know. And the dad's a hospital porter. Once he was nearly an astronaut himself, so Wilfie tells me. That's were Wilfie gets it from, I suppose. Odd change of job if you ask me. Couldn't I just tell Wilfie myself, whatever it is?'

Skillern's eyes glinted as he told her the news.

'The final five?' repeated Mrs McDuff. 'Oh my.'

She plumped down, uninvited, onto Skillern's easy chair.

'So what happens next? How do they choose?'

'The final takes place this weekend on *Saturday Smash*. The children will be accompanied by their headteacher. So I will be going too.'

'*Saturday Smash*? You? Oh, I'm sorry Mr Skillern, but you on *Saturday Smash*?' Mrs McDuff was stifling bubbles of laughter. 'I mean, they do all sorts of funny things to the contestants.'

'I am not a *contestant*. I am simply chaperoning Wilfie on the show.'

'But he can't go,' cried Mrs McDuff, her laughter dissolved by a thought. 'You can't go either. It's the school trip to the tin mines, remember? You asked me to fix it up. It's in the diary.'

Skillern was halted in his tracks. Of all the people in the school, he and Wilfie should be going to the tin mines.

'I suppose the show is in the morning,' said Mrs McDuff. 'Could you and Wilfie join us afterwards? Let's think. We're leaving by coach first thing. We'll have a play on the mining experience adventure playground as soon as we arrive – it doesn't matter if you miss that. Then a go in the mining labyrinth – that's a maze. A bit of fun. It doesn't matter if you miss that either.'

Skillern tutted impatiently. There was no stopping Mrs McDuff once she started.

'Apparently,' she continued, 'you can spend hours in there if you get lost. Then there's the picnic lunch. We could save you some. And then we have a talk. Now that will be interesting. It's going to be by someone whose grandfather was actually down the mines. I'm going to ask him if he knew my grandfather. That would be quite a thing, wouldn't it? Then we go down the mine after that—'

'We'll join you for the talk and the trip down the mine. We can miss the rest.'

'But what if Mrs Whisper doesn't want him to go on *Saturday Smash*? Don't you need her permission?'

Skillern suspected Mrs Whisper would not want Wilfie to go on the show. He could not risk her scuppering the entire enterprise. They had tried to get in touch but without success so, he, Wilfie's headmaster, acting in loco parentis, would make the decision. After all, he knew what was best for Wilfie. Wilfie would go.

57. Weird purple
Roundabout: the Moon orbits the Earth every 27.3 days.

On Friday at five o'clock, the night before *Saturday Smash*, Weston gave one of his drinking pals a ring. He was nervous about the programme. Needed to go out and relax. The other line rang. Miriam answered it, her voice like honey. He could hear her quite clearly, even above his own conversation. The walls in Ostrich HQ were paper thin. And anyway, he always found himself listening to her, wanting to hear what she had to say.

'I'm sorry, Mr Black. Weston's on an important call. Media. Big day tomorrow.'

Weston gave a little sigh of relief. She was smart at keeping up pretences; maintaining the successful agency profile. He would give her credit for that. But why was she talking in that clever sort of voice? A cultured voice. Must be because she thought Franklin was clever and cultured – she never spoke to him like that. She was laughing now. The culture bit had gone. She was laughing her silly, girly laugh. Giggling.

She was flirting with Franklin!

'Sorry, Mr Black. Just the idea of you and Weston, I mean Mr Wright, sitting on the sofa watching *Saturday Smash* together... I mean grown men... and you don't sound the sort of person to… oh, I am sorry… I'll pass on the… I'm so sorry!'

Miriam put the phone down. Overwhelmed by laughter, she had actually put the phone down on Franklin Black. Their top client. Ever. And now her laughter was louder than ever. She had completely lost control.

Weston cut his conversation.

'Call you back.'

He stormed into reception.

'Miriam!'

The phone rang again. Miriam tried to compose herself, but she could not. She was clearly in such a state she was incapable of carrying out the simplest of tasks. Weston reached across her desk and answered the ringing phone to demonstrate the point.

'Weston, Franklin Black here. Got cut off speaking to one of your staff. Miriam? Would you come and watch *Saturday Smash* with me tomorrow? I'd value your opinion. How we should handle the publicity. And well done for getting us on. A triumph.'

Weston looked at Miriam, shaking in the corner. What was she doing, her hand stuffed in her mouth like that, and why was she wearing that weird purple outfit?

'Miriam actually booked the show,' he said.

'In that case, it would be a good for her to come along too.'

'Miriam?'

'Yes, Miriam. One of your account execs?'

'No. Yes,' said Weston. 'Account exec. Of course. One of our best. Tip top. Razor sharp.'

'Then bring her along. If she fixed it up, she's earned her spot on the sofa. See you both tomorrow.'

58. Going live

Venus weather forecast: metal snow followed by sulphuric acid rain.

On Saturday, as dawn broke, Agatha slid her hand across the bed to where Peter should be, willing him to be there, for him to wake and turn to her, to kiss her, to touch her, for them to be together. For him to have forgiven her. But the coolness of the sheets only made her feel more alone and the ache of missing him more intense. She would wake the boys soon to get them to school early for the tin mine trip, but for now she would think of Peter. Tell him she was sorry. Sorry for being angry. Not understanding. For not working things out with him when they had the chance. It was four days since she had picked up the envelope. The pain was still acute, but she was dealing with things like Peter would: cheering up the boys, finding a bright side.

'Reconstruction only happens to special people after all,' she said. 'We should be proud of dad.'

'Really?' said Pip.

'Really,' said Agatha. 'And he'll want to hear all about the mining trip. Remember everything.'

When Wilfie and Pip arrived at school, Mrs McDuff was waiting for them.

'Morning, Pip. On the coach, poppet. Now, Wilfie dear, you're going with Mr Skillern. He'll explain everything and we'll see you later at the mine. Very best of luck, dear.'

To Wilfie's surprise, Mrs McDuff wrapped her arms around him, squeezing him against her woolly coat.

'Very, very best of luck, dear. Oh, I think Mr Skillern wants you now.'

Mr Skillern was shouting at Wilfie from his car.

'Get in, Wilfie, We haven't got much time.'

Seconds later, Wilfie was staring at the thin lines of hair on the back of his headmaster's head as they sped out of the school car park. In the mirror, Mr Skillern looked stern. He didn't speak. Wilfie, used to being taken out of lessons for special checks, contained his disappointment, still excited to be going on the school trip later. He hoped they would make it in time for the labyrinth. He had been especially looking forward to that. They left the village, drove through open countryside and into the outer circles of the city. Mr Skillern stopped from time to time to check a map and then drove on again. Then he seemed to be trying to drive and look at the map at the same time. Wilfie thought he perhaps ought to offer to help.

'Mr Skillern, do you—'

'Just be quiet. I'm trying to concentrate.'

So Wilfie sat back in his seat and gazed up at the increasing number of high-rise office blocks and apartments, and at the blue sky beyond. The same blue sky that dad would be able to see. He wished his dad was with him now.

They swung down an alley, cutting the sky to a sliver. Rubbish kicked about, sprinkled like confetti, paintwork on windows was patchy, render on walls peeling. Mr Skillern was muttering to himself about being lost, the wrong part of the city, this couldn't be right when he suddenly came to a halt and reversed back into a space between two parked cars.

'Hurry,' he said getting out and marching down the street. Wilfie followed and they came to a halt beside an off-white door, scuffed at the edges. A notice, held in a plastic folder, swung on a single staple: Island Studios. There was a grubby plaque next to the door with a set of buttons, the lettering faded: Studio 1–19. Mr Skillern pressed the studio seven button.

'Yep,' came a confident young voice.

'Mr Skillern, Headmaster Fellows Light School here with Wilfie Whisper.'

'Cutting it a bit fine, aren't you? Come straight on up. And get your skates on. We kick off at ten o'clock.'

There was a buzz and a click and the door opened. Stairs, chipped and stained, the edges stuck with peeling red and white safety tape, rose from a gloomy stairwell. And it stank of mice. Wilfie wished more than ever that he was on the school trip. His classmates would be larking about in the adventure playground, climbing the shaft ladder, wriggling through the underground tunnel experience. And here he was climbing up a stinking staircase. He wished he wasn't a Slow Learner.

As they reached the seventh floor, a door with a big green circle saying Studio 7 in whirly writing was flung open and Evie Blick-Foxton rushed out, black curls bouncing, cheeks pink, flustered. Wilfie's heart leapt when he saw her: it explained a lot. She must be doing the test and the last test hadn't taken long. Perhaps they would get to the labyrinth after all.

Wilfie!' she cried. 'Thank goodness. You're late. Where's your mum? Dad?'

'Couldn't make it,' said Skillern, breathless from the climb.

'Shame,' said Evie. 'Never mind. Put this on Wilfie. Quick.'

Evie looped a silver apron over Wilfie's head and fastened it behind his back.

'Excited, Wilfie?'

'About the tin mines?'

'Tin mines? No, being on *Saturday Smash*.'

Wilfie, confused, wasn't sure what to say.

'Mr Skillern, don't tell me you've not told him? Oh, I... Come on Wilfie, follow me.'

Wilfie stared in wonder at Evie's high black heels as she led him at speed into a small room where two girls and two boys, also wearing silver aprons, were sitting with seven or eight adults on tatty purple sofas and pouffes watching a large TV screen. On the screen was a puppy, all wrinkles and folds of fat. A little girl was cuddling and patting it, encouraged by cooing sounds coming from a young studio audience. Everyone in the room turned to stare at Wilfie. One boy half smiled and raised a hand in welcome. The rest looked hostile.

'Right, quickly everyone. This is Wilfie. Wilfie this is Callum, Grace, Trent and Flick. Mr Skillern, Wilfie's headmaster, other headteachers, parents. Sorry, but that's all the introductions we have time for,' said Evie.

The four children nodded at Wilfie and mumbled hellos. Only Trent, the boy who had smiled, said 'Hey' and gave another wave. Evie looked up at the clock, above which was a blue bulb and a red bulb.

'I'm afraid we've already done the warm up, Wilfie, but you'll be fine. OK everyone, three minutes until you're on. Watch the coloured bulbs. When the blue one lights up, it means we are about to go. When the red light flashes, you'll be taken onto the set. And don't forget from that point on it's live. Do your best and enjoy it. And let the best astronaut win.'

'Mr Skillern,' said Wilfie, 'what's happening? Why am I wearing this?'

Skillern was staring at the clock, ignoring him. Evie grabbed Wilfie's hand and sat down with him on a purple sofa, leaning close, her voice breathy, her bright eyes close to his. She was looking right into him.

'Listen, Wilfie. Remember when I came to see you about the second round of the space competition?'

'The slow learner test you mean?'

'Right. No. Oh, this is ridiculous. You should have… oh, this is too much. Listen.'

The blue bulb went on.

'Listen. You have got through to the final of the space competition. Down to the last five. This is the final. Live on TV. *Saturday Smash*.'

'*Saturday Smash*?'

'Oh, Wilfie. The TV programme? Everyone watches it.'

'We don't have a TV. It broke. Mum doesn't like telly, anyway.'

'But the briefing? What you're meant to do?'

An assistant was lining up the other contestants, pairing them with their teachers, ready to go.

'Contestant Four. Wilfie Whisper. Headmaster Mr Skillern. Over here please.'

Evie seemed upset.

'Don't worry,' Wilfie said. 'I'll be fine.'

Wilfie lined up behind Trent. Mr Skillern standing to his side was breathing heavily.

The blue bulb went off. The red light flashed.

'Just be yourself,' whispered Evie, giving Wilfie's arm a squeeze.

Then they were off, out from the dark into the bright lights of the *Saturday Smash* studio.

And, to Wilfie's amazement, the final.

59. Lonely as one

Comets have a visible coma. Asteroids do not.

Agatha sat at the wooden table in Grey Cottage staring at the half-open kitchen door, willing Peter to charge in. 'The hens are out again,' he'd say. Or 'I'm going to fix that banging stable door once and for all.' Or he'd grab her hand and cry, 'Come on Agatha, let's go and lean against the wind on the moor.' She could only ever imagine him like this. Not as the man she had argued with. Love had eclipsed anger.

But the door only swung a little on the breeze and, with the boys away, for the first time ever at Grey Cottage she felt the quiet and a fog of loneliness descend. She wandered out to the vegetable garden, her place of solace – but not today. Tears were too close. Her bicycle, propped against the wall from yesterday, beckoned. She pushed it up the track to the lane and, without a plan, cycled fast, feeling the pressure in her legs, the rising beat of her heart, the labouring of her breath. It was what she needed.

A coach lumbered up the hill towards her, filling the narrow lane. She stopped and pulled her bike onto the verge, flattening herself against the hawthorn hedge. It was the school trip: Fellows Light pupils on their way to the tin mines. The coach passed too fast for her to make out her own children, but she waved anyway, glad they were there, glad they had a distraction. Then she cycled down into the village, past the school, up the main street and out towards the split in the hills where the road fell away, the city lying in the green folds, glistening, bright white.

The circular layout was clear from her high vantage point. She could even make out the hospital far away in circle four. It seemed a long time since they had held such high hopes of Peter becoming a surgeon. It even seemed an age since he had been working as a hospital porter. Loneliness threatened to overwhelm her again. The view of the hospital drew her thoughts to Penelope. Was she still alive? If she was, she would be alone in some bed, in some ward, waiting for the end. Why hadn't she gone to visit her? Why had she ignored someone so special? Oh, she should have gone! Any good friend would have gone when they still had the chance. Chances were not to be missed. Agatha started pedalling hard, her breath coming in short bursts, tears for Peter, for Penelope, blurring her vision. She hoped she wouldn't be too late.

It was not easy to find someone in the hospital if you only knew they were called Penelope. And especially if you didn't know if they were alive.

'I've come to visit Penelope. Probably in her eighties. Nineties. I don't know.'

The elderly hospital volunteer on reception squinted at a screen, trying to read the illuminated green and prodded at a few keys, arthritic fingers bent and shaking.

'There's a Penny in Ward 34. Penelope in Ward 2. No, that's children. Might be this one. Ward 72. A Penelope there. Ward 72 is for the likes of me. Old.'

Agatha hurried off to find Ward 72. Coming down the corridor towards her was a hospital porter pushing a trolley at speed. He must know Peter. She wanted to stop him. Ask him if he knew her husband, what he thought of him. If he was liked. She was sure he was. Did they ever have a coffee together? Discuss the patients? Maybe he knew why Peter was in Reconstruction. Or when he would come home. Come home. The phrase swirled. The trolley was coming fast. Under control, but fast; an emergency.

'He has red hair. Tall. Green eyes. Loud laugh.'

But the trolley, patient and porter swerved round her, an obstacle to be avoided. The patient, a young woman propped up on white pillows, eyes closed, hollow-cheeked, jaw dropped, mouth ajar, was rushed away. How could she have thought the porter would have time to stop, to talk to her about Peter? Agatha, feeling foolish, turned and entered the lift, pressing number seven. Peter might have used this lift, taking his patients up to surgery, reassuring, caring for them. But she could not feel his presence. He had been stolen from this place.

The door opened on level seven. Ward 72 was through grey swing doors with little windows on each side. The windows had netting within the glass, so when you peered through it was like looking into a cage. Agatha could make out a long room with twenty or so beds. Thin green curtains were drawn over large windows, subduing daylight and spreading a watery hue. Most of the beds were shrouded with curtains in the same pale green. One or two were left open, the beds occupied by the elderly – wisps of hair, wrinkled skin, mouths open, eyes rheumy. All passive, waiting.

Agatha pushed open the door. As it squeaked, two or three patients turned their heads, slowly, wearily. What were they thinking? Was it the tea tray? Or time for more medication? Or was someone about to be wheeled off for treatment. Perhaps their last.

Agatha walked down the ward, looking right to left. An old man lifted two or three fingers in a gesture of welcome. It was a small movement but Agatha noticed it and, encouraged, ventured towards his bed.

'You don't know where I can find a patient called Penelope, do you?'

The man nodded.

'Penelope is swimming.'

He closed his eyes.

'Thank you. You're very kind.'

She moved on, looking at those she could clearly see, peering at others through gaps in surrounding curtains. Someone turned on a television. The noise was brash and cut through the breathy hush of the watery underworld.

A nurse entered from the far end of the ward, small, neat and walking fast across the blueish yellow linoleum floor. She had no idea where Penelope was and tut-tutted at the system; everyone should have better labelling. She darted in and out of the beds until at last she saw a name tag. 'Penelope' was found. She pulled back a curtain with a screechy sound to reveal Agatha's Penelope fast asleep.

'Here's Penelope. Alright darling?'

The nurse clacked off down the ward, leaving Agatha alone with her friend. Tears sprang to her eyes. She wasn't too late after all.

'I am awake, you know,' said Penelope, eyes still closed. 'How are the gooseberries?'

'Bountiful. I'll bring you some next time.'

'I knew you'd come eventually.'

She failed to elaborate and Agatha felt appalled she had not been before. It was good to meet up again; to feel a friendship, a special bond. Agatha felt she had been given a second chance. And now she could see a precious brimming of life as Penelope's eyes opened, just a little.

'Lovely to see you, dear,' said Penelope, smiling at her.

'How are you feeling?'

'I feel as if I am walking on a bridge that's swaying and getting narrower and narrower until it becomes so narrow it is a tightrope and I will lose my balance and fall. But I don't mind falling.'

Penelope seemed as lucid as ever.

'Have you made any friends?'

'Impossible, dear. We're all islands here, trapped in our beds. No communication across the waters. And even if we could hail one another, it's not the place for long-lasting friendship. In this ward, people come and people go and, generally, they don't come back. Although they do keep us going as long as possible. Look at me. I thought I would have fallen weeks ago and I'm still here.'

'Thank you for what you said,' said Agatha. 'About the wool. It made a difference.'

'I knew it would. Your mind is open and you let the burden fall. You will do great things.'

Agatha was confused. Perhaps the old lady's mind was slipping, but her words held wisdom and were comforting. Challenging. In the silence that followed, Agatha's eyes rested on a glass vase overflowing with feverfew on the table by Penelope's bed; daisy-like white petals, yellow centres, dark lime green leaves: the promise of the outdoors.

'Lovely, aren't they?' said Penelope. 'Frankie brought them. He's a good boy. Comes every day. Picked from my garden.'

Penelope closed her eyes and dozed.

'Bye, Penelope,' whispered Agatha. 'I'll come again. I promise.'

'Wait.'

Without opening her eyes, the old lady slid her hand under her pillow and pulled out a leather-bound book.

'Take this. Let it breathe. It needs to breathe.'

The book frightened Agatha: a blatant defying of authority. It didn't even have a yellow cover.

'Could you give it to Frankie?'

Penelope chuckled.

'He knows it by heart. Word for word. Matthew, Mark, Luke, John and the rest. It will look after you. Just remember, stand firm in the faith, be courageous, be strong. Take it, dear.'

Reluctantly, Agatha took the volume. Instantly she felt a surprising joy merely from holding it: the softness of the leather, the way it bent in her hand and, above all, the promise of its power in which Penelope so firmly believed. But it was dangerous to hold in the open. She tucked it into her pocket where it sat lumpy, obvious.

'He will never leave you nor forsake you,' whispered Penelope.

From behind a curtain surrounding another bed floated the sound of a TV theme tune, all pops and whistles. It seemed completely out of place.

Agatha, conscious of the book in her pocket, the danger it posed, got up and hurried down the ward. She needed to get outside. Get away.

60. Razor sharp
Hello? Hello? Is there life on Mars?

Franklin, Miriam and Weston sat in a row on the sofa in Franklin's office watching the opening credits of *Saturday Smash*.

'How did you get the programme sorted, Miriam?' asked Franklin.

'Persistence.'

'Good on you.'

Weston could tell Franklin was impressed. That he thought Miriam was smart. She had succeeded where expensive PR agencies had failed. And she looked stylish in her orange shirt. Too stylish maybe. Sitting next to Franklin. Close. Franklin kept looking at her. Yes, there was no doubt, he fancied her. Weston cursed – he should have sat in the middle.

'Oh,' said Miriam. 'This is so exciting.'

To Weston's surprise, she surreptitiously took his hand and gave it a squeeze. A sign they were allies or something more? He returned the squeeze. She giggled. She definitely giggled. But before he could analyse what the squeeze meant, the *Saturday Smash* theme tune – inane, jolly and irrepressibly catchy – blasted into the room and Miriam let go and began, embarrassingly, clapping along. But the atmosphere was contagious so, like thousands of children round the country, inhibitions slipped and the three were soon having fun, bouncing a little on the sofa, shouting out, caught up in the pure fun that was *Saturday Smash*. They sang along to Glasshouse Riding's musical number, cooed at the adorable puppy feature and, when it came, were pumped up for the big feature. The KISS final.

61. Studio Seven

Chilly. Uranus hits the coldest temperatures of any planet with a minimum atmospheric temperature of -224°C.

'Now we are going to smash history!'

Sim, the presenter of *Saturday Smash*, was hyping up the studio audience. Wilfie was trying to keep up, watching the programme on the screen.

'Are you qwackers?' interrupted Sim's sidekick, an unfortunate dressed as a duck.

'Duckface, I am super smashing serious. And here they come. The finalists of KISS. Live here on *Saturday*

Smash. Let's give them the smashing greatest welcome in the universe and bee-yond!'

The young studio audience screamed over the *Saturday Smash* theme tune as Wilfie and his fellow contestants ran through an arch of flashing lights and a few puffs from a smoke machine.

'Let's smash it for Callum! Grace! Trent! Wilfie! And, last but not least, Flick!'

Wilfie followed Trent and copied his moves, waving at the audience, waving at the cameras and everyone watching at home: friends, school, the nation. Along with the other contestants, Wilfie hopped, skipped and grinned his way across the studio floor to a line of five tables, each with a sign dangling from the front proclaiming the name of a child and their school.

'So, kids, to your tables and rev yourselves up. This is it! The final frontier,' announced Sim. 'The final frontier before one of you will be the first child in the world to go into space. How does that feel?'

From behind their tables the children and their teachers raised their arms in the air and shouted 'Smashing!'. Wilfie tried to cotton on, aware of Mr Skillern beside him staring firmly at the floor.

'Soooo, here we go with your *Saturday Smash* task. Listen carefully. The stakes are high. Before you are five tables. One each. On each table is a tub. And in each tub there are nine balls of different sizes with a hole drilled from side to side. There are eight wires. The wires are of different lengths and some are thicker than others. One ball has no wires. Your task is to thread the wires through the balls and put them in the right order. Whatever that is. As soon as you've finished, race back to your start position and hit – smash bang! – on that buzzer. The first to get the correct answer is the winner. And will be the first child in space!'

Wilfie focused on the balls and wires before him.

'To make it a little trickier, your headteachers will spray your rivals with foam while you're working it out. So watch out. It's gonna get *Saturday Smash* messy, messy, messy! Ready? Smashing. Five, four, three, two, one. We have lift off!'

62. Carrot or lemon?

The great storm on Jupiter raged for three hundred and fifty years. On and on. It became known as The Great Red Spot, so immense that Earth could fit across it three times. And still it rages.

The coach taking the Fellows Light pupils to the tin mines had been making an odd flapping noise. The driver pulled in at a motorway service station and jumped out to see what was wrong. Mrs McDuff pressed her face to the window to see what he was up to.

'Can you believe it?' he said, hopping back aboard. 'Puncture. Tyre needs changing but I can't get the bloomin' nut off. Spanner's missing.'

'Can we get another spanner?' asked Mrs McDuff. She looked around, as if a spanner might magically appear.

'Nope, it's a specialist spanner. We've got loads back at the depot but, it being Saturday, there won't be anybody in the office. I'll have to drive back and pick one up myself.'

'Drive?'

'Well, not drive. Hitch a lift. Shouldn't take me more than an hour. Wait here and have tea and buns.'

Mrs McDuff felt a shiver of alarm as the driver, whistling, strode off towards the bridge to the other side of the road. She shuffled out of her seat to face the children and Mr

Chillworth, who had been sitting behind her, breathing down her neck the whole journey. Mr Skillern was meant to be coming, of course. Why Mr Chillworth had volunteered to take his place was beyond her. He was useless.

'What's happening, Mrs McDuff?'

'Aren't we going to the tin mines?'

Someone started crying. This would not do.

'Come on children, off the bus. Hold hands. Stay in line. Could you take the rear please, Mr Chillworth?'

Mrs McDuff herded the children towards the cafe. Inside, a whiff of cooking fat hung in the air. Bright yellow and red plastic chairs and tables patterned the cavernous room. Posters advertising carbohydrate laden snacks adorned the walls, interspersed with large TVs all running the same programme. The children flooded in and sat down in groups, chattering non-stop.

'You have to order from the self service counter.'

A girl in jeans and a yellow T-shirt with a red slogan across her chest reading Pleased to Serve materialised before Mrs McDuff.

'Thank you, dear, but we're not ordering anything. Our bus has a puncture, can you believe, so we're stranded, waiting for it to be mended.'

'You can't wait here. This is a cafe, not a waiting room.'

'Oh dear. I wonder, could you make an exception just this once? We won't be long.'

'You can only stay if you buy something. The trays are over there.'

'I'll have a cup of tea,' said Mr Chillworth, heading across to put in his order.

'Any kids not ordering anything will have to wait somewhere else,' said Pleased to Serve.

Mrs McDuff, already flustered, felt her irritation with

Mr Chillworth reach boiling point as she watched him take a tray from the stack, slither it along silver runners and poke about at the plastic wrapped sandwiches, buns, slices of cake, and chopped fruit as if he had all the time in the world. Mr Chillworth was, in her opinion, untrustworthy, always hovering round her office wanting custard creams and not suited to teaching.

'Anyone not ordering anything, make your way out to the foyer,' shouted Pleased to Serve.

A few of the children stood up, but most did not hear over the noise of the chatter and TVs.

'No, wait,' said Mrs McDuff. 'Please wait.'

She scrambled round her handbag for her purse. She only had enough money to buy something for five or six pupils. Certainly not an entire bus load.

What an earth was she going to do?

Mr Chillworth reappeared with two cups of tea.

'I've had a word with the manager and he said that, in the circumstances, it would be fine to wait here as long as the children behave themselves. I've bought you a cup of tea. And a slice of carrot cake or a slice of lemon drizzle. You choose.'

Mr Chillworth carefully placed the tray, laden with a teapot, milk, sugar, two cups and saucers, and two slices of cake onto the red plastic table. Mrs McDuff looked at him in wonder: his long thin face, his long thin hands – such sensitive hands – and long thin tie, and felt like hugging him. Really hugging him. He was actually smiling at her. A thin line of a smile, admittedly, but with the light catching his aquiline nose, his well-defined jaw and cheek bones and high, intelligent brow he looked quite – dare she admit it – attractive. Noble even. Had she misjudged him all these years?

'Mr Chillworth, you are a love,' she said, overcome.

'Shall I be mother?' Mr Chillworth replied and proceeded to pour.

'I suppose,' he said, looking at her over his teacup, 'you could call this our first date. I've been trying to pluck up the courage since parents' evening. I overheard what you said, I'm afraid. Remember? Soft spot for me. Custard creams. And then you saved me from choking. And now here we are. Fate.'

'Parents' evening?' Mrs McDuff was trying to remember. Of course – the tie episode. But what had she said? She knew he liked custard creams. He came into her office enough times asking for them. But a soft spot?

Mr Chillworth reached out and gave her plump fingers hovering over the lemon drizzle a little squeeze.

'To us,' he said.

Mrs McDuff blushed, her world turned upside down.

'To us,' she replied, without knowing what she was saying. 'I'm so sorry. I don't have any custard creams.'

'I don't like custard creams,' replied Mr Chillworth. 'It was just a ruse.'

'Oh, Mr Chillworth!' spluttered Mrs McDuff, laughing into her tea. 'You are a dark horse. My, oh my.'

As Mrs McDuff composed herself, a murmur of appreciation swept across the room. A news programme had finished, replaced by the intro to *Saturday Smash*, captivating the children of Fellows Light. Mrs McDuff barely noticed. Right now, her pleasure was in a simple cup of tea, a slice of cake and a rosy glow that her future might somehow be a little less lonely and a little more jolly.

Fifteen minutes passed pleasantly. Then, out of the blue, the room erupted. All the children were shouting and pointing at the TV.

'Look! Wilfie Whisper!'

Seconds later, another shout went up.

'Mr Skillern! It's Mr Skillern!'

Only one child, Pip Whisper, was silent, wide-eyed and open mouthed, unable to speak.

63. Final frontier

How small is the messenger? The smallest planet in the solar system, 4.879 kilometres across the equator for Mercury. Earth is 12,742.

The *Saturday Smash* contestants dashed to their tubs; the race to the final frontier had begun. Callum, Grace, Flick and Trent tipped out their balls to start sorting, but that was a mistake; the balls rolled off the table and time was lost hunting for them across the studio floor. Wilfie had a different strategy, searching for the one he needed first, the bright orange one. Then he took the smallest ball and the shortest wire. It linked up perfectly.

Wilfie worked methodically and made good progress until his world was smothered in a white, wet foam: foam in his face, in his eyes, slippy on his hands. The wire and balls slid off his table in a waterfall of bubbles. Through the onslaught, he glimpsed the headteacher standing in Flick's lane, the one behind the Bucksworth Primary sign, firing directly at him. The studio had been reduced to perfect *Saturday Smash* mayhem: headteachers squirting pupils, the floor a slippery ice rink of foam, balls rolling all over the place, children skidding about, chasing them. Sim was dancing around, shouting 'Smashing! Smashing!' every time a headteacher struck a direct foamy hit on one of the young contestants. The studio audience was screaming with laughter at every slip and slide. Wilfie turned his back to the Bucksworth Primary teacher, defending himself as best he could. As he did so, he caught the eye of Mr Skillern, the only adult standing still amongst the chaos. Wilfie took another direct hit. The attack seemed to propel Skillern into action; he grabbed his gun and started firing wildly at the other contestants.

Could Mr Skillern be defending him?

Did he really want him to win?

Mr Skillern, spraying contestants like a madman, was screaming: 'For the glory of Fellows Light, Wilfie, hurry up! Hurry up!'

Wilfie focussed. He had seven wires linked. Nearly there. He knew what he was doing. Then, above the noise, the chaos, he heard a buzzer. Grace from Bucksworth was back at her station. Wilfie was too late. It was all over.

'It's a necklace,' shouted Grace.

Whack, whack, worm!

Wrong. Grace was wrong.

The chance to be the first child in space was still wide open.

Wilfie concentrated. He ignored the madness, connecting the wires and balls, making sense of them. Sun. Mercury. Venus. Earth. Mars. Jupiter. Saturn. Uranus. Neptune. How many times had he ordered the planets on the beam of his bedroom, the peas on his plate, the bubbles in his bath? All for this.

Finished.

He rushed to his buzzer and slammed down his fist.

Time stood still in the service station as the pupils from Fellows Light waited to see if Wilfie had got the right answer. Mrs McDuff clasped her hands tight round her cup of tea. Even Mr Chillworth was gripped by the moment;

his pointed jaw set firm in anticipation. Pip, watching his big brother covered in foam, hand on buzzer, eyes bright, knew he had got it.

'Solar system,' whispered Pip.

'Solar system,' said Wilfie.

He smiled directly at the camera.

Directly at Pip.

'The answer is solar system.'

There was a bang from above and little silver stars cascaded down. The *Saturday Smash* music blared out. The game was over.

'We have a *Saturday Smash* winner,' Sim shouted. 'So, you are…'

'Wilfie. Wilfie Whisper,' whispered Wilfie, hardly able to speak. Could he really, truly, honestly be going into space? Could something he had dreamed of day and night actually be about to come true? He would see shooting stars close up, after all. He felt faint from excitement, his legs trembled, his mouth was dry, and he felt conscious of a choking, a sobbing that he couldn't control. Above all, his heart was bursting at the thought of doing a spacewalk for his dad. His eyes brimmed with tears and he wished beyond everything that his dad could be with him, right now, to share the moment.

'Wilfie Whisper,' repeated Sim. 'Smashing! Remember that name. Remember you heard it first on *Saturday Smash*: the first child to be going into space. Let's smash it for Wilfie Whisper!'

The studio audience went wild.

Off stage, Evie Blick-Foxton did a little skip and a hop, clapped and wiped away a tear as the five young contestants shuffled off set to make way for a magician. She hugged Wilfie.

'Wilfie! You've done it! You've actually done it. You are going to be the first child in space. How does it feel?'

'It feels… it feels… I don't know. Mum and dad…'

Wilfie saw his parents arguing in the garden. He saw his dad watching his mum run off onto the moor. And he saw the photo of his dad in a spacesuit, alone in a capsule, a capsule that turned into a cell and he was there alone, unable to escape, his dreams trapped between four walls.

'I want to go for my dad,' burst out Wilfie. To his shame, he started sobbing. Somehow, winning made him unbearably happy and sad at the same time and he just couldn't hold back the tears.

'Oh, Wilfie!' cried Evie. 'That's cute. That's so cute.'

She gave him another hug.

'Fellows Light are delighted to have the honour,' interrupted Skillern.

'Well done, Mr Skillern,' said Evie, letting go of Wilfie and shaking Skillern's hand. 'A good day for Fellows Light.'

'A smashing day,' said Skillern, smiling awkwardly at his attempt to make a joke.

'And you'll need this,' said Evie, handing Wilfie a file. 'It's the winner's briefing file. It includes details of the two-day pre-flight training, and what to expect aboard the launch rocket and in No 49 Pennyside. There are a few tasks the people at OSH would like you to carry out when you are up there. Nothing serious. Just normal, everyday things like what it's like brushing your teeth, cooking, that sort of thing. But don't worry – it all takes place in No 49. Apart from your spacewalk. There are special notes on that. Now, let's talk about dates. There are regular flights taking six passengers each time. Scientists, geologists and some techie people I expect. It's booked up for the next few weeks, but we are on standby. Rather, you are on standby. So, plenty of time to get you trained up, suit fitted. Any questions? Permission for Wilfie to have the time off school Mr Skillern? There will probably be a fair bit of press coverage. OK for us to have interviews at Fellows Light, Mr Skillern?'

Franklin flicked off the TV.

'So what do you think, guys?'

After the laughter, the hysteria, the foam, the silence in the OSH office felt heavy. Weston shuffled his feet, wondering what to say. He could hear the faintest noise of traffic from the street below and wished he was out there. Anywhere but on that sofa. He willed Miriam to answer the question.

'Sorry,' said Miriam.

She was looking intently at her nails. Had she painted them lilac? Or would you call it mauve? It was hard to say where the nail finished and the cuticle started. Funny word – cuticle. But 'sorry' wasn't a very good answer. The whole thing was a humiliating disaster.

'I'm not sure it was the sort of coverage we were really after,' muttered Weston.

He picked up a cushion he had thrown on the floor during the excitement and hugged it.

'What's the matter with you guys? I thought it was terrific,' said Franklin. 'Smashing even. I loved the show. And we've got a winner. What did you think of Wilfie Whisper, Miriam?'

So, Franklin thought it was OK – and if it was OK with Franklin, it was, supposed Weston, his spirits rising, OK with him

'Impressive. But small. Mr Black…'

What on earth was Miriam about to say now? Weston could tell by her tone it would be trouble.

'Franklin, I can't believe you are actually going to send a child into space. I've been reading about it and quite honestly, now I see the actual little boy and think of him alone up in that black, black nothingness, it breaks my heart. I'd rather he didn't go but if it's too late I think we should at least go and check him out. And his family. I really do.'

Miriam was right of course. Those dark eyes of hers – so enormous, so serious, so earnest. She really did care. But what could they do? It was too late to backpedal on the whole thing. The winner had been announced on national TV.

'What do you think, Weston?' asked Franklin.

'Miriam's right.'

It was an automatic response. She was right, but he was not sure what should be done.

'Great. Try and get a realistic impression. Use a bit of subterfuge so you'll get the real picture. Go running and pitch up at their door for a glass of water. Anything – just find out what makes the family tick.'

'What? Why am I going?'

'You're the best person for the job,' said Miriam.

'But I don't run.'

'You could always start,' said Franklin. 'Young man like you. Keep you in shape. Mind sharp.'

'I'll sort you out some kit,' offered Miriam.

Weston knew she would think it would be good for him. Running.

'Better than meeting those creepy friends of yours after work,' she said, a little directly, thought Weston. He liked his creepy friends. And anyway, they weren't that creepy.

'Develop your physique,' she added.

Why would Miriam, of all people, care about his physique?

'Good work, Wilfie,' said Skillern as they started the drive back.

Wilfie was reading the briefing file. He skipped the pages on the tests and jumped to the section entitled 'Spacewalk'. There were detailed instructions about oxygen levels, how to attach the tether, just like in the bathroom at home.

'I said good work, Wilfie,' repeated Skillern.

'Thank you,' said Wilfie looking up. In the driver's mirror he could see Mr Skillern's normal frown had been replaced by something. Excitement? Wilfie had never seen him look like that. The whole world seemed to have changed since he got up that morning.

'Mr Skillern, will I go, really?'

'I'm not going to stop you.'

The way Mr Skillern said it made Wilfie think that someone else might.

'Mr Skillern, would you mind not telling mum about this? Not yet. I'm not sure if she likes things like space trips.'

'Of course, Wilfie. Our secret.'

For some reason he tapped his nose.

'At this rate we should make the school tin mining trip this afternoon, so you can tell your mum all about that instead.'

On the trip back from the tin mine, Wilfie made Pip promise to keep the competition a secret. Sharing the secret made Pip part of it.

'It's such a big, enormous, gigantic secret, it'll be easy,' said Pip. 'I mean mum's not going to suddenly say "I wonder if Pip has a secret that Wilfie has won the space competition?" is she?'

Wilfie agreed. Although it seemed that everyone else knew about it except mum. She lived in a different world. No television. No radio. No friends visiting. He liked their life out on the moor and was happy mum wanted to live like that. To make it special for them. He just wished dad could be there too.

64. Reconstruction (2)
Hot topic. Fifteen million degrees Celsius: the temperature inside the Sun.

Agatha, piercing light reddens my awakening. It is the same every day. I try to stay in my dreams a moment longer, eyes closed. 'Time to get up. Wilfie. Pip,' you are calling. I see you. Soft tread down narrow wooden staircase. Blue dress, slim bare arm out to balance, hand light against cool plaster wall. Barefoot dance over cold grey flagstones. White feet straight into black boots. Chill of the yard. Up with the iron latch. Hens out. One. Two. Three. Four. Five. Corn sprinkled. Eggs. Return to kitchen. Voice floating up wooden stairs. 'Wilfie. Pip. Are you up?' Your voice rings clear. But did you stop the form, Agatha? I hope you stopped it. What if Wilfie goes and things go wrong? I open my eyes to stop such thoughts. There lies madness and I need to fight for my sanity. 'Five,' I say aloud. 'Seven?' I am already losing count of the days.' The door clicks open and the woman places a bowl of porridge on the small plastic table and leaves. The porridge is colourless. I want to throw it against the wall. Make a mess. But I am hungry. And I want my dignity. So I sit on the bed and eat it, slowly. The second I have finished she comes in again. Knowing, perfect timing. Without speaking, she leads the way to my four-hour unburdening session. Small room. Two chairs. One table. She begins the session the same way every day. 'What do you want to tell me?' 'Nothing,' I say. I just want to leave, but I know there is no point fighting. Many are sent on Reconstruction. You just have to put up with it. So I am running with the process as best I can. But today I am worried. I can feel myself softening, accepting. Falling into a vacuum. My mind is emptying, ready to be rebuilt. Reconstructed. This is how they work. I follow the woman back to my room. I've seen no one else since I arrived. Everything is set up to leave you empty. Even the food is bland: milk, cauliflower, white rice, yoghurt. But today, Agatha, something happens that gives colour. I am in the library for the afternoon's activity – it is the same every day. The library is extensive. Bookshelves floor to ceiling, filled with regimented pale blue books, spines identical. On the first day, I was told to choose one. None had titles. I pulled one out at random. Empty white pages. And the next. And the next. 'Here,' says the woman holding out a pencil. 'Write,' she says. 'Write what?' 'Your thoughts, feelings. Drawings are permissible too.' 'I don't know what to write.' 'That is significant too.' I choose a book. I sit all afternoon and write nothing at all. At the end of the session, I am told to keep the book. It is for my 'expression'. 'You must bring it to each session.

Keep it with you at all times,' she says. I do not mark the pages. But today, as I sit at the table, the empty pages before me, I see something that makes my heart leap: the reflection of another candidate catches in the window. It is only a fraction of a second, but I am certain who it is. Dorcas. So, that's why I'm here. Why we are both here. The patients in the lift. The vulnerable. The broken on their way out. All Dorcas and I did was deliver them to surgery, holding out a little hope for them on the way up. What's wrong with that? Of course, everything is wrong with that. If a patient's hospital notes say they have cancer, the authorities want the surgeon to open up that patient and find the cancer. If the cancer has gone, it unnerves them: the system is failing, they are losing control. Someone must be to blame. I see faces of patients on trolleys, the silver of the lift, Dorcas saying 'when two are gathered together', her hand touches theirs, my hand touches theirs… how many did we save? And for this we are being punished. Dorcas! Why do they punish a woman of such incomparable beauty of heart and soul? I stare at the blank pages before me and start to write. It is the only thing I can do. I love you Agatha. You are my beginning. Before, I was lost to darkness.

65. Damson cheese

The Sun will consume the Earth. And Venus. And Mercury. After the Sun has burned all the hydrogen, it will go on burning helium for one hundred and thirty million more years, expanding and expanding and expanding to engulf Mercury, Venus and Earth.

When Agatha returned from the hospital, she shut the leather book Penelope had given her in the drawer along with the Child Assist Order (1) and (2). She would need to keep it hidden. Perhaps she might dare to read it one day. But not yet. Its power, once unleashed, could be dangerous. It had transformed people's lives before and it could do again. And the authorities did not like that. Reading banned books at university had been such a joy, giving her such delight, but things were different now. So much more was at stake.

Over the past few days, a heavy crop of damsons in the orchard had brought a phrase from one of the university books to mind. How odd that a string of words, a smell, a sound could live within you. And how she had puzzled over this one: the 'venerable hardness' of a damson cheese. How could damsons become cheese? What sort of transformation took place? And why had it gone hard?

Agatha would make damson cheese for Peter. She was filling Grey Cottage with good things, focusing on his return, not his absence. It was the only way she could deal with things. Her tutor group had looked up how to make damson cheese and the recipe had stayed with her: boil the damsons in sugar until the mixture is so thick you can scrape the bottom of the saucepan with a wooden spoon and see, for a second or two, the shiny base before the thick purple liquid covers it again.

'What are you doing?' asked Pip, as he and Wilfie came in from school.

'Making damson cheese. Come and help me pick.'

The boys followed Agatha into the orchard. She didn't mind – they could do their homework later. And they were dealing with the Reconstruction well. Ever since the tin mines trip last Saturday, Pip had been giving Wilfie secret looks and Wilfie always pretended he hadn't seen. She noticed things like that. She knew her boys. Perhaps it was a surprise for Peter. Whatever it was Pip seemed excited and that was a good thing.

Agatha gave Wilfie a bucket and Pip a basket. She tapped her palm on the sharp upright stone that had injured Peter's hand. She didn't like to pass the place without doing so. Wilfie had once asked her why.

'It doesn't feel right not to.'

'Is it a spell?' asked Pip.

'No, not a spell, but it keeps everything just so.'

So today, as normal, she tapped the wall. It was always sharp – a tiny pierce of pain in her palm. Sometimes she tapped down harder to increase the pain. Especially now Peter was in Reconstruction. Wilfie and Pip tapped it too. Right in the centre of their palms. Pip would often look to see if it had left a red mark. And it always did.

Some mothers might take the sharp, knife-like danger away to protect their children, but Agatha liked it there. Its sharpness challenged her as life challenged her. She liked to prove to herself she could deal with things and she liked to see her children being brave, forming the habit.

Damson fruits hung together in deep blue-black clusters, lowering the branches of the tree.

'Easy to reach,' said Pip. The fruits were small and had to be picked one by one but they were plentiful. Soon, the bucket and basket were full.

'That'll do. Now for the cooking.'

Back in the kitchen, they pulled off leaves and little woody stalks from the damsons then tipped them into the deep white sink. Water from the tap bounced the fruits round, ducking them down under pressure until they escaped and rose again to float on the surface. Insects losing their grip scurried to save their lives, some trying to climb the slippery white rock face, others flailing for seconds beneath the water until, lifeless, they sank to join the debris of earth and grit at the bottom of the sink.

Agatha put the stainless steel cauldron used for cooking stews and soups on the kitchen floor and the three of them gathered the damsons in their hands, shovelling them from the sink into the cauldron. A few fruits escaped, rolling across granite slabs, hiding under wooden chairs, tucking in between boots. But they were all found and returned to the cauldron.

'No escapes,' said Pip, enjoying the hunt.

Agatha lifted the cauldron onto the range and brought the fruity mixture to a tumbling boil, watching with anticipation. The boys lost interest and trotted off to lark about outside. But Agatha was entranced: hard little fruits gave up the ghost and softened, their blackened skins splitting open, bleeding a soft orange pulp. And from deep within, hard stones, stripped of their flesh, popped to the surface. She picked them out with a metal spoon, one by one.

The sieve had gone missing. Agatha went out to the vegetable garden. She had probably left it there, meaning to pick something small and coming back with a cabbage instead, leaving it behind, forgotten. Things were always getting moved and lost, but never lost forever. Scissors, trowel, bucket, basket – a continuous flow, back and forth, from kitchen to garden to kitchen. As natural a progression as seed to plant to seed. Everything in its place, in its time. Sometimes gone but never forgotten.

She could see the boys running out on the moor.

'Craw! Craw!' they shouted.

A sideways jump by Wilfie made Agatha think of Peter: redness of the hair, twist of the body, flinging up of the arms, a visual thread that made her drop her head and weep. Reconstruction was something many families went through. People knew that. Accepted that it was a good thing. The state caring. But Agatha also knew if she thought about it too much, she would scream. She could scream and scream and never stop. Not until Peter was back.

Through tears, she saw the silver sieve tucked under a collapsed runner bean plant. The mix of branches she had taken from the orchard and made into a wigwam of support, all bends and wrong angles, had snapped under the weight of climbing beans. The plants that had made their way up into the sunlight, born from the dark world of seeds, had grown into a mass of twirling, creeping vines that wound their way upwards, sprouting great leaves and red drop-shaped flowers and pods. She must have left the sieve when she had been out picking the long, elegant, finger-like beans that hid amongst the green. Perhaps Peter had arrived home and she had gone to greet him, forgetting the beans, forgetting the sieve. She picked it up now and walked back to the kitchen, pained by loneliness.

Agatha set the sieve over a large ceramic bowl and poured in the steaming damson mixture. Deep purple liquid and pulp flooded into the bowl beneath, leaving stones and skins trapped above. With the back of a metal spoon, she pushed the remaining pulpy mixture through, so it dropped in soft lumps into the dark pool. She would serve the damson cheese to Peter the day he returned. It would surprise and delight him. Happiness crept back into the task. She removed the sieve from the bowl to reveal a rich black liquid. It sloshed and slopped as she poured it back into the cauldron.

'Now simmer, I think.'

Agatha spoke aloud. She enjoyed the sound of her voice mixing with cries of birds, children, the bubbling of her mixture. Peter would be back in a few days, she felt certain. And then she would put on a dress for him and dance with him and eat damson cheese with him and go to bed with him. Together. Reconstruction could not separate them forever.

Agatha tipped sugar into the mixture. The white crystals held for a moment, pure and clean against the dark waters, then a crimson red crept amongst them, staining dark and sucking down, until they disappeared. The boiling began again. Tumbling, turning, evaporating.

'Where does the moisture go?'

She placed the palm of her hand flat against the cool, softly white plastered wall of the cottage. Could it be absorbing the evaporated damson juice? Surely it would go a little pink. And what of spinach? Would it go green? Raspberries? Beetroot? What would people think if they knew she had such thoughts? They would think her mad. But she didn't care. She wanted to own her own thoughts. She spun round.

'Oh, wall of beetroot, damson and spinach, how I honour thee!'

She bowed to the wall, then took a spoonful of the hot damson liquid and allowed it to cool a moment. She dipped her finger into the purpleness, still hot, and painted a heart on the wall. A child would be scolded for such an act. But she loved the heart. She loved doing it because it was her impulse, her wall, her home: the freedom to act as instinctively as a bird rises in flight. Agatha knew that was precious.

Wilfie and Pip came in for tea. Grey Cottage was so familiar to them that they noticed changes instantly. Straight away they saw the heart.

'What's that?' asked Pip.

'It's a message from me to your daddy.'

'Is it in blood?'

'No, damson juice. Do you want a go?'

Wilfie and Pip dipped their fingers in the purple juice and dabbed it on the wall. They tried to draw but the liquid dried fast, absorbed into the plaster, so they only got the first bit of a line done before it ran out. Spots seemed easier. Wilfie dotted a neat line curving upwards.

'A rocket?' asked Agatha.

She returned to her boiling. The mixture was reducing and thickening. She drew the wooden spoon across the bottom of the pan, but only got a split second of silver. You needed to see the silver clearly. And then, there it was. The mixture was firming and a silver path was visible, the red holding each side before flooding in. Agatha greased pots, mugs, egg cups and ladled in the mixture. She left it to cool, to set. The cheese would be turned out and eaten with a strong blue cheese. She could not wait to give Peter a slice. Sharp and sweet.

On Sunday, as the three were finishing their gooseberry tea, there was a tap on the half-open kitchen door.

Agatha cried out in surprise. A man was standing there, his tall, pencil-like figure splitting the frame, his shorts spattered with mud, his face flushed red.

'Sorry. Didn't mean to make you jump,' he said.

'What do you want?' demanded Agatha.

'Just wondering if I could have a glass of water. Been running.'

'Wilfie, get a glass of water,' said Agatha, wanting to keep an eye on the stranger, not turn her back as she reached for a glass. But her voice was softer. The man seemed pleasant. Even a little anxious.

'Why are you running?' asked Pip.

'To keep fit. Get out. See the countryside.'

Wilfie handed him the water. He drank it in two long gulps.

'Thanks.'

He smiled at Wilfie as he handed back the glass.

A silence followed. Was he going to go now? Agatha realised she didn't want him to. She had missed adult company.

'Would you like a cup of tea? Maybe mint tea? We have so much in the garden, we have to do something with it. And it's probably good for runners. I used to drink it myself, when I was running. Not when I was actually doing the running. Afterwards. Or before.'

'Thanks. Mint tea would be great.'

Agatha pressed past him to pick the pungent leaves growing in out-of-control mounds near the kitchen door.

'Don't you love that,' she said, rubbing the green between her fingers, releasing fresh mint as she went back into the kitchen. The man, still hovering near the door, was staring at the stone slabbed floor.

'Granite,' Agatha said. 'Three hundred million years old. Still beautiful.'

'I've not seen a floor so worn as that before. So walked over.'

'If you walk on the moon your footsteps stay there for thousands of years. There's no climate. That's why. Nothing to blow them away. So they stay there.'

It was the first time Wilfie had spoken. The man seemed interested.

'That so? Your floor is a bit the same I suppose. These dips and rises from hundreds of footsteps in and out, in and out.'

'Except not hundreds of people have been to the moon.'

'You're right there. Not yet anyway.'

Agatha knelt down and slid her hand over the granite.

'It's so smooth. So friendly.'

'It's a miracle. Flowing molten rock to this, a kitchen floor. Ordinary,' said Weston.

'Not ordinary. Special. Crystalline rock.'

Agatha felt animated, enjoying conversation, the sound of another adult, the presence.

'Minerals battling in a great swirling, boiling mass for prominence. White feldspar. Glassy quartz. Black shiny mica. Don't you love their names?'

'Mica,' said Pip. 'Mica. Mica. Mica. Our black hen is called Mica. After the floor.'

'Aren't hens girls?' said the man.

'Mica is a girl's name,' said Pip.

'Suppose. So what's your name?'

'Pip. So I would be a girl's name with an 'a'.'

'Pip-a. Pippa,' said the man testing it, trying to keep up. 'Are you Wilfie's younger brother?'

'I'm Wilfie's only brother. And no sisters.'

'Only brother. No sisters.'

He seemed struck by the idea of there being only one sibling.

'What's your name?' asked Pip.

'Weston.'

'Weston-a,' said Pip. They all laughed.

Agatha handed him a mug of mint tea.

'Come and sit down.'

'Do I drink it with the leaves in?'

'You can or you can't,' said Pip.

There were four chairs around the kitchen table. The boys ate their gooseberries and giggled as Weston dipped the mint leaves in and out. It was strange to see another man sitting in Peter's chair. They were about the same height but this man had a slender frame – so different from Peter's well-built physique. Agatha's heart pounded. Thoughts about Peter were merging with thoughts about this stranger. What was she thinking? Appalled, she got up and hurried to the larder.

'Where are you running to?' asked Wilfie.

'I'm not,' said Agatha, colouring as she realised Wilfie was speaking to the runner, not her. Her heart hammered; she felt embarrassed to the core.

Weston pulled a crumpled map from his pocket.

'I got a bit lost, but I've been running from here to here,' he said, pointing at the village and Grey Cottage.

'Why were you running to our house?' asked Pip.

'Well, I wasn't. I mean, I was, but only because it's good to have something to aim for.'

'Would you like some damson cheese?' called Agatha, trying to keep her voice steady. The cheese was still in moulds, waiting to be turned out onto baking paper. She planned to wrap them up, store them in the fridge; little presents ready to be enjoyed on special occasions – like when Peter returned. But she had an overwhelming desire to share one right now. Nothing wrong with that, was there?

'Yes, I'd love some. What is it?'

Agatha brought out a round circle of just set purple, along with a slab of blue cheese.

'Cheese and cheese. Both cheese. Very different but perfect together,' she said, her voice light.

The blue-veined cheese crumbled as she placed it on a small plate for Weston. Then she took a sharp knife and sliced off a crescent of damson cheese. It sat like a clear purple jewel, rich against the roughness of white-blue. As Weston tasted the sweet sharpness, the crumbly smoothness, she felt a surprising pleasure from seeing the look of delight on his face.

Later, as he was leaving, Weston lingered at the door as if there was something he wanted to say. He seemed to be taking everything in – the granite floor, the beams, the marks on the wall, the moulds of damson cheese sitting in the larder, the boys – as if he wanted to remember it all, hold on to the experience.

'Bye then,' said Agatha, wanting to add, 'Come again if you're running past.'

'Don't forget your map,' shouted Wilfie, going outside to give it to Weston.

'My map. Be lost without that. Thanks.'

'You could follow the stars,' said Wilfie. 'You can see loads from here.'

'That right?'

'North Star,' said Wilfie, pointing.

Agatha, standing in the doorway, looked upwards. Dusk was only just falling but, already, the North Star, bright and brilliant, was visible.

'I'll not get lost now, Wilfie,' said Weston. 'Map. North Star. All set. Ready to go.'

'Ready for take-off,' replied Wilfie.

Agatha smiled, glad the man was going, feeling somehow that she had escaped and was left wanting Peter more than ever.

Weston waved as he jogged up the track. Agatha turned back into Grey Cottage to wrap up the damson cheeses, ready for her husband's return.

66. Seat space

Nuclear fusion creates the energy at the sun's core, as hydrogen converts to helium.

On Tuesday morning, Mr Skillern had an urgent call from Evie.

'Is Wilfie Whisper in school, Mr Skillern?'

'Yes, as far as I know.'

'Good. Get him ready. There's a seat with his name on it on this afternoon's launch.'

'This afternoon?'

'Yes, this afternoon. 16.50 departure.'

'Are you saying he might go up today?'

'No, Mr Skillern, I'm saying he *is* going up today. Some geologist booked on this afternoon's flight can't make it. Got the sniffles or something. They don't want to waste the seat, so, hey presto. A golden opportunity for Wilfie. Not to be missed. We'll send a car. It'll be with you at ten thirty. And there might be some press. Put your best tie on.'

'What about the space training day? Or was it days?'

'They can explain everything in the car and then run through a few last details at the launch. Don't worry, we'll be in constant communication with Wilfie. Video screens. Two way. If he goes today, he'll be back in class this time next week, done and dusted.'

Skillern wanted to say something but had no idea what.

'Look,' said Evie, 'if we don't take this chance the whole thing might never happen. It's not easy to get a seat – they can be booked up for months. I know it's sooner than expected but we've got to go for it, Mr Skillern.'

It was all happening too fast. Much too fast.

'Mr Skillern?'

He noted irritation in Evie's voice. She thought he was dithering, like Firth used to dither. Surely he couldn't be turning into Mr Firth?

'I'll make sure Wilfie is ready.'

'Good. And tell his mum. We want her there. It all adds to the human interest of the story.'

'Yes, of course, of course,' said Skillern. His hand shook as he replaced the receiver. He had not anticipated this. Not at all. Not so soon. He rang through to Mrs McDuff.

'Get Mrs Whisper on the phone. And get Wilfie sent to my office. Right now.'

The occasion had arisen and Skillern would rise to the occasion. Be a leader. A great leader. He sat lost in thought about his emerging greatness. He strode across to the window. The empty playground of Fellows Light spread before him; children in class, learning. A well-ordered, disciplined school.

A door in the classroom block at the far end of the playground opened and a little boy with red hair stepped out, closing it behind him, struggling with the dodgy latch.

Wilfie Whisper.

The boy started across the black tarmac, tightrope walking the white lines of the netball court. Skillern snorted; the boy was ambling.

No idea. No idea.

Halfway across Wilfie stopped, crouching to tie his shoelace.

Hurry up, for goodness' sake.

Skillern, impatient, tapped on the window, but Wilfie failed to look up. He finished doing up his lace and continued to make his way along the white line, taking jumps over the black tarmac whenever the line ran out.

What an earth was he playing at?

And where was his mother?

Why had Mrs Whisper not answered the phone? It would be better to have things ticked off properly. But then, Wilfie had asked him not to tell his mum. Skillern would take the boy at his word. Wilfie knew what was best for his mum and Skillern knew what was best for Wilfie. Perhaps it was better not to have the mother involved. He shuddered at the memory of the tie episode. The woman was too emotional. As headmaster of Fellows Light it was his duty to make decisions, take responsibility. And he would not shirk responsibility. He had the grit, the courage to step up to the mark. Oh yes, he would step up to the mark and show the world what he was made of.

67. Jacob's ladder

No landing: Jupiter, Saturn, Uranus and Neptune have no solid surface.

When Agatha free-wheeled down the track to Grey Cottage after a morning's cleaning, she was chilled by the sight of a white van in the yard. So out of place. So wrong in her landscape. The whine of drilling was coming from the cottage. Agatha flung her bike against the stone wall and rushed in.

A young man in blue overalls and goggles was up a stepladder leaning against a powerful, screeching drill, which was biting its way into the oak beam that ran the length of her kitchen. The beam, in protest, puffed out little showers of sawdust, which floated down, coming to rest as a fine dust on the flagstone floor.

'What's going on? How dare you? Stop that! I said stop that!'

Agatha shook the stepladder. The operative, frog-eyed, looked down in alarm and released the trigger on his drill.

'What are you doing to my beam? Why are you in my house?'

'Sorry darlin'. The door was open. And there was no one around so I thought I'd crack on. Jacob, by the way,' he added, pointing at the red lettering embroidered on his chest that read *Jacob* and, underneath, *Technical*.

'What? There is no job. I've not asked for anything.'

'Sorry love, but someone has. My boss sent me straight out this morning to come and fix up a screen in your kitchen.'

'What are you talking about?'

'I've got the job sheet.'

Jacob jumped down from the ladder and produced a piece of paper from his pocket.

'There you are darlin'. Sorry if there has been a misunderstanding. I'm nearly done anyway.'

He climbed back up his ladder and started twisting a hook into the drilled hole.

'Nearly finished, then I'll be gone and leave you in peace. It's all peace and quiet out here, isn't it? Those views. Don't often get to come out to such open spaces. Bit special, isn't it?'

Agatha only half heard. She was reading the job sheet, trying to understand.

Jacob twisted the hook again, sinking it deeper and deeper into the beam.

'No!' cried Agatha.

'Good hold on that hook,' Jacob said, hopping down and trotting out to his van.

Agatha stormed after him.

'Look, this order, it's a mistake. A video link? I never ordered such a thing. We don't even have a radio. It's broken. And Peter's not here now. He should be here, then none of this would be happening.'

Agatha knew she was talking too much but she couldn't help it. This seemed wrong, so very wrong. A stranger sent to her house. Doing things to the house. The place where only she and Peter and Wilfie and Pip should be.

'Stop! What are you doing now?'

Jacob was carrying a screen into Grey Cottage. He whistled as he climbed back up the ladder and hoisted a ring at the back of the screen onto the hook. The screen dangled on the beam, swinging. He whistled as he made an adjustment, getting it to hang straight, and he whistled as he attached a power cable to the back and down into a socket on the worktop. Whistling. Not listening to her. Not listening at all.

'I'll just tap in the wires. Don't want any splashes from your sink getting it wet. Fizz! Buzz! Poooosh!' he said, grinning.

He hammered in a few u-shaped nails, attaching the wire along the ceiling and down the wall, where it lay like a wound, a scar on Grey Cottage.

'Good job. All done. Happy?'

'No, not happy at all. I don't want a screen. This order isn't from me.'

'Maybe it's complimentary, direct from OSH. Right-ho, let's get you tuned in. Six channels to set up for you. You can see one at a time or split the screen into two, or even six. Pretty incredible, hey?'

Jacob pointed a remote control at the screen.

'One is OSH technical. Two, OSH management. You might even get the big cheese on that, Mr Black himself—'

'I don't know what you're talking about—'

'Three, launch,' continued Jacob. 'We're setting one

up at the launch site so you can watch the take-off from Growlers Drop. Should be able to watch that anytime from four o'clock onwards...'

'Take-off? What are you—?'

'Four, personnel,' continued Jacob. 'That's your direct link to your School Liaison Officer. Five is No 49 Pennyside, external. And six – the real cherry on the top – is No 49 Pennyside, internal. That's where your lad is. Or will be. Let's see if it all works.'

'What do you mean, "my lad"?' whispered Agatha, with dread in her heart; knowing what he meant, but not wanting to believe it, not wanting the terrifying thought to be acknowledged, to become reality.

'Let's see if we can get OSH technical. Nope. Nothing there yet. Probably not switched on. How about four? Personnel.'

The face of a young woman with black curls filled the screen.

'Oh, gosh! Is that you Jacob? Gosh, this thing works. I've been carrying it round with me all morning then suddenly I got a beep. Can't believe it works. Just a little mobile screen. I can see you. Can you see me? Gosh, how exciting. Oh, hello! Who's that with you, Jacob?'

'Agatha Whisper,' said Agatha, hardly able to breathe as the horror unfolded before her.

'What's going on? Tell me. Please, tell me.'

'Mrs Whisper, at last. Wow! So thrilled to meet you. Evie Blick-Foxton, School Liaison Officer on the KISS space competition project.'

'Space competition? Oh no...'

'How do you do and all that. Wilfie is just adorable. Take off not long now – can you believe it? Sorry we haven't met but it's all happened in such a rush, hasn't it?

Gosh, there was quite an excitement at Fellows Light this morning. Mrs McDuff and Wilfie heading off in a taxi. I'm sorry I couldn't be there myself – and obviously you neither – but it was all so unexpected, wasn't it? Right out of the blue. Your little lad is quite the hero, isn't he?'

'But Wilfie didn't enter the space competition. I wrote "No Way" on the form.'

'I'm sorry? You definitely signed the form. I have it here in my file somewhere. Hang on. Yes, here we go. Signed.'

'Signed and saying "No Way"?'

'Ah, maybe… looking at it…'

'Yes?'

'Look, Mrs Whisper, it's been signed by Peter Whisper. Quite clearly. There seems to be some other stuff rubbed out, but it doesn't matter now. Wilfie's won. He's going into space. The first child ever!'

'Into space? No, he can't be…'

'I'm sorry Mrs Whisper, I really am. But he left school at ten thirty this morning.'

'This morning?'

Agatha's knees buckled. It was real. The fear of Wilfie being taken had become a reality.

'Yes, the school tried to contact you but it was all such a mad rush. A seat on the launch shuttle coming up out of the blue like that. What a golden opportunity. Couldn't be missed. Look, keep your telly on as well as the screen. Might see him on newsflashes. It's a big super-duper breaking news story. Actually breaking right now. Mrs Whisper, are you still there? Can you hear me? Can you switch on your telly?'

'I don't think she has a telly,' said Jacob.

'No telly? Gosh, can we get OSH Technical in on this conversation please, Jacob? They might help explain things.'

The screen split into two. The second screen beamed straight into a busy office, filled with eager faces.

'It's on!'

'Hey, hello!'

'OSH techie team here, alive and kicking.'

'I'm sorry if you're a teeny bit anxious, Mrs Whisper. Only natural of course,' said Evie, 'but we are so thrilled Wilfie won because we believe in him. We believe in Wilfie.'

'Oh yes,' shouted a techie. 'We believe in Wilfie.'

'Our little space hero,'

A bald, bearded man from OSH Technical lent forward, filling his side of the screen.

'Hello Mrs Whisper. A momentous day, is it not? Young Wilfie heading for the stars. He'll be home in a few days. But in that time he will have changed the world. There are riches out there beyond our wildest dreams. Not just to create wealth but to enrich human life. Cures for childhood diseases. Cancer. Blindness. One day, these will all be things of the past. Think of that, Mrs Whisper, think of that.'

'I don't care. I just want Wilfie back now. Home. Safe and sound.'

'The trip is one hundred percent safe, Mrs Whisper. Listen, we understand your concerns, of course we do. Any parent would feel a little anxious right now. But Wilfie has had full training. He knows exactly what to do. Nothing has been left to chance. Believe me. And you can watch it all live from the safety of your kitchen. Don't forget to tune in.'

Agatha knew she was beaten. She pressed her knuckles over her eyes, trying to suppress the great sobs that were threatening to swamp her.

Don't scream and shout and get hysterical.

Don't react as any mother would whose child has been stolen away.

'Don't worry, Mrs Whisper. He's in safe hands. The best. Talk later.'

The bald, bearded man disappeared and the other techies surrounding him returned to desks and keyboards.

'Jus' one more job,' said Jacob, holding out a form on a clipboard. It was marked with two crosses.

'Sign here and here please.'

One. I am satisfied with the standard of the screen.

Two. I am happy with the position of the screen.

'But I don't know what standard—'

'It's a good one,' said Jacob.

Confused, in shock, all Agatha knew was that the screen provided a sliver of a link to Wilfie, so, against all her better judgement, she signed.

'Good stuff,' said Jacob. 'Oh, to turn the screen off, click the blue button. Don't worry darlin', you'll soon get the hang of it. All the best to Wilfie. Don't forget, screen three, four o'clock. Be seeing ya.'

Jacob, whistling, hopped back into his van and sped off up the track.

68. Splashed in glory

Once upon a time, 14 billion years ago, a bubble a thousand times smaller than a pinhead exploded. The universe was born.

Agatha pressed her hand on the sharp stone, gasped in pain, and stared at the blood on her palm, flowing from split skin. She wiped it across her face, marking her own failure.

She took a spade to turn the heavy earth, to work out her anger. But she couldn't dig, numbed by events. Grey clouds scowled above, filling the skies. Oh, how she wished to see the hidden blue. The blue that linked her to Peter. The blue Wilfie would be hurtling through into the above and beyond, carrying the future of humankind on his little shoulders.

I am going you know, mum.

As if in answer the clouds started to disperse. The sun's rays warmed the lingering vapours, filling the arc of the sky with a haze and casting a brilliant shimmering light over the landscape, shining silver off the stone of the cottage, glittering yellow on trembling leaves and, beyond, splashing glory over the moor's deep green mantle, reflecting bright on its yellow jewels of gorse and rich swathes of heathery purple.

I am going you know, mum.

The gentle, persistent voice was unmistakable. Wilfie telling her, as he had told her so many times before, of his covenant, his promise to use the gifts he had been blessed with. But only now did she understand.

Washed in the beauty of her world, transformed by understanding, Agatha felt her spirit transcend all she had been fighting. She felt a rush of joy and started to cry, her tears an outpouring of relief. Wilfie had been born special, different, a visionary, and now everything he had known was coming true. Not as she would have wished. Not as she had expected. They had taken him against her will. That was her battle. Not Wilfie going. Her exceptional, wonderful son. It was Wilfie's will, his vision. All as it should be. As Peter had understood. How right and knowing he had been. How she had misunderstood them both. But they would forgive her. Love would see to that. Hope flooded upon her.

I am going you know, mum.

'Yes, Wilfie, I know,' whispered Agatha. 'We're so proud of you. Dad and I. So very proud.'

She rubbed her hands across her face, wiping away the tears, the stain of blood. Beside her, broad beans grew thick amongst the spindly canes, which were still holding firm. She picked a leathery pod and split it open. Inside, on the blankety-bed, lay four beans, perfectly formed, each a pearly pale green with a luminous lime umbilical strip. One by one, she ate each seed, loving the texture of the silky skin splitting, the softness of the pulpy flesh. She picked more; a host more, filling a pot that was lying abandoned in the greenery. She took the beans inside.

The screen looked out of place but she was glad of it now. Her link to Wilfie. She hoped above all that Peter was watching. Peter who had always had faith in their little boy. And if he couldn't watch, she would remember every detail to tell him when he returned. When he came home. When they were all home.

She started splitting the beans open. The leathery pods reminded her of something. She hurried upstairs, pulled open the drawer that held the Child Assist Orders, the Reconstruction letter and took out Penelope's book. It felt beautiful, comforting: the softness of the leather, the way it lay cupped in her hand. She felt a thrill at the thought of the words within. Powerful. Not dangerous. Powerful. Back in the kitchen she sat at the table and paused, staring a moment or two at the little volume before her. Then she opened it. Black type sat dense on thin translucent pages. And throughout, verses were underlined in pencil, sections circled, comments written in the margins. A spidery hand. Penelope.

Be on your guard; stand firm in the faith;
be courageous; be strong.

Let love be genuine. Abhor what is evil;
hold fast to what is good.

Now faith is the assurance of things hoped for,
the conviction of things not seen.

He gives power to the weak
and strength to the powerless.

And now these three remain: faith, hope, and love.
But the greatest of these is love.

The phrases tumbled from the pages – resonant, mysterious, mighty, poetic – promising something beyond all comprehension

And then a sentence made her gasp:

Though your sins are like scarlet,
they shall be as white as snow;
though they are as red as crimson,
they shall be like wool.

Singing above the words was Wilfie.

I am going you know, mum.

The clarity of his words chimed with the writing, both full of hope, of certainty. Agatha paused, understanding, not understanding, believing, not believing.

Let it breathe, Penelope had said. *Let it breathe.*

Agatha hurried to the oak chest, tucked under coats, that held the children's old schoolbooks, scribblings, stories, drawings. She flicked through an exercise book, searching for unused pages and tore them out – twelve pages in all, lined in faintest blue. Back at the table, she copied out verses, loving the words, listening to their message, believing their power.

For I know the plans I have for you…
plans to prosper you and not to harm you,
plans to give you hope and a future.

There is no fear in love; for perfect love casteth out fear.

Our faith can move mountains.

Train up a child in the way he should go,
and when he is old, he will not depart from it.

Above all else, guard your heart,
for everything you do flows from it.

She copied the same texts again and again. Remembering them. Letting them become part of her. She imagined places she would leave copies: houses she cleaned, hospital, school. She saw the words spreading to others, coming to life. Perhaps she could even get one on Mr Skillern's desk? She laughed out loud at the thought. Wouldn't that be a wonderful thing for Mr Skillern? For Fellows Light?

And she hoped all day that the minibus would not be late. She wanted Pip home so they could watch the launch together. It would be too much to do it alone.

69. Growlers Drop

How smooth is the Moon? Its surface is pitted with craters from collisions with comets and asteroids. Not smooth at all.

'I just can't believe it,' said Mrs McDuff. 'I just can't believe you actually won.'

Wilfie pressed his lips firmly together. There was a stinging behind his eyes and his breathing felt out of control. He stared at a black mole, a tiny planet, on the back of the taxi driver's neck. Did the man know it was there? He was about to discover things in space and the taxi driver might not even know that he had a planet growing on his neck.

'You the lad that won the space competition?' asked the driver.

'Yes, he is,' said Mrs McDuff. 'We're awfully proud of him.'

Wilfie didn't want to talk. He had wanted to go home, get Stuffy Ted, hug his mum tight. But Mr Skillern had said there was not enough time.

'I need to see Pip,' Wilfie had blurted out when he had been pulled out of maths and told to hurry: the launch was that afternoon. It didn't feel right. All a bit panicky. But if he could just see Pip before he left maybe it would be OK. Mr Skillern had tutted and sent for Pip.

'Say sorry to mum for me, Pip. I'll be back soon so she needn't worry.'

'Yep.'

Pip's face was red and he was breathing in gulps.

'Look after Stuffy Ted for me.'

'Yep.'

Then Pip had grabbed hold of Wilfie and held him tight.

'In the car, Wilfie,' Mr Skillern was saying.

Wilfie had climbed into the car and that was it; he was off to space.

Now Mrs McDuff was hunting around in her bag. She pulled out a scrap of paper.

'Listen dear, I've got Mr Skillern's notes here. He took them down from that lovely Evie over the phone. Let's have a look. Terrible writing. Mr Skillern has terrible writing for a headmaster. I'm always telling him. Scribbles. If only Mr Chillworth was here to decipher. Let's see. Your spacesuit is waiting for you at the terminal. Evie will meet us there if she can make it in time. Turn and wave when you get in the tram and wave again when you walk up the steps into the launch shuttle. Then there is a whole load of stuff about decompression, but you can read that later. It's beyond me. Now Wilfie dear, anything you want to ask me? Nothing too technical. I'd need Mr Chillworth here for that.'

'Could you tell my mum I've had to go? Say bye to her for me.'

'Of course, dear. Oh, look. I say. We're being followed. I feel like a film star!'

Wilfie turned. Tight on their tail was a van. On top of the van was a camera. Wilfie slid down in his seat. Mrs McDuff squeezed his hand.

'Take no notice of them, dear. I've got a present for you.'

She reached in her bag and pulled out a tin.

'Not biscuits, dear. Not this time.'

Wilfie took off the lid. The tin was stuffed with little pieces of folded paper.

'Messages from your classmates,' said Mrs McDuff. 'Mr Chillworth had a whip round as soon as he heard you were off. Dear man. Well, open them.'

Wilfie unfolded the first.

Bring us back a bit of moon.
Have fun!

His eyes brimmed with tears as he took out a stripy yellow and white paper sweet bag. *Don't let the sherbet explode. Ha! Ha! Boom! Boom! Sam* was written in pencil on the outside. Inside were six lemon sherbets.

'You alright, dear?' asked Mrs McDuff. Wilfie could not help himself. A tear fell.

'Open this one,' she said, picking out a pink note.

Wilfie opened the homemade envelope. Inside was a lock of blond hair and a message: *Forever Together Out There. Omani Sponge xxx.*

'Goodness,' said Mrs McDuff. 'I didn't know you had a girlfriend.'

'I don't,' said Wilfie. 'I've never spoken to Omani.'

'What's in the big envelope?'

Wilfie pulled out a tie. A Fellows Light prefect's tie. Blue and yellow diagonal stripes.

'Does that mean I'm a prefect?' asked Wilfie. He had never, ever thought he would be a prefect. His mum would be really, really pleased if he was.

'I suppose so. Well done you. And look a note from Mr Skillern himself.'

Remember, Fellows Light is a Light for the World.

Wilfie put his precious gifts back in the tin and held it tight.

'Been to Growlers Drop before, have you?' asked the taxi driver.

'No, never,' said Mrs McDuff. 'It's all quite an adventure for us.'

'Did you know the departures lounge used to be a sports pavilion?'

'No, I never knew that. Goodness me.'

'Yep. Used to be the pavilion for the village cricket pitch. You know, local matches, sporting triumphs, golden ducks, cream teas. Right on the very edge of land still lethally contaminated.'

'Oh dear,' said Mrs McDuff. 'Sounds rather dangerous.'

'Yep. Since the meteorite smashed the area to smithereens there's been a high wire fence round the edge to stop people wandering about. Course, it's safe enough, so they say, if you're properly kitted up. Do you know how much they've spent running the tram line from the terminal to the launch pad?'

'No, I've no idea,' said Mrs McDuff.

'Mind-boggling amount. But they haven't spent a penny on the pavilion. It's an old fashioned tongue-and-groove sort of place. Pock marked with splinters from flying debris. Looking forward to your trip are you, laddie?'

An hour later, the taxi drew to a halt before a tatty wooden building. Mrs McDuff struggled out, Wilfie sliding across the seat after her.

'I told you it needed a lick of paint, didn't I,' said the driver.

'Oh, my,' said Mrs McDuff, clasping Wilfie's hand, as she pushed open the door of Growlers Drop Departures.

In his dreams, Wilfie had imagined a modern building, gleaming white, buzzing with scientists looking at screens, commentaries of take-offs, chat in funny voices coming from astronauts as they floated in the unknown. But this room was rundown and stank of something wet. Brown tiles lay curling and patchy on the floor. On the wall above a battered door, a faded sign, painted in green letters, outlined in black, read: Players Changing Room – Visitors. Someone had scrawled below in thick black pen: Departures. Not what Wilfie had expected at all. He reeled round. On the opposite wall was another door with another green sign: Players Changing Room – Home. And there was a wooden board with the names of cricket captains listed in gold lettering. This was cricket, not space travel at all.

'I say, an honours board from days gone by. That's a bit special,' said Mrs McDuff. 'I can remember—'

But Wilfie wasn't here for cricket. He trotted across the room to the window, footsteps squeaking on sticky flooring. He cleared a patch from the film of grime that shadowed the glass. In the distance, hazy and pale against the sky, he could make out a silver grey needle pointing upwards, a lonely vertical on a horizontal landscape. His heart leapt.

The shuttle.

'Look, Mrs McDuff. Look!' he cried.

Mrs McDuff bustled over to join him.

'Is that what you're going up in?' she said, squinting. 'Goodness, it looks such a small thing to be going such a long way.'

'Yes! Up and down,' said Wilfie. 'It doesn't burn up on re-entry. That was the big step forward dad says. Going up and coming back down.'

'Burning up? Goodness, these scientists. What will they think of next?'

Mrs McDuff turned from the window and dropped down into a sagging chair, the leather torn, yellow stuffing fluffing out.

'Come and wait here, dear,' she said as she thumbed through a grubby pile of magazines left to entertain passengers waiting for lift-off. 'Goodness, I can't understand a word of these. But you might like to take one for the journey. Read all about how a giant elliptical galaxy forms if there's a collision of the Andromeda galaxy and the

Milky Way. Gobbledygook to me.'

But Wilfie stayed at the window, entranced by the shuttle and all it promised.

From outside came the noise of hooting, the screech of vehicles, voices.

'Oh my. The press are descending,' said Mrs McDuff. 'All trying to get a winning shot of the first child in space in his flying gear. It could get nasty.'

A shout of laughter came from Departures.

'I say, dear, I think there's someone in there,' said Mrs McDuff. 'Why don't you pop in and get ready? I'll wait here. Don't you worry about me.'

For a moment, looking at Mrs McDuff on the chair with her magazine, so safe and homely, Wilfie wished he could stay with her, but he knew his destiny lay on the other side of that door. He took a deep breath and crossed the threshold.

The changing room smelt of sweat, of rubber, of aftershave. And it was so untidy. The chaos frightened Wilfie: clothes, equipment, empty food packaging scattered all over the place. But what terrified him the most were the five or six men strolling about semi-naked. This was alien territory for him. One man was reading a newspaper. Another was shaving, watching him from his mirror, his eyes flitting from Wilfie, back to his chin, to Wilfie, to his chin.

'Hey, you the kid that won that competition?' asked the man. 'The famous Wilfie Whisper? Congrats. Nervous?'

'Bit,' said Wilfie.

'Don't worry. I spend half my life up there. It's not that bad. No trees though. I miss seeing green. I'm Luke.'

Luke bounded over to a row of spacesuits hanging on a rail. He pulled out the smallest.

'This arrived about an hour ago. Special delivery. Special size.'

The other men laughed as Luke held the suit up against his own long, lean body.

'You know what this is?'

'A spacesuit,' whispered Wilfie.

'It's your lifesaver and it's awesome,' said Luke 'It'll save you from freezing to death at minus two hundred and fifty degrees or frying up at plus two hundred and fifty degrees. It'll supply you with beautiful oxygen in the vacuum of space, stop you dying of thirst, bat away space dust coming at you faster than a bullet, protect you from deadly levels of radiation. So look after it.'

'Don't frighten him,' a woman's voice shouted from behind a changing room door.

'Put it back, Luke, before you get a hole in it,' said another, and they both screeched with laughter.

'Woman astronauts,' said Luke. 'Shouldn't be allowed.'

He grinned at Wilfie and Wilfie grinned back, trying to shuffle off his anxiety, wanting to enjoy the moment. And wanting to remember everything. Everything to tell dad.

Luke hung the spacesuit back on the rail and took down a rucksack from the locker above.

'This rucksack came too,' he said, opening it and taking out a file. 'So, you're staying at 49 Pennyside. Cosy. These are your living-in-space instructions. Best look after this. It tells you everything you need to know up there, like turning on the kettle. Although I guess at your age you're not bothered about cups of tea. Ha, look at this.'

He held up a T-shirt that said *OSH Little Miner*.

'Love it,' said one of the women as she opened her cubicle door.

'Cute,' said the second woman, ruffling Wilfie's hair as she passed.

Wilfie smiled. He didn't mind the teasing. Not too much anyway. They all seemed to be treating a trip into space like a normal day out. Which was good, he supposed.

Luke zipped up the rucksack and threw it to Wilfie.

'Better get kitted up.'

Wilfie took the spacesuit. It was heavy and dragged on the floor.

'Careful. These things cost a fortune. Although yours, of course, will be half price.'

The changing room rocked with laughter. Wilfie carried his stuff into a cubicle, wanting to be alone. He dragged on the leggings and long sleeved white T-shirt. They fitted snug to his body as if someone was hugging him. It was a good feeling. He stared at the suit. This was a big moment, but it didn't feel real: more as if he was getting ready for a fancy dress party.

'Smart,' said Luke when Wilfie emerged. 'Feels like wearing cardboard to begin with, but you'll get used to it. You'll need a helmet. Try this one.'

As Luke lowered the helmet over his head, Wilfie felt like he was being crowned, being changed in some significant way. There was a clicking as the helmet connected round his neck to the suit.

'You OK in there? Good man. Keep it on until you get to your Pennyside. Wait until you are inside and pressure has levelled. OK?'

Wilfie tried to nod but his head was big and clumsy. It was a simple task but he couldn't do it. The suit had become a prison, his body trapped, everything out of control. His eyes filled with tears.

'Don't worry, pal,' said Luke. 'I was scared stiff first

time I went up but now I don't even give it a second thought. Enjoy yourself!'

A recorded announcement, high-pitched and tinny, spluttered on the airwaves.

'Shuttle doors locking for take-off in thirty-two minutes. Proceed to tram transfer.'

Thirty-two minutes. The competition, the adventure, the actual idea of going into space, which had seemed an unreal dream, was becoming an unstoppable reality and Wilfie was scared. But he couldn't turn back. He looped the rucksack over his shoulder and waded out to reception. The sight of Mrs McDuff sitting there, soft and comfortable, holding the biscuit tin on her lap, made his eyes sting with tears again.

'Oh my goodness. Look at you. A real astronaut at last. I'm so proud of you, dear.' She tried to hug him but the suit got in the way. She gave him a little wave instead.

'Look after yourself and come back in one piece.'

She was talking louder than usual. She tapped on his visor.

'Can you hear me in there?'

'Yes. Easily.'

'Don't forget this,' she said, thrusting the biscuit tin into Wilfie's gloved hand. 'Best of luck, dear. Best of luck.'

'Don't worry, miss,' said Luke. 'We'll keep an eye on him. Come on Wilfie. Let's get going.'

Luke headed for the exit. Wilfie followed, clumsy.

On the other side of the wire fence, the media were waiting.

'Give us a wave, kid,'

'Bring us back a golden nugget.'

'Hey, little astronaut. Good luck.'

It was too much. The people, the shouting, the saying goodbye. He needed air. Fresh air. He fiddled with the catches on the helmet round his neck. He needed to pull it off. Just for a second.

'Hey kid,' someone shouted. 'Leave your helmet on. It's toxic out there.'

Wilfie, fighting claustrophobia, willed himself to calm down, not to mess things up. He walked on, the spacesuit forcing him to walk with long, slow steps. The movement swept him back to the airlock of Grey Cottage. Standing in the bath with his dad and Pip. Pip too small to reach the lock. Floating out into the corridor. Gravity free. His dad fighting off aliens. The memory flooded him with a burst of joyful energy, a thrill of excitement. He could do this. He could do this and make his dad proud.

'Wilfie! Take this.'

Wilfie turned. Amongst the crowd, he could see a tall man pressed against the wire, waving something. It was the man who had run to their house, who didn't know how to drink mint tea, who had eaten mum's damson cheese. Weston. What was he doing here? Wilfie had liked him. It was good to see someone who was a link with home amongst so many strangers. Wilfie took slow steps towards him.

'Wilfie,' Weston seemed flushed, out of breath. 'We – that's me and Miriam my... well Miriam – wanted to give you this. A map of the moor. Grey Cottage.'

Weston was struggling to stuff the map through the fence. Miriam, beside him, took over with small, nimble fingers.

'Turn round Wilfie and I'll push it into your rucksack,' she said.

Wilfie rocked as Miriam tucked the map safely home.

'Done,' she said.

'Just a good luck thing. Help you find your way home,' said Weston, his voice punctuated with little squeaks. 'Although you could just follow the North Star, of course. Just wanted to make doubly sure… that you… that you… come… that you—'

'Weston wanted to wish you all the luck in the world,' said Miriam, smiling.

'Thanks,' said Wilfie. The lady had a lovely smile.

'It's a wonderful thing you're doing,' said Miriam. 'Good luck.'

She wrapped her arms tight around Weston's waist and Weston put his arm round her shoulder and pulled her to him. They looked so together. Wilfie wished he had someone special coming with him. Like his dad.

'Bye then.'

Wilfie turned and trudged towards the tram. On the first step, he paused and waved. The cameras behind the wire clicked and clicked and clicked.

The tram, powered by an overhead cable, set off to the centre of the Growlers Drop.

'Incredible isn't it,' said Luke, nodding at the landscape. 'To think, one meteorite hit did all that. Fields, woodlands, farms, villages – boosh – thrown aside; those closest to the centre – boosh – vaporised. Lucky for us. We got the perfect launch pad.'

'Yes,' said Wilfie, not understanding.

'Just imagine,' said Luke, 'when that meteorite smashed into the earth – bam! – ancient bedrock, undisturbed for millennia, was instantly compressed by the impact and then rippled out becoming fluid, spreading like a puddle of thick cream.'

'Here we go,' said one of the other astronauts.

'Poor kid. Captive audience,' said another.

'That meteorite was suicidal. It smashed into earth, was

blasted and shattered by shock waves from its own impact and then, whoa, then things really started to hit off. It roared into a ferocious nuclear heat, taking out great chunks of target rock. And then,' Luke waved his arms, gesticulating, despite the awkwardness of his spacesuit, 'then the cream turned and flowed back into the dip, leaving collapsed crater walls. As it met in the centre, it rose up, up, up but, whoa, at the same time started cooling, sinking back, leaving a flat, circular plateau. Like I said, the perfect launch pad.'

'So now you know,' said a voice from the front.

Wilfie was glad to know. It was the sort of thing he wanted to know – craved to know. He was only distracted from the moment by his gloves, which were too big, and the good luck biscuit tin which kept slipping off his lap.

The tram came to a jolting stop. His fellow passengers got out, not bothering to listen to the recorded destination message.

Watch your step.

Remember to take all your belongings.

Wilfie clambered out, stumbled and fell. The shuttle towered above him, no longer a sliver of a silver spike, but a majestic gleaming structure of power and wonder. Charged with excitement, his dreams on the brink of coming true, Wilfie climbed onto the first step. Reaching the eighth, he remembered to turn, to wave. Far away, behind the fencing, was the blurred line of the media. A wave he hoped would go to his mum, to Pip and maybe even his dad.

70. Tiny dot

Look up and see a shooting star. A meteoroid burning up as it enters the Earth's atmosphere. A meteor is born and dies. A bright light to nowhere.

Skillern was on fire. Mr Chillworth had rigged up a projector to connect a TV to the big screen on the stage in Founder's Hall. The whole school was going to watch the launch live at a special after-school assembly. On his instruction, Mrs McDuff had invited the local paper. This was big news for Fellows Light and Skillern did not, on any account, want to miss the opportunity to put the school – and his inspirational leadership – on the map. Teachers were instructed to escort parents, arriving to pick up their children, into the hall. The local journalist and a trainee photographer turned up. Pupils, teachers, Skillern, even mums and dads were pressed for interviews and to pose for photographs: 'arms straight up to the sky, make yourself look like rockets'; 'take giant space steps'; 'pretend you're floating without gravity'. Children who caught school buses were allowed to go home, but Skillern made sure everyone else stayed. By four-fifteen, Founder's Hall was packed – it was quite a party atmosphere. Skillern made a speech, but no one was listening. They were glued to the screen, which showed a reporter outside a tumbledown pavilion.

'Inside, our young astronaut is changing into his spacesuit. What could be going through his mind? Ah, I think they're coming out. Their tram will soon be heading to the launch pad with Wilfie Whisper aboard.'

Children in the hall were getting restless.

'Is that the moon?'

'Where are they going?'

'Shhh. Look.'

The shuttle came into view. Tall, white, other worldly. The hall fell silent.

Five astronauts got out of the tram and climbed up into the shuttle.

'Which one's Wilfie?'

'Wait. Just wait,' commanded Mr Skillern.

A smaller figure was still getting out of the tram. He tripped and fell. A murmur swept around the hall. A couple of youngsters cried out. The figure pulled himself up and took slow steps forward. He made it to the shuttle steps. On the eighth step, he turned and looked straight at the cameras facing him far, far away from the other side of the perimeter fence. The picture on the school screen zoomed in on his helmet and there you could see the small face of Wilfie Whisper peeping out.

'Ohh, it's Wilfie,' cried the children, giggling and pointing. 'Look! Look, it's Wilfie!'

Wilfie waved, as if he could hear them, and smiled. The entire hall waved back – even Mr Skillern. Then Wilfie turned and climbed the last steps and disappeared through a doorway into the shuttle. A metal plate slid across the opening, sealing the astronauts inside.

And then nothing.

Chatter started in the hall.

'What's he doing, Mr Skillern?'

'Has he forgotten to turn the engine on?'

Everyone laughed, then a red light seeped out from the base of the shuttle.

'Look!'

The hall fell deadly silent, all eyes on the screen, transfixed.

Agatha was clicking at the remote. How could she have wasted time writing when Wilfie was about to launch?

And now the screen wasn't working. She tuned and retuned from the remote trying to remember what Jacob had said. At last, the screen flicked on and split into six, but each square was fuzzy. She placed a chair under the screen. It wobbled as she reached up to turn the dials.

'Mum! Mum!'

Pip burst in, throwing down his school bag.

'Mum! Wilfie… what's that?'

'A screen,' said Agatha. 'To watch Wilfie. But I can't get it to work.'

'Quick mum. I want to see him.'

Agatha fiddled, twisting and turning the dials again. The screen suddenly burst into life. She clicked to screen three and there, in the centre, was the shuttle.

'Oh Pip!'

She jumped down, mesmerised by the thin sliver of silver, knowing inside was Wilfie, their beloved, adored Wilfie, son and brother: the little fellow with green eyes, bright red hair and freckles, who had lived and breathed space from the moment he was born. Green eyes, bright red hair and freckles like his dad, who had lived and breathed space but whose dreams had been shattered. And now Wilfie was carrying the torch.

Dreams to reality.

Earth to the above and beyond.

From now to the future.

Passing all understanding.

71. Shaken to pieces

Not so strange. Millions of meteors are burning up in the Earth's atmosphere every day.

Inside the transfer shuttle the other passengers were strapped into their seats, tipped back to horizontal, ready to go.

'Put your tin in the locker, young man,' said Luke. 'Don't want it flying around pulverising us. Then get strapped down. Best get a move on. Not long before take-off. This thing doesn't hang around.'

Wilfie pushed his tin into a locker and climbed onto the last empty seat. It tipped him back to horizontal. Straps clicked fast around his small body, holding him down: ankles, legs, diagonally across his stomach and chest, his arms and his head.

A message buzzed: 'Prepare for take-off.'

Way below him, Wilfie felt vibrations build. Gentle at first. Then fierce. They took hold of the capsule and shook it – thousands of tiny movements, back and forth, back and forth. The capsule fought as the engine built up thrust to a terrific level while holdbacks clamped the shuttle down – until finally they gave in and released. A roar and the capsule shot away.

The acceleration pressed Wilfie deep into his seat, pummelled the breath out of him, violently shook his small body. Without warning, the forward acceleration stopped. Wilfie's head smashed against the front of his helmet, the straps drove painfully into his limbs, his stomach, his chest. Then the capsule, vibrating wildly, blasted away again. Wilfie tried to stay motionless, but his body was thrown against the straps holding him down. Noise was inside and around his head: he was panting hard, yelling. The second acceleration peaked and slowed. The pressure of the straps eased, and where the yelling had raged in his head, there was now silence.

Wilfie closed his eyes, overwhelmed by the momentous events of the last three minutes. He had made history. But it didn't feel as if he was there: he felt detached, floating outside his own being, as if watching – rather than being – the first child to travel out of the Earth's atmosphere. Floating before him he saw the smiling faces of hundreds, thousands, billions of children turning into brilliant stars. One was moving towards him. His own face. Wilfie Whisper, sixty-two miles above Earth, crossing the Karman Line which pinged as he raced through, snapping like an elastic band. Out of Earth's thermosphere into the exosphere: the sphere words combining and circling, turning into a three dimensional turning sphere, sphere, sphere. Wilfie tried to drag himself back to full consciousness, to break out of whatever dream world he had fallen into. Open your eyes. Open. The effort was immense. Half-open, lids flickering, he could see the white of the capsule and he knew it was real. He focussed on the porthole, which was moving. No, not moving. It's cover sliding open, revealing a circle of perfect blackness; the infinity of space. Space. Right outside. A light, dazzling white, crept into the circle. He tried to pull himself awake. Following the light came turquoise: the most intense turquoise imaginable – brilliant and beautiful, curving into the circle, filling its space. Wilfie had never seen it before, but he knew it like a friend, like someone he loved. Earth. But its brilliance forced him to close his eyes. And with eyes closed, he couldn't hold onto consciousness. He began to drift away. To travel on. To travel further into space.

Down on Earth, away from the city, up from the village, across the moor, down the track to Grey Cottage, Agatha held Pip as they watched the screen, mesmerised by the light blasting from the shuttle's base, deafened by the sounds of a groan that might be a roar, a sigh that might be thunderous and the shimmer of metal that held a child so precious, rocketing at an inhuman speed into the nothingness of above. The shuttle became a tiny dot on the screen and was gone. The vision had become a memory.

72. Airlock

Gravity holds together the stars, the dust, the gas, the dark matter to create galaxies. Millions or even trillions of stars.

A gentle tapping on his helmet brought Wilfie round. He was floating, bobbing against the shuttle wall.

'Hey, how are you doing?'

'You took that launch pretty rough.'

Luke and the other travellers were floating as if it was normal.

'You gave us a fright there. Been out for hours. Just floating around. All curled up like a baby in the womb.'

Confused, Wilfie could only make out a blur of white metal, shadows, shapes of grey, bright whites, moving and drifting in and out of one another. His head ached and the taste of meat in his mouth rolled his stomach. It reminded him of the pork lunch at Fellows Light. But he wasn't at school. He was floating. He took off his helmet and let it go. It hung there, barely moving. Excited, despite the throbbing in his head and bruising of his body, Wilfie propelled himself over to a porthole.

And there it was. Not a dream anymore. Actually there.

Space.

Wonderful, incredible space!

Wilfie pressed his face close to the glass. He cupped his hands tight around his eyes to cut out the internal light. The blackness was out there. Deep, haunting, velvety blackness. As his eyes adjusted to the dark, the blackness filled with stars. Not just the number of stars you see from Earth, but millions and billions of stars. Not twinkling, but holding still and bright. This was what he had come for. This was what he had dreamt about.

'We're due for docking at No 49 in six minutes,' said Luke. 'Better get that helmet back on.'

The shuttle closed in on No 49 Pennyside and locked on to the outer airlock door. A complex manoeuvre simply done: the shuttle and No 49 travelling at the same speed took the speed away and made it as easy as driving a car into a car wash. The door to the shuttle slid open.

'Have fun.'

'Cheerio.'

'See ya' later.'

'Hey, don't forget this.'

Luke handed Wilfie his tin. Passengers waved and gave him the thumbs up. One didn't even look up from his book. His departure seemed as normal as getting off a school bus.

Wilfie, still lightheaded from the flight, waited in the airlock, unnerved to find himself alone. On one side, the shuttle rumbled and roared, detached and moved off. On the other lay his new home. Wilfie waited for the inner door to open. But it didn't. He knew there would be a delay. He knew that from standing in the bath at home with dad and Pip, giggling, full of excitement, expectation. He knew the delay was a to ensure pressure was synchronised, oxygen levels corrected. In the bathroom, they waited and it was fun, but here it was claustrophobic. Breathing was hard. Small, sharp little gasps.

Not giving him enough.

The sound of the speedy sucking in of air, the rapid rising and falling of his shoulders, scared him. There was tightness in his chest, round his throat. His breathing came faster, faster, but his lungs seemed emptier. Cries of 'Mum!' 'Mum!' merged with his outward breaths. His eyes stung and tears came, working their way down his chin, his neck. He pushed the handle to the inner door but couldn't grasp it, his hands slipping inside the gloves. He wanted to pull them off, but they were part of his suit; his life support system. He was shouting now. Screaming. Screaming over the pounding in his chest. The squeezing. The unbearable crushing. He couldn't breathe yet in his terror he was panicking, wasting his last breaths. He gasped and sucked. Gasped and sucked. Above the noise in his head, the noise of his fear, echoing round the airlock, he heard a banging. Rhythmical. One beat a second. Then a beep and clicks. The inner door swung open, revealing a glowing light. Striped. Colourful. Bright. Wilfie stopped shouting. He stopped crying. He breathed. Calmer and with a final effort, he dragged himself through the hatch and collapsed into No 49 Pennyside.

He had arrived.

73. Up there

Think of everything you can think of and you will think of the Universe. The Universe is everything that exists: planets, stars, galaxies, all forms of matter and energy. Absolutely everything.

Wilfie's new home was colourful. The usual shades of white, grey and silver had been banished in the specially designed No 49. Gee & Gee had gone to town and their colour selection was bizarre. Horizontal stripes started as dark red at base level and moved up through oranges to pale yellow and white at the top. Although, in orbit, the top could be the bottom. It was like living inside a giant lollipop. It was fun – Wilfie loved it.

It was also clever. When you were floating about, you knew what level you were at and which way up you were. Dark for the lower levels, light for the top. A simple device but useful for a novice astronaut.

'Looks amazing, hey, Wilfie?'

A voice floated, disembodied, into the cabin. Wilfie swivelled round.

'Screen one. Your friendly techie team is here ready to welcome you aboard. Can you pull yourself down?'

Wilfie turned to look at the six screens positioned midway up the capsule an orange stripe. He turned upside down to pull himself closer. The movement made his stomach contract, nausea sweep over him. But the thrill of hearing a human voice, of seeing human faces, made him euphoric.

'Yes! Yes! I see you.'

Wilfie gave them an upside down wave.

There was a second or two delay as Wilfie's message flew home. His simple gesture sparked a frenzy of delight: the technical team, squeezing together to get a look into Wilfie's cabin, waved back, yelping and hitting high fives.

'You can take your launch suit off now. T-shirt and shorts are fine. Take your helmet off first, then pull at the toggle to release your suit.'

Wilfie removed the helmet – flicking up the clips left him exhausted. He grasped the toggle that hung behind his back and pulled down. The suit released and peeled off easily. He let it hang in the air.

'You need to keep tidier than that. What would your mum say?'

'Can I see mum?'

'Yes. Switch on screen six. Should be showing already.'

Screen one showed the OSH Technical team. Four had Evie waving and laughing, but no sound. The rest were blank.

'Six is not showing anything.'

'Have a go at tuning it.'

There were lots of dials, none labelled. Wilfie twiddled a few but didn't dare go too far. One might be an ejector seat. Or decompress the cabin.

'I don't know how to tune it.'

'Didn't you cover that in your training?'

'We didn't have time for communication training,' interrupted another techie. 'I can talk you through it, Wilfie. On screen six, see the second dial to the left? Turn it clockwise. No anti-clockwise.'

Wilfie turned the dial. Nothing.

'It might be the third dial. I'll check.'

So Wilfie spent his first ten minutes in space trying to tune in from the above and beyond down to earth, to the moors, to the screen hanging in the kitchen of Grey Cottage.

Eventually someone found the right page in the manual.

'Wilfie, I've got it. Tune dial three and four at the same time.'

Screen six flickered. And then there it was: a black and white version of the kitchen in Grey Cottage. He could see a mug on the table, Pip's school bag on the floor, a stool in the wrong place with the sieve on it and his old pencil case. What was that doing out? The objects gave him a piercing feeling in his side.

'Mum. Mum?'

After the launch, Agatha and Pip ran outside and looked up to the skies as if they might see the rocket. Something tremendous had happened, but what could they do about it? Agatha was in turmoil: ecstatic in her exhilaration, fearful of the perils Wilfie faced.

'Where is he? Where is he?' shouted Pip.

But he could see nothing, so he ran back in to the house and looked at the screen. Then out again.

'Can you see him, mum?'

'No, but he's somewhere up there.'

'If you look and you're looking in the right place but you don't know you are, you might be looking straight at him and not even know,' said Pip,

'Maybe. Let's look really hard.'

Agatha and Pip looked up to the sky and tried to converge their view on the same spot miles and miles away, hoping they might be looking straight at Wilfie.

Then Pip ran into the house to check the screen again.

'Mum! Quick! Quick!'

Agatha ran.

Wilfie was there.

'Mum. Mum?'

For a split second, she saw him. Wilfie grinning. Wilfie anxious. Wilfie on his great adventure. Wilfie saving mankind.

Then screen six clicked off again.

'Home's gone,' said Wilfie to the techie team, 'Can you get it back? Please.'

'Nope, not now. We'll fix it in the morning when the team are back on site. If you need anything before then, ask Sinai.'

'But I do need something. I want to see my mum.'

'Sorry, we only do emergencies after hours. Have something to eat.'

'How do I do that? And who's Sinai?'

Agatha flicked to technical.

'Screen six isn't working.'

'Mrs Whisper. You just caught us. We've been chatting to Wilfie. He's doing fine.'

'Why can you see him and I can't?'

'Probably because you have a home screen – nowhere near as powerful as ours, I'm afraid. Did you sign to say you were happy with it when it was installed?'

'Yes, but I didn't know. Can you get me a better one? Please.'

'We'll never get one in time. And the home screens are never much good anyway. You could watch on normal telly? The flight's being covered on all channels.'

Agatha knew there was little she could do. She tried to hold the picture of Wilfie in her heart, that moment of joyous connection, but the image was slipping away. All too soon. She felt a rising panic. And desperate to do something she took a school exercise book from Pip's bag and tore out the empty pages. Then she opened Penelope's leather book and started copying out texts again. There were so many places to leave the powerful words, so many people who needed them.

She searched Grey Cottage for more paper: paper bags, blank end pages in books, the edge of an old newspaper, the back of official forms, the bottom of a letter fining them for failing to send in Pip's medical update on time, the side of a school report. She worked on and on, tens of texts multiplied into hundreds. Far too many for one pencil case so she packed them into empty cartons, old boxes, anything she could carry round with her, to be taken to unknown destinations – the texts to be hidden in secret crevices, discovered and their words released, flung out into the world to do their work: changing hearts and minds. Those not stuffed away, she stuck to the walls of Grey Cottage, pinning them to the kitchen beams, pegging them out on string like bunting. It was a risk having them out in the open like this, but it felt right.

Seeing the words hovering in the air made her feel closer to Wilfie and Peter and all that was precious to her.

74. Woolly hats and constellations

Beware. If you get too close to a black hole you'll get sucked in and can never escape.

After the launch broadcast, gifts for Wilfie started mounting up at OSH. Go. 4. It. on reception had the pleasure of sorting them out. She updated Franklin every time he walked past.

'Look at this, Mr Black.'

She was wearing a woolly hat patterned with constellations.

'It came with a note: *To the little lad heading for the stars. I knitted this hat for you and hope it will keep you warm should it be chilly up in space. I have no idea, but I do know it's generally cold when I go out for a walk before bedtime. Much love. Gladys*'.

'And chopsticks, Mr Black. Honestly, they want Wilfie to see if he can eat space ready meals with chopsticks. Bit late for that.'

'Did you know, Mr Black, that other countries are interviewing kids to send up? Don't want to get left behind, do they? But it's nothing like as good as being first. And Wilfie will always be first. To the end of time.'

75. Ostrich flying

What am I? I orbit the Sun, but I'm not a planet or even a dwarf planet. But I could be a comet or an asteroid. Or some other sort of small body. Yes. I'm a small solar system body.

Ostrich Advertising Agency felt the benefit of Wilfie's flight immediately. News spread that the genius behind the idea to send a child into space was Weston W B Wright.

'Better response than our normal marketing mailshot,' said Miriam, carrying a coffee into Weston's office. 'I've had call after call after call all morning.'

Weston was euphoric, not because of the calls, but because Wilfie had arrived safely at No 49 Pennyside – a moment of overwhelming relief. And yes, phones ringing at Ostrich HQ were also a cause for celebration. At last, he was making a name for himself. He allowed himself some satisfaction in that. Things were looking up. He even considered taking on an assistant.

'Watch it,' said Miriam. 'Don't get too big for your boots. The bubble could burst.'

Weston put his index finger in his mouth, pulled at his cheek and let go, making a popping sound.

Miriam returned to her desk, trying to restrain her laughter.

Weston couldn't resist. He made the popping sound again.

'You big baby,' she called. The door was ajar and Weston could see that she had got out her mirror and was putting on some more make-up. Why on earth did she need any more make-up? There was only him to impress.

'I'm pleased for you, Weston,' she called. 'You're becoming quite a sensation.'

'So, do you think it's a good idea after all? After what you said about a kid in space?'

'If he comes back safe and sound – well, yes, I do. And to think it was all your idea. That really is something. I'm proud of you.'

Weston did not know how to reply. Proud of him. Miriam was proud of him. He still couldn't think of anything to say.

He made the popping sound again and was rewarded with a peal of laughter.

76. Feverfew
What is a dwarf? An object orbiting the Sun that is rounded by its own gravity but is not gravitationally dominant in its orbital area is a dwarf planet. Unless it's a moon.

The day after the launch, Agatha awoke early – the spectacle of the shuttle propelling itself into the endless blue had filled her dreams and was still vivid in her mind. And what of Peter? What was he thinking? Perhaps he didn't even know? What madness that was – something so close to him, of such significance – for him not to know. But what could she do about it? The best thing was not to make a fuss. Let things take their course and then Peter would be home. Best to fight her battles under the radar. Her heart skipped a beat as she imagined how, later that day while cleaning, she might slip a text between some cans of beans in one home, behind a picture frame in another. It might make a difference.

After Pip got on the minibus, Agatha cycled to the village and then on to the hospital to visit Penelope. She cycled fast, enjoying the burn in her legs, the pounding in her heart – feeling empowered by physical exercise. Penelope was wide awake, alert, and they discussed plants, flowers, growing and took an imaginary walk around the old lady's garden.

'What's happened?' asked Penelope, after a moments silence. 'Something has.'

Peter always said he could tell what she was thinking. Penelope seemed the same.

'I've read the book,' said Agatha.

Penelope smiled.

'Good. That's very good. I'm pleased for you.'

'I've been writing notes too,' said Agatha. She reached into her bag to get out the pencil case, confide in Penelope, but at that moment the doors to the ward swooshed open followed by the squeak of trainers on linoleum.

'Frankie,' said Penelope without looking. 'He's read it. Many times.'

Frankie, athletic, compact, strode towards them. Agatha thought of all the verses that must be stored in his mind. She imagined she could see them coming out of his head. Like speech bubbles. Knowing all those words, carrying them around with you would make you different, wouldn't it?

He kissed Penelope on her hollowed cheeks and pulled out a bunch of white and yellow feverfew from his rucksack.

'For you, Auntie Penny. Another offering from your garden. A bit bashed, I'm afraid.'

He hunted around for a vase to put the flowers in.

'Sorry, dear. Vases are always on the move,' said Penelope. 'As soon as the flowers have died, they whisk the vase off to another patient. Sooner if the patient dies first.'

They all laughed.

'One day, I'll bring in your own vase, Auntie, or maybe two or three. Twenty should do it. One for everyone in the ward.'

'Lovely, Frankie. You're a good boy. You look after me. And everyone else when you're not off working all hours. This is Agatha, my only other visitor and the dear girl who keeps my house clean and tidy. She talks to me about gardening and family and even you, Frankie.'

Frankie laughed.

'Good to meet you at last, Agatha.'

They shook hands across Penelope's enfeebled body.

'Sit me up a bit, would you?'

From either side of the bed, Agatha and Frankie puffed up her pillows, propping her up.

'I never had the operation, you know. When I got into surgery, they said I didn't need it. There was some mistake. That's probably why I'm here now. The operation might have killed me.'

Frankie held his Auntie's hand.

'You're looking good, Auntie.'

'You look tired Frankie. Not doing too much running, are you? Or looking after everyone else and forgetting about yourself. Or is it the job? Or your girlfriend?'

'I don't have a girlfriend. Not exactly.'

'Oh?'

'It's early days.'

'The job then?'

'There's a project. It's challenging.'

'He never tells me what he does,' said Penelope, turning to Agatha. 'Doesn't like to talk about it. Or doesn't think an old lady like me will understand.'

'You would understand, Auntie,' interjected Frankie. 'I've told you. It's property. And mining. A big company. But there's nothing more to say – apart from I'm leaving as soon as I can. I'll look for something nice and local to my circle. Perhaps apply to Wigmore's. What do you think?'

'You'd be hopeless. You'd take too long asking everyone their life story. And you could do better than that.'

'But I've spent years doing better and you get trapped. You know that.'

'Yes, yes, I was horribly trapped once. Top of my tree and supposedly in control. But the funny thing was that I was actually being controlled by the organisation that I was meant to be controlling. I didn't realise it to begin with, but I was losing myself and morphing into the person they wanted me to be – not me at all. One day, I woke up and realised that they controlled everything about me. Where I lived, what I wore, even what I ate.'

She coughed. Frankie passed her a glass of water.

'Thank you, Frankie.'

'Talking too much, Auntie.'

'But I shouldn't have worried,' she went on, 'because they got rid of me in the end. Yes, they even controlled my demise. One minute I was respected and living in circle five – it went with the job – then I was shooed out to circle fifteen where Frankie insists on living. But I wasn't going to languish there. So I used my savings and moved out to the village where I could be happy with my little garden and my gooseberries. I don't regret my downfall one bit. My mind's my own again. Be strong enough to hold on to that, dear. Don't let them take your mind. It's yours, and that's the way it should be. Otherwise it's curtains.'

'So, there you are,' said Frankie. 'Better your own life where you want to live. Normal places. Normal people.'

Penelope laughed. 'If you want normal don't go to Wigmore's. They're all barking. Especially Mr Wigmore himself.'

'How about you, Agatha?' said Frankie. 'How's your husband? Your boys? You've got two, Auntie Penny told me. It must be a noisy household.'

The questions came so out of the blue that Agatha barely knew how to answer them.

'It is, when we're all there.'

'So, where are they?'

'Where? My husband is, well, not home. And my son is... One is at school.'

'And the other one?'

'The other one is so far away, I don't know if he will ever return.'

It was the first time she had voiced her fears. It felt like a confession, and a dangerous thing to say. Spoken out loud, her worst fear seemed to become more real. She stared at the tiny blue veins on Penelope's hand. Life so fragile, moments together so precious. And this could be one of the last for Penelope and Frankie. She felt her presence was wrong; aunt and nephew should be alone. But she was too late, Frankie was standing up to go.

'I hope things work out for your son, Agatha. I really do.'

'So you're off, dear?' said Penelope.

'Yes, I'm afraid so. Work to do.'

'Off down the tin mine?'

Frankie kissed Penelope. She took his hands.

'Soft as a feather. That's office work. You can't fool me.'

Frankie kissed her again.

'Bye auntie. Keep reading your detective novels.'

'Frankie,' said Agatha.

'Yes?' said Frankie, turning back.

'Would you give these to someone. Anyone.'

Agatha hand shook as she unzipped the pencil case, stuffed with ten, twenty, thirty pieces of paper. She thrust a fistful into his hand.

'Put them anywhere. People's pockets. On a bus. Through car windows. We've got to do something.'

Agatha watched him stride down the ward and disappear through the swing doors, her heart racing.

The hospital was busy when Agatha left Penelope's bedside half an hour later. She felt emboldened by her encounter with the old lady and her nephew and her fear of doing the wrong thing, making things worse, dissipated.

Words spilled from Agatha's lips before she had even considered what she was about to do. Like Peter, like Wilfie, like Penelope, like Frankie, she would choose her own path again, try to do the right thing.

'Staff Welfare?' replied a passing nurse. 'Level Four.'

Agatha raced up the stairs. The door to Staff Welfare was closed. *Entry Strictly By Appointment Only*. Agatha ignored the sign and pushed open the door.

An elderly man leapt up from his desk and marched towards her, sought to block her way, trying to intimidate her with the fury of his beady black eyes.

'You can't just come in here without an appointment. You need an appointment. It says on the door,' he started, his voice high-pitched, aggressive. 'You must have—'

'Peter Whisper,' interrupted Agatha, striding towards him. 'I've come about my husband, Peter Whisper. There is something you must do.'

'You can't just come…'

Agatha pushed past him and sat down at the meeting table in the centre of the room.

She was ready.

77. First night, first day

Speeding through the solar system: the fastest meteoroids race through at twenty-six miles per second.

'Bedtime. Change and wash. Lie down. Night night. Lights out.'

Sinai, the inflight vocal timetable, was fast becoming Wilfie's closest friend. Obediently, Wilfie lay down on the seat that tipped back to be his bed and the straps closed around him, cocooning him for his first night in space. Exhausted, he was happy to drift into sleep.

Eight hours later, the straps released, waking him. Sinai was calling him for breakfast, and he was starving.

'Breakfast. First meal of the day. Set you up. Don't skip it.'

Wilfie explored his larder, trying to work out what the food was. Fossilised in transparent plastic were slabs of cottage pie, fish pie, chicken casserole, beef stew and macaroni cheese, flattened cheeseburgers, strips of dried fish and sealed boxes of sandwiches and packets of biscuits, chocolate bars, sliced apples, peanuts.

Wilfie chose a ham sandwich and chocolate, too hungry to work out how to heat anything up. Before he had finished eating, the techies came on screen.

'Morning. Morning. Today we want to get some tests done. Then we'll film you living in your new environment. Show how easy it is for the body to adapt to space. Then on to some fun activities. Capture you enjoying free time in your home-from-home. A piece of cake. How does that sound Wilfie?'

Wilfie was in his element. His heart raced as he thought of the days ahead. Tomorrow, OSH Technical was going to send No. 49 on an asteroid mining trip, a routine remote-controlled exercise. All Wilfie had to do was sit and watch from the safety of the Pennyside. But the promise for the day after that was what thrilled him beyond measure: a spacewalk. His stomach knotted at the thought of telling his dad. Peter would throw him up and down in the air, telling him he was champion. There would be risks of course; Wilfie knew OSH were testing him, checking he was capable. Of course he was capable.

'If it all goes well, we'll send you out onto the asteroid with your hammer, bucket and spade. Chip a bit off and bring it home,' said a techie.

'Show those big burly miners it's just like a day at the seaside,' said another. 'Child's play.'

Wilfie spent the first morning doing tests and activities. They became boring: timing his breathing, lifting weights that had no weight while the OSH Technical team watched him and recorded his results. He couldn't see the point, but he did his best.

Mundane everyday activities followed. He brushed his teeth three times. Smiling. They wanted to get a good shot. He threw a ball in the air five times and caught it. Having fun. Although the ball just floated. No momentum. It was hard to make it look like a good game. For an hour, he lay on his bed reading a comic, moving position again and again, so he looked comfortable. Relaxed. He was not.

'Lunchtime.' came the voice of Sinai.

Wilfie did not need reminding.

'Can I have something hot?'

Bored by the tasks, he was starting to feel lonely. Comforting food would help. Something homely.

There was an exchange on the techie screen.

'Where's Ginger? Ginge, can you show Wilfie how to heat up something for his lunch.'

A peaky young man buzzed in.

'Don't see why not. Hello, Wilfie. I'm your dietician for the voyage. I'll help you prepare a range of delicious meals to keep you bright and breezy throughout your flight. How about a high protein cheeseburger? I'll take you through how to heat it up. No proper cooking involved. Just heat and unwrap. Hang on a sec.'

All Wilfie had to do was take a packet and pop it in the microwave. He had never used a microwave before but it seemed pretty simple, and anyway, the temperature would be set and controlled from Earth. Not like in the pictures he had seen of the first astronauts squirting liquid borscht from tubes into their mouths to stop it floating all over the place. These days you could heat up a decent meal. Like a cheeseburger.

'Right, pick up the packet and put it in the microwave. Ok, I see you've done that. Ten seconds should do it. Good. It's ready… now. Press the release button to the left. Your right. I meant to the right. Good. Good. You will need to eat the cheeseburger straight from the packet. Strap yourself down in a sitting position. Careful it's not too hot.'

Wilfie took the cheeseburger out of the microwave

and pushed himself down to strap himself into the seat. Accidentally, he let go of the cheeseburger and it floated out of reach. It took five minutes to unstrap himself, retrieve it, get strapped back in again and peel open the packaging. The cheeseburger tasted of cardboard. His mum never let him eat cheeseburgers. She said they tasted of cardboard and she was right.

As Wilfie took a second bite, there was a terrific bang. The whole Pennyside vibrated. Chunks of the inner walls fell off, fragmenting into tiny mites of dust, filling the capsule with fog. The nutritionist screamed as Wilfie's straps snapped open and he pitched forward, face first, into the screen, splattering it with lumps of burger, bread, cheese and tomato sauce. The travel capsule had been hit or had exploded.

Within three seconds, all communication with Earth was lost.

78. The swirling black
Rings round my planet. Gas giants Jupiter, Uranus and Neptune have rings but Saturn's are the most visible.

Weston W B Wright straightened his tie and tried to smooth down his spiky hair as he bounded into the offices of OSH, ready for his meeting with Franklin Black.

'Hello, Mr Wright. How are we today?' said the brunette on reception. 'Take a seat on the pod and I'll ring through to Mr Black to let him know you're here. Would you like a glass of iced lime water with a sprig of fresh mint?'

Weston was fidgety. The whole idea of having a kid up in space was getting to him again. Wilfie was up there – they had got that far. Now they needed to get him back. It was an exhausting roller coaster of excitement and terror. OK, it had been his idea, but since Miriam questioned it, he had felt as though he was on the edge of some unspeakable catastrophe. Even though she now kept saying it was wonderful and she was proud of him.

The difference was that she hadn't shared damson cheese with the family. It was no longer just a kid. It was Wilfie. The boy who had told him how to follow the North Star back home. Danger for the little fellow lurked perilously close to glory. Last night, Weston had been tormented by a recurring nightmare: Wilfie being sucked into a black hole, swirling, pulled down into a deep vacuous nothingness. Skinny white arms reached out to him, a high, squeaky voice begging to be saved, imploring, barely heard over the rush of swirling black. The child whirled round faster and faster and faster, his red hair burning up in flames, getting further and further and further away until all Weston could see was a tiny speck of red circling round and round, pulled by an immense centrifugal force, and then – pop! – gone. Panicking, Weston had fumbled for his bedside lamp. A click and light flooded his bedroom. For a moment, everything seemed normal, then in an insane moment he had rushed to the window: the child was standing on the window ledge, tapping, wanting to come in. All Weston had to do was open the window and grasp his tiny hand – it was tiny, fairy-like – and pull him in to safety. But Weston had been mistaken. There was no child at the window for him to save, just twinkling stars mocking him. The child was up there in peril and he, Weston W B Wright, put him there.

Today – walking to work, sitting at his desk, eating a garibaldi, taking the bus to the OSH offices – the image of Wilfie, trapped, swirling down a black hole, pounced again and again. He should have listened to Miriam. But as he lost confidence, she seemed to be gaining confidence in the project: Wilfie had, after all, made it safely to No. 49 Pennyside. And OSH had promised it was one hundred percent safe. They had said so from the start. It would all be fine.

Weston declined the iced lime water and paced over to the pod area. The bank of TV screens hanging to the left of the large window were on mute. All of them were tuned in to the state news channel. Why, thought Weston, are newsreaders' teeth always so white? Their hair so annoyingly perfect? Weston pushed his fingers through his thick hair. He must get it cut. Short. Sharp. Look the part. He yawned. Boy, was he tired. The info line running along the bottom of each TV screen flashed. A big news story must be coming in. He watched as the words ran at speed.

Breaking news. First child in space. Breaking news.

Weston tensed. He tried to lipread the newsreader. The tape ran on.

Breaking news.

First child in space goes missing.

Internal explosion or collision?

'Turn it up!' Weston yelled. The receptionists looked up, shocked.

'Never mind.'

Weston ran to the lift and stabbed at the button. Twice. Three times.

'You can't go up alone. Wait.'

But Weston was already on his way.

The lift only took eight seconds, but it felt like an eternity. The poor little guy. What had happened? How could he have ever suggested such a stupid, stupid idea?

He had been playing with a kid's life.

Wilfie Whisper.

Lost in space.

It was all his fault. Just to make a bit of money. Just to prove that he could come up with a good idea. Good idea? The kid was probably dead. His little body burnt up. Or exploded into a million fragments. Scattered about the universe. Or compressed until he popped. The door slid open. Weston stormed out, straight into Franklin's swanky office.

79. Open wound

Which team are you? Inner or outer? Terrestrial or gas giant? Smaller or larger? Rock and metal or hydrogen and helium? Mercury, Venus, Earth and Mars or Jupiter, Saturn, Uranus and Neptune?

Wilfie had not been enjoying the cheeseburger, but that wasn't a problem now. He would never get to eat the whole thing. The microwave had overheated and blown up, causing an instant drop in internal pressure. As he was thrust against the screen, Wilfie inadvertently flicked a switch, turning off contact with the technical team. Fear, arguments, panic broke out back on Earth. The press who had made camp in the techies' office at OSH sent notices to their teams around the world that there had been a catastrophic explosion or a collision and that the first child in space had gone missing. Probably lost forever.

For Wilfie, the smoke-filled cabin was disconcerting. But he knew what to do. He remembered his dad's words from times working in the woodshed.

'Find the source of the problem and switch it off.'

The microwave, a tiny rectangular box set into the wall, had blown out. An opening like a wound in the neat panelling was sending out crackles and sparks. Wilfie had no idea how to turn it off. But he did know how to turn contact with Earth back on. He cleared the screen of cheeseburger with his sleeve and reconnected with OSH.

'That you Wilfie? You OK?'

'I'm OK. But I lost my cheeseburger. And can you see the microwave? It exploded.'

'Who the hell left that on?'

'I'm a dietician, not a technician.'

An argument broke out amongst the OSH techie team. Whose fault was it? Who was in charge of health and safety? How could they have lost contact? Nearly blown up the capsule?

'Sorry, Wilfie mate. Cold meals for you from now on.'

'That's OK.'

Wilfie gave them the thumbs up.

And back down on earth a phone rang in Franklin's office to confirm all was back under control.

80. Look your best

Watch out. If you are a comet and fly too close to the Sun, frozen water and carbon dioxide on your surface will rapidly change to gas, forming a coma. A tail and a glow. Sublime.

'Invitation,' said Weston, grinning and waving a card at Miriam. The ups and downs of the day at had left him reeling. Remembering how he had charged into OSH HQ that morning, thinking they had the blood of a kid on their hands when it was just an exploding cheeseburger, left him deeply embarrassed. Still, he had only been reacting to what he had seen on the news. And Franklin had taken his outburst well. So well, in fact, that he had given him an invitation. The invitation he was now waving at Miriam, if only she would pay attention.

'Reception for the OSH team this evening. World history has been made and all the movers and shakers who have made it happen are on the guest list. And that, Miriam, includes Weston W B W of Ostrich Advertising.'

Miriam looked up, her eyes darker and deeper than ever, brimming pools of loveliness within her perfect oval face.

'Wonderful news, Weston. You are on the way up.'

'It says "plus guest".'

Lazarus raised his head from his work looking hopeful. But Weston was definitely not going to take Lazarus.

'What would they think if I took along an ostrich?' Weston said, trying to bat away the possibility. 'As a joke, obviously.'

Miriam had returned to her typing. Her breathing had deepened, the rise and fall of her floaty orange shirt trying to keep up with the rise and fall of her chest beneath.

'Don't suppose you would like to come, would you, Miriam?' said Weston, fiddling with a pile of paper clips on her desk.

'I would like that very much.'

She was looking at him, taking him in with her beautiful dark eyes. Perhaps she really did want to come. With him. Weston found it hard to believe.

'Excellent,' he said. 'So… well… that's fixed then. We'll go straight after work.'

'No, I'll meet you there. I need to change first.'

'But you look spot on as you are. Just perfect.'

Her orange shirt was flamboyant, artistic, challenging. He liked it.

'I'll see you there, Weston. I want to look my best. It's not every day you're asked out by a superstar.'

Weston could hear the admiration in her voice, see desire – was it desire? – in her look. Miriam desired *him*? If Lazarus hadn't been there, he might have taken her in his arms and kissed her and... who knows what? But Lazarus was there.

'OK,' said Weston. 'I'll wait for you in reception. They have these big green pods. I'll be sitting on one of those. Might even have time to retrieve my pen lid.'

Weston strode into his office and stared out of the window. Things were looking up. He thrust his hands into his pockets. In the left was a piece of paper. Where on earth had that come from? *Pure in heart. Peacemakers.* Rather beautiful. Had a good ring to it. He would try and drop it into conversation. Might impress Miriam. Yes, it might be just the thing.

Space mining or two people falling in love – which is the greater of the two? Franklin Black was expected to make a speech at the party. All the big chiefs were gathering: government officials, industry leaders, the press. And there was plenty to say. Wilfie Whisper's arrival at No. 49 Pennyside was a triumph for the kid, for OSH, for the world. Incredible. And the effect on the industry had been dynamite; interest from mining companies was flooding in. He would push this, talking about the endless supply of precious metals out there. Transforming life on Earth. Big issues. Exciting stuff.

The lift door opened. Weston and Miriam made a messy entrance, tripping over each other, awkward in each other's presence: a couple yet not a couple, smiling, catching each other's eye, looking and not looking, taking each other's hand, slipping as one into a relationship. Bert Weinberg, the lead OSH designer, made a beeline for Miriam and was soon blasting her with space talk. She was holding her own and Weston, a step behind, was watching her every move, listening to her every word. Weston threw in a comment, interrupting Bert and making Miriam giggle – a delightful pop of laughter. Weston was proud to be with her – anyone would be proud to walk into a room with a woman like her.

Franklin decided there and then that as soon as this project was over, as soon as Wilfie had returned to Earth, he would make his escape from public life, from big business, from circle five. He had been preparing his exit for a long time. He knew where to go. He knew the people. The place. Nothing special, but, equally, very special.

He folded his speech in half. Folded it again. As a waiter passed by carrying a tray of used champagne flutes, Franklin slipped the unwanted speech on board. It was a cracker of a speech, bound to impress, and he did not want to risk being headhunted again, to be tempted away from happiness. He stepped forward for the last time as the man at the top to welcome the guests. After the party, as soon as the last guest had left, he hurried out of the building. He had to get to circle fifteen, to Wigmore's, before it closed. His heart raced as he planned what he was going to say to the woman with the beautiful smile on checkout seven.

81. Artichokes

You can never get to the edge of the Universe however hard you try. Walk in a straight line indefinitely. On and on. On and on. And you will end up where you began. It's because the Universe bends.

Agatha, I love you. If I lie on my bed, my head touches the wall and I can see out of the high window opposite. The full moon floods my enclosed world. Familiar brightness, an unfettered freedom to just be, overwhelms me in a wash of sadness. I have had bad thoughts about asking to leave. I know it's wrong. Nobody asks if they can leave. It is a privilege to take part. But Agatha, I have had enough. If I was as small as Pip, I would squeeze through that letterbox window and float away. If I shrink, I can push out the glass and metal surround and squeeze through the gap, float away over the lake, across the pine forest, over the city, the villages, out over the moor and home to Grey Cottage. To you, Agatha. I'll lie beside you between cool sheets, holding you, feeling the smoothness of your skin, listening again to the rise and fall of your breathing. Be close to all things precious. I try not to think like this too much. It is destructive. Undoing my Reconstruction. But tonight the moon makes it impossible. The light is throwing pictures on the wall. I see the garden at Grey Cottage, and you Agatha. Yes, you! I call out, but you don't reply. You are busy breaking off a long dead stem from an artichoke plant, which stands tall and eccentric against the skyline. I see its giant spiky purple flowers, black in the night light, and its truncated stalks, beheaded by an earlier harvest, waiting, uncertain. You are pulling at one.

It looks strong, but its use as a bearer of fruit has long gone, its base no longer fed or protected. It gives up with ease, thick stalked but hollow. You break it in two and tie a string round one half, pushing it into the warm earth. You walk in a straight line, unravelling the string, then make a knot round the second stick and, like the first, push it into the ground. From your apron pocket you take your sharp knife and cut, releasing the ball. And now you have seeds. A jam jar of seeds. You are pressing them into the earth, keeping in line with the string. You do your best for each seed, planting now when it has the best chance of fulfilling its life, the moon working with you, encouraging the start, the growth. All the while you are humming, talking to each seed as you put them to bed. And now you are you. Washing the dirt from your hands. Climbing the stairs. Running a bath. You sit in steaming water, back bent forward, bumps of spine, bubbles of soap running from your shoulders. Strands of black hair, tied back, escape over the white nape of your neck. As you stand, naked, I am ready to wrap a towel round you and take you to bed. But somehow the boys are in the bath too, playing the spacewalk game. A piece of paper floats above. You are trying to catch it. 'The form,' you are crying. 'Don't let them take the form.' You jump, trying to snatch it, leaving the boys alone in the bath to wait for the pressure in the airlock to readjust. Pip is pointing at the door, begging Wilfie to open it. 'It's too high. I can't reach.' But Wilfie is no longer there, and the door to the landing is open, swinging on its hinges. 'Wait. Wait for me.' Pip is clambering out of the bath to follow Wilfie. But the landing has vanished and Pip perches on a tiny ledge of floorboard, in danger of being sucked away into the black infinity of space that has opened up below and above and around him; a vast, gaping void, punctuated with billions of stars, not twinkling, but still and staring. Pip cries into the deadening silence. But there is no sign of his brother. Wilfie has disappeared, swallowed by infinite nothingness.

82. Catching ducks

Three quarters of the universe is missing. Dark energy. Dark matter.

'OK, Wilfie. Day two. Your mining trip. Up for it?'

Wilfie was certainly up for it. He was impatient for adventure.

'So, the idea is you'll travel to a near asteroid which we know has palladium deposits. Silvery white stuff. We'll try and scrape some off the surface. Not exactly sinking a shaft – for now, it's crumbs from the surface. But even that's pretty exciting.'

'Really exciting,' said Wilfie. 'I can't wait. What do I need to do?'

'Not much. Attach yourself to your bed while we lift off from the rim. Could be a bit of rocking around on release. Then it should be a smooth ride until we reach the asteroid. You'll get an out-of-this-world view from the window.'

Lift off from the rim was rough. Despite the straps, Wilfie was shaken about, knocked again and again against the side of the shuttle, pain chipping away at his excitement, building his fear.

But it was over in less than five minutes – the battering stopped, the straps released.

'Hooray, we're off,' said the techie. 'Look at that beauty float on its way. What a dream machine.'

'All OK there, Wilfie?' said another. 'Give us a thumbs up. We've got the press in. They'd love a picture.'

Recovering, Wilfie did his best to smile. Turning to the window, he forgot his bruises, his homesickness. He was travelling through space all by himself. A space explorer! An adventurer! He squinted, trying to focus on a single star. But each star split and become two, then he was looking at ten, no, hundreds at a time. He tried to see to the end of things, to peer as far as he could – knowing it was impossible – but driving himself to look deeper and deeper, the question that always fascinated him, rolling in his mind: what is past that? And that? And that? What was on the other side of everything?

It was going to be a short expedition: an hour to reach the asteroid, an hour on the surface with the automatic scrappers, and two hours back – something about it being slower to travel backwards in space.

'Another world record,' said the techie, as No. 49 touched down on the asteroid.

'Look at that. A perfect landing.'

Wilfie's heart was in his mouth as he gazed down at the asteroid, only feet away. He was captivated by the beauty of its ruddy, pitted surface, the mystery of its birth, its very existence in the solar system. He could see lustrous streaks of silver worming their way through the rocky surface. He could see palladium. Palladium! No wonder people kept saying space mining was the future. Gripped by the wonder before him, Wilfie barely noticed the grunting, the juddering as the Pennyside cutters were lowered. Then the scrapping started, sharp blades scything back and forth, back and forth, rocking Wilfie like a baby in a cradle, making the hour pass by in a heartbeat.

'Time to return to the rim. Straps on, Wilfie.'

The techie's voice brought Wilfie's thoughts – floating out way beyond the capsule – back to the practicalities at hand. He strapped himself in as No. 49 Pennyside rose and headed back smoothly, perfectly under control. But when the moment came to reattach to the rim, the buzzing chat from the technical team fell silent.

'Hi. Hello. Anyone there?' said Wilfie. 'Hurry... the rim... it's right... someone...quick! Oh please. Be quick.'

'Watcha, young man,' came a voice at the last second. 'Sorry to give you a fright. Just changing shifts back here. Looks like the last lot missed that docking. Have to go round again. Hold tight.'

So No. 49 was forced to go round again. And again.

'Those guys should never have checked out,' came the complaints from Technical. 'If you mess it up once, it's darn hard to get these things to attach.'

Again and again, the technical team tried to dock No. 49 onto the rim but, again and again, they missed. And again and again the press in the studio fired questions.

'Can you tell me how you're feeling right now, Wilfie?'

'What do you reckon your chances are of a successful reconnection?'

Time and again, the techies tried to reassure.

'Don't worry, Wilfie, we'll catch it next time.'

To Wilfie, pushed about, battered and bruised, their voices, their questions, were torture; he was desperate for the terrifying hit and miss to be over. A nightmarish memory of his dad trying to catch something and repeatedly missing wormed its way into his mind. A little boy squeezed in a crowd of strangers, pushing and jostling him, the sickly smell of sugar and cooking fat hanging in the air. Everyone was laughing at lots of jolly ducks, whirling round and round on a current of water; bright yellow ducks with scary smiles pressed into their orange beaks and little wire hooks on their heads. His dad had a long pole with a hook on the end. He was trying to catch a duck for Pip, but he kept missing. He kept missing and everyone was laughing at him. Strangers laughing because even little children could catch a duck and this big tall man with bright red hair couldn't do it – too clumsy. He got close but then – whoops! – he missed. Every time, the duck escaped, bobbing off to go round again. But the people laughing didn't know that the man was Wilfie's dad and he was trying to catch a duck with his left hand because his right hand had been in a bad accident. Wilfie really, really wanted his dad to catch a duck and show people he was clever and had nearly been an astronaut – but wasn't because he was too tall – and then had nearly been a surgeon – but wasn't because of an accident – and was a hospital porter and did lots of pushing and pulling even though he had a bad hand. Wilfie hated the people laughing at his dad. He hated being jostled by them. Pushed about. But his dad didn't seem to mind. He was laughing too. Wilfie willed his dad to catch a duck to prove himself, but he never did. And now, every time the OSH technical team missed the rim, Wilfie felt that same helplessness, the same tears of frustration – now mingling with terror – threatening to fall.

On the eighth attempt, No. 49 looked as if it was going to make it.

'Nicely done. Nicely done. Hold steady.'

'Hey, we're too close on the near side. It'll never lock on.'

'No way.'

'Prepare yourself, Wilfie.'

'Brace.'

'Look out!'

'What?' yelled Wilfie.

No. 49 smashed into the rim. Contact with Earth was lost, the lights went out and the temperature in the capsule began to drop.

83. Hitting the rim

What is the Universe? Mainly dark energy. Some dark matter. And a bit of ordinary matter.

Agatha's muscles screamed as she cycled fast to Fellows Light, the revolutions of her wheels chiming with her breathing: Wilfie, asteroid, Wilfie, asteroid. The shoddy screen in her kitchen had failed her again. No sharp image, just a grainy flicker, on, off, on, off. Off. Despairing, she grabbed her bicycle and cycled to school. She would witness Wilfie's moment of glory there, his wonderful adventure, his incredible, history making asteroid mission. She might make it in time. She had to make it in time.

Skidding into the car park, she cast aside her bike, raced across the playground and down the long corridor of the classroom block. Ahead were double doors into the hall. Through the glass panes, she could make out rows of pupils, chattering, fidgeting, flittering like the pieces of paper on her kitchen beams. There was a blank screen on stage, facing them, waiting. She entered. The back row was empty save two figures on the left of the aisle. From the thin outline of one and the comfortable outline of the other, she recognised the detestable Mr Chillworth and the likeable

Mrs McDuff huddled together, deep in conversation. Agatha crept to a back row seat on the right. Any minute now, she would be able to share Wilfie's adventure and she could not wait. She hugged her bag to her chest as if it was Wilfie. Knowing it was stuffed full of texts, she felt comforted.

Mr Skillern marched onto the stage. He was grinning, rubbing his hands, his forehead glistening.

'This is a great and glorious day for Fellows Light,' he announced. 'I am…'

The live stream came on, interrupting his speech. An image, clearer than any Agatha had watched in her kitchen, flooded the screen: a view of space outside the Pennyside. The exact same view as Wilfie's. And it was beautiful. An infinity of black. Stars holding still in their brilliance. Fairy dust of the Milky Way. And, close up, the edge of the capsule – a gleaming silver grey.

Agatha gasped, her sound lost in the noise from the schoolchildren who cried out, bounced on chairs, jumped up, pointed – all thrilled beyond measure.

'And remember, as the Pennyside journeys from rim to asteroid, from asteroid to rim, with its precious cargo, we are seeing the future of mining.'

The TV commentary cut a stark contrast with the mysteries on screen; the voice so normal, so everyday.

Agatha could have watched forever, but the children in the hall were not so patient. After the initial excitement, they were restless.

'Is Wilfie nearly there?' piped a child near the front.

'What's happening?'

'Mum,' whispered Pip. Her heart leapt as she saw her younger son creeping along the empty back row of seats towards her. 'I saw you coming in. I want to watch with you.'

Pip squeezed up close to her.

'I think we've missed it,' announced Mr Chillworth, standing up. 'I think the capsule is returning from the asteroid, not going to the asteroid.'

What did Mr Chillworth mean? How could they have missed it? Was the programme on too late? Did the trip take less time than planned? The confusion brought with it a prickle of fear.

'We could watch the capsule attach to the rim,' suggested Mr Chillworth.

'You can now see the rim to the bottom right of the picture,' said the commentator.

The fuzzy outline of some sort of red metal object dipped in and out of focus.

'Reattaching to the rim is a tricky manoeuvre, but the OSH team is well trained and … oh! I don't believe it, the Pennyside has hit the rim but failed to attach…'

'It's missed,' cried someone, as the capsule hit the rim and bounced away.

'Watch it. Watch it. Oh, it's missed again. The capsule has missed the rim again,' came the commentary.

'Will it catch it next time?'

The children started shouting, pointing at the screen.

'Missed it.'

'Missed it again.'

'I don't like it.'

'Come on, Wilfie,' breathed Agatha. 'Come on.'

'Wilfie,' said Pip, his face white, tears brimming.

'Things are looking a little serious up there. If the Pennyside doesn't attach soon…'

As the capsule tried yet again, it hit the rim and rocked violently.

'Poor Wilfie.'

'Don't like it.'

'Why's it not working?'

'Wilfie!' Agatha's shrill cry of fear went unnoticed. Nobody turned to look. They were all transfixed by the drama on screen.

'I wouldn't like to be in that little boy's shoes right now,' said the commentator.

'Is Wilfie alright?'

'Is he going to die?'

'Will it explode?'

'No, no,' breathed Agatha, squeezing Pip.

The capsule smashed into the rim again with such violence that it ricocheted away, spinning at dizzying speed and out of sight. The screen filled with the blackness of space, then froze.

'It's gone! I'm not saying we've lost it but it's not looking good. Not looking good at all.'

Pip dug his fingers into Agatha's arm.

Children were shouting, wanting answers from their teachers. For everything to be alright.

'Is Wilfie lost in space?'

'Where's it going?'

'What a tragedy. What a tragedy. First child in space lost.'

'No,' screamed Agatha.

Children started crying.

'He's dead, isn't he?'

'Turn it off. Turn it off.'

Mrs McDuff hurried on to the stage.

'Well, children,' she said. 'Wasn't that exciting? I'm sure Wilfie will be safe and sound any minute now, back on the rim. What do we think he found on the asteroid? Hands up.'

Agatha, paralysed by fear, stared at the blackened screen. A figure moved into the black. Skillern. Of the blackness but separate. He marched across the stage, down the central steps and up the aisle towards her, his jaw clenched, eyes bulging, face contorted in a nightmarish grimace. He was coming to tell her news she already knew, news so dreadful she wanted to close her mind off, turn back time to Grey Cottage, to the family, whole again: Peter, Agatha, Wilfie, Pip.

But Skillern didn't stop. He marched straight past her and out of the hall.

Agatha's mind was racing. Wilfie needed help. Right now. What were they doing? OSH. The people who sent him. They must help. Do everything possible. Fast.

Agatha grabbed Pip's hand, pulling him to his feet, and tore out through the double doors. They ran down the corridor, across the playground, up three flights of stairs and burst into Skillern's office.

Skillern was already there, but in the wrong place. He was perched on the edge of the open sash window, one leg over the sill, his eyes bloodshot. Fear emanated from his whole being.

'No!' cried Agatha, rushing across. 'Don't you dare.'

She pulled at his jacket so he fell backwards into the room. He crashed heavily to the floor and lay there, motionless, as if the fight had gone out of him.

'Get Evie on the phone right now,' she hissed. 'Right now! Find out what's happening. Where Wilfie is. Right now.'

As the Pennyside smashed into the rim, there was a roar of screeching metal then silence, darkness, cold – an intense cold that stole away Wilfie's breath and became an agony. He tried to feel his way to the controls, to get help, hear a human voice, find out what to do, but the blackness and freezing cold disorientated him. Shivering, he curled up into a ball, trying to hold onto the last remnant of warmth in his body. But the shivering would not stop – his body not his anymore, just a vehicle of pain and spasm. Locked in his foetal state, he floated in the black. Drifting.

And then it didn't matter anymore.

He was back at Grey Cottage: a winter's night, the window open – freezing cold in the room but warm in bed. He liked it like that.

'Pip, are you awake? Are you there?'

Pip was coming towards him holding a candle, his eyes bright, merry.

'Shall we play the spacewalk, Wilfie? Or make another planet? You choose, Wilfie. You choose.'

Spacewalk? Planet? Planet? Spacewalk?

The candle was too close to Pip's face. It might hurt him. Burn his skin.

'Pip!'

The candle was burning brighter now, so bright he couldn't see his little brother anymore. It had become an exploding brightness that was everywhere, hurting his eyes, painful, and then it became the brightness of the lights of the capsule and the stripes and the screen and his shivering stopped and the pain of the cold was leaving him and someone was talking to him, asking him things he couldn't answer.

'You OK, Wilfie? Sorry about that? You OK? Say something, Wilfie.'

But Wilfie, his head throbbing, body exhausted, could only curl up and fall asleep, just as he used to in Grey Cottage.

'He's back on the rim,' whispered Skillern.

Agatha snatched the phone from him.

'Mrs Whisper?' said Evie. 'Gosh, that was a close call, wasn't it? But yes, back on track now. Pictures looking good. You might be able to chat to Wilfie from your screen when you get back home.'

Agatha felt the tightness round her throat, the unbearable cramping in every muscle and sinew of her body release with such force that she thought she might fall. She clung to Pip, both laughing and crying, hurrying as one to the window to see the sky, to be closer to Wilfie. Agatha leaned her forehead against the bar of the sash, giving thanks.

The doors were opening across the far side of the playground and children were dribbling out – quiet, heads down, some crying, like ghosts of their former selves, bewildered by fear and dread. Agatha lent out, shouting to them, breaking the spell.

'Wilfie has attached to the rim. He's alive. He's safe.'

The children, as one, stopped and stared up at the window, pale-faced, suspicious.

Pip, tucked between Agatha and the window, cupped his hands to his mouth.

'Wilfie!' he shouted, waving to the skies. 'Hello, Wilfie!'

The children lifted their faces, scrunching up their eyes against the brightness, as if they might see Wilfie looking down at them.

'It's true,' yelled Pip. 'Wilfie made it to the rim. Hello, Wilfie!'

Belief spread amongst the children and they began to wave, to chatter, to laugh, to shout along with Pip.

'Wilfie. Hello, Wilfie!'

The sounds of life floated up to the window, to Agatha and Pip and, beyond, to Wilfie in the skies above.

Agatha, euphoric, reached into her bag and took out a fistful of texts and threw them out of the open window, where they spread out and came fluttering down onto the playground. Pip joined in and together they scattered the texts like seeds over a field as the children below leapt and danced to catch them.

You are the light of the world.

Be kind to one another.

Children, obey your parents in all things.

Love one another.

Every good gift and every perfect gift is from above.

'Take them home,' laughed Agatha. 'Take them home.'

Turning from the brightness of the window, the inside of Skillern's office was dark, oppressive. The headmaster, sitting ramrod straight in his chair, was staring at the wall, his cheeks white as chalk.

'I apologise,' he said, without looking at Agatha.

'I apologise,' he repeated. 'I thought I was doing the right thing.'

The right thing? He had put his own ambition before the life of her son. He had lied to her. Deceived her. Tricked her. And then – what was he doing by the window? On the brink.

'I still think I was,' he added.

He put his head in his hands and sobbed, his entire body shaking.

Agatha would not judge Mr Skillern. He had a cause

and he was passionate. But the way he had gone about it had been wrong. She knew he would suffer.

At her feet, Pip was gathering stray texts.

She bent to pick one up. The words on the scrap of paper dipped and danced, swam and soared in her mind, chasing a memory: *sins like scarlet… crimson… wool…*

With hope in her heart, she placed the paper on Skillern's desk; a forbidden text fired right into the heart of authority, a text that had the power to heal.

84. Sharp stones

The Sun is white. Not yellow. From Earth it looks yellow because of the Earth's atmosphere. But at six thousand degrees centigrade, it can only be white.

A click at his door woke Peter. It was the smallest of sounds but in Reconstruction all sounds had meaning, all were significant. Click. A card was being pushed in and out of the lock. He waited for the door to open, for the woman to come in and order him to the library or exercise or a counselling session. But the door didn't open. Peter tentatively pushed down on the handle. The act surprised him. He was not used to doing things for himself. It felt dangerous.

Holding the handle down, he pushed against the door. It opened, revealing a dimly lit featureless corridor stretching away. At the far end, just before a turn, he thought saw the shadow of a figure slip away but he couldn't be sure. Otherwise it was empty.

Was this a chance to leave Reconstruction? To escape? Images of people he loved, of the possibility of being with them again, swirled before him in a rising vortex of hope. Agatha, Wilfie, Pip.

And Dorcas. Dorcas was somewhere in this labyrinth. Should he try and find her? Escape together. Was it a chance to escape? Or was he being released? Perhaps it was a trap. Confusion gave him courage. He had been given a glimpse of freedom and he would take it. Later, he would demand Dorcas's freedom too. And all the other poor souls. His book. He would need his book. He picked it up and started down the grey tube corridor.

But something felt wrong. He turned the other way, hurrying. A fork. A T-junction. Left? Right? Right? Left? An endless curving corridor. And then space opened up before him: the reception area, softly lit. And the lockers where he had left his clothes. Each opened to his touch, but each was empty. He needed his clothes. He stood for a moment, unsure what to do, head bowed, feeling the chill of his bare feet on the cold concrete floor. Then he strode to the door – to the outside world – pushed on the steel handle. Lightly, willingly, the door swung open.

Peter stepped out into the darkness.

He was going home.

85. So far
Moonmoons are moons that have moons.

Sinai woke Wilfie for day three.

'Wakey, wakey. Dress and breakfast.'

Wilfie, head thudding, floating in and out of dreams, could hear the techie team talking to him from the screen. He pulled himself from sleep.

'Sorry, Wilfie mate. After yesterday's performance, there's no chance of returning to the asteroid. I'm afraid your bucket and spade spacewalk is off. Can you hear me,

Wilfie? The spacewalk is off.'

'What do you mean?'

'Look, I know you're disappointed but there's nothing we can do about it. Orders of the chief technical officer. He reckons it's enough of an achievement for you to be up there. He doesn't want any stunts or tricks. Just wants you back safe. Mission accomplished.'

'So, what are we doing today?'

'Playing safe. A rerun of day one. Tests. Activities. Just get through the day. Pick-up is scheduled for tomorrow morning. You'll be back home for the weekend. Safe and sound. Project over.'

Wilfie turned away from the screen. Not doing the spacewalk was a bitter blow. To be up here in space, but not out in space felt like a failure. He was failing his dad – not fulfilling the dream. He tried to picture his father but the images vaporised before they could form. He put one hand in the other and squeezed, trying to recapture the safe feeling of holding his dad's hand. He knew his dad would always look for another way. Surgeon to porter. But what could he do?

The techie was droning on about tests.

'Hey, are you listening, Wilfie? Wilfie?'

Wilfie turned, not to acknowledge the man on the screen, but to look at the bank of dials to the left. To one in particular. Decompression.

He could hear his dad's voice in the bathroom playing the spacewalk game: 'Decompression. Takes a long time. Don't want to get the bends.'

He remembered the night his dad had lurched from side to side on the landing, grasping his elbows, his knees.

'Oh, I feel dizzy! Oh, the pain in my arms, my legs, my joints. Oh, the pain.'

He had fallen to the ground, rolling and groaning.

'I have the bends! Pip, you didn't decompress the cabin. Now look at me! Ah!'

Wilfie would give it more time. He flicked the switch to start decompression. He didn't want to make the same mistake as Pip.

'Wilfie, are you with me?' asked the techie.

'Yes.'

'Right, let's start with your breathing. Blow into the oxygen tube and I'll take your measurements.'

That was another thing. He would have to start pre-breathing pure oxygen. It was one hundred percent out there. He needed to be prepared.

At the end of day three, Sinai called bedtime. The techie team had gone off at lunchtime, having run out of steam, bored with the tests and activities. Wilfie, left to his own devices, checked his spacesuit, looking for holes, weak points.

'Night night,' said Sinai as the lights in the capsule dimmed.

Wilfie closed his eyes and did his best to imagine his dad, his mum and Pip. He knew what he was about to do was dangerous and wanted to say sorry to them in case it went wrong.

'I'm going to do the spacewalk, mum,' he said, as he had in his bedroom, in the kitchen, in the garden, on the moors. And the sound of his voice talking to his mum made her real.

'Yes,' she replied. 'Of course you are. And I'm proud of you. So very proud.'

'So you don't mind, mum?'

She was picking blackcurrants, the bush heavy with berries.

'For you,' she said, smiling, holding out her hand.

Clustered on her pale, delicate palm were four currants, each black as space, round as a planet.

Perfectly ripe at that very moment.

He took the blackcurrants, one by one. Sweet, sharp, delicious.

'Thanks, mum.'

She raised her hand and waved at him, her eyes bright with love.

The time had come. Wilfie pulled himself to the screen and broke all the OSH rules. He flicked the bank of screens off, cutting off contact with Earth. For the first time, he was all alone in space. Alone, yet his confidence was growing. He put on his spacesuit – easier this time, familiar. He picked up the helmet, the white space gloves, opened the capsule door and pulled himself into the airlock. He closed the door behind him, pulled the oxygen feed mask from the wall and started breathing in pure oxygen. He guessed – hoped – about an hour would be enough.

'This is the big adventure,' his dad was saying.

He was standing in the bath with Pip. Dad was building up expectation.

'Team Whisper. Prepare for exit. Concentrate on your breathing. Concentrate on keeping calm for the first few minutes outside, then we'll go exploring. Final check. Helmet: check. Tank: check. Tether: check. Five. Four. Three. Two. One. Wilfie to exit. Wilfie to exit.'

Wilfie took a giant step out of the bath and pulled back the lock.

'Ready to exit,' reported Wilfie.

'Good luck, Team Whisper,' said dad. 'Look out for aliens.'

Then the hatch opened and Wilfie Whisper floated out of the airlock into the unknown.

I am part of space at last. I am of space, but separate. I am existing in this endless void. I see Earth to one side, beautiful and blue, a crescent, a light and a blackness beyond. I think of the lands of the world and can see them all: white arctic to endless orange deserts; hot green jungles and their living creatures – the ant on a leaf bound by the same instinct to live as a fleeing antelope, a blue whale in the deep, a cormorant diving from cliffs, flying over the oceans that swell from flattest calm to stormy seas. There, on the blue, are the people of the world, with all their strange differences. Can I see the billions moving about their daily life? Can I stretch out and hand food to the hungry, water to the thirsty? And people stretching back in time. Where are they? Died on Earth, but still of the Earth? I think of my family. The invisible links. The closeness, even when we are so far away. Life binds us together – an existence outside our existence. And turning, I see in a blackness that is not a colour but a beauty that you breathe, these planets, these stars existing out here in space, so far on and on and on. Are they waiting to be discovered, to exist because we know of them? I turn and look at objects lit by the sun. Planets, stars, moons, the glow of the Milky Way, great dust clouds, planetoids, asteroids. So many it is hard to face them, going on further and further away. And I know more exist beyond that and that and that. Objects, places, great vacuums of blackness that have no life. But their dance gives them life: turning, spiralling, orbiting, exploding. Somewhere amongst the millions are my friends, first known hanging from the beam in my bedroom –

Mercury, Venus, Mars – the terrestrials linked to the Moon. And beyond are the outliers – Jupiter, Saturn, Uranus, Neptune. Known and unknown. Their life is a different one. Different from mine and the invisible thread that links me to those below. To mum and dad and Pip. That is life.

It is true that what Wilfie did was thought impossible. Astronauts train hard for spacewalks: hundreds of hours underwater, running on the treadmill, building muscle, obtaining peak fitness. Yes, they are among the fittest people on Earth. And the training is relentless: for emergencies, mechanical failure, breakdown of portable life support systems. And always, always they maintain second by second contact with ground control.

But that was the past.

Wilfie's mission was to prove the future – that space belongs to everyone. And, for Wilfie, it was even more than that; he would take on what had been denied to his father. So, when Wilfie stepped out into the blackness, he knew there was a chance he might not come back. But that was a chance he wanted to take. For his family.

86. Top of the track

Where do you come from, cosmic ray? From deep in outer space. What are you made of, cosmic ray? Highly energetic particles. Highly energetic particles. Highly energetic particles.

Agatha was washing clothes. She loved to wash. She wasn't good at collecting clothes in an orderly way or sorting them into particular piles. She just washed whatever needed doing at the time. Items lying on the floor, draped on a chair, left on the bed as she made her way to the washing machine. A discarded shirt. A pair of Pip's pants. A sock left on the landing. Like picking flowers, she would stop and take anything that caught her attention. Every item was a pleasure to Agatha, a link to those she loved. She gathered an armful of clothes, took them downstairs and across the stone slabbed kitchen and pushed them into the mouth of the washing machine. They lay in the silver drum waiting to be tossed and turned, whizzed around backwards and forwards, hot, cold, spun and rinsed until they were done, waiting to be plucked out and hung out on the line to dry.

Peter's journey was long and painful, his bare feet cut and bleeding. But he forced himself onwards, jogging when he could, never stopping, night or day. No one bothered him. Homeless people were a common sight. He found his way out of the pine forest to a main road which led to the city. He followed the outer city road until it peeled off through the gap between the hills, down into the village, past Fellows Light and onto the road that led out to the moor. Close to home, he marched on, his mind fixed on his return, holding tight to the book, ignoring the sharpness of stones that sliced into the soles of his feet or grazed his elbows, his knees, when he stumbled and fell.

The moor stretched out before Peter, a beautiful, living green, bright with yellow gorse and purple heather. Flocks of birds swooped black against the pale skies, showing off their freedom. Peter struggled up the lane to the top of the track. When he saw Grey Cottage below, like a mirage, he wanted to cry out, to call for his family, to share his joy. But his lips were cracked and his mouth so dry that no sound came. He looked in wonder: the vegetable patch, full and rambling, the kitchen door ajar, Agatha's bike against the wall, the washing line pegged with clothes – the story of a family. But the washing line disturbed him. Something wasn't right. There were not enough clothes. Clothes that belonged to Agatha. Clothes that belonged to Pip. Nothing of Wilfie's.

Wilfie had gone.

Peter cried out, his throat dry, rasping, and collapsed to the ground, too afraid to go down the track, too afraid to go home.

Across the valley came the drone of the school minibus. It reached the top of the track. A small boy hopped off and hesitated. There was a man hunched on the grass, his red hair matted, his clothes filthy, his feet blackened and bleeding.

'Dad?' the little boy said.

The man turned to look at him.

'Pip.'

Peter put out his arms and Pip rushed to hug him, careless of the smell of sweat, the filth, the unfamiliar roughness of the cheeks. Father and youngest son.

Then a boy standing behind Pip came forward and put his arms round Peter and hugged him tight.

'Dad, I did it for you. I did the spacewalk,' he whispered.

'Wilfie. Oh Wilfie… you…'

Peter could not speak anymore. He held his two boys close, pulling the three of them into one. And there they stayed awhile, a trinity of love.

'Mum,' said Wilfie, breaking the spell. 'Come on Pip, we should get mum.'

The boys peeled away and raced down the track.

Peter struggled to his feet, wanting to follow but, feeling the pain, the exhaustion, he waited.

Agatha, alerted by the boys, ran out of the house. She stopped in her tracks when she saw Peter, taking in the shadow of the man she loved, the man she so desired to be with, to kiss, to hold. Risk had been rewarded at last.

She hurried towards him and took his familiar hands in her own, transfixed by the sight of their entwined fingers. He seemed unable to look at her.

'You've been away a long time,' she whispered.

'You were right, Agatha,' he said. 'About Wilfie. I should never have risked his life. It was a terrible thing to do.'

'He wanted to go' said Agatha. 'He did it for us, Peter. And now he's home. And so are you.'

Peter stooped to pick up the book he had carried for so long from the grass. He handed it to Agatha.

'It explains everything.'

Agatha caressed the book's cover as if the contents were already known and beloved. She then took his hand and led him down the track into Grey Cottage, pulled off his filthy grey shorts, shirt and underwear and dropped them on the kitchen floor. Peter stood before her, thin, naked, wounded, while hundreds of little pieces of paper, stuck to the walls, pinned to the beams, pegged along strings, fluttered and rustled, whispering a welcome home. Peter followed Agatha upstairs, where she filled the bath and washed the dirt and mud, the sweat and tears from his battered body. Clean, he stood while Agatha dried him, cherishing his nearness, loving the promise of times to come. She dressed him in clothes that felt so much like home that he cried.

'Sit down. Let me see your feet.'

Kneeling before him, she held his feet in her hands, turning them to look underneath. Shredded from walking barefoot, his cuts bled softly.

'I need a bandage,' said Agatha. 'Oh, I'm sorry Peter. I still haven't got any.'

'Doesn't matter. Doesn't matter a bit.'

Agatha put her head on Peter's lap and he lay his hand on her neck. She thrilled at his touch, so longed for. Then she stood up and took him by the hand, wanting him to fill the space in their bed, for her to feel him there, know that he was home, know that they were together again, tender touch to tender touch, stroke of skin to stroke of skin, loving heartbeat to loving heartbeat.

87. Porter. Cleaner. Wilfie. Pip.

How far is it for you to travel our galaxy, brave Sun? One hundred thousand light years. Prepare for my return two hundred million years from today. Farewell.

Much later, when the moon was up and the sun pale, Peter went with Wilfie to the workshop. Home had revived him and love had given him strength, and now there was something he needed to do. Something to protect his family, to keep them to together until the wide world beckoned again. He lifted a chain and padlock that, at one time, had locked the gate at the top of the track from a hook where it had hung since Agatha and Peter had decided they had no need for it. The padlock was rusty. Peter took down the dark green oil can with its long spout and little lever. It had been in the shed long before Peter and Agatha had arrived at Grey Cottage, its life once busy, then forgotten and unused. But now, like everything, it was needed again. Thick oil poured into the lock. Peter waggled the key back and forth. The lock loosened and opened. Back to life.

Agatha, busy tying up beans, watched as Peter, with the lock in his hand and chain over his shoulder, headed up the track. Wilfie was bobbing alongside him, red hair blowing in the evening breeze. He disappeared behind the height of the wall but she could still see Peter.

'Where's dad going?' asked Pip.

'Not far. He'll be back in a minute.'

The soil beneath her feet was bright with green shoots – life pushing itself up through crumbled earth. Agatha cleared weeds from around a young spinach plant to give it a chance. Pip was hiding in a row of blackcurrant bushes. She pretended she couldn't see him.

'Pip? Pip? Where are you?'

There was no answer but she knew he was there.

At the top of the drive, Peter dropped the chain onto the tussocky grass. Against the wall was the wooden five-bar gate where, as far back as Wilfie could remember, it had lain, unused. Now, with his dad, he pulled at the grass, the thistles, the weeds that held it fast.

'So you did the spacewalk then.'

'I couldn't have done it if you hadn't been there to tell me what to do, dad. The decompression. The oxygen. They tried to stop me going. But I had to go. For you, dad.'

Together they rocked the gate, pulling hard. The grasses, ripped from their roots, let the gate burst free, throwing Peter and Wilfie onto their backs. Laughing, Wilfie wriggled to rest his head on his dad's chest. The sky was darkening, the stars coming out, one by one. Wilfie stretched out a freckled hand as if to touch the dreamy infinity and the inky blackness beyond.

'I did it, dad. I did it for you. But I'm glad I came back. I'm glad we both came back.'

Wilfie jumped up and pulled his dad to his feet. Together, they dragged the gate shut and circled the chain round the post. Wilfie threaded the padlock shackle through the chain then back into its bar, clicking it too. Locked.

'Have you got the key, dad?'

The key sat on the flat of Peter's hand, a sliver of silver.

'You look after it,' said his dad, folding Wilfie's hand around the key. 'It'll be safe with you.'

Wilfie gripped it tight and together they looked out at the moor, at Grey Cottage and all it held. It was good to be home. Good to have their world back to themselves, for now.

Porter.

Cleaner.

Wilfie.

Pip.

Acknowledgements

Setting out to write about the first child in space has been quite a journey and I have many people to thank: my friend Carol for our bet that we could both write a novel – we both did!; Ralph for his giant leap that became a story; Anna, my mentor at Cornerstones; Lynn, Matthew, Heather, Helen, Dominic, Garry, Chris, Wayne, Mark, Sophie, John, Alice and the many kind friends who read first drafts and advised from their professional viewpoints, from the scientific to the spiritual; the Mslexia Novel Competition for selecting *Precious Matter* for their longlist, encouraging me onwards and upwards; the pioneering team at Lendal Press and Valley Press; and, above all, my family who have gone above and beyond in cheering me on. You're all stars!

About the Author

Belinda Roberts is a designer and illustrator. She has written a number of plays and written and illustrated books for children including *MoonMouse* and the *Daisy Drama Club* series.